ANGEL

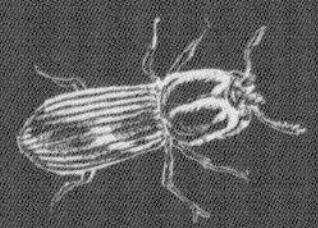

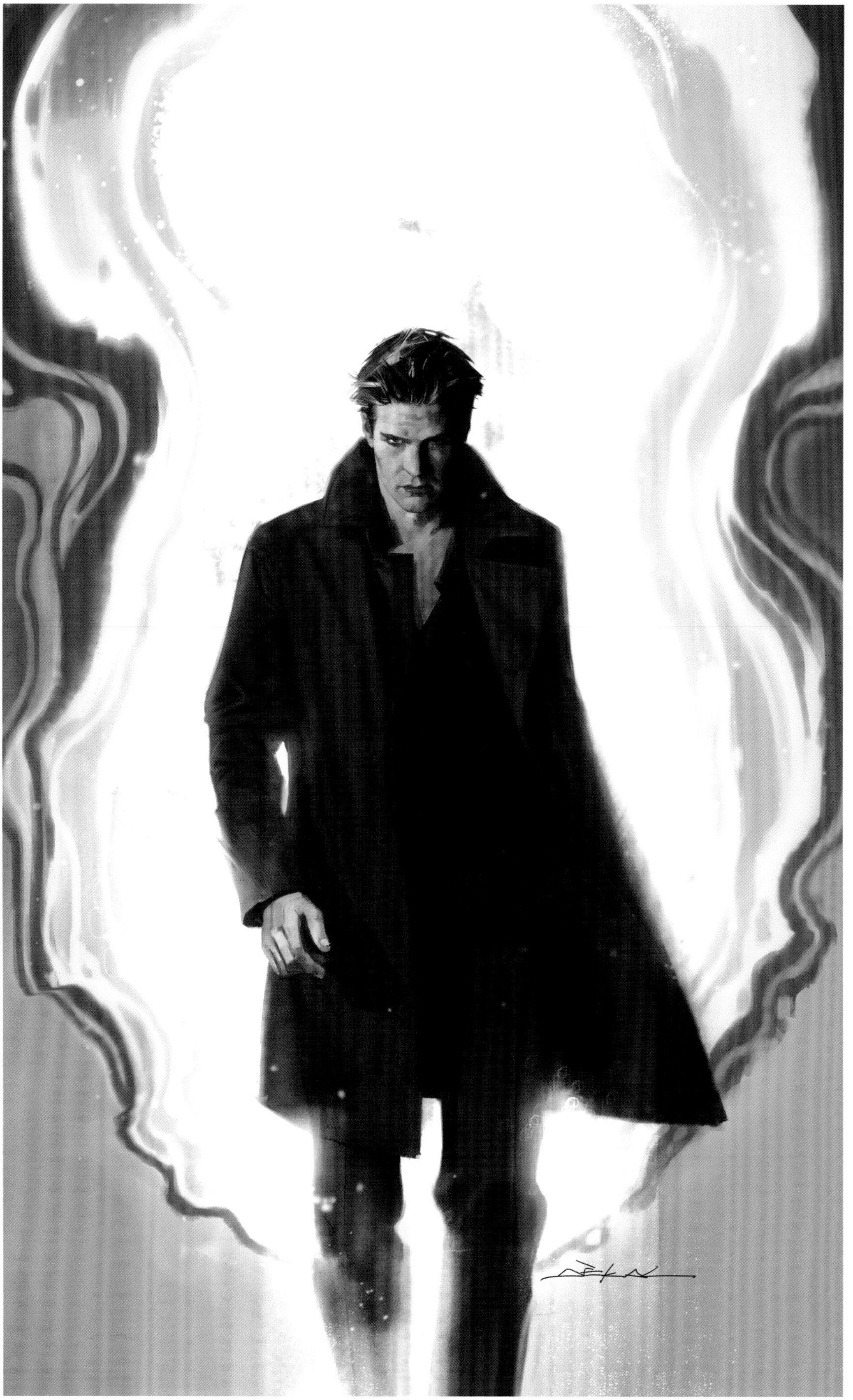

ANGEL

SEASON 11, VOLUME 1
OUT OF THE PAST

Script
CORINNA BECHKO

Art
GERALDO BORGES

Colors
MICHELLE MADSEN

Letters
**RICHARD STARKINGS
& COMICRAFT'S
JIMMY BETANCOURT**

Cover and Chapter Break Art
SCOTT FISCHER

Executive Producer
JOSS WHEDON

DARK HORSE BOOKS

President and publisher **MIKE RICHARDSON**

Editor **FREDDYE MILLER**

Assistant editor **KEVIN BURKHALTER**

Designer **ANITA MAGAÑA**

Digital art technician **CHRISTIANNE GOUDREAU**

Special thanks to Nicole Spiegel and Carol Roeder at Twentieth Century Fox, Becca J. Sadowsky, Andrew Chambliss, Christos Gage, Ruth Gage, Sierra Hahn, Bob Harris, and Randy Stradley.

The art on page 2 is the variant cover art from *Angel* Season 11 #1, by Jeff Dekal.

This story takes place after the events in *Angel & Faith* Season 10, created by Joss Whedon.

This volume reprints the comic book series Angel *Season 11 #1–#4 from Dark Horse Comics, originally published January through April 2017.*

Published by
Dark Horse Books
A division of Dark Horse Comics, Inc.
10956 SE Main Street
Milwaukie, OR 97222

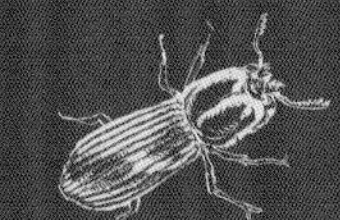

DarkHorse.com

To find a comics shop in your area, call the Comic Shop Locator Service toll-free at 1-888-266-4226.
International Licensing: (503) 905-2377

First edition: August 2017
ISBN 978-1-50670-346-6

10 9 8 7 6 5 4 3 2 1
Printed in China

When young Liam was turned into a vampire, he became incredibly *good* at being exceptionally *bad*. Under the name Angelus, for hundreds of years he reveled in killing and left horror in his wake. In 1898, he received his comeuppance through a gypsy curse that returned to him his soul and his conscience. Now known as Angel, he has been trying to make up ever since for all that he did as a soulless, evil monster.

Among Angel's friends is Winifred "Fred" Burkle, a brilliant and quirky physicist who has been through her own series of mystical events and works with Angel to make the world safer. Fred shares her body with an Old One, a goddess named Illyria; it's weird, but it seems to be working out.

Right now, Angel and Fred are visiting Ireland to perform a small exorcism . . .

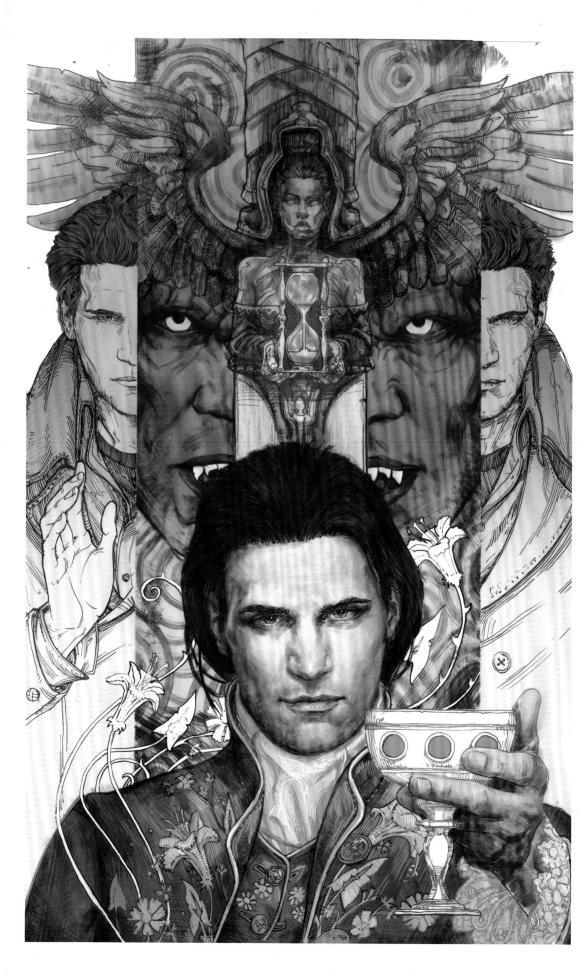

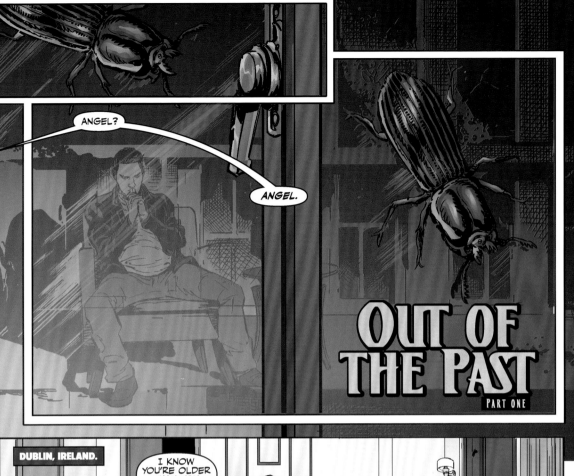

ANGEL?

ANGEL.

OUT OF THE PAST
PART ONE

DUBLIN, IRELAND.

I KNOW YOU'RE OLDER THAN YOU LOOK...

...BUT I THOUGHT YOUR KIND WAS IMMUNE TO HEARING LOSS.

HUH?

SUN'S ABOUT TO GO DOWN. WE SHOULD GET TO IT.

SORRY, FRED.

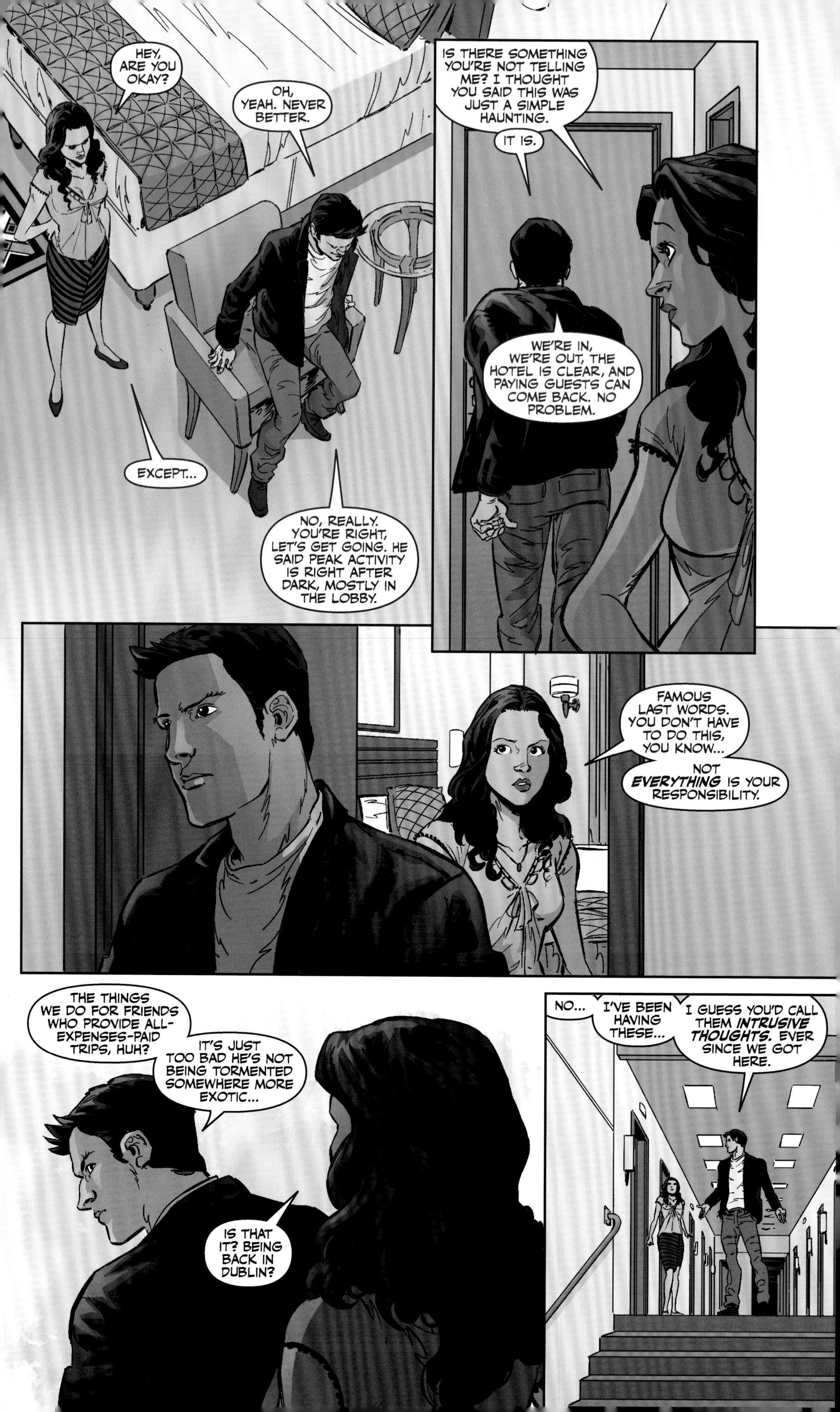
HEY, ARE YOU OKAY?
OH, YEAH. NEVER BETTER.
EXCEPT...
NO, REALLY. YOU'RE RIGHT, LET'S GET GOING. HE SAID PEAK ACTIVITY IS RIGHT AFTER DARK, MOSTLY IN THE LOBBY.
IS THERE SOMETHING YOU'RE NOT TELLING ME? I THOUGHT YOU SAID THIS WAS JUST A SIMPLE HAUNTING.
IT IS.
WE'RE IN, WE'RE OUT, THE HOTEL IS CLEAR, AND PAYING GUESTS CAN COME BACK. NO PROBLEM.
FAMOUS LAST WORDS. YOU DON'T HAVE TO DO THIS, YOU KNOW...
NOT *EVERYTHING* IS YOUR RESPONSIBILITY.
THE THINGS WE DO FOR FRIENDS WHO PROVIDE ALL-EXPENSES-PAID TRIPS, HUH?
IT'S JUST TOO BAD HE'S NOT BEING TORMENTED SOMEWHERE MORE EXOTIC...
IS THAT IT? BEING BACK IN DUBLIN?
NO...
I'VE BEEN HAVING THESE...
I GUESS YOU'D CALL THEM *INTRUSIVE THOUGHTS.* EVER SINCE WE GOT HERE.

INTRUSIVE THOUGHTS?

KIND OF. IT'S NOTHING, FRED. LET'S GO.

THEN WHY ARE YOU LETTING IT BOTHER YOU?

LET'S JUST FORGET IT, OKAY? FORGET I SAID ANYTHING.

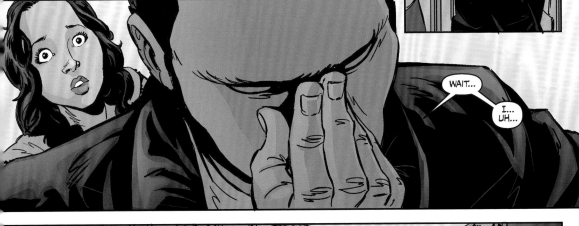

WAIT... I... UH...

ANGEL?! WHAT'S HAPPENING?

IS IT A VISION?

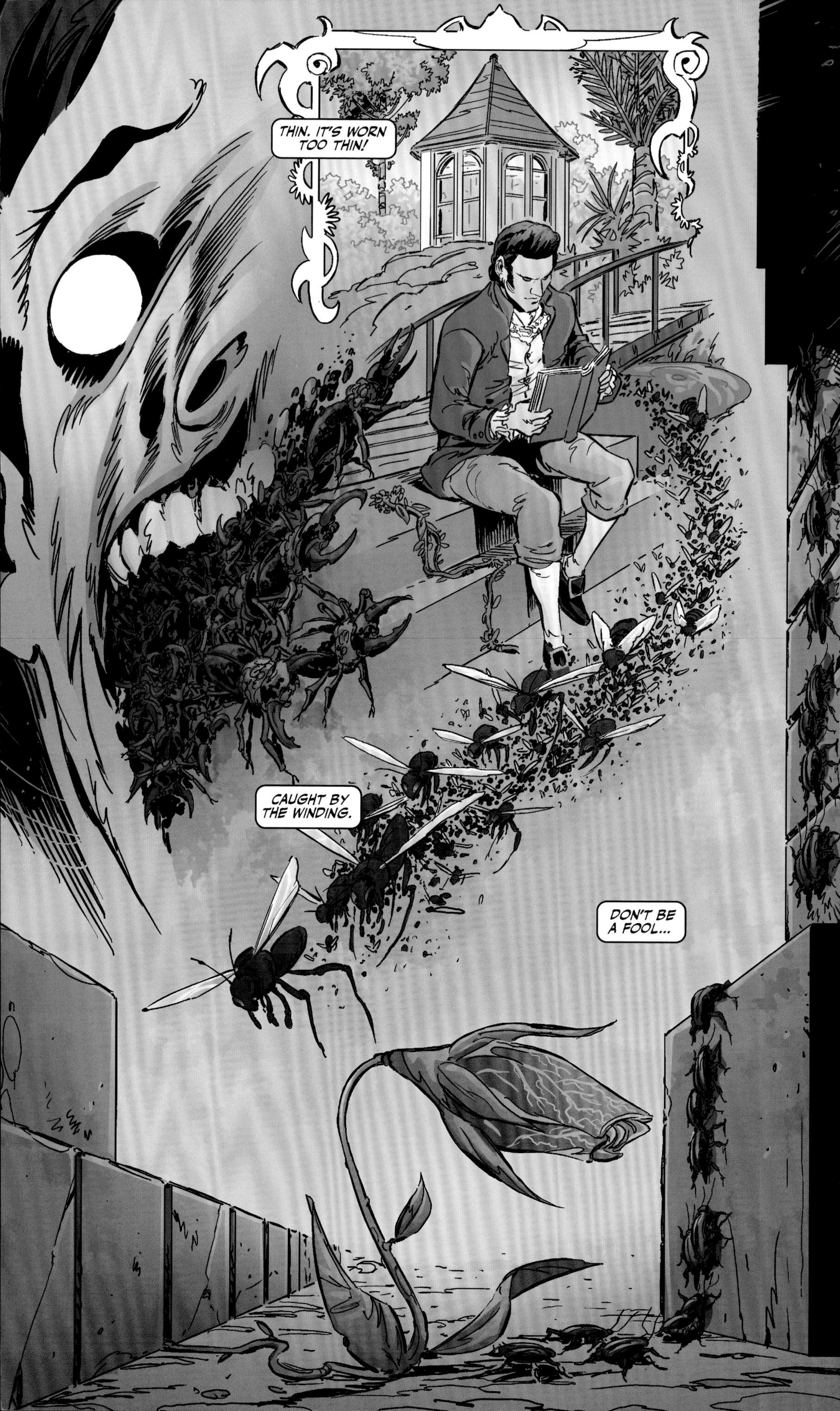
THIN. IT'S WORN TOO THIN!
CAUGHT BY THE WINDING.
DON'T BE A FOOL...

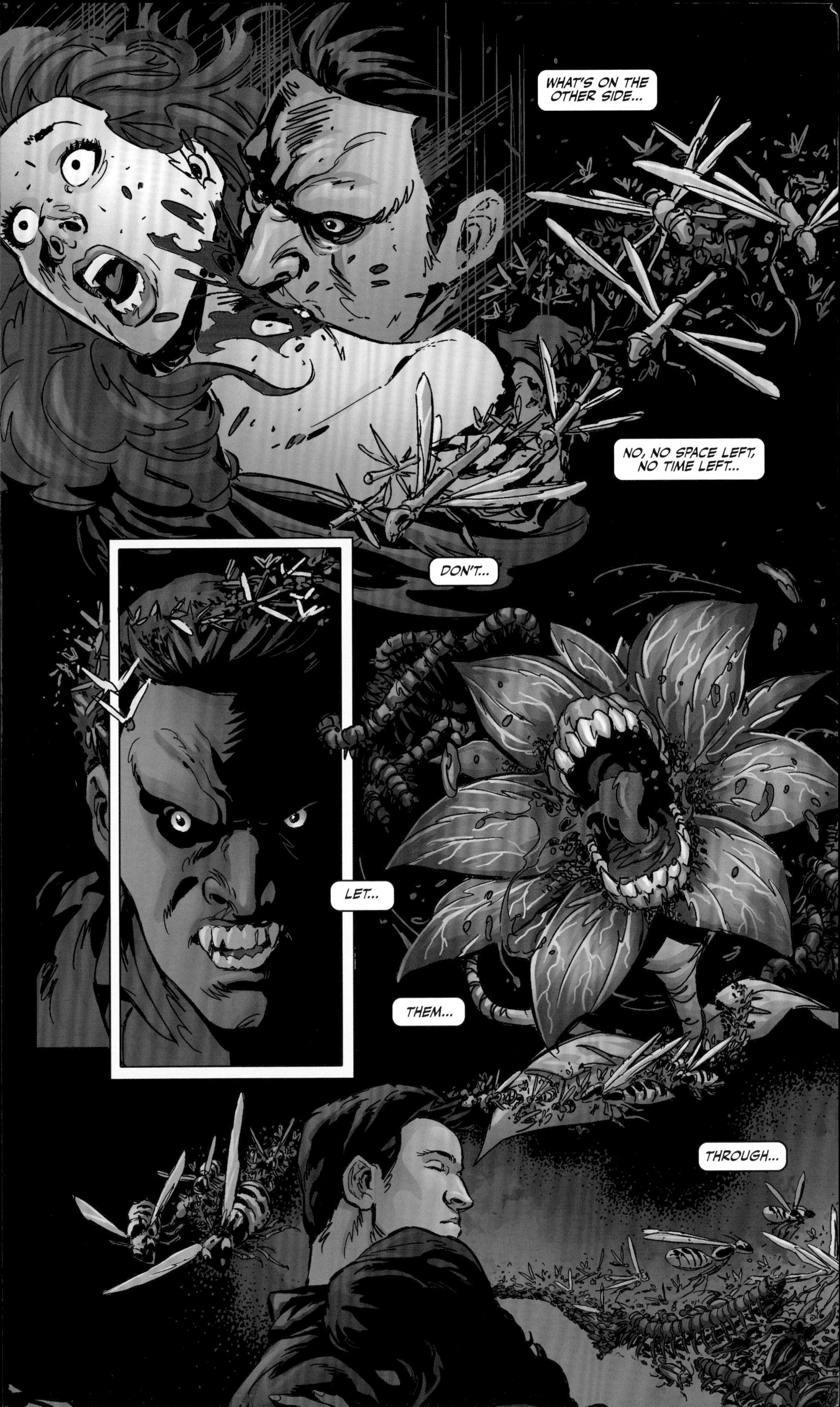
WHAT'S ON THE OTHER SIDE...
NO, NO SPACE LEFT, NO TIME LEFT...
DON'T...
LET...
THEM...
THROUGH...

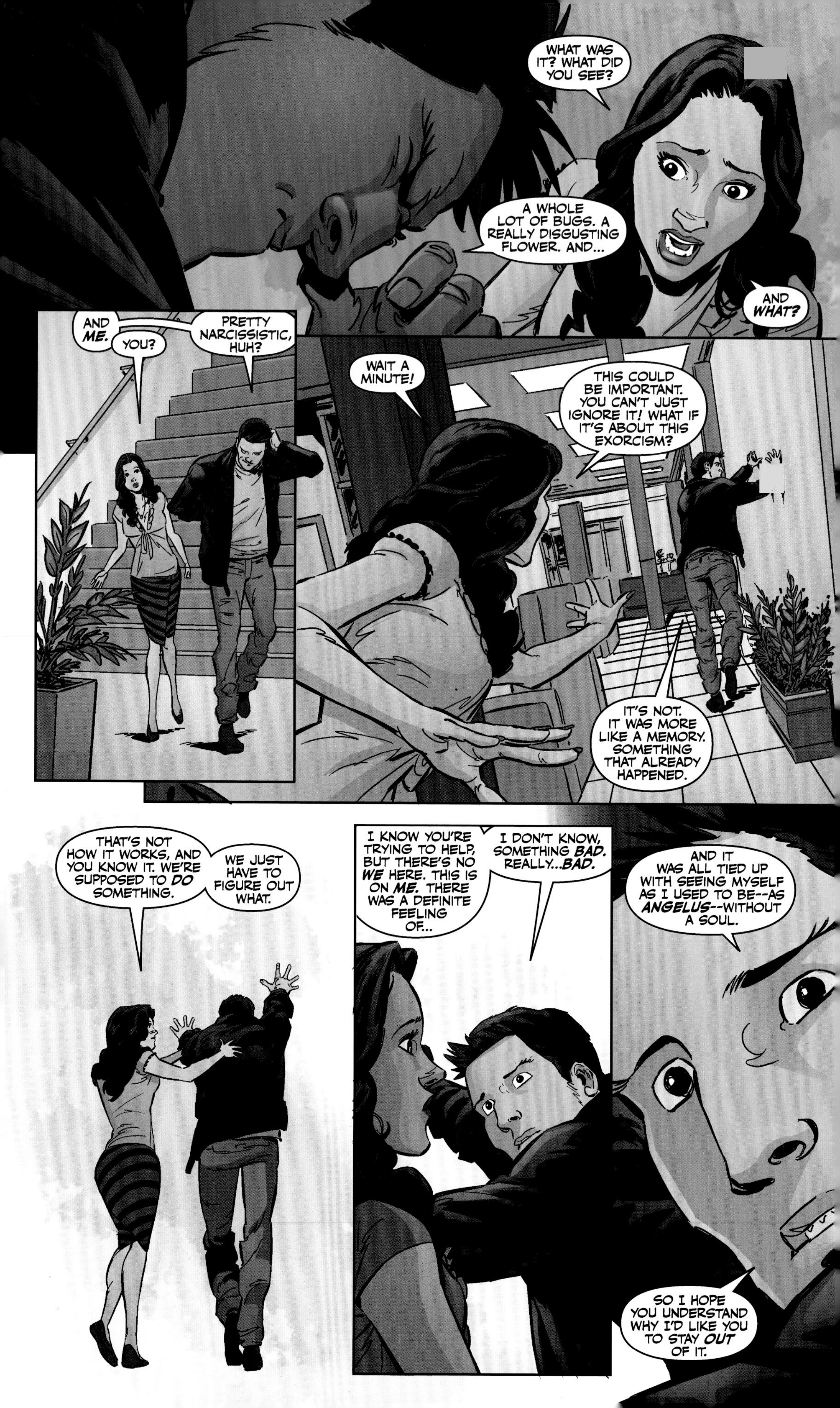
WHAT WAS IT? WHAT DID YOU SEE?
A WHOLE LOT OF BUGS. A REALLY DISGUSTING FLOWER. AND...
AND WHAT?
AND ME.
YOU?
PRETTY NARCISSISTIC, HUH?
WAIT A MINUTE!
THIS COULD BE IMPORTANT. YOU CAN'T JUST IGNORE IT! WHAT IF IT'S ABOUT THIS EXORCISM?
IT'S NOT. IT WAS MORE LIKE A MEMORY. SOMETHING THAT ALREADY HAPPENED.
THAT'S NOT HOW IT WORKS, AND YOU KNOW IT. WE'RE SUPPOSED TO DO SOMETHING.
WE JUST HAVE TO FIGURE OUT WHAT.
I KNOW YOU'RE TRYING TO HELP, BUT THERE'S NO WE HERE. THIS IS ON ME. THERE WAS A DEFINITE FEELING OF...
I DON'T KNOW, SOMETHING BAD. REALLY...BAD.
AND IT WAS ALL TIED UP WITH SEEING MYSELF AS I USED TO BE--AS ANGELUS--WITHOUT A SOUL.
SO I HOPE YOU UNDERSTAND WHY I'D LIKE YOU TO STAY OUT OF IT.

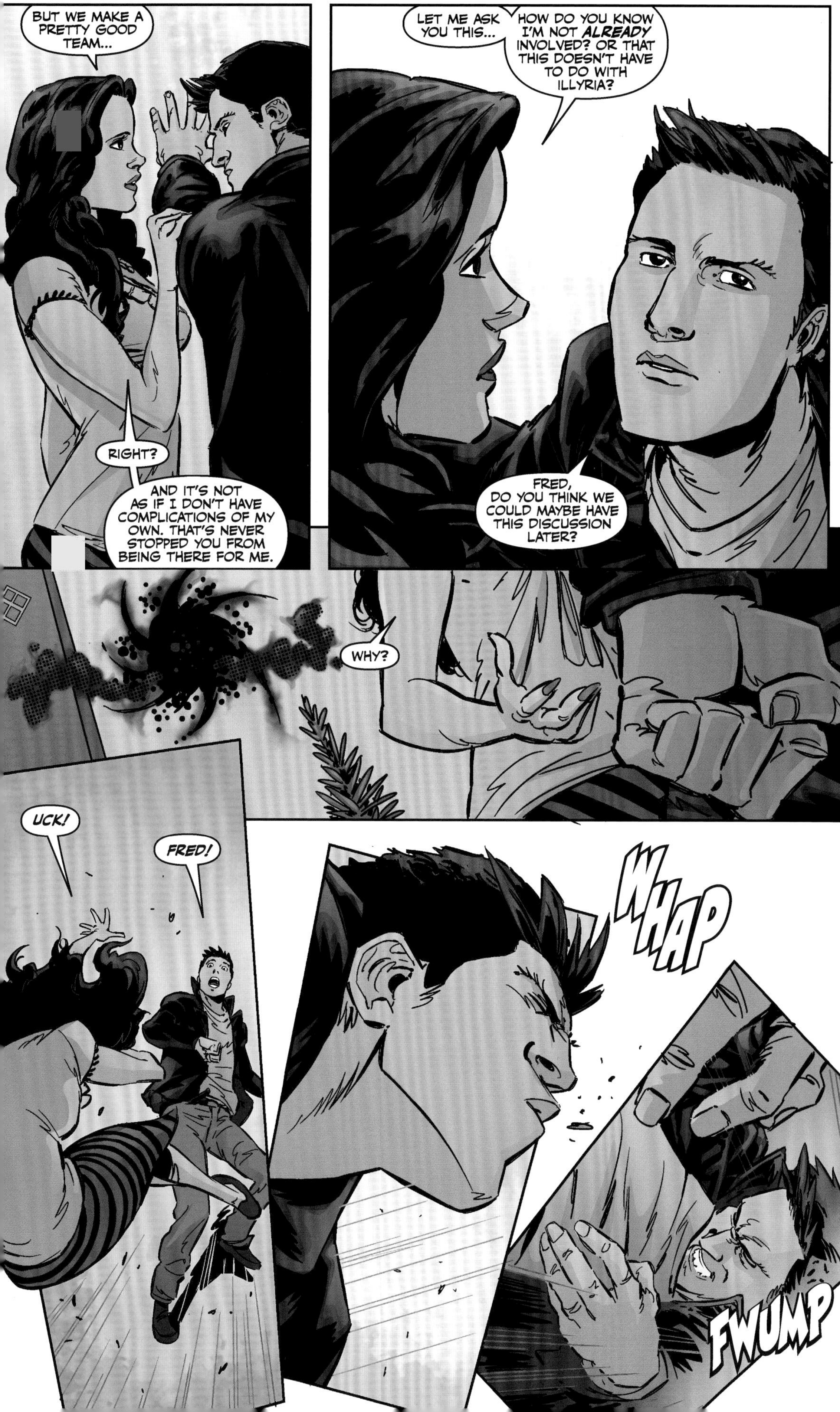
BUT WE MAKE A PRETTY GOOD TEAM...
RIGHT?
AND IT'S NOT AS IF I DON'T HAVE COMPLICATIONS OF MY OWN. THAT'S NEVER STOPPED YOU FROM BEING THERE FOR ME.
LET ME ASK YOU THIS...
HOW DO YOU KNOW I'M NOT ALREADY INVOLVED? OR THAT THIS DOESN'T HAVE TO DO WITH ILLYRIA?
FRED, DO YOU THINK WE COULD MAYBE HAVE THIS DISCUSSION LATER?
WHY?
UCK!
FRED!
WHAP
FWUMP

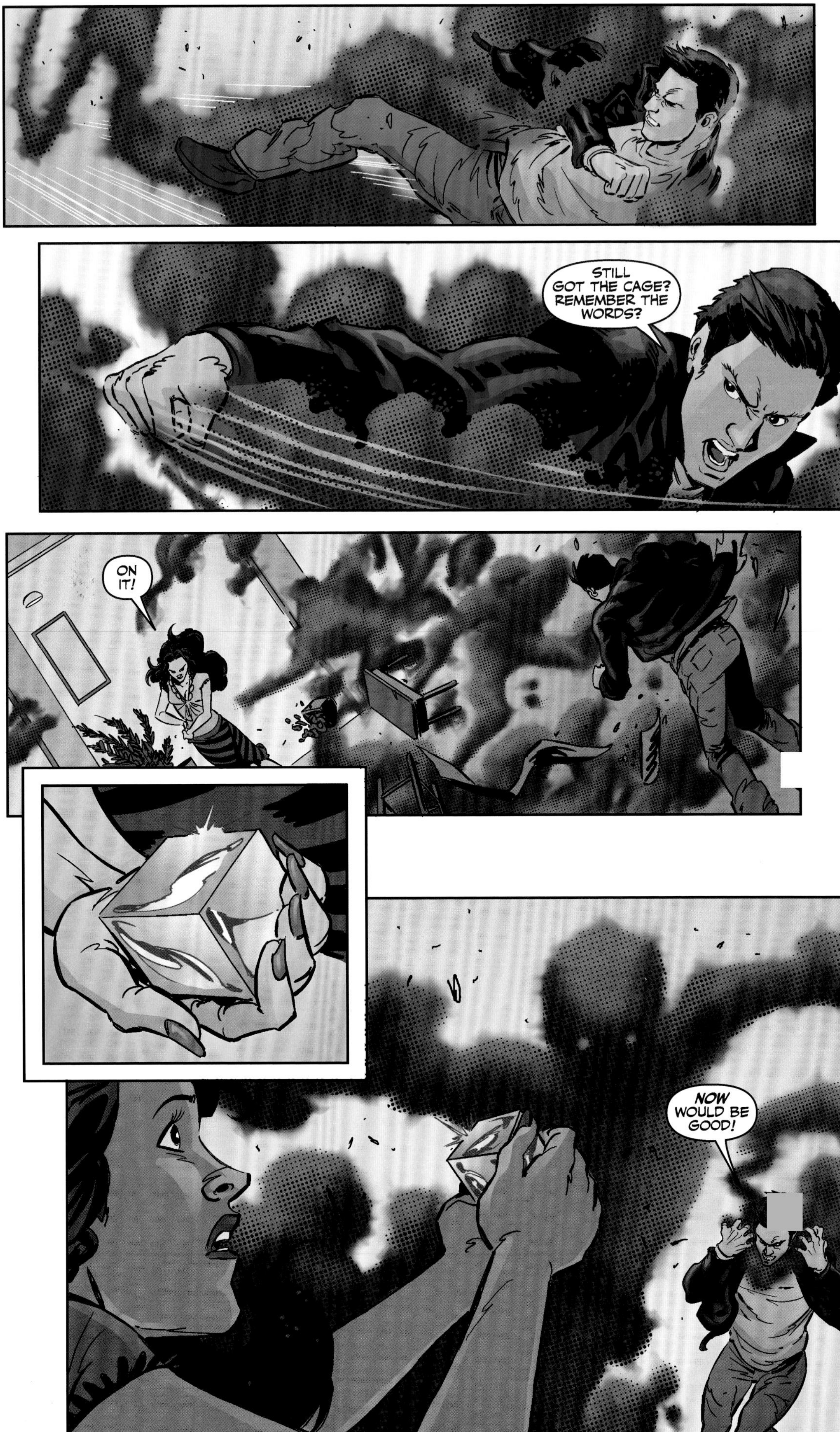
STILL GOT THE CAGE? REMEMBER THE WORDS?
ON IT!
NOW WOULD BE GOOD!

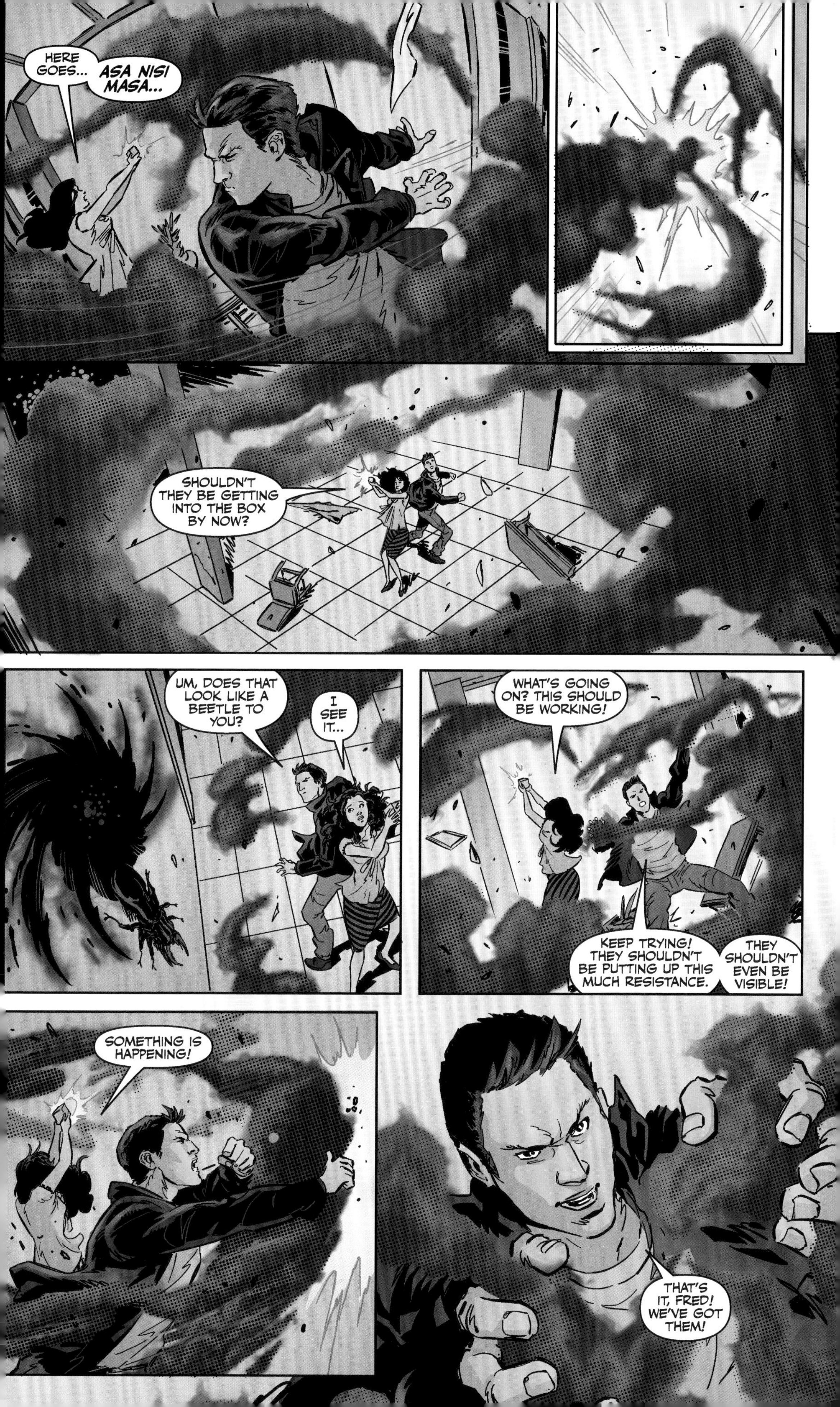

HERE GOES...
ASA NISI MASA...
SHOULDN'T THEY BE GETTING INTO THE BOX BY NOW?
UM, DOES THAT LOOK LIKE A BEETLE TO YOU?
I SEE IT...
WHAT'S GOING ON? THIS SHOULD BE WORKING!
KEEP TRYING! THEY SHOULDN'T BE PUTTING UP THIS MUCH RESISTANCE.
THEY SHOULDN'T EVEN BE VISIBLE!
SOMETHING IS HAPPENING!
THAT'S IT, FRED! WE'VE GOT THEM!

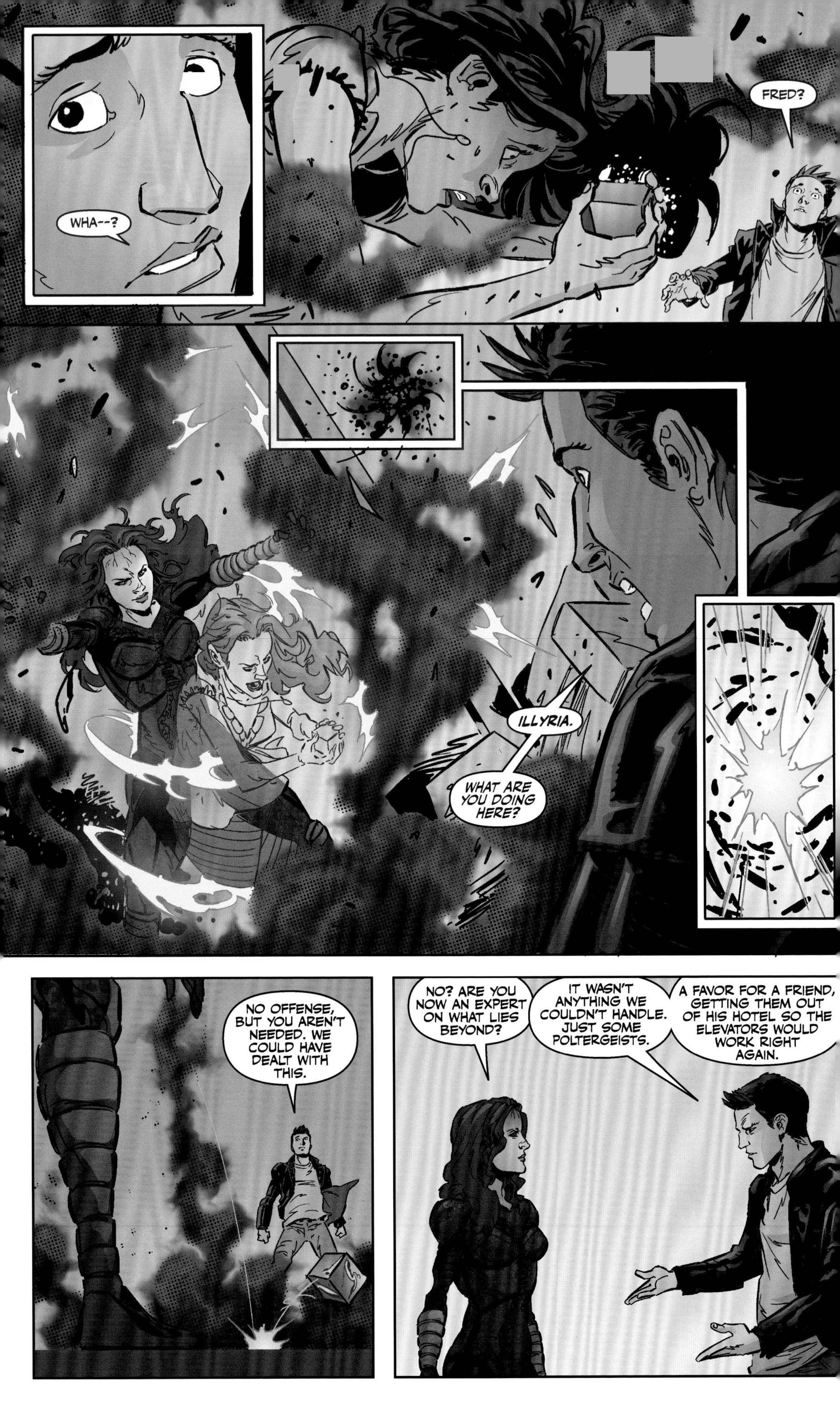

WHA--?
FRED?
ILLYRIA.
WHAT ARE YOU DOING HERE?
NO OFFENSE, BUT YOU AREN'T NEEDED. WE COULD HAVE DEALT WITH THIS.
NO? ARE YOU NOW AN EXPERT ON WHAT LIES BEYOND?
IT WASN'T ANYTHING WE COULDN'T HANDLE. JUST SOME POLTERGEISTS.
A FAVOR FOR A FRIEND, GETTING THEM OUT OF HIS HOTEL SO THE ELEVATORS WOULD WORK RIGHT AGAIN.

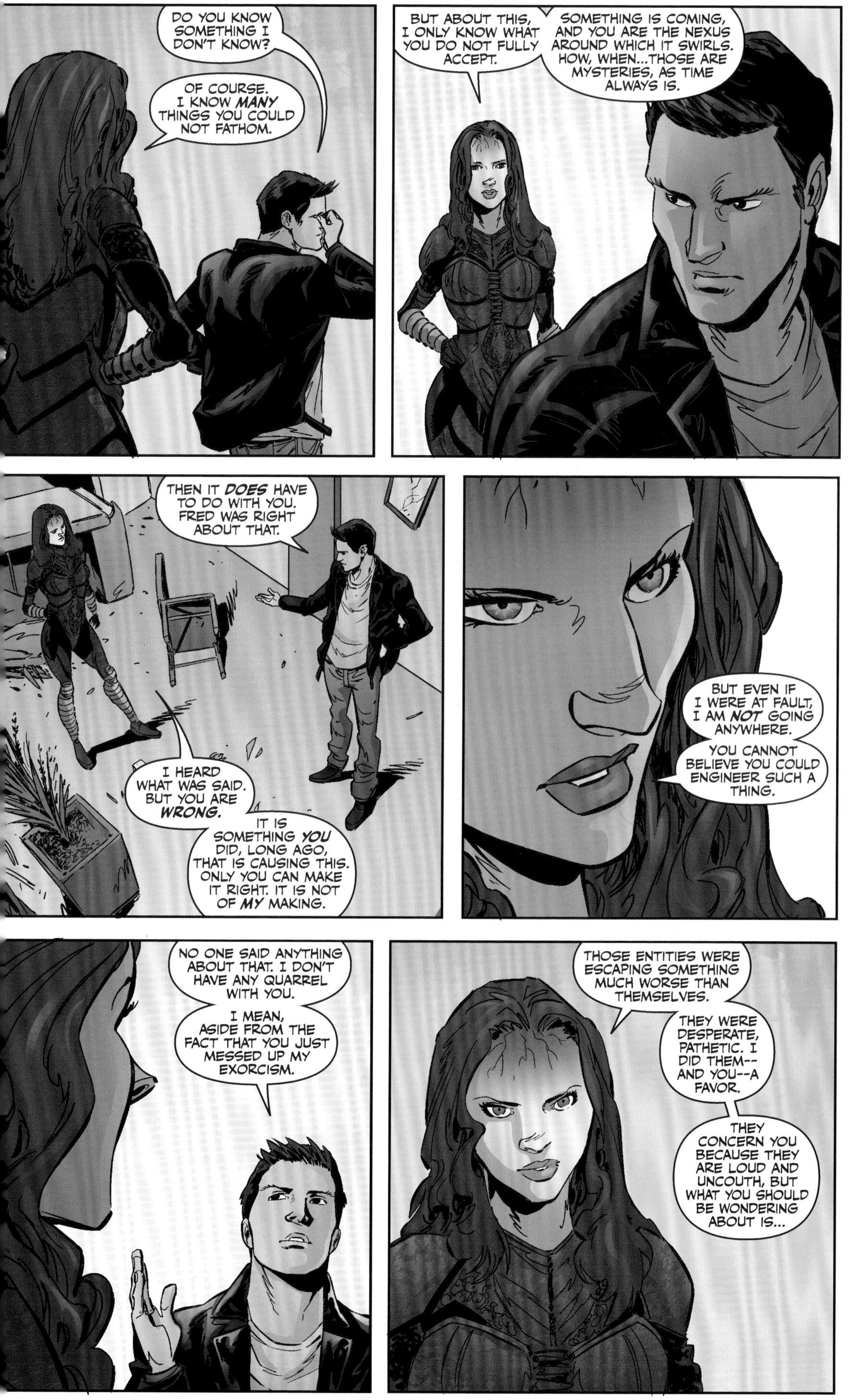
DO YOU KNOW SOMETHING I DON'T KNOW?
OF COURSE. I KNOW *MANY* THINGS YOU COULD NOT FATHOM.
BUT ABOUT THIS, I ONLY KNOW WHAT YOU DO NOT FULLY ACCEPT.
SOMETHING IS COMING, AND YOU ARE THE NEXUS AROUND WHICH IT SWIRLS. HOW, WHEN...THOSE ARE MYSTERIES, AS TIME ALWAYS IS.
THEN IT *DOES* HAVE TO DO WITH YOU. FRED WAS RIGHT ABOUT THAT.
I HEARD WHAT WAS SAID. BUT YOU ARE *WRONG.*
IT IS SOMETHING *YOU* DID, LONG AGO, THAT IS CAUSING THIS. ONLY YOU CAN MAKE IT RIGHT. IT IS NOT OF *MY* MAKING.
BUT EVEN IF I WERE AT FAULT, I AM *NOT* GOING ANYWHERE.
YOU CANNOT BELIEVE YOU COULD ENGINEER SUCH A THING.
NO ONE SAID ANYTHING ABOUT THAT. I DON'T HAVE ANY QUARREL WITH YOU.
I MEAN, ASIDE FROM THE FACT THAT YOU JUST MESSED UP MY EXORCISM.
THOSE ENTITIES WERE ESCAPING SOMETHING MUCH WORSE THAN THEMSELVES.
THEY WERE DESPERATE, PATHETIC. I DID THEM--AND YOU--A FAVOR.
THEY CONCERN YOU BECAUSE THEY ARE LOUD AND UNCOUTH, BUT WHAT YOU SHOULD BE WONDERING ABOUT IS...

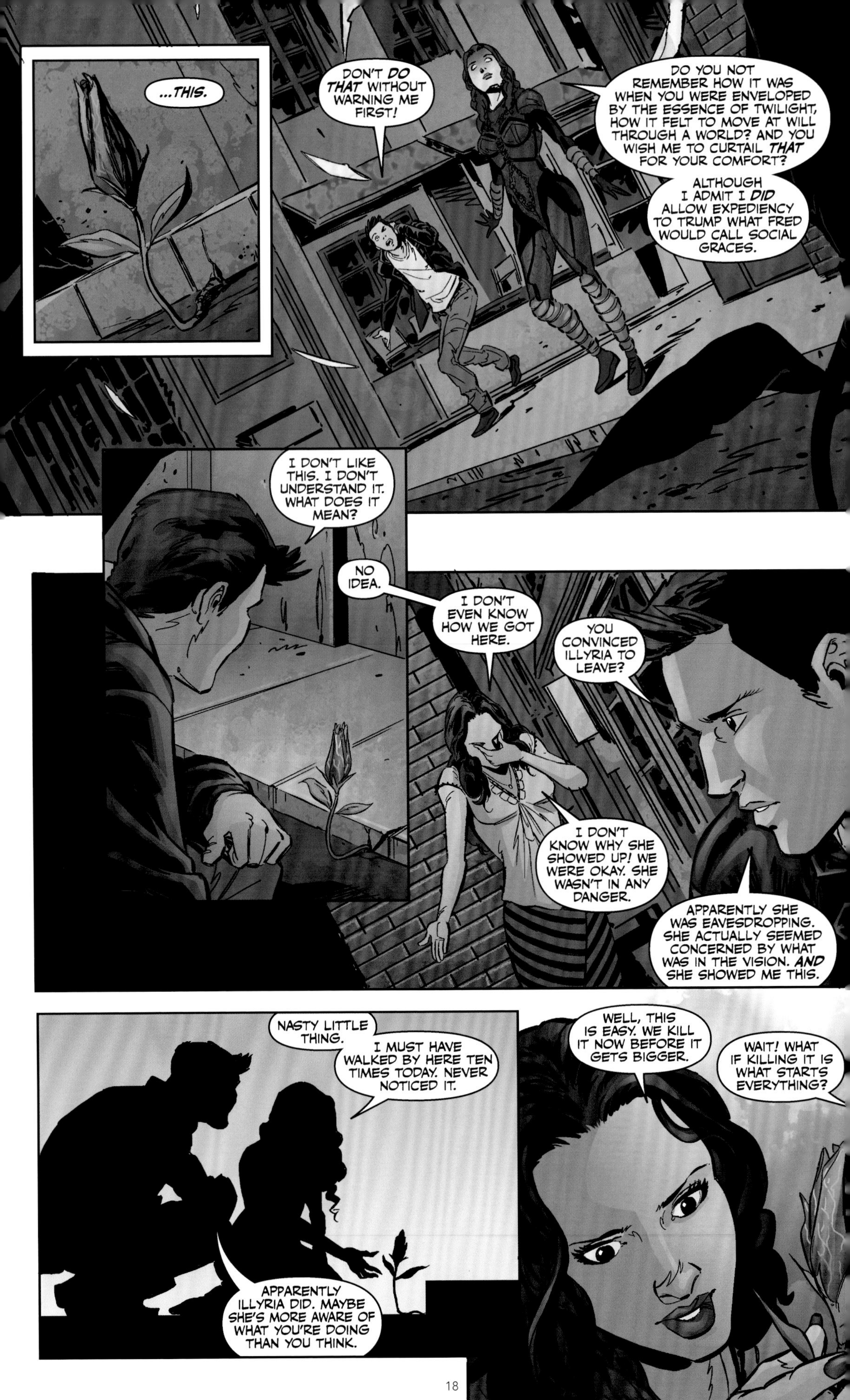

...THIS.
DON'T DO THAT WITHOUT WARNING ME FIRST!
DO YOU NOT REMEMBER HOW IT WAS WHEN YOU WERE ENVELOPED BY THE ESSENCE OF TWILIGHT, HOW IT FELT TO MOVE AT WILL THROUGH A WORLD? AND YOU WISH ME TO CURTAIL THAT FOR YOUR COMFORT?
ALTHOUGH I ADMIT I DID ALLOW EXPEDIENCY TO TRUMP WHAT FRED WOULD CALL SOCIAL GRACES.
I DON'T LIKE THIS. I DON'T UNDERSTAND IT. WHAT DOES IT MEAN?
NO IDEA.
I DON'T EVEN KNOW HOW WE GOT HERE.
YOU CONVINCED ILLYRIA TO LEAVE?
I DON'T KNOW WHY SHE SHOWED UP! WE WERE OKAY. SHE WASN'T IN ANY DANGER.
APPARENTLY SHE WAS EAVESDROPPING. SHE ACTUALLY SEEMED CONCERNED BY WHAT WAS IN THE VISION. AND SHE SHOWED ME THIS.
NASTY LITTLE THING.
I MUST HAVE WALKED BY HERE TEN TIMES TODAY. NEVER NOTICED IT.
APPARENTLY ILLYRIA DID. MAYBE SHE'S MORE AWARE OF WHAT YOU'RE DOING THAN YOU THINK.
WELL, THIS IS EASY. WE KILL IT NOW BEFORE IT GETS BIGGER.
WAIT! WHAT IF KILLING IT IS WHAT STARTS EVERYTHING?

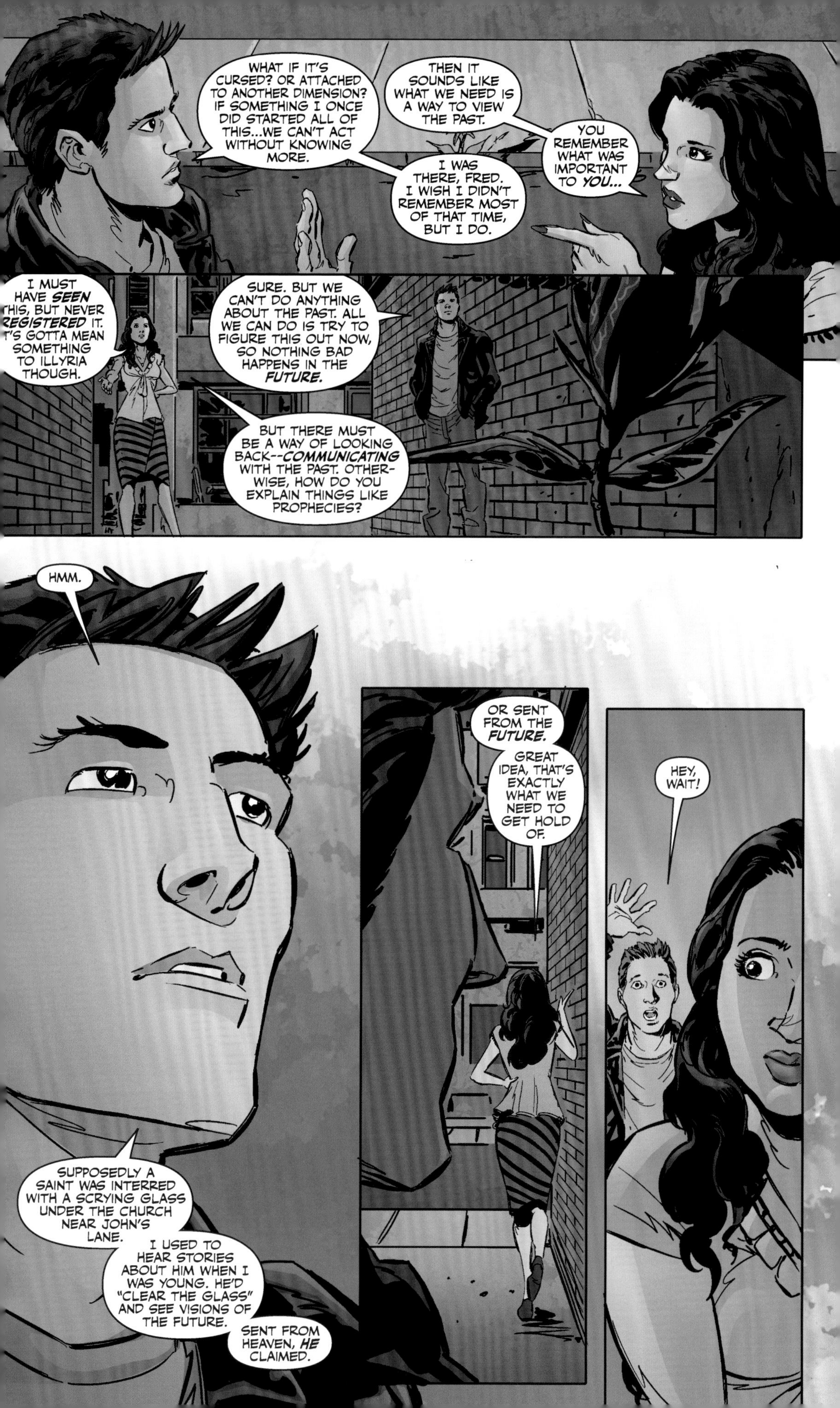

WHAT IF IT'S CURSED? OR ATTACHED TO ANOTHER DIMENSION? IF SOMETHING I ONCE DID STARTED ALL OF THIS...WE CAN'T ACT WITHOUT KNOWING MORE.
THEN IT SOUNDS LIKE WHAT WE NEED IS A WAY TO VIEW THE PAST.
YOU REMEMBER WHAT WAS IMPORTANT TO *YOU...*
I WAS THERE, FRED. I WISH I DIDN'T REMEMBER MOST OF THAT TIME, BUT I DO.
I MUST HAVE *SEEN* THIS, BUT NEVER *REGISTERED* IT. IT'S GOTTA MEAN SOMETHING TO ILLYRIA THOUGH.
SURE. BUT WE CAN'T DO ANYTHING ABOUT THE PAST. ALL WE CAN DO IS TRY TO FIGURE THIS OUT NOW, SO NOTHING BAD HAPPENS IN THE *FUTURE.*
BUT THERE MUST BE A WAY OF LOOKING BACK--*COMMUNICATING* WITH THE PAST. OTHERWISE, HOW DO YOU EXPLAIN THINGS LIKE PROPHECIES?
HMM.
SUPPOSEDLY A SAINT WAS INTERRED WITH A SCRYING GLASS UNDER THE CHURCH NEAR JOHN'S LANE.
I USED TO HEAR STORIES ABOUT HIM WHEN I WAS YOUNG. HE'D "CLEAR THE GLASS" AND SEE VISIONS OF THE FUTURE.
SENT FROM HEAVEN, *HE* CLAIMED.
OR SENT FROM THE *FUTURE.*
GREAT IDEA, THAT'S EXACTLY WHAT WE NEED TO GET HOLD OF.
HEY, WAIT!

UM, HOW DO WE KNOW WHERE TO LOOK?

JOHN'S LANE CHURCH.

THIS IS PROBABLY A WASTE OF TIME, YOU KNOW.

ONE WAY TO FIND OUT!

I LOOSENED IT FOR YOU.

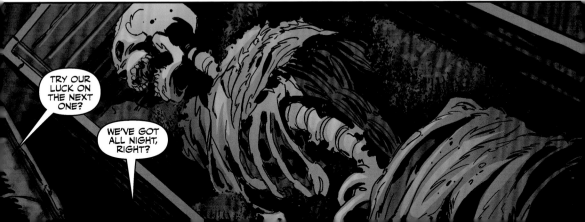

TRY OUR LUCK ON THE NEXT ONE?

WE'VE GOT ALL NIGHT, RIGHT?

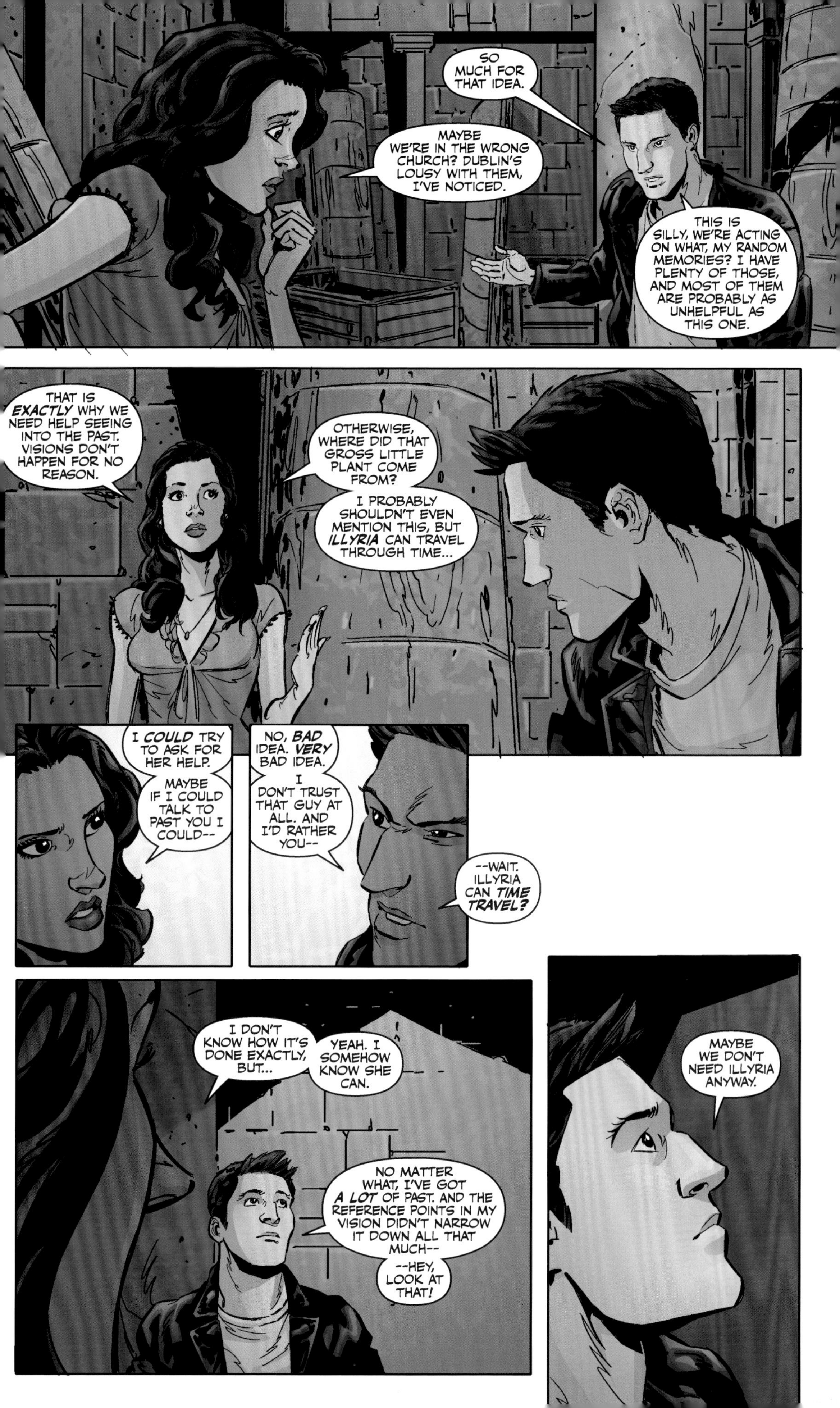
SO MUCH FOR THAT IDEA.
MAYBE WE'RE IN THE WRONG CHURCH? DUBLIN'S LOUSY WITH THEM, I'VE NOTICED.
THIS IS SILLY, WE'RE ACTING ON WHAT, MY RANDOM MEMORIES? I HAVE PLENTY OF THOSE, AND MOST OF THEM ARE PROBABLY AS UNHELPFUL AS THIS ONE.
THAT IS *EXACTLY* WHY WE NEED HELP SEEING INTO THE PAST. VISIONS DON'T HAPPEN FOR NO REASON.
OTHERWISE, WHERE DID THAT GROSS LITTLE PLANT COME FROM?
I PROBABLY SHOULDN'T EVEN MENTION THIS, BUT *ILLYRIA* CAN TRAVEL THROUGH TIME...
I *COULD* TRY TO ASK FOR HER HELP.
MAYBE IF I COULD TALK TO PAST YOU I COULD--
NO, *BAD* IDEA. *VERY* BAD IDEA.
I DON'T TRUST THAT GUY AT ALL. AND I'D RATHER YOU--
--WAIT. ILLYRIA CAN *TIME TRAVEL?*
I DON'T KNOW HOW IT'S DONE EXACTLY, BUT...
YEAH. I SOMEHOW KNOW SHE CAN.
NO MATTER WHAT, I'VE GOT *A LOT* OF PAST. AND THE REFERENCE POINTS IN MY VISION DIDN'T NARROW IT DOWN ALL THAT MUCH--
--HEY, LOOK AT THAT!
MAYBE WE DON'T NEED ILLYRIA ANYWAY.

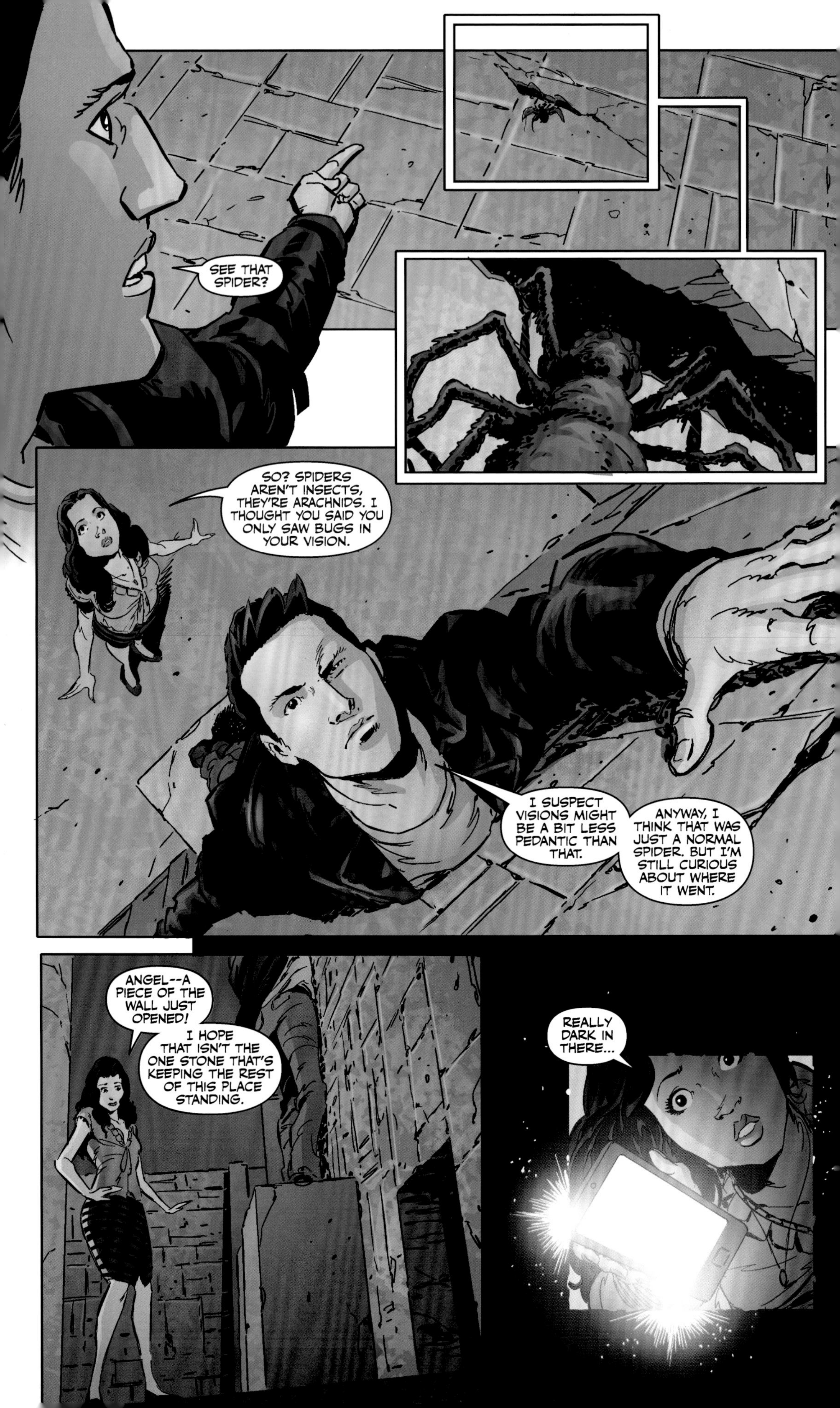
SEE THAT SPIDER?
SO? SPIDERS AREN'T INSECTS, THEY'RE ARACHNIDS. I THOUGHT YOU SAID YOU ONLY SAW BUGS IN YOUR VISION.
I SUSPECT VISIONS MIGHT BE A BIT LESS PEDANTIC THAN THAT.
ANYWAY, I THINK THAT WAS JUST A NORMAL SPIDER. BUT I'M STILL CURIOUS ABOUT WHERE IT WENT.
ANGEL--A PIECE OF THE WALL JUST OPENED!
I HOPE THAT ISN'T THE ONE STONE THAT'S KEEPING THE REST OF THIS PLACE STANDING.
REALLY DARK IN THERE...

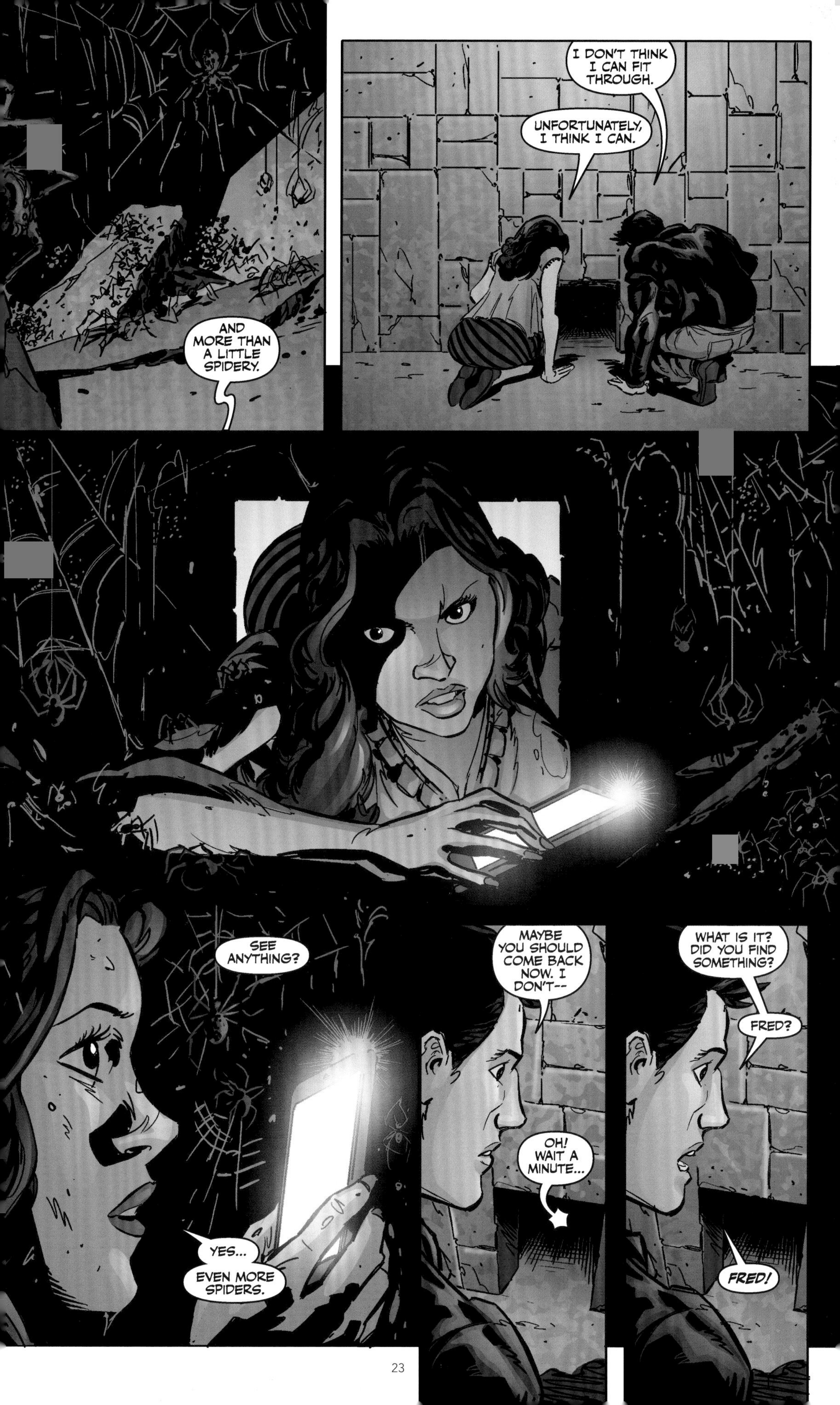
AND MORE THAN A LITTLE SPIDERY.
I DON'T THINK I CAN FIT THROUGH.
UNFORTUNATELY, I THINK I CAN.
SEE ANYTHING?
YES...
EVEN MORE SPIDERS.
MAYBE YOU SHOULD COME BACK NOW. I DON'T--
OH! WAIT A MINUTE...
WHAT IS IT? DID YOU FIND SOMETHING?
FRED?
FRED!

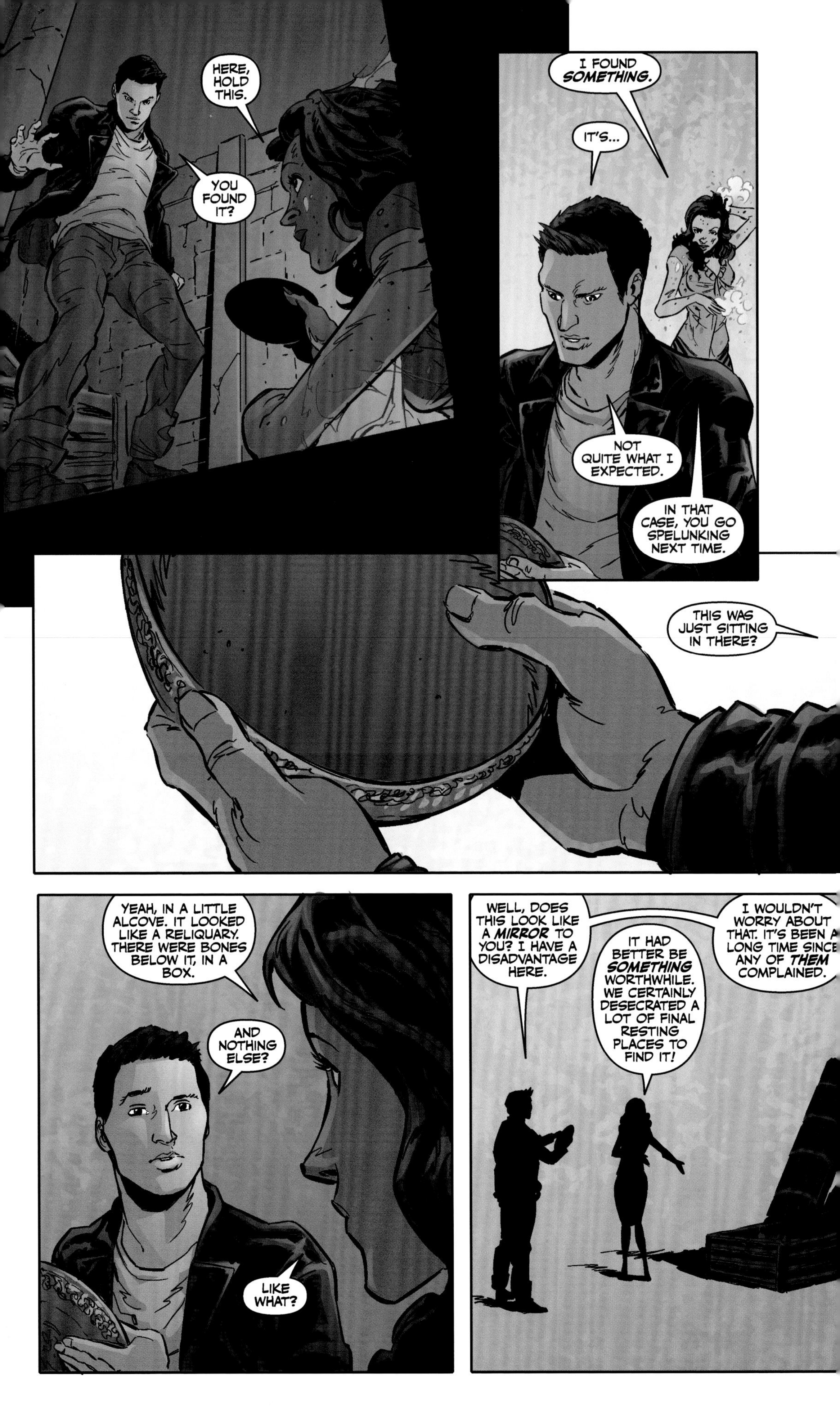
HERE, HOLD THIS.
YOU FOUND IT?
I FOUND SOMETHING.
IT'S...
NOT QUITE WHAT I EXPECTED.
IN THAT CASE, YOU GO SPELUNKING NEXT TIME.
THIS WAS JUST SITTING IN THERE?
YEAH, IN A LITTLE ALCOVE. IT LOOKED LIKE A RELIQUARY. THERE WERE BONES BELOW IT, IN A BOX.
AND NOTHING ELSE?
LIKE WHAT?
WELL, DOES THIS LOOK LIKE A MIRROR TO YOU? I HAVE A DISADVANTAGE HERE.
I WOULDN'T WORRY ABOUT THAT. IT'S BEEN A LONG TIME SINCE ANY OF THEM COMPLAINED.
IT HAD BETTER BE SOMETHING WORTHWHILE. WE CERTAINLY DESECRATED A LOT OF FINAL RESTING PLACES TO FIND IT!

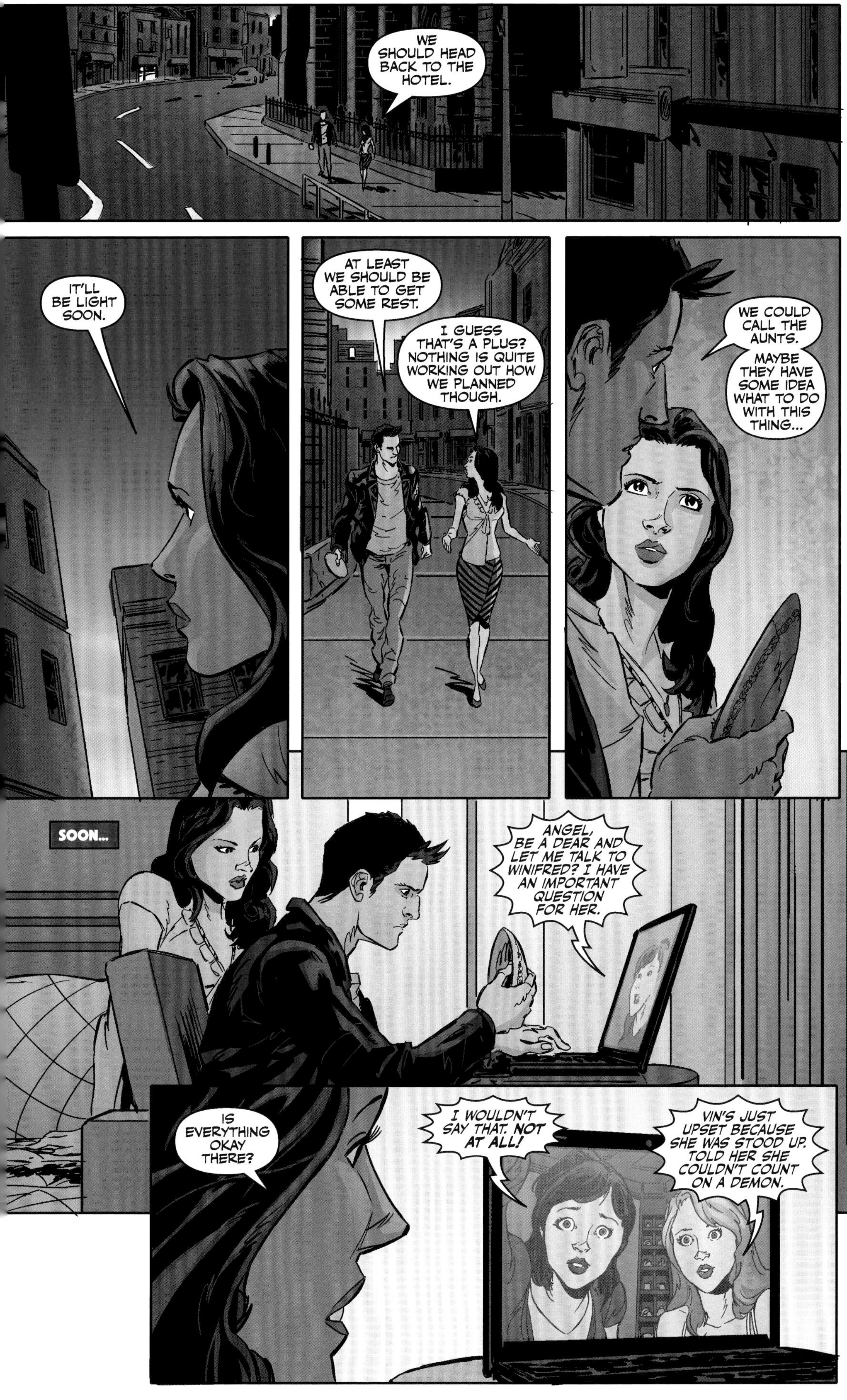
WE SHOULD HEAD BACK TO THE HOTEL.
IT'LL BE LIGHT SOON.
AT LEAST WE SHOULD BE ABLE TO GET SOME REST.
I GUESS THAT'S A PLUS? NOTHING IS QUITE WORKING OUT HOW WE PLANNED THOUGH.
WE COULD CALL THE AUNTS.
MAYBE THEY HAVE SOME IDEA WHAT TO DO WITH THIS THING...
SOON...
ANGEL, BE A DEAR AND LET ME TALK TO WINIFRED? I HAVE AN IMPORTANT QUESTION FOR HER.
IS EVERYTHING OKAY THERE?
I WOULDN'T SAY THAT. NOT AT ALL!
VIN'S JUST UPSET BECAUSE SHE WAS STOOD UP. TOLD HER SHE COULDN'T COUNT ON A DEMON.

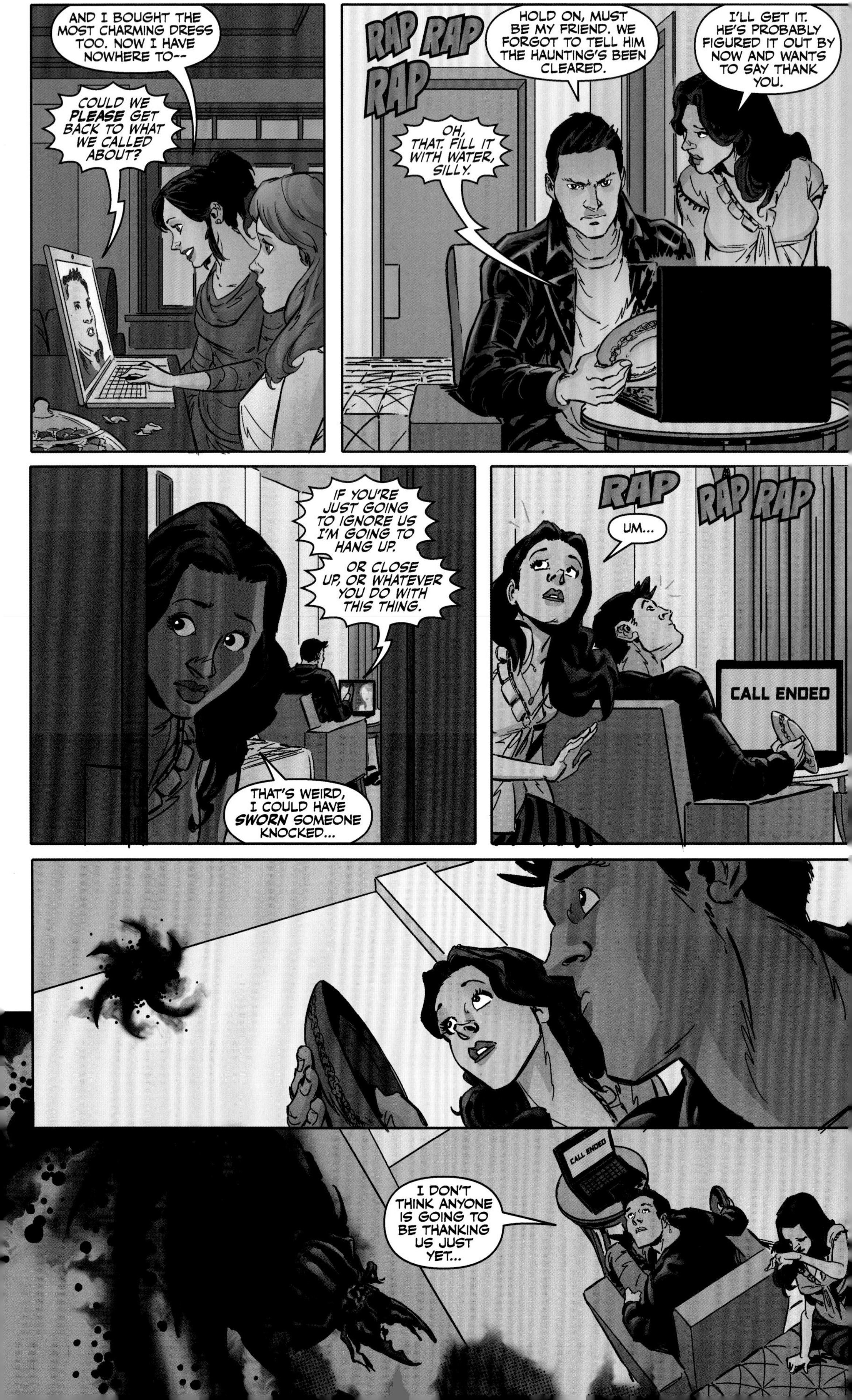
AND I BOUGHT THE MOST CHARMING DRESS TOO. NOW I HAVE NOWHERE TO--
COULD WE PLEASE GET BACK TO WHAT WE CALLED ABOUT?
RAP RAP
RAP
OH, THAT. FILL IT WITH WATER, SILLY.
HOLD ON, MUST BE MY FRIEND. WE FORGOT TO TELL HIM THE HAUNTING'S BEEN CLEARED.
I'LL GET IT. HE'S PROBABLY FIGURED IT OUT BY NOW AND WANTS TO SAY THANK YOU.
IF YOU'RE JUST GOING TO IGNORE US I'M GOING TO HANG UP.
OR CLOSE UP, OR WHATEVER YOU DO WITH THIS THING.
THAT'S WEIRD, I COULD HAVE SWORN SOMEONE KNOCKED...
RAP
RAP RAP
UM...
CALL ENDED
CALL ENDED
I DON'T THINK ANYONE IS GOING TO BE THANKING US JUST YET...

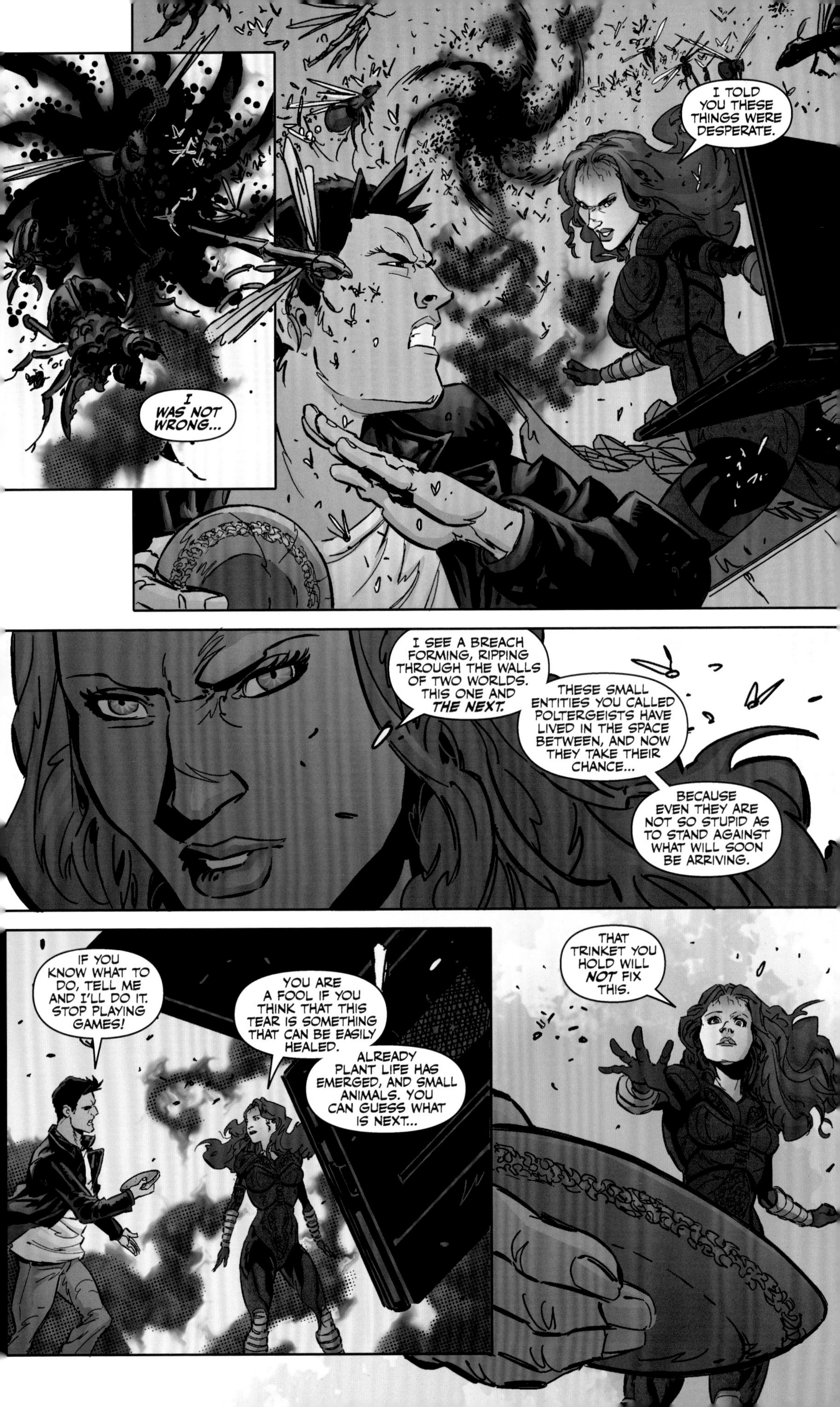
I WAS NOT WRONG...
I TOLD YOU THESE THINGS WERE DESPERATE.
I SEE A BREACH FORMING, RIPPING THROUGH THE WALLS OF TWO WORLDS. THIS ONE AND THE NEXT.
THESE SMALL ENTITIES YOU CALLED POLTERGEISTS HAVE LIVED IN THE SPACE BETWEEN, AND NOW THEY TAKE THEIR CHANCE...
BECAUSE EVEN THEY ARE NOT SO STUPID AS TO STAND AGAINST WHAT WILL SOON BE ARRIVING.
IF YOU KNOW WHAT TO DO, TELL ME AND I'LL DO IT. STOP PLAYING GAMES!
YOU ARE A FOOL IF YOU THINK THAT THIS TEAR IS SOMETHING THAT CAN BE EASILY HEALED.
ALREADY PLANT LIFE HAS EMERGED, AND SMALL ANIMALS. YOU CAN GUESS WHAT IS NEXT...
THAT TRINKET YOU HOLD WILL NOT FIX THIS.

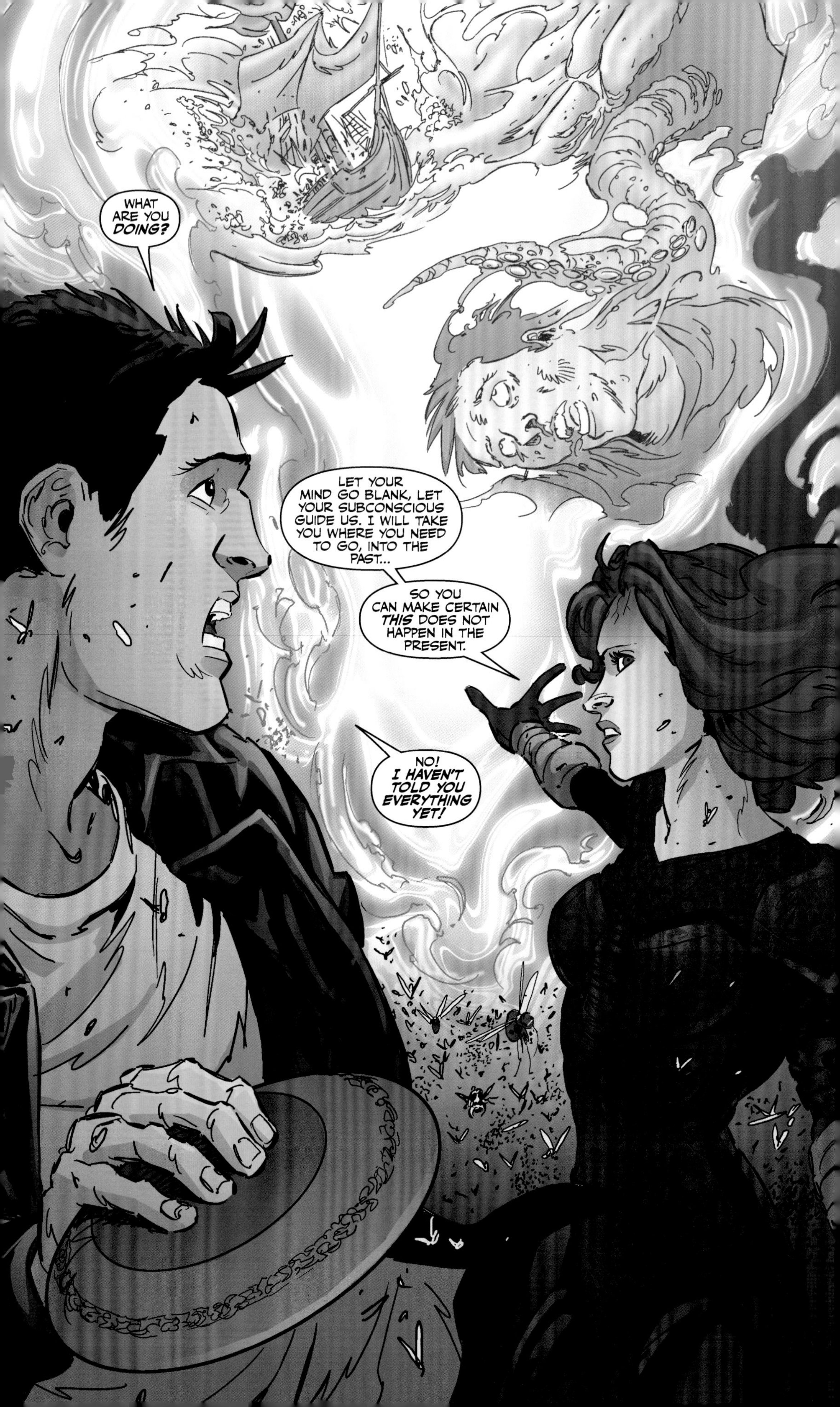
WHAT ARE YOU *DOING?*
LET YOUR MIND GO BLANK, LET YOUR SUBCONSCIOUS GUIDE US. I WILL TAKE YOU WHERE YOU NEED TO GO, INTO THE PAST...
SO YOU CAN MAKE CERTAIN *THIS* DOES NOT HAPPEN IN THE PRESENT.
NO! *I HAVEN'T TOLD YOU EVERYTHING YET!*

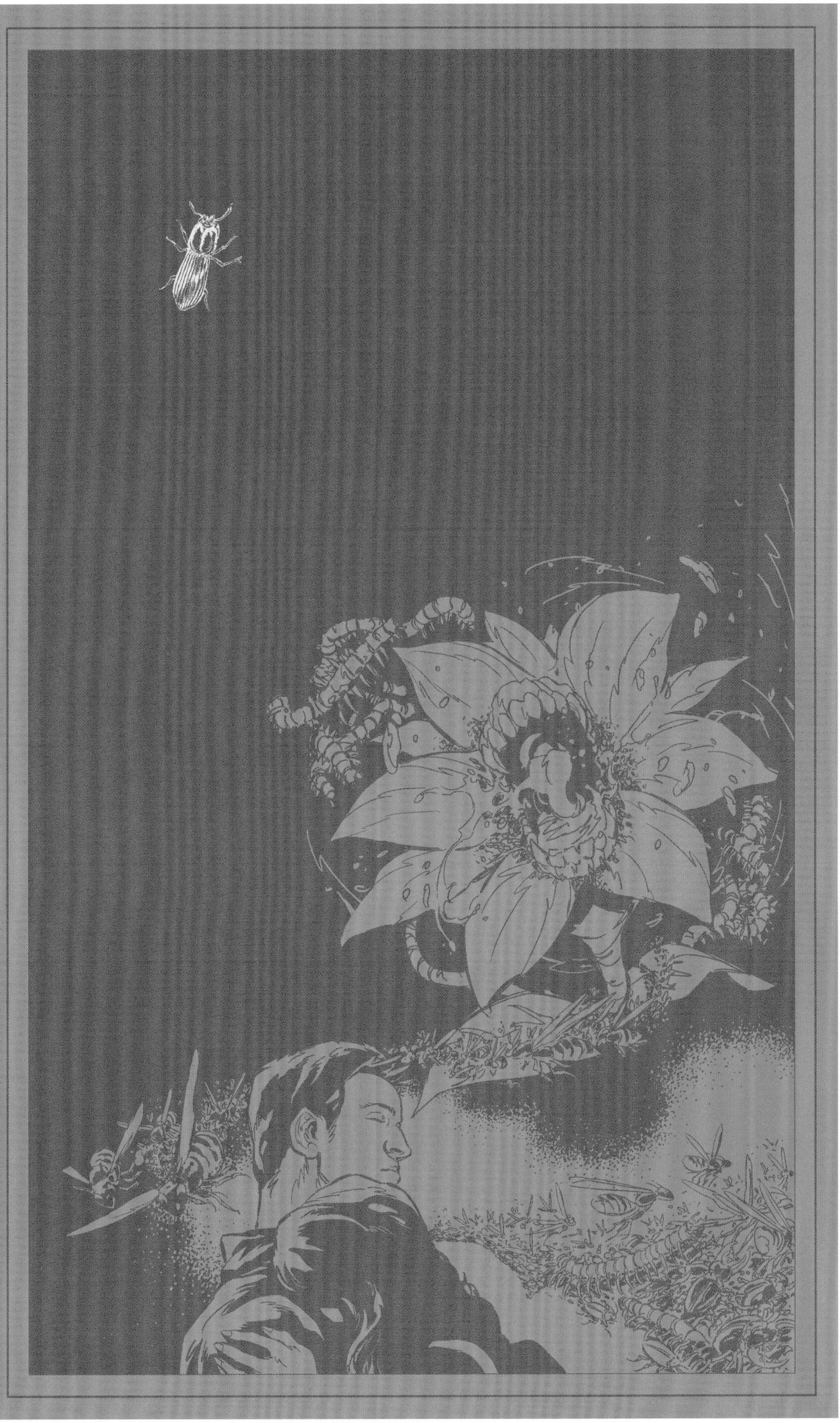

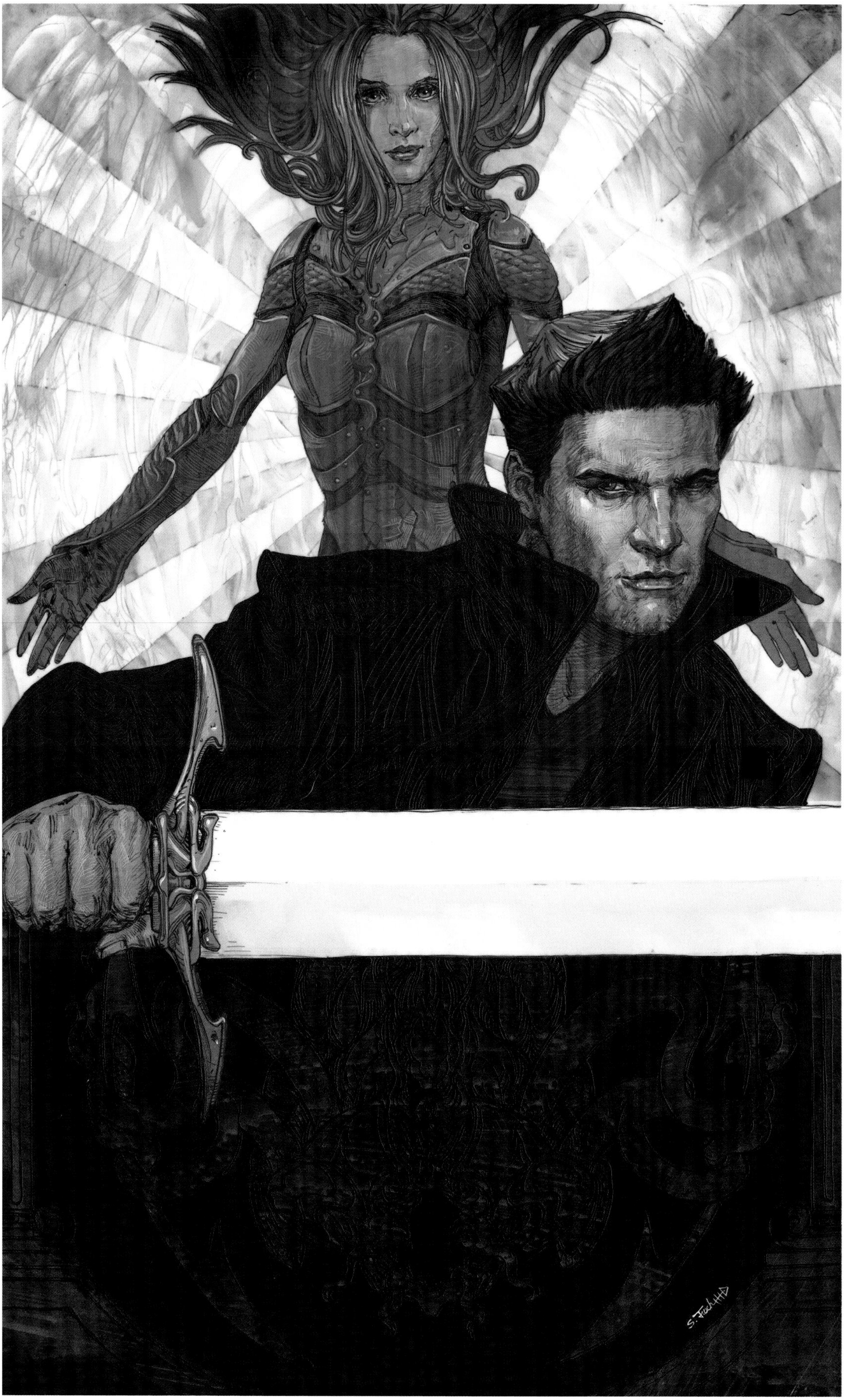

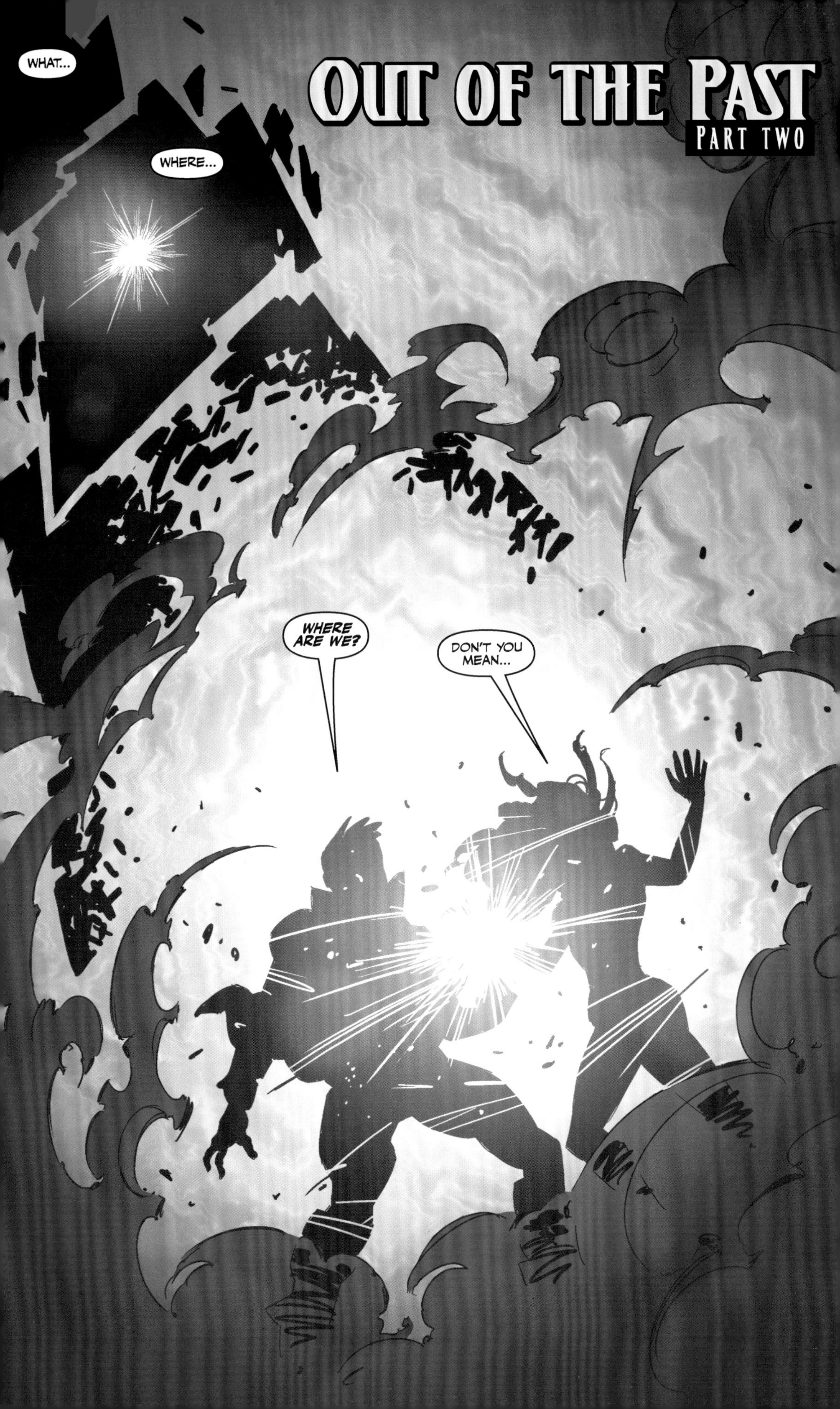
WHAT...
OUT OF THE PAST
PART TWO
WHERE...
WHERE ARE WE?
DON'T YOU MEAN...

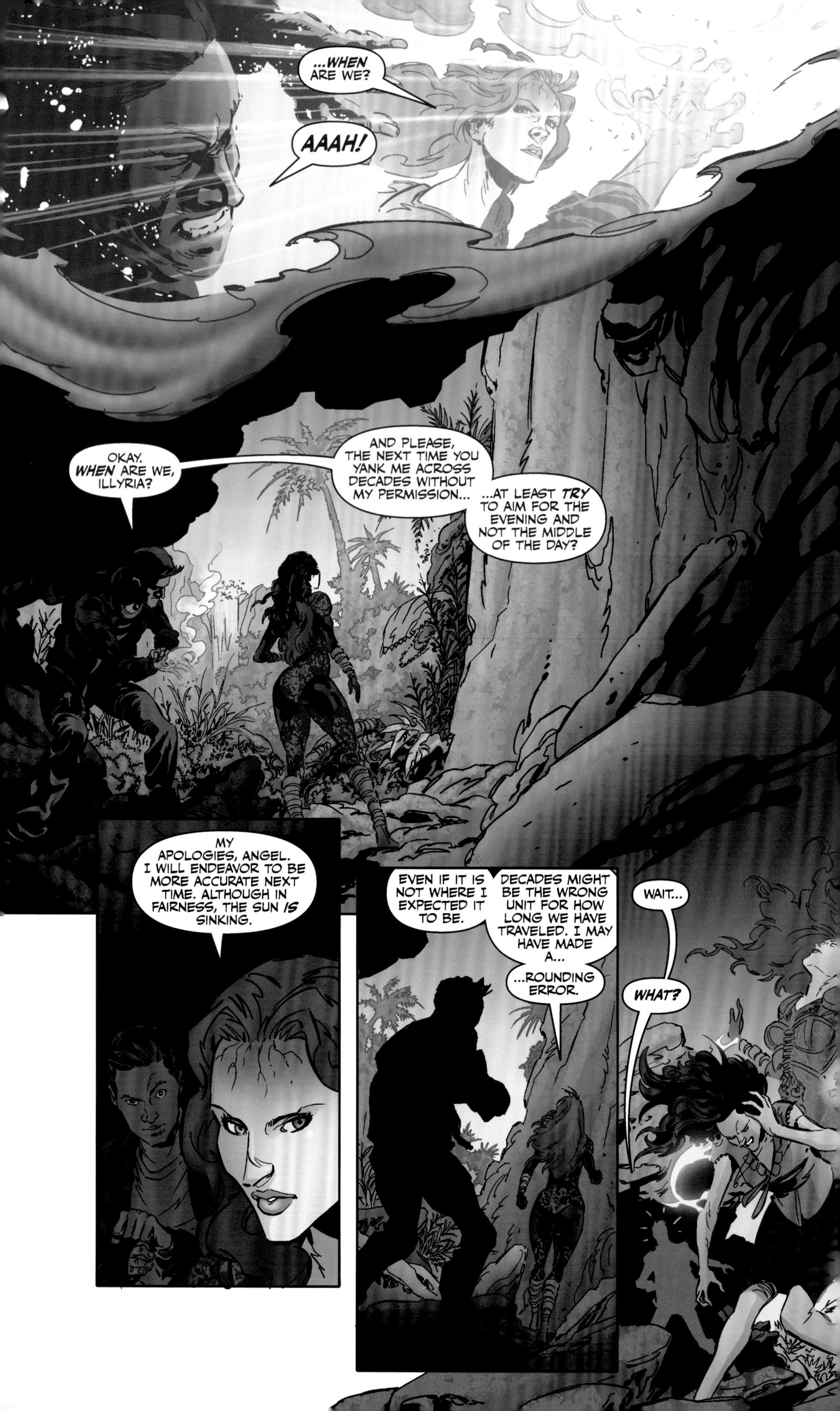
...WHEN ARE WE?
AAAH!
OKAY. WHEN ARE WE, ILLYRIA?
AND PLEASE, THE NEXT TIME YOU YANK ME ACROSS DECADES WITHOUT MY PERMISSION...
...AT LEAST TRY TO AIM FOR THE EVENING AND NOT THE MIDDLE OF THE DAY?
MY APOLOGIES, ANGEL. I WILL ENDEAVOR TO BE MORE ACCURATE NEXT TIME. ALTHOUGH IN FAIRNESS, THE SUN IS SINKING.
EVEN IF IT IS NOT WHERE I EXPECTED IT TO BE.
DECADES MIGHT BE THE WRONG UNIT FOR HOW LONG WE HAVE TRAVELED. I MAY HAVE MADE A...
...ROUNDING ERROR.
WAIT...
WHAT?

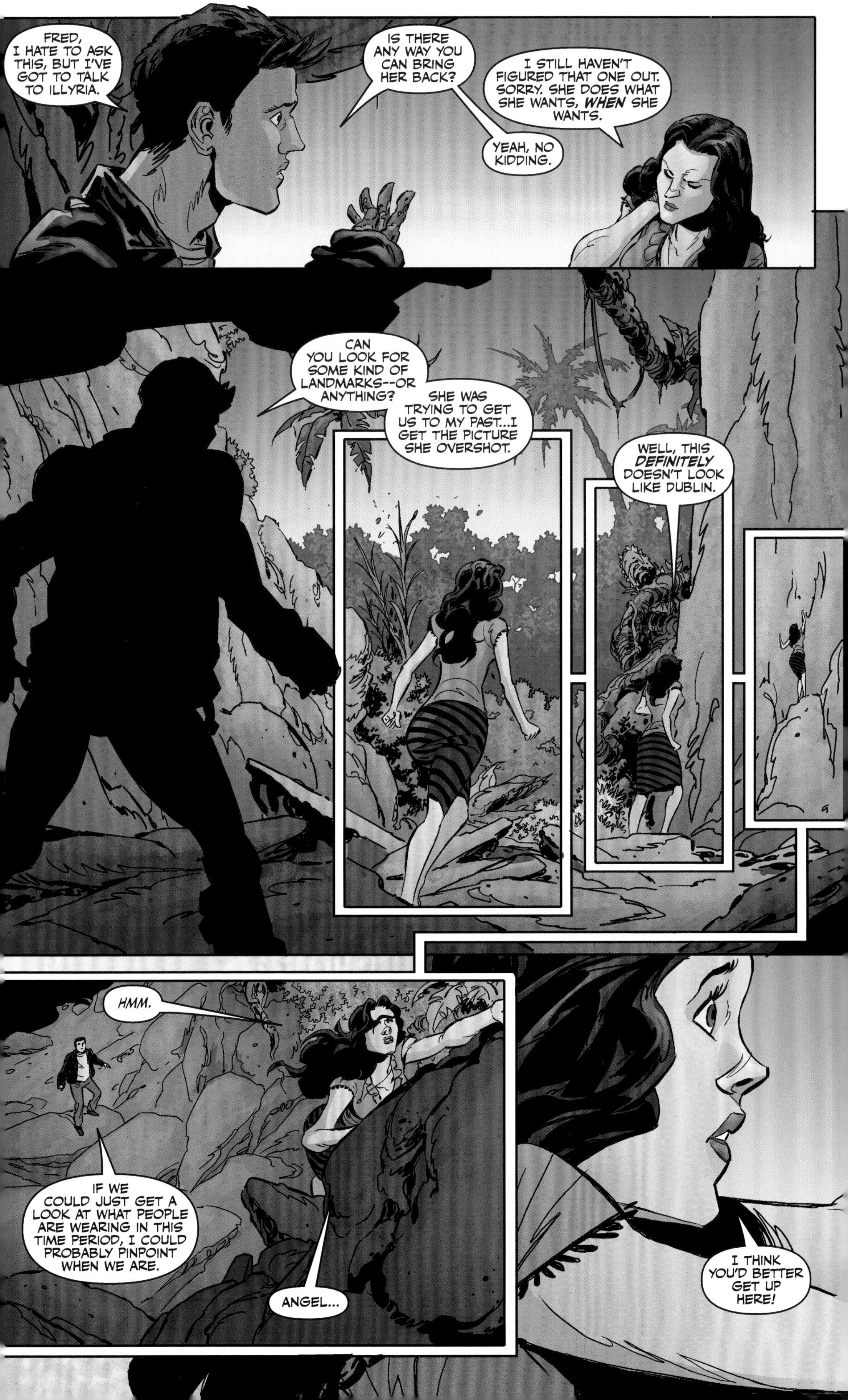
FRED, I HATE TO ASK THIS, BUT I'VE GOT TO TALK TO ILLYRIA.
IS THERE ANY WAY YOU CAN BRING HER BACK?
I STILL HAVEN'T FIGURED THAT ONE OUT. SORRY. SHE DOES WHAT SHE WANTS, *WHEN* SHE WANTS.
YEAH, NO KIDDING.
CAN YOU LOOK FOR SOME KIND OF LANDMARKS--OR ANYTHING?
SHE WAS TRYING TO GET US TO MY PAST...I GET THE PICTURE SHE OVERSHOT.
WELL, THIS *DEFINITELY* DOESN'T LOOK LIKE DUBLIN.
HMM.
IF WE COULD JUST GET A LOOK AT WHAT PEOPLE ARE WEARING IN THIS TIME PERIOD, I COULD PROBABLY PINPOINT WHEN WE ARE.
ANGEL...
I THINK YOU'D BETTER GET UP HERE!

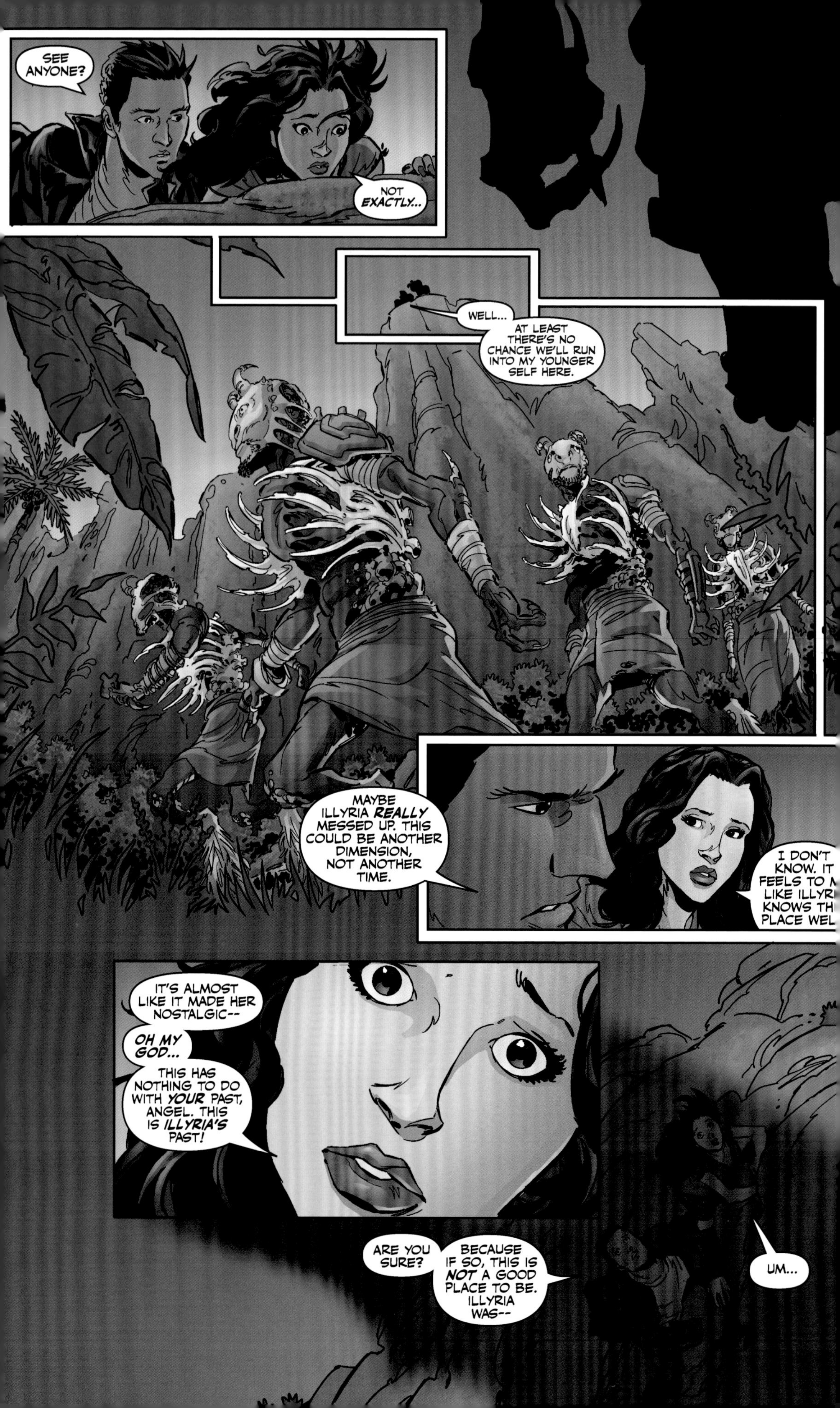
SEE ANYONE?
NOT EXACTLY...
WELL...
AT LEAST THERE'S NO CHANCE WE'LL RUN INTO MY YOUNGER SELF HERE.
MAYBE ILLYRIA REALLY MESSED UP. THIS COULD BE ANOTHER DIMENSION, NOT ANOTHER TIME.
I DON'T KNOW. IT FEELS TO M LIKE ILLYR KNOWS TH PLACE WEL
IT'S ALMOST LIKE IT MADE HER NOSTALGIC--
OH MY GOD...
THIS HAS NOTHING TO DO WITH YOUR PAST, ANGEL. THIS IS ILLYRIA'S PAST!
ARE YOU SURE?
BECAUSE IF SO, THIS IS NOT A GOOD PLACE TO BE. ILLYRIA WAS--
UM...

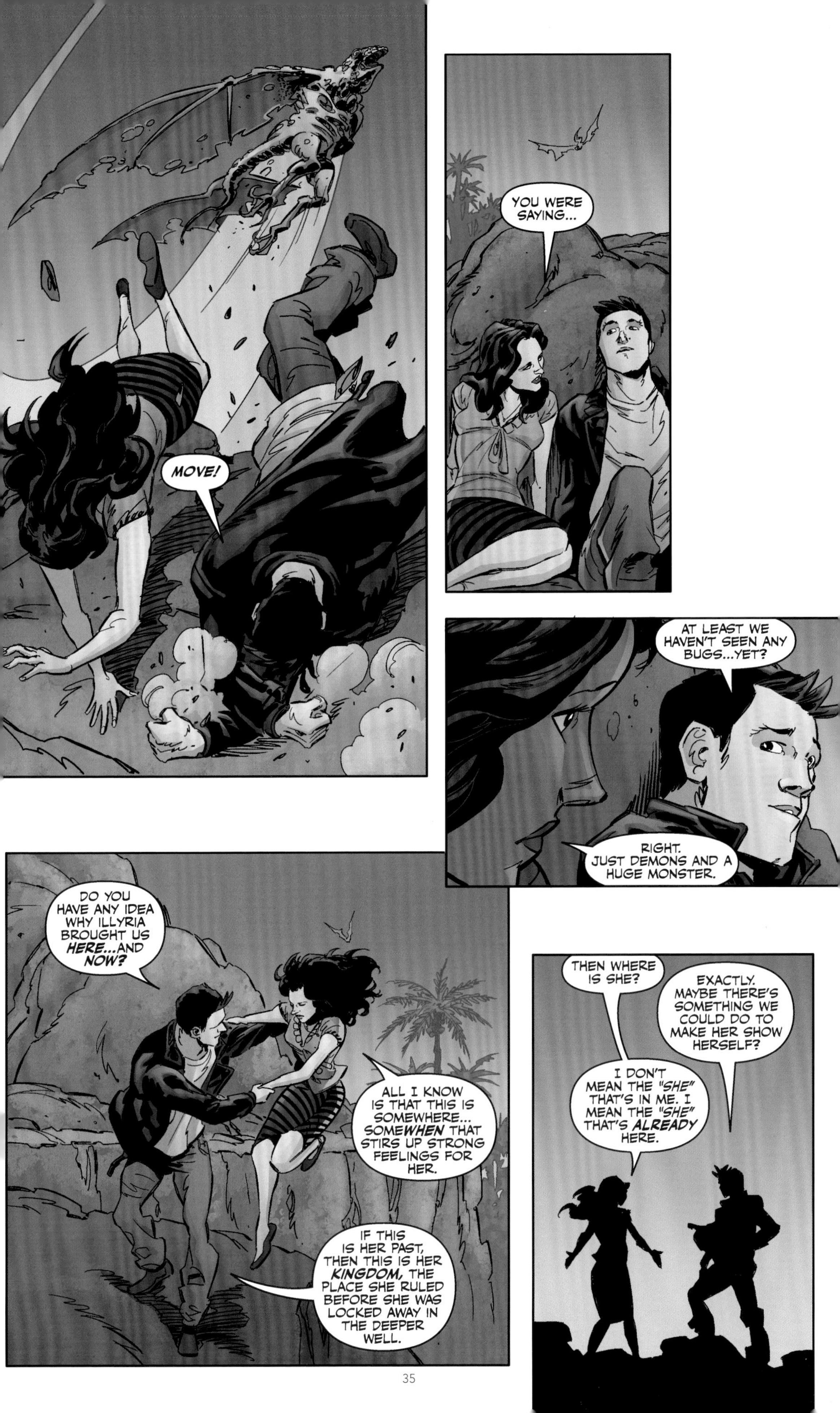
MOVE!
YOU WERE SAYING...
AT LEAST WE HAVEN'T SEEN ANY BUGS...YET?
RIGHT. JUST DEMONS AND A HUGE MONSTER.
DO YOU HAVE ANY IDEA WHY ILLYRIA BROUGHT US HERE...AND NOW?
ALL I KNOW IS THAT THIS IS SOMEWHERE... SOMEWHEN THAT STIRS UP STRONG FEELINGS FOR HER.
IF THIS IS HER PAST, THEN THIS IS HER KINGDOM, THE PLACE SHE RULED BEFORE SHE WAS LOCKED AWAY IN THE DEEPER WELL.
THEN WHERE IS SHE?
EXACTLY. MAYBE THERE'S SOMETHING WE COULD DO TO MAKE HER SHOW HERSELF?
I DON'T MEAN THE "SHE" THAT'S IN ME. I MEAN THE "SHE" THAT'S ALREADY HERE.

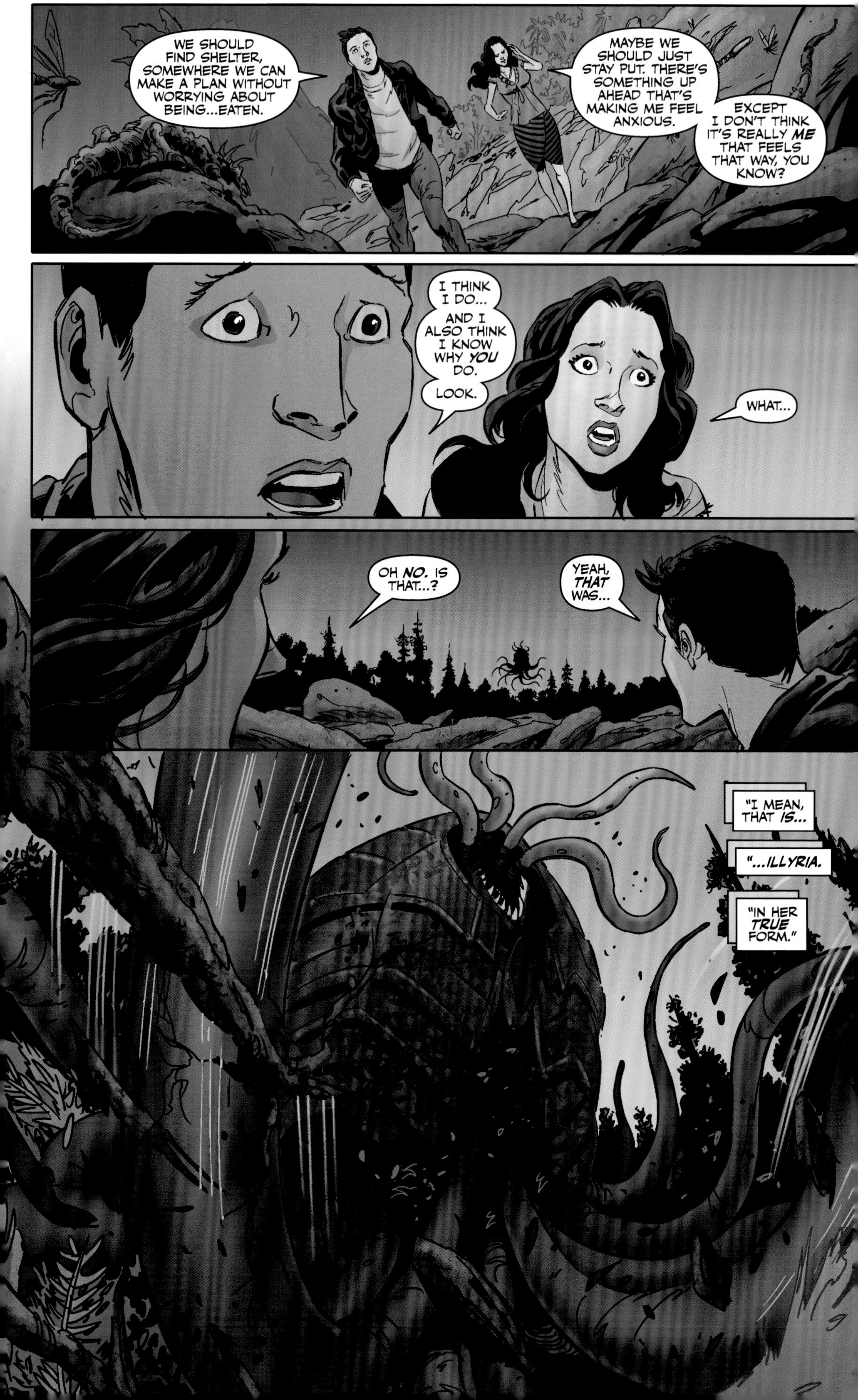
WE SHOULD FIND SHELTER, SOMEWHERE WE CAN MAKE A PLAN WITHOUT WORRYING ABOUT BEING...EATEN.
MAYBE WE SHOULD JUST STAY PUT. THERE'S SOMETHING UP AHEAD THAT'S MAKING ME FEEL ANXIOUS.
EXCEPT I DON'T THINK IT'S REALLY *ME* THAT FEELS THAT WAY, YOU KNOW?
I THINK I DO...
AND I ALSO THINK I KNOW WHY *YOU* DO.
LOOK.
WHAT...
OH *NO.* IS THAT...?
YEAH, *THAT* WAS...
"I MEAN, THAT *IS...*
"*...ILLYRIA.*
"IN HER *TRUE* FORM."

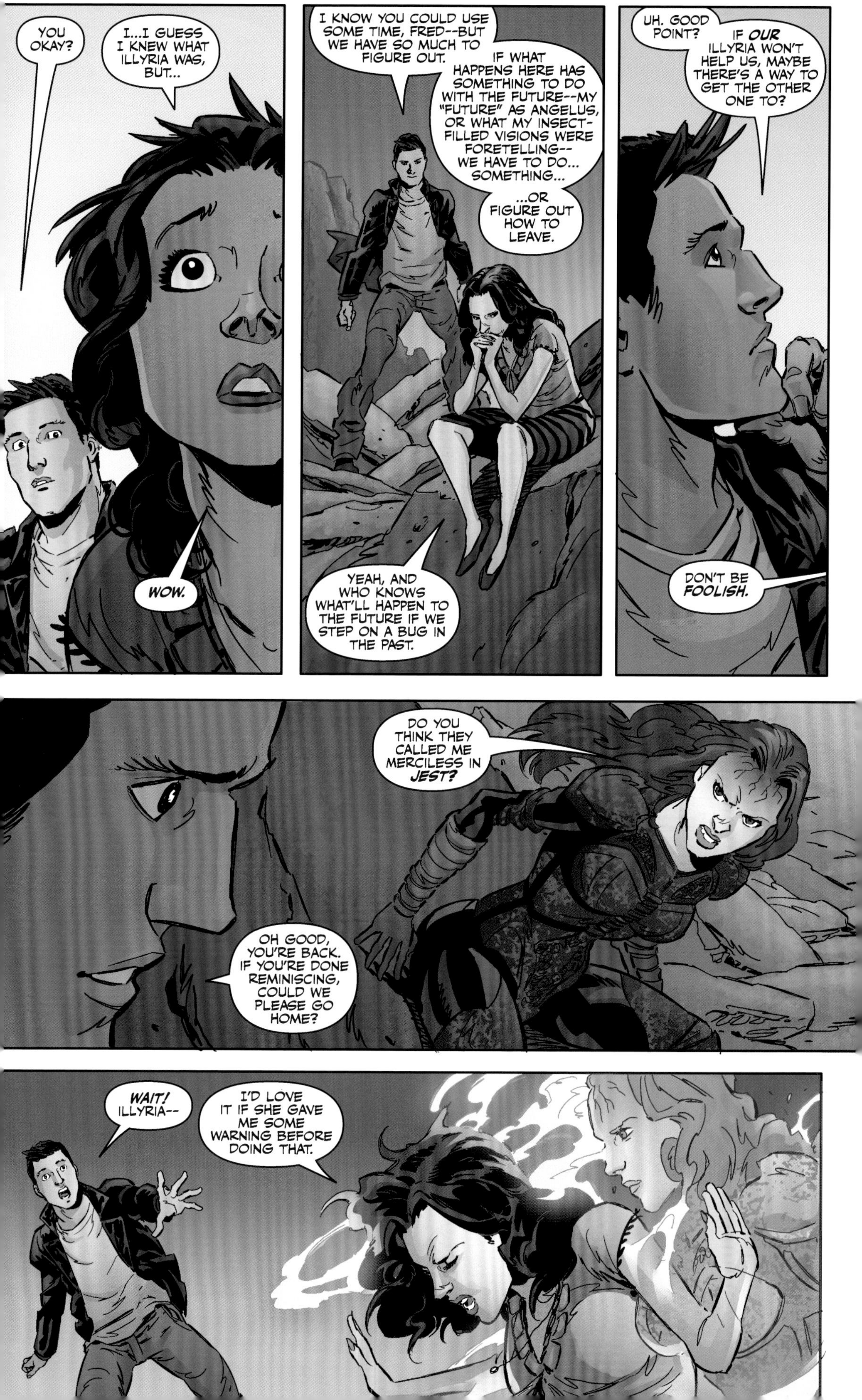
YOU OKAY?
I...I GUESS I KNEW WHAT ILLYRIA WAS, BUT...
WOW.
I KNOW YOU COULD USE SOME TIME, FRED--BUT WE HAVE SO MUCH TO FIGURE OUT.
IF WHAT HAPPENS HERE HAS SOMETHING TO DO WITH THE FUTURE--MY "FUTURE" AS ANGELUS, OR WHAT MY INSECT-FILLED VISIONS WERE FORETELLING-- WE HAVE TO DO... SOMETHING...
...OR FIGURE OUT HOW TO LEAVE.
YEAH, AND WHO KNOWS WHAT'LL HAPPEN TO THE FUTURE IF WE STEP ON A BUG IN THE PAST.
UH. GOOD POINT?
IF OUR ILLYRIA WON'T HELP US, MAYBE THERE'S A WAY TO GET THE OTHER ONE TO?
DON'T BE FOOLISH.
DO YOU THINK THEY CALLED ME MERCILESS IN JEST?
OH GOOD, YOU'RE BACK. IF YOU'RE DONE REMINISCING, COULD WE PLEASE GO HOME?
WAIT! ILLYRIA--
I'D LOVE IT IF SHE GAVE ME SOME WARNING BEFORE DOING THAT.

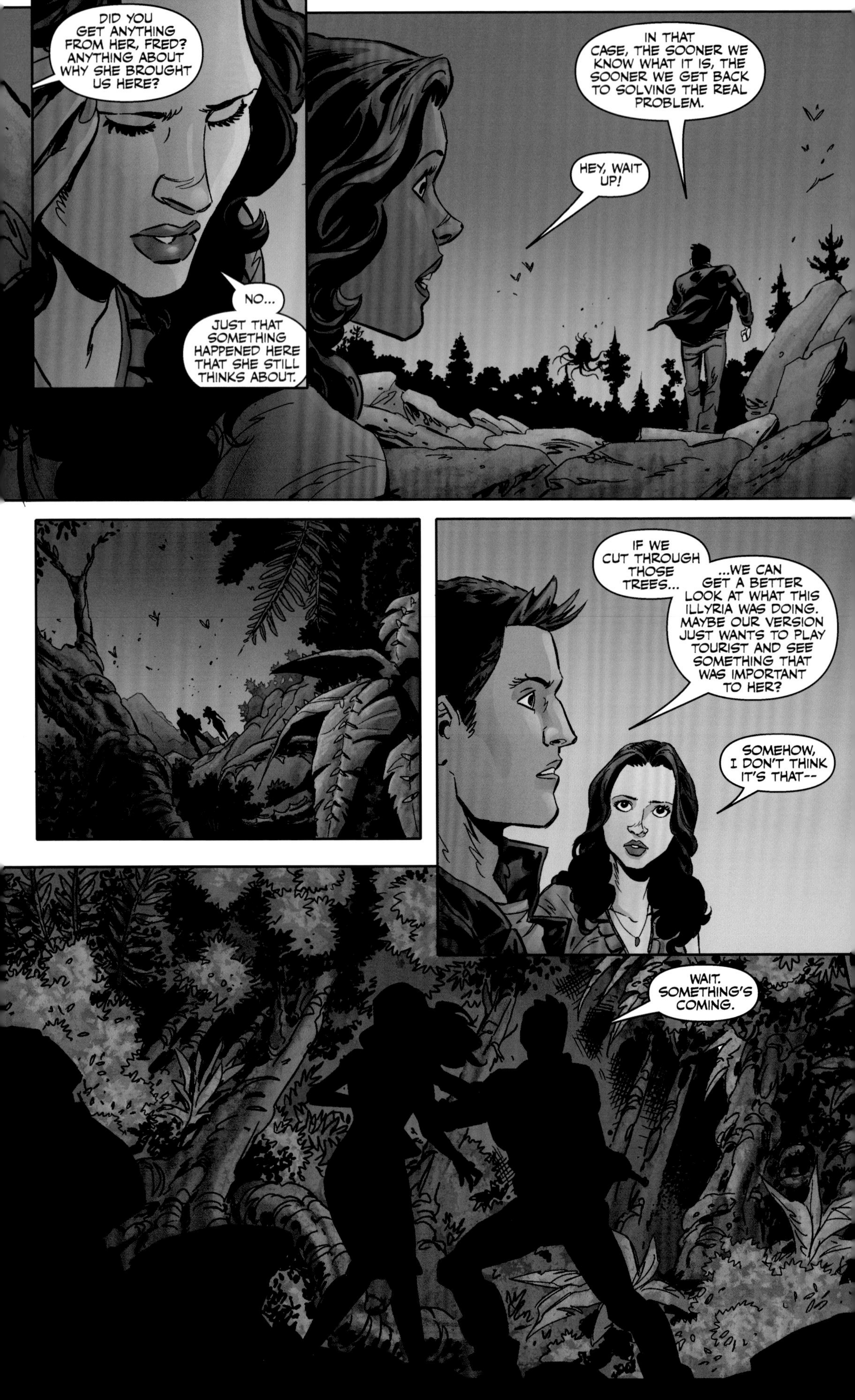

DID YOU GET ANYTHING FROM HER, FRED? ANYTHING ABOUT WHY SHE BROUGHT US HERE?
NO...
JUST THAT SOMETHING HAPPENED HERE THAT SHE STILL THINKS ABOUT.
IN THAT CASE, THE SOONER WE KNOW WHAT IT IS, THE SOONER WE GET BACK TO SOLVING THE REAL PROBLEM.
HEY, WAIT UP!
IF WE CUT THROUGH THOSE TREES...
...WE CAN GET A BETTER LOOK AT WHAT THIS ILLYRIA WAS DOING. MAYBE OUR VERSION JUST WANTS TO PLAY TOURIST AND SEE SOMETHING THAT WAS IMPORTANT TO HER?
SOMEHOW, I DON'T THINK IT'S THAT--
WAIT. SOMETHING'S COMING.

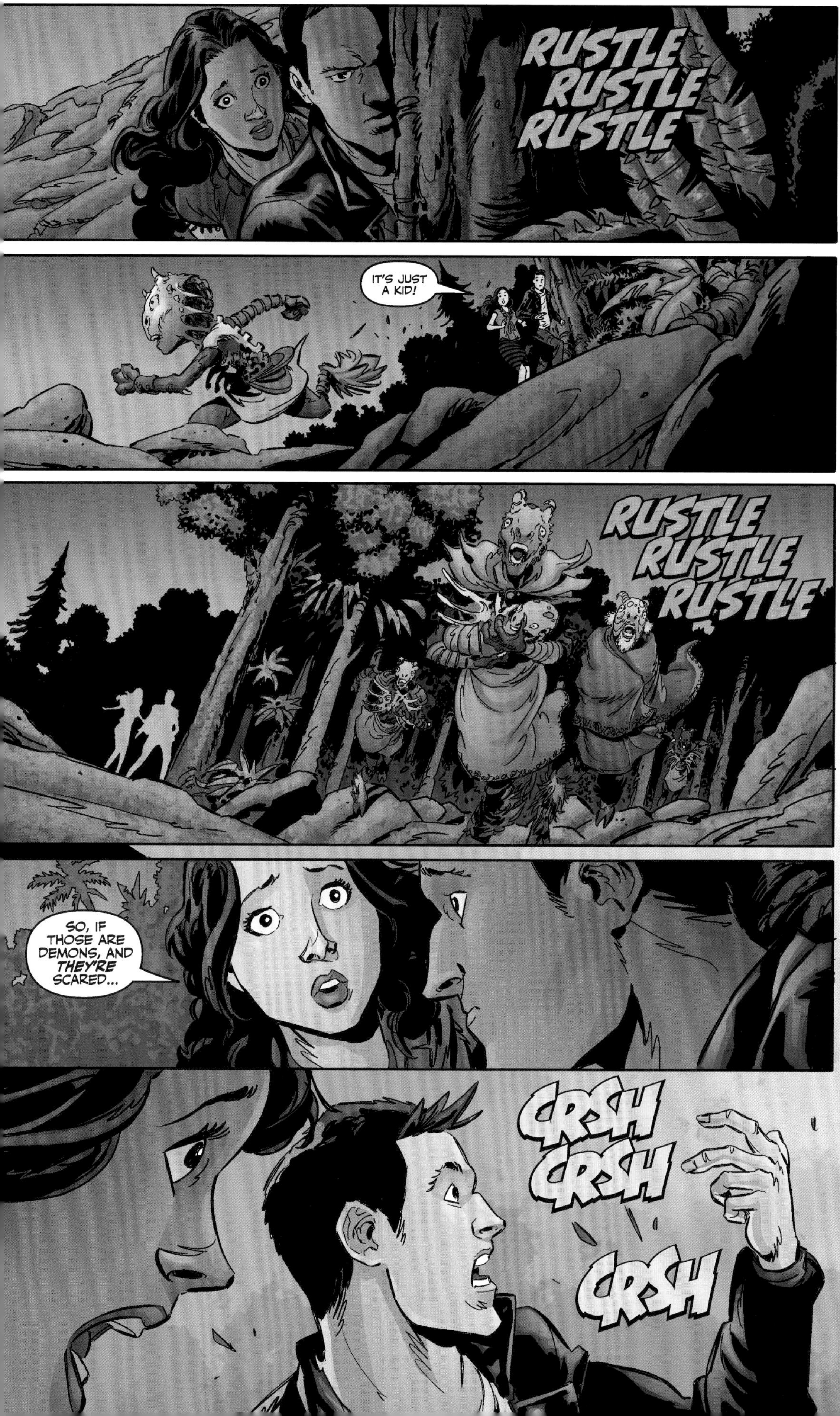

RUSTLE RUSTLE RUSTLE
IT'S JUST A KID!
RUSTLE RUSTLE RUSTLE
SO, IF THOSE ARE DEMONS, AND *THEY'RE* SCARED...
CRSH CRSH CRSH

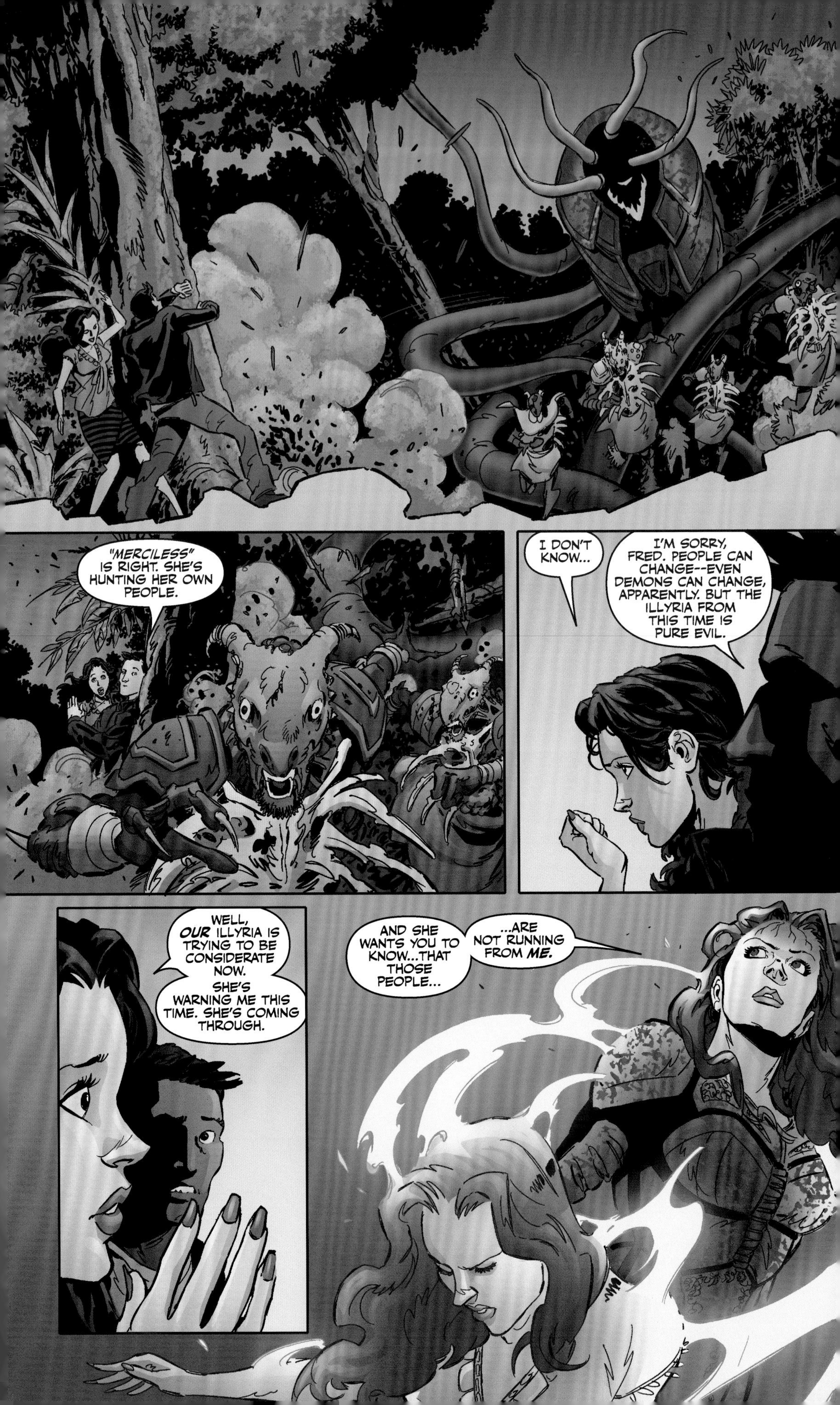

"MERCILESS" IS RIGHT. SHE'S HUNTING HER OWN PEOPLE.
I DON'T KNOW...
I'M SORRY, FRED. PEOPLE CAN CHANGE--EVEN DEMONS CAN CHANGE, APPARENTLY. BUT THE ILLYRIA FROM THIS TIME IS PURE EVIL.
WELL, OUR ILLYRIA IS TRYING TO BE CONSIDERATE NOW.
SHE'S WARNING ME THIS TIME. SHE'S COMING THROUGH.
AND SHE WANTS YOU TO KNOW...THAT THOSE PEOPLE...
...ARE NOT RUNNING FROM ME.

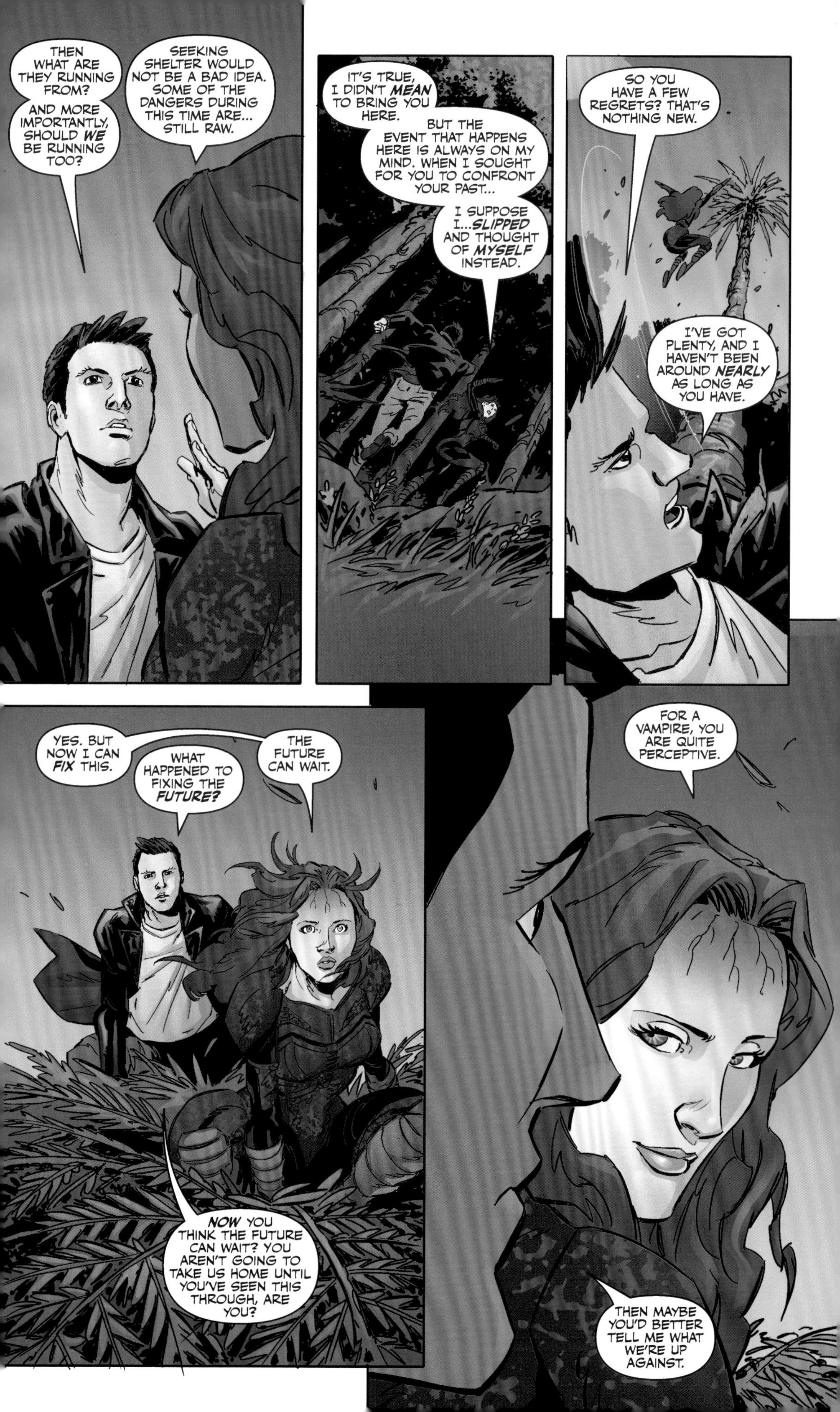
THEN WHAT ARE THEY RUNNING FROM?
AND MORE IMPORTANTLY, SHOULD *WE* BE RUNNING TOO?
SEEKING SHELTER WOULD NOT BE A BAD IDEA. SOME OF THE DANGERS DURING THIS TIME ARE... STILL RAW.
IT'S TRUE, I DIDN'T *MEAN* TO BRING YOU HERE.
BUT THE EVENT THAT HAPPENS HERE IS ALWAYS ON MY MIND. WHEN I SOUGHT FOR YOU TO CONFRONT YOUR PAST...
I SUPPOSE I...*SLIPPED* AND THOUGHT OF *MYSELF* INSTEAD.
SO YOU HAVE A FEW REGRETS? THAT'S NOTHING NEW.
I'VE GOT PLENTY, AND I HAVEN'T BEEN AROUND *NEARLY* AS LONG AS YOU HAVE.
YES. BUT NOW I CAN *FIX* THIS.
WHAT HAPPENED TO FIXING THE *FUTURE?*
THE FUTURE CAN WAIT.
NOW YOU THINK THE FUTURE CAN WAIT? YOU AREN'T GOING TO TAKE US HOME UNTIL YOU'VE SEEN THIS THROUGH, ARE YOU?
FOR A VAMPIRE, YOU ARE QUITE PERCEPTIVE.
THEN MAYBE YOU'D BETTER TELL ME WHAT WE'RE UP AGAINST.

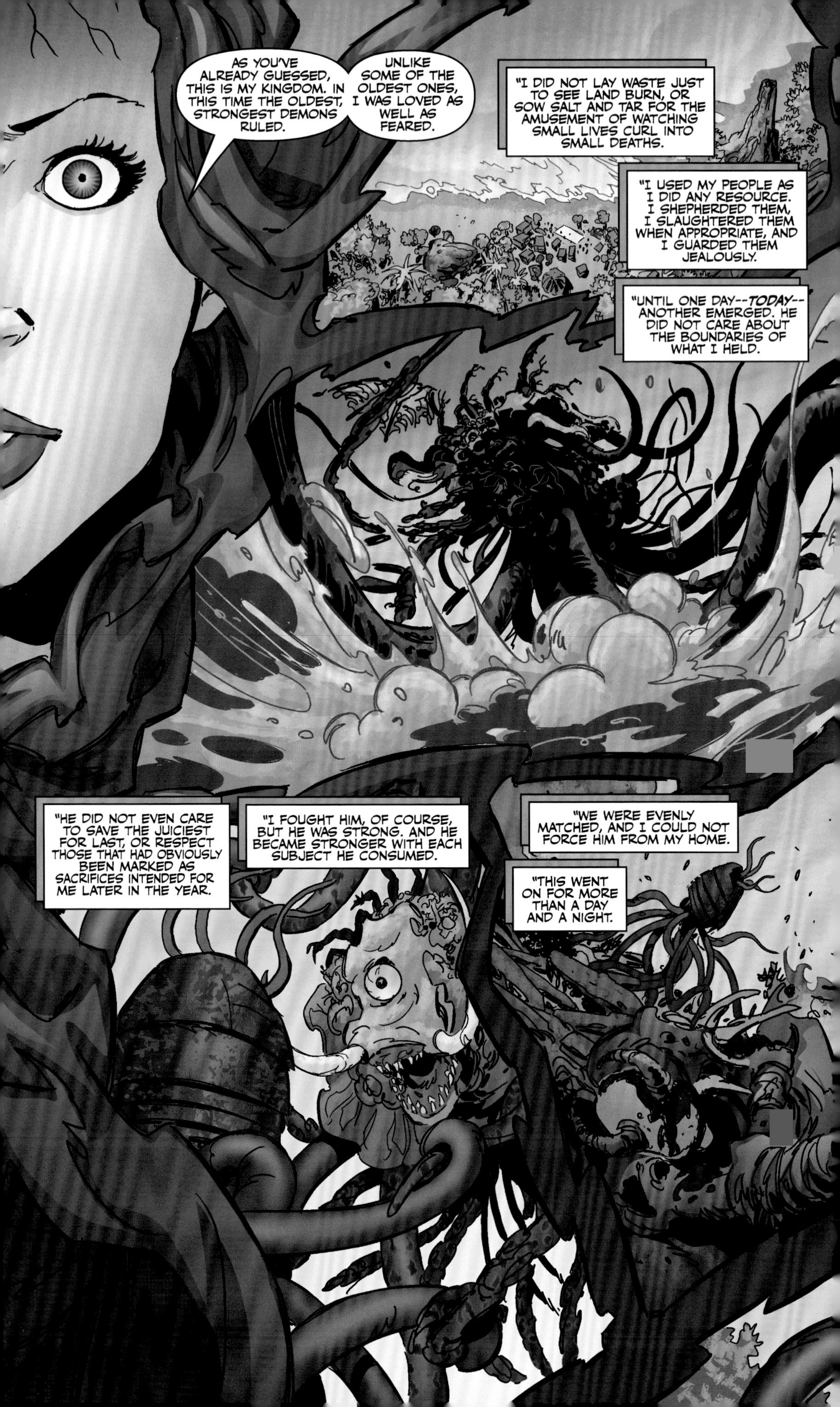
AS YOU'VE ALREADY GUESSED, THIS IS MY KINGDOM. IN THIS TIME THE OLDEST, STRONGEST DEMONS RULED.
UNLIKE SOME OF THE OLDEST ONES, I WAS LOVED AS WELL AS FEARED.
"I DID NOT LAY WASTE JUST TO SEE LAND BURN, OR SOW SALT AND TAR FOR THE AMUSEMENT OF WATCHING SMALL LIVES CURL INTO SMALL DEATHS.
"I USED MY PEOPLE AS I DID ANY RESOURCE. I SHEPHERDED THEM, I SLAUGHTERED THEM WHEN APPROPRIATE, AND I GUARDED THEM JEALOUSLY.
"UNTIL ONE DAY--*TODAY*--ANOTHER EMERGED. HE DID NOT CARE ABOUT THE BOUNDARIES OF WHAT I HELD.
"HE DID NOT EVEN CARE TO SAVE THE JUICIEST FOR LAST, OR RESPECT THOSE THAT HAD OBVIOUSLY BEEN MARKED AS SACRIFICES INTENDED FOR ME LATER IN THE YEAR.
"I FOUGHT HIM, OF COURSE, BUT HE WAS STRONG. AND HE BECAME STRONGER WITH EACH SUBJECT HE CONSUMED.
"WE WERE EVENLY MATCHED, AND I COULD NOT FORCE HIM FROM MY HOME.
"THIS WENT ON FOR MORE THAN A DAY AND A NIGHT.

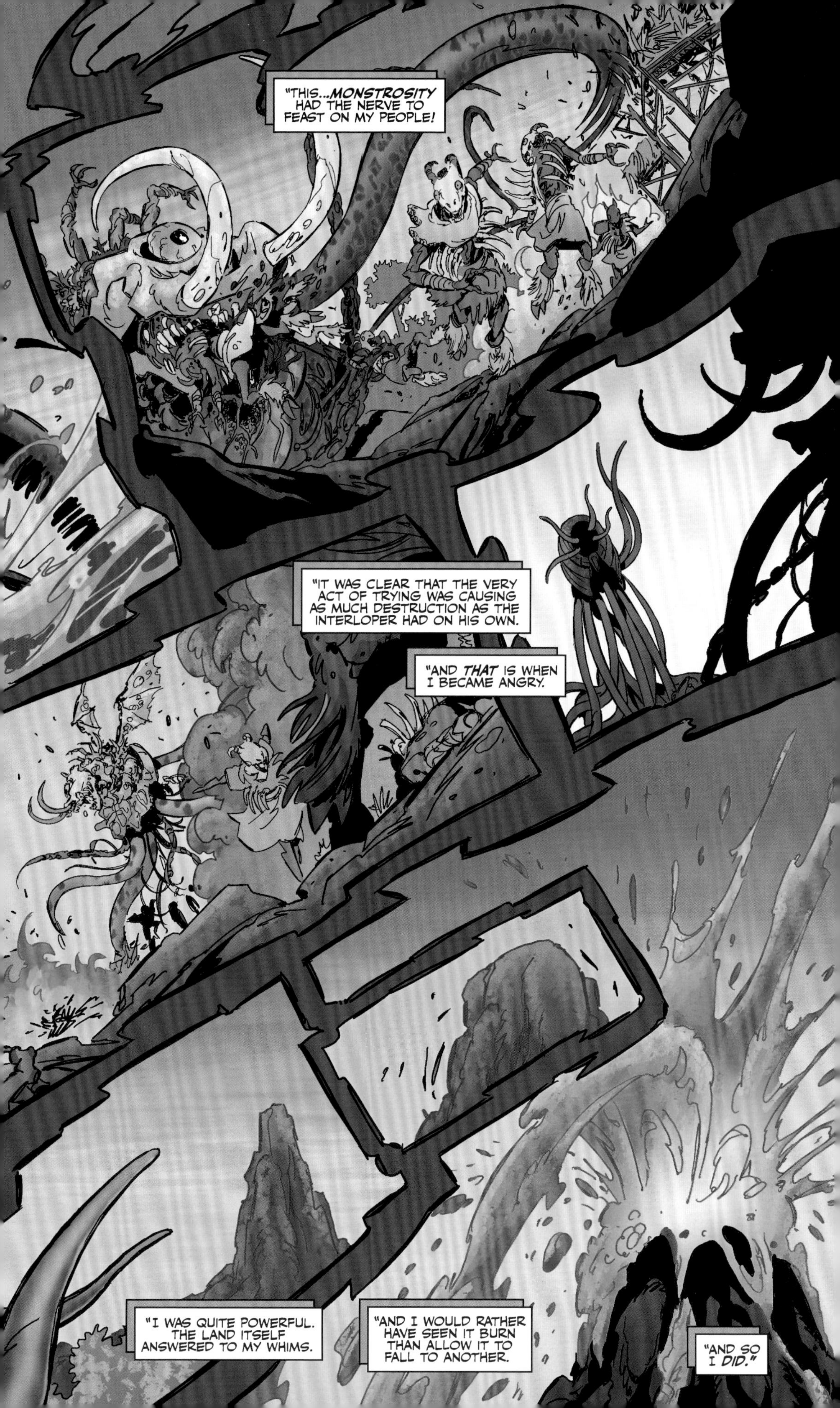
"THIS...*MONSTROSITY* HAD THE NERVE TO FEAST ON MY PEOPLE!
"IT WAS CLEAR THAT THE VERY ACT OF TRYING WAS CAUSING AS MUCH DESTRUCTION AS THE INTERLOPER HAD ON HIS OWN.
"AND *THAT* IS WHEN I BECAME ANGRY.
"I WAS QUITE POWERFUL. THE LAND ITSELF ANSWERED TO MY WHIMS.
"AND I WOULD RATHER HAVE SEEN IT BURN THAN ALLOW IT TO FALL TO ANOTHER.
"AND SO I *DID*."

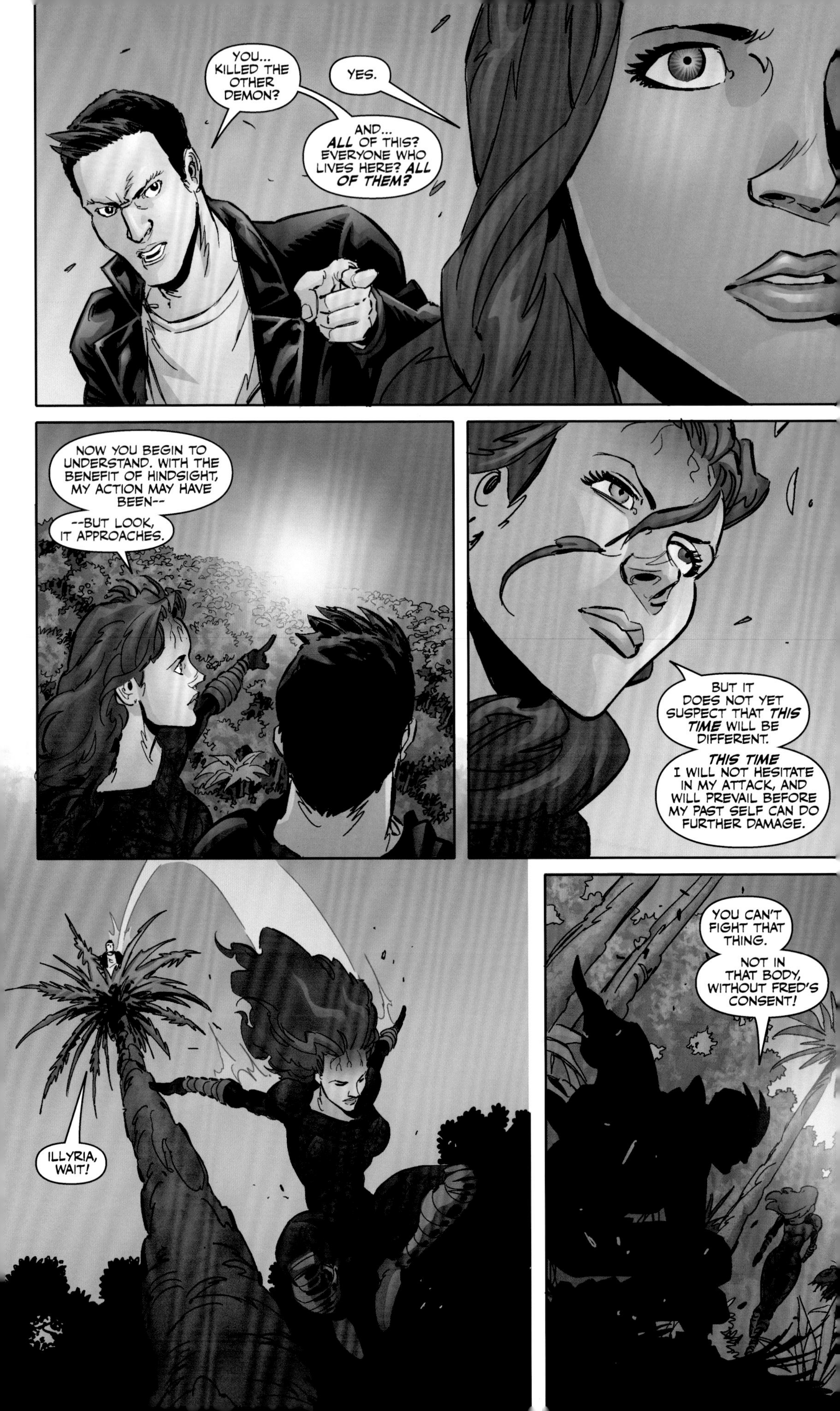

YOU... KILLED THE OTHER DEMON?
YES.
AND... ALL OF THIS? EVERYONE WHO LIVES HERE? ALL OF THEM?
NOW YOU BEGIN TO UNDERSTAND. WITH THE BENEFIT OF HINDSIGHT, MY ACTION MAY HAVE BEEN--
--BUT LOOK, IT APPROACHES.
BUT IT DOES NOT YET SUSPECT THAT THIS TIME WILL BE DIFFERENT.
THIS TIME I WILL NOT HESITATE IN MY ATTACK, AND WILL PREVAIL BEFORE MY PAST SELF CAN DO FURTHER DAMAGE.
ILLYRIA, WAIT!
YOU CAN'T FIGHT THAT THING.
NOT IN THAT BODY, WITHOUT FRED'S CONSENT!

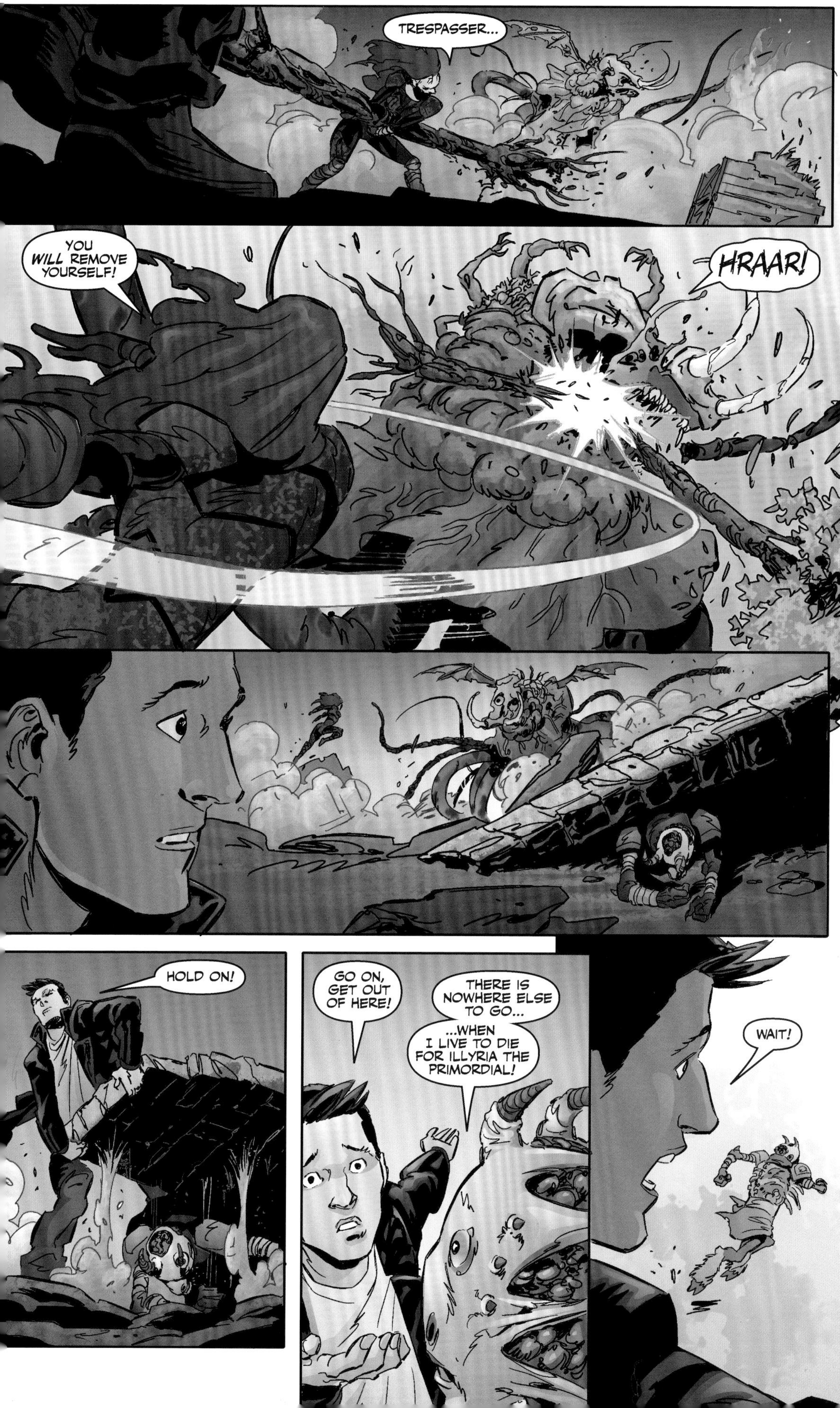
TRESPASSER...
YOU *WILL* REMOVE YOURSELF!
HRAAR!
HOLD ON!
GO ON, GET OUT OF HERE!
THERE IS NOWHERE ELSE TO GO...
...WHEN I LIVE TO DIE FOR ILLYRIA THE PRIMORDIAL!
WAIT!

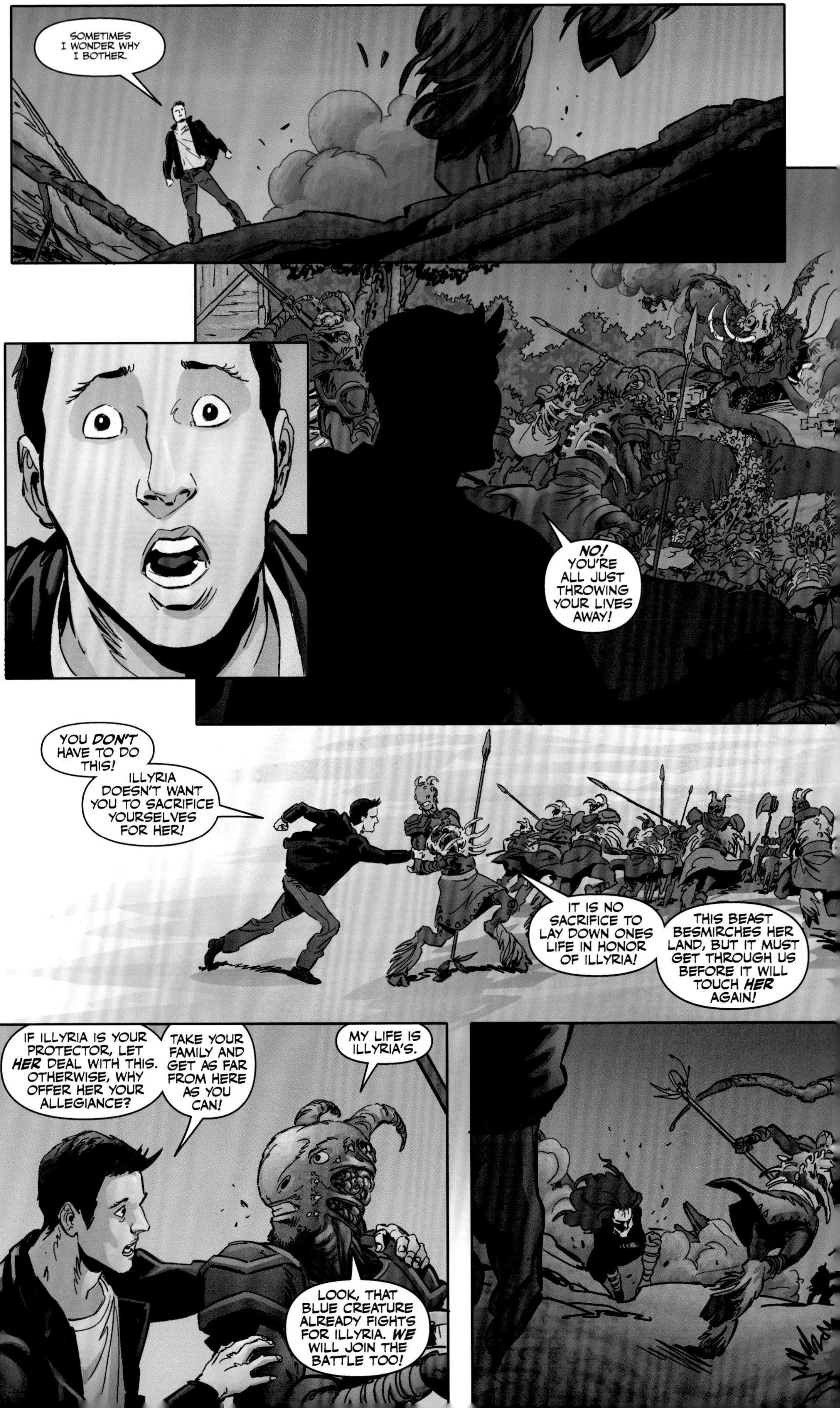
SOMETIMES I WONDER WHY I BOTHER.
NO! YOU'RE ALL JUST THROWING YOUR LIVES AWAY!
YOU DON'T HAVE TO DO THIS!
ILLYRIA DOESN'T WANT YOU TO SACRIFICE YOURSELVES FOR HER!
IT IS NO SACRIFICE TO LAY DOWN ONES LIFE IN HONOR OF ILLYRIA!
THIS BEAST BESMIRCHES HER LAND, BUT IT MUST GET THROUGH US BEFORE IT WILL TOUCH HER AGAIN!
IF ILLYRIA IS YOUR PROTECTOR, LET HER DEAL WITH THIS. OTHERWISE, WHY OFFER HER YOUR ALLEGIANCE?
TAKE YOUR FAMILY AND GET AS FAR FROM HERE AS YOU CAN!
MY LIFE IS ILLYRIA'S.
LOOK, THAT BLUE CREATURE ALREADY FIGHTS FOR ILLYRIA. WE WILL JOIN THE BATTLE TOO!

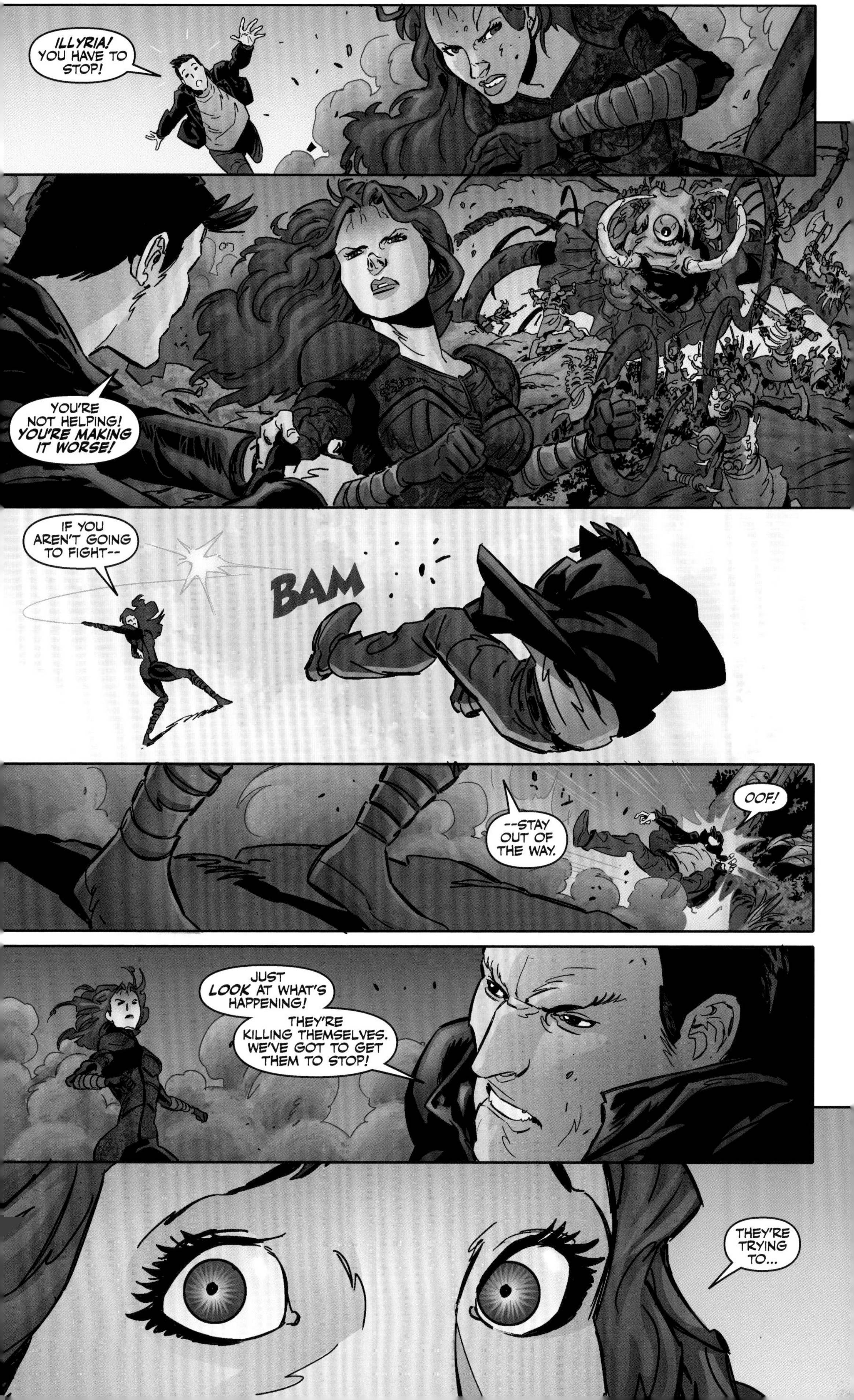
ILLYRIA! YOU HAVE TO STOP!
YOU'RE NOT HELPING! YOU'RE MAKING IT WORSE!
IF YOU AREN'T GOING TO FIGHT--
BAM
--STAY OUT OF THE WAY.
OOF!
JUST LOOK AT WHAT'S HAPPENING!
THEY'RE KILLING THEMSELVES. WE'VE GOT TO GET THEM TO STOP!
THEY'RE TRYING TO...

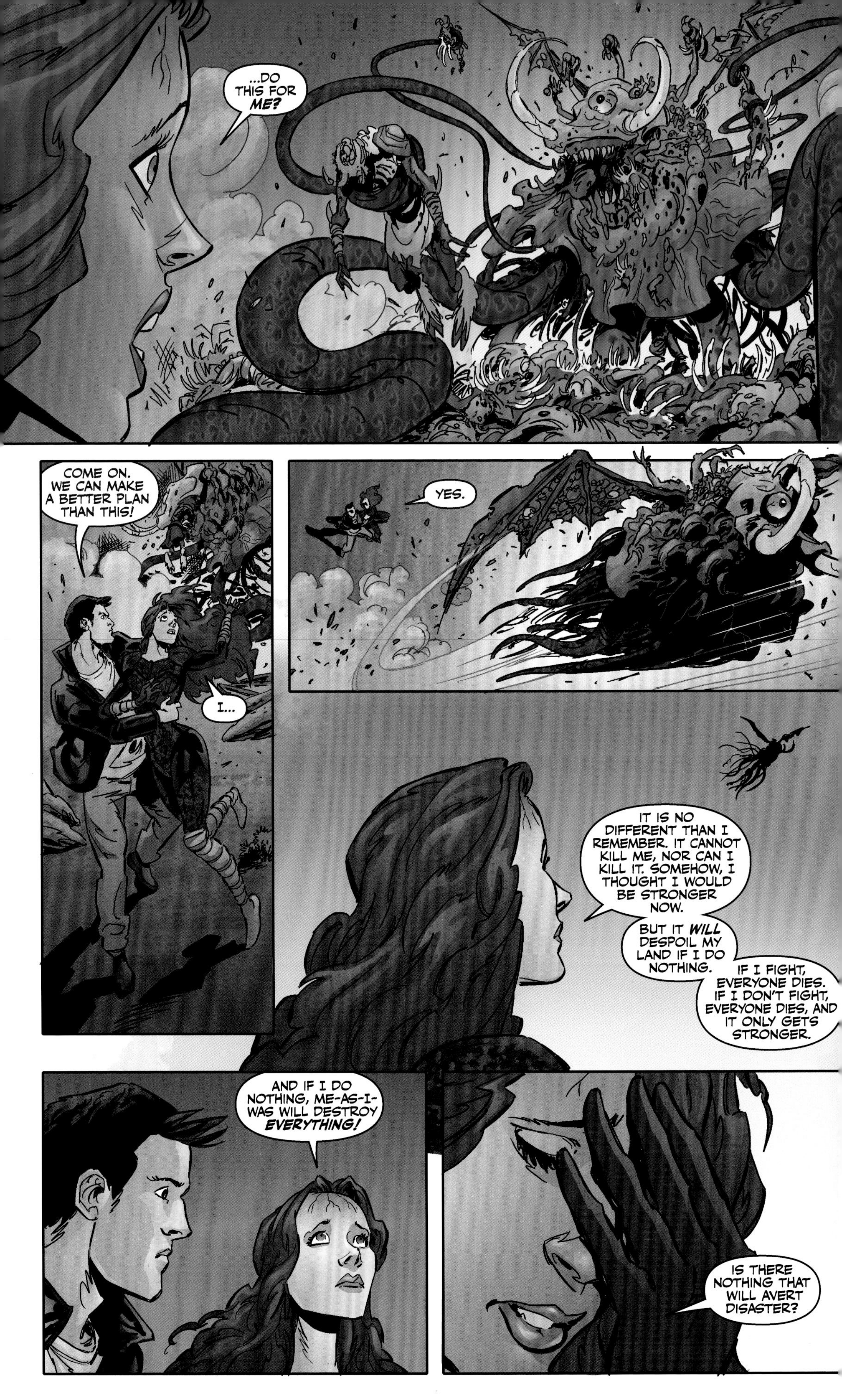
...DO THIS FOR *ME?*
COME ON. WE CAN MAKE A BETTER PLAN THAN THIS!
I...
YES.
IT IS NO DIFFERENT THAN I REMEMBER. IT CANNOT KILL ME, NOR CAN I KILL IT. SOMEHOW, I THOUGHT I WOULD BE STRONGER NOW.
BUT IT *WILL* DESPOIL MY LAND IF I DO NOTHING.
IF I FIGHT, EVERYONE DIES. IF I DON'T FIGHT, EVERYONE DIES, AND IT ONLY GETS STRONGER.
AND IF I DO NOTHING, ME-AS-I-WAS WILL DESTROY *EVERYTHING!*
IS THERE NOTHING THAT WILL AVERT DISASTER?

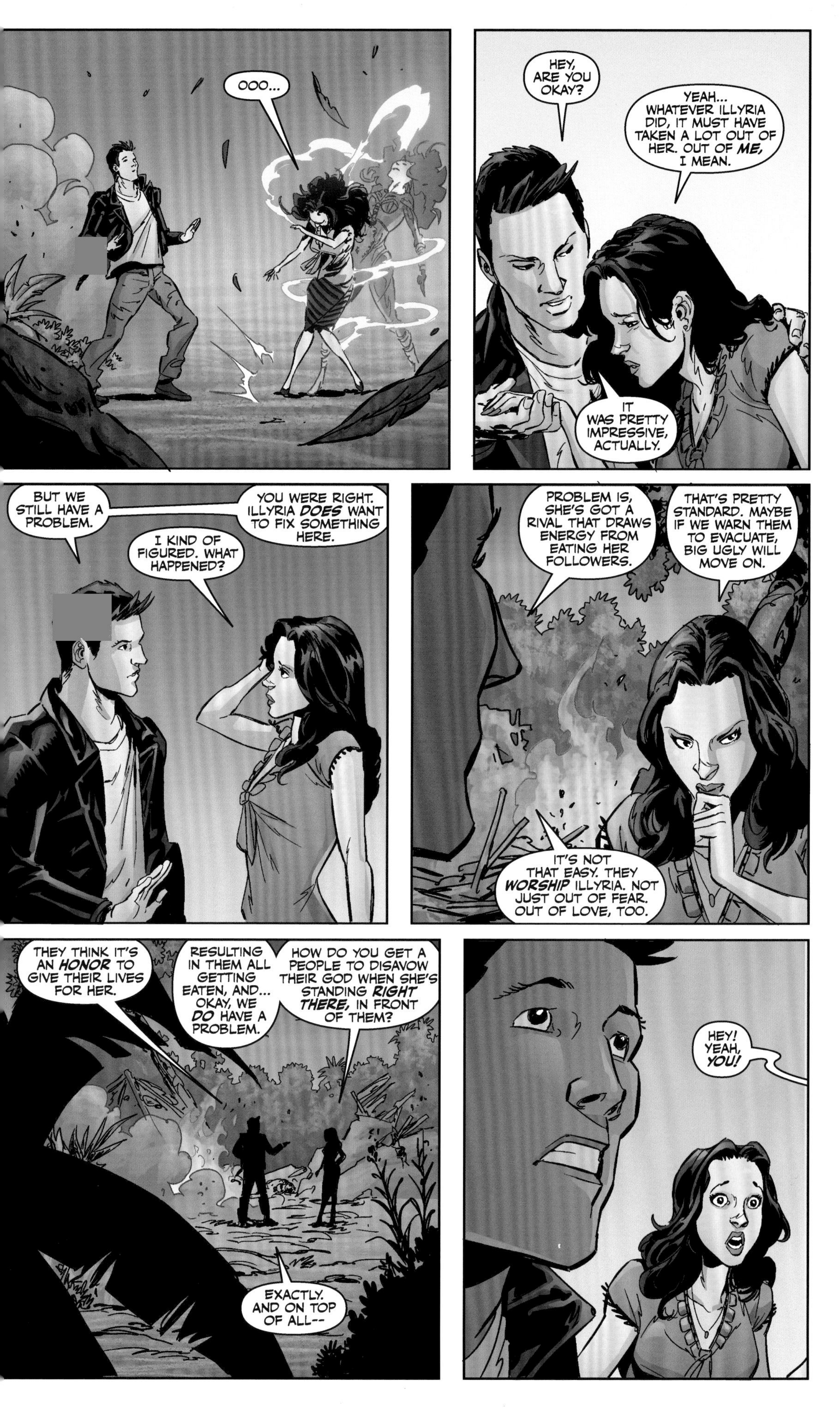
OOO...
HEY, ARE YOU OKAY?
YEAH... WHATEVER ILLYRIA DID, IT MUST HAVE TAKEN A LOT OUT OF HER. OUT OF *ME,* I MEAN.
IT WAS PRETTY IMPRESSIVE, ACTUALLY.
BUT WE STILL HAVE A PROBLEM.
YOU WERE RIGHT. ILLYRIA *DOES* WANT TO FIX SOMETHING HERE.
I KIND OF FIGURED. WHAT HAPPENED?
PROBLEM IS, SHE'S GOT A RIVAL THAT DRAWS ENERGY FROM EATING HER FOLLOWERS.
THAT'S PRETTY STANDARD. MAYBE IF WE WARN THEM TO EVACUATE, BIG UGLY WILL MOVE ON.
IT'S NOT THAT EASY. THEY *WORSHIP* ILLYRIA. NOT JUST OUT OF FEAR. OUT OF LOVE, TOO.
THEY THINK IT'S AN *HONOR* TO GIVE THEIR LIVES FOR HER.
RESULTING IN THEM ALL GETTING EATEN, AND... OKAY, WE *DO* HAVE A PROBLEM.
HOW DO YOU GET A PEOPLE TO DISAVOW THEIR GOD WHEN SHE'S STANDING *RIGHT THERE,* IN FRONT OF THEM?
EXACTLY. AND ON TOP OF ALL--
HEY! YEAH, *YOU!*

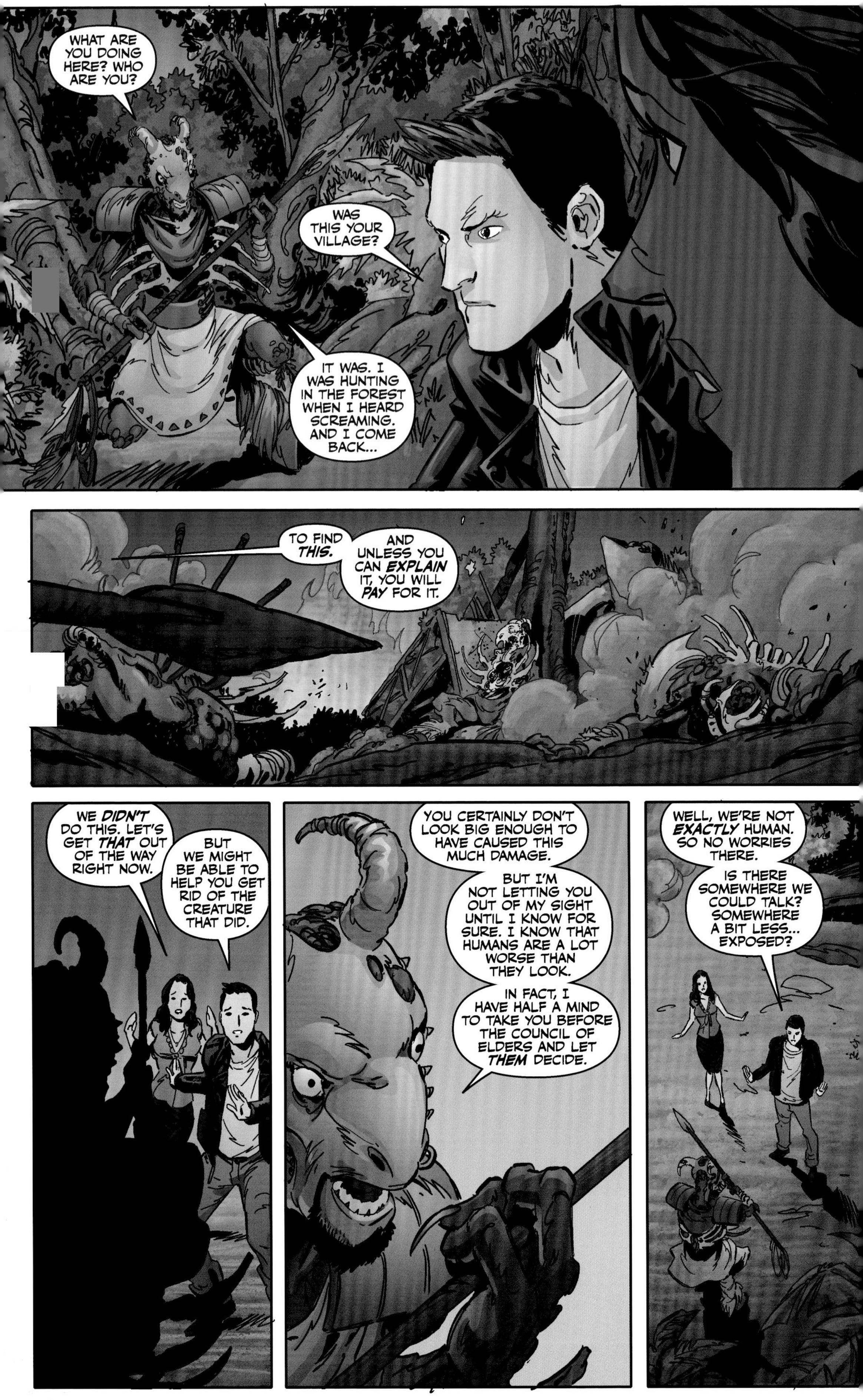
WHAT ARE YOU DOING HERE? WHO ARE YOU?
WAS THIS YOUR VILLAGE?
IT WAS. I WAS HUNTING IN THE FOREST WHEN I HEARD SCREAMING. AND I COME BACK...
TO FIND *THIS.*
AND UNLESS YOU CAN *EXPLAIN* IT, YOU WILL *PAY* FOR IT.
WE *DIDN'T* DO THIS. LET'S GET *THAT* OUT OF THE WAY RIGHT NOW.
BUT WE MIGHT BE ABLE TO HELP YOU GET RID OF THE CREATURE THAT DID.
YOU CERTAINLY DON'T LOOK BIG ENOUGH TO HAVE CAUSED THIS MUCH DAMAGE.
BUT I'M NOT LETTING YOU OUT OF MY SIGHT UNTIL I KNOW FOR SURE. I KNOW THAT HUMANS ARE A LOT WORSE THAN THEY LOOK.
IN FACT, I HAVE HALF A MIND TO TAKE YOU BEFORE THE COUNCIL OF ELDERS AND LET *THEM* DECIDE.
WELL, WE'RE NOT *EXACTLY* HUMAN. SO NO WORRIES THERE.
IS THERE SOMEWHERE WE COULD TALK? SOMEWHERE A BIT LESS... EXPOSED?

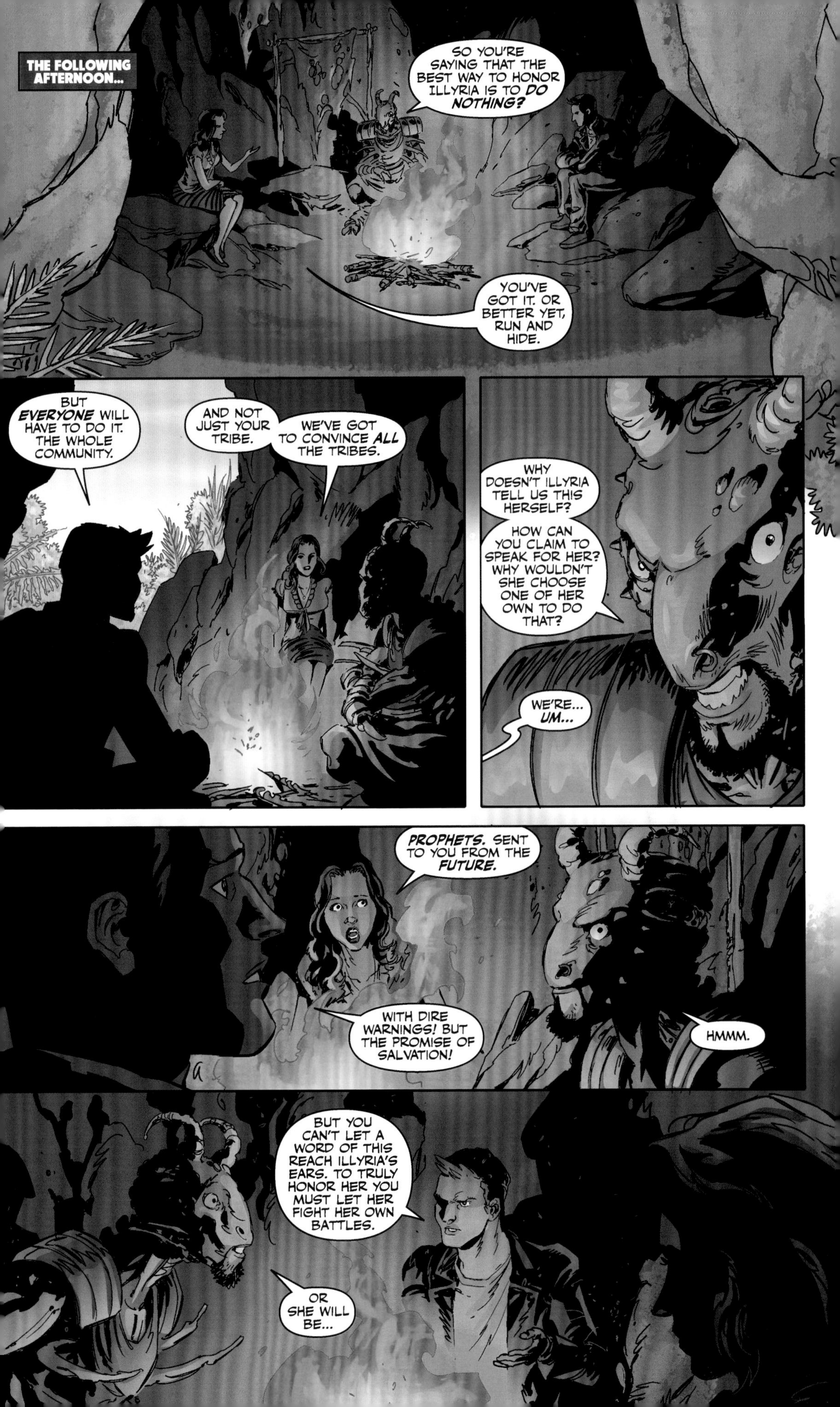

THE FOLLOWING AFTERNOON...
SO YOU'RE SAYING THAT THE BEST WAY TO HONOR ILLYRIA IS TO DO NOTHING?
YOU'VE GOT IT. OR BETTER YET, RUN AND HIDE.
BUT EVERYONE WILL HAVE TO DO IT. THE WHOLE COMMUNITY.
AND NOT JUST YOUR TRIBE.
WE'VE GOT TO CONVINCE ALL THE TRIBES.
WHY DOESN'T ILLYRIA TELL US THIS HERSELF?
HOW CAN YOU CLAIM TO SPEAK FOR HER? WHY WOULDN'T SHE CHOOSE ONE OF HER OWN TO DO THAT?
WE'RE... UM...
PROPHETS. SENT TO YOU FROM THE FUTURE.
WITH DIRE WARNINGS! BUT THE PROMISE OF SALVATION!
HMMM.
BUT YOU CAN'T LET A WORD OF THIS REACH ILLYRIA'S EARS. TO TRULY HONOR HER YOU MUST LET HER FIGHT HER OWN BATTLES.
OR SHE WILL BE...

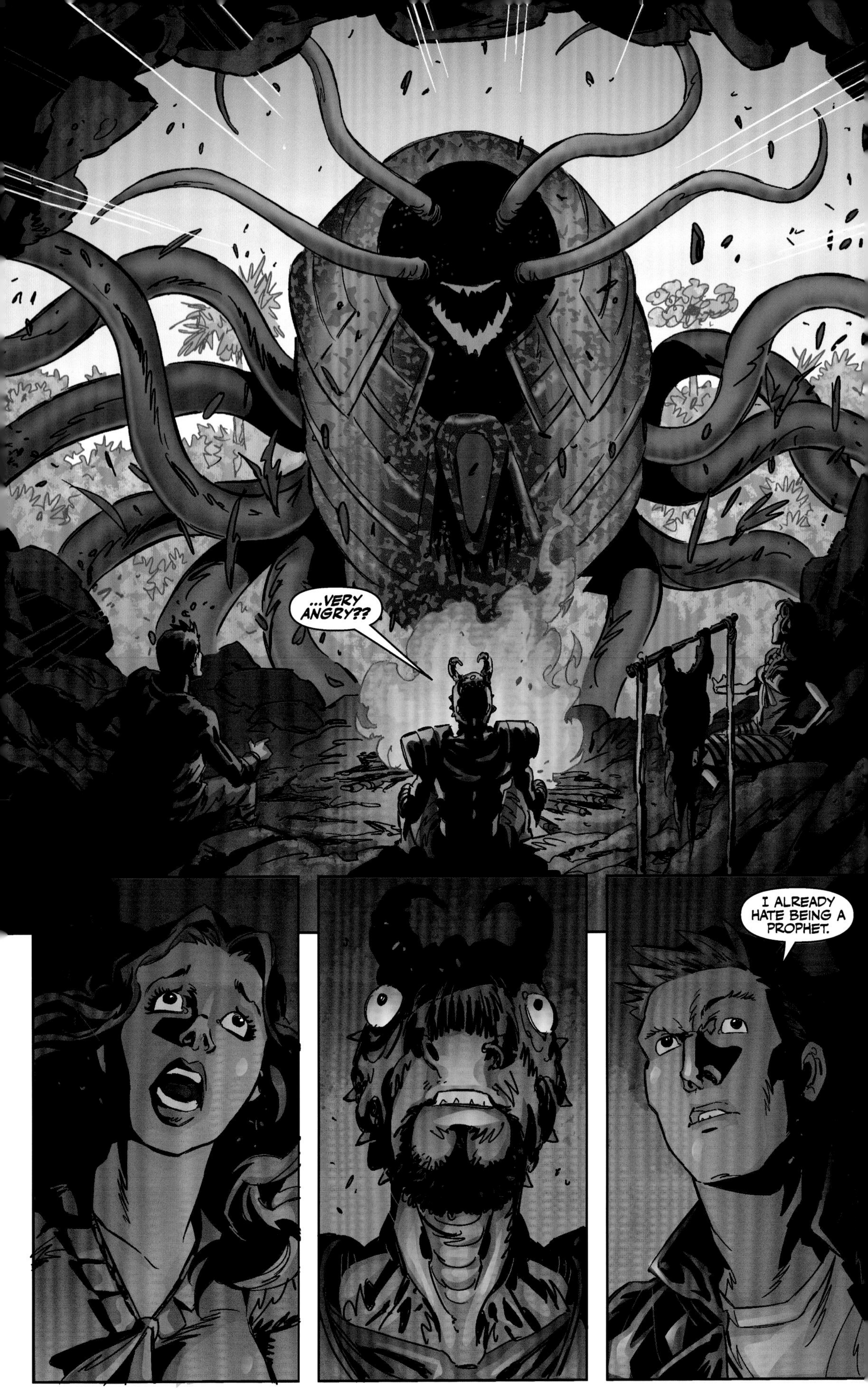
...VERY ANGRY??
I ALREADY HATE BEING A PROPHET.

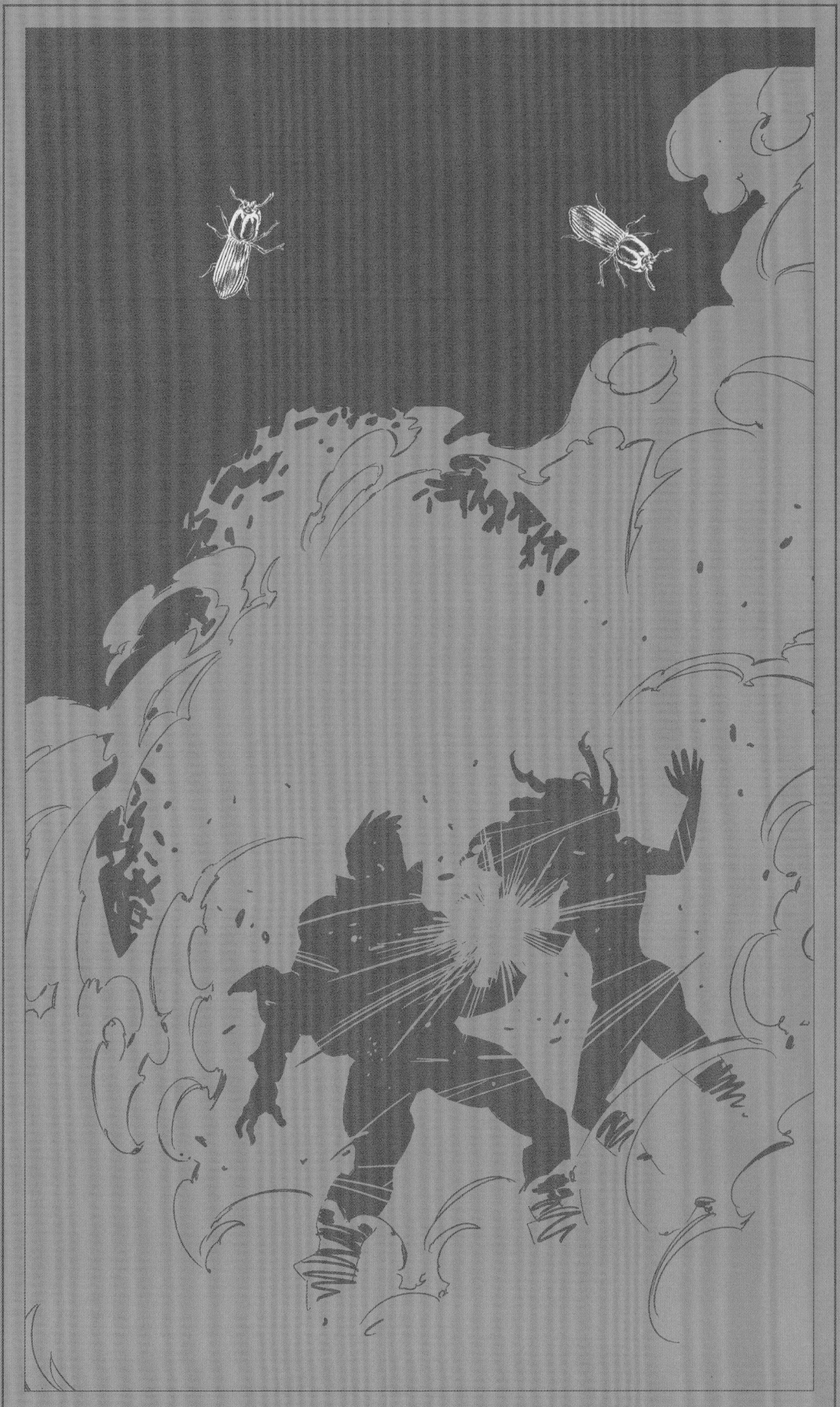

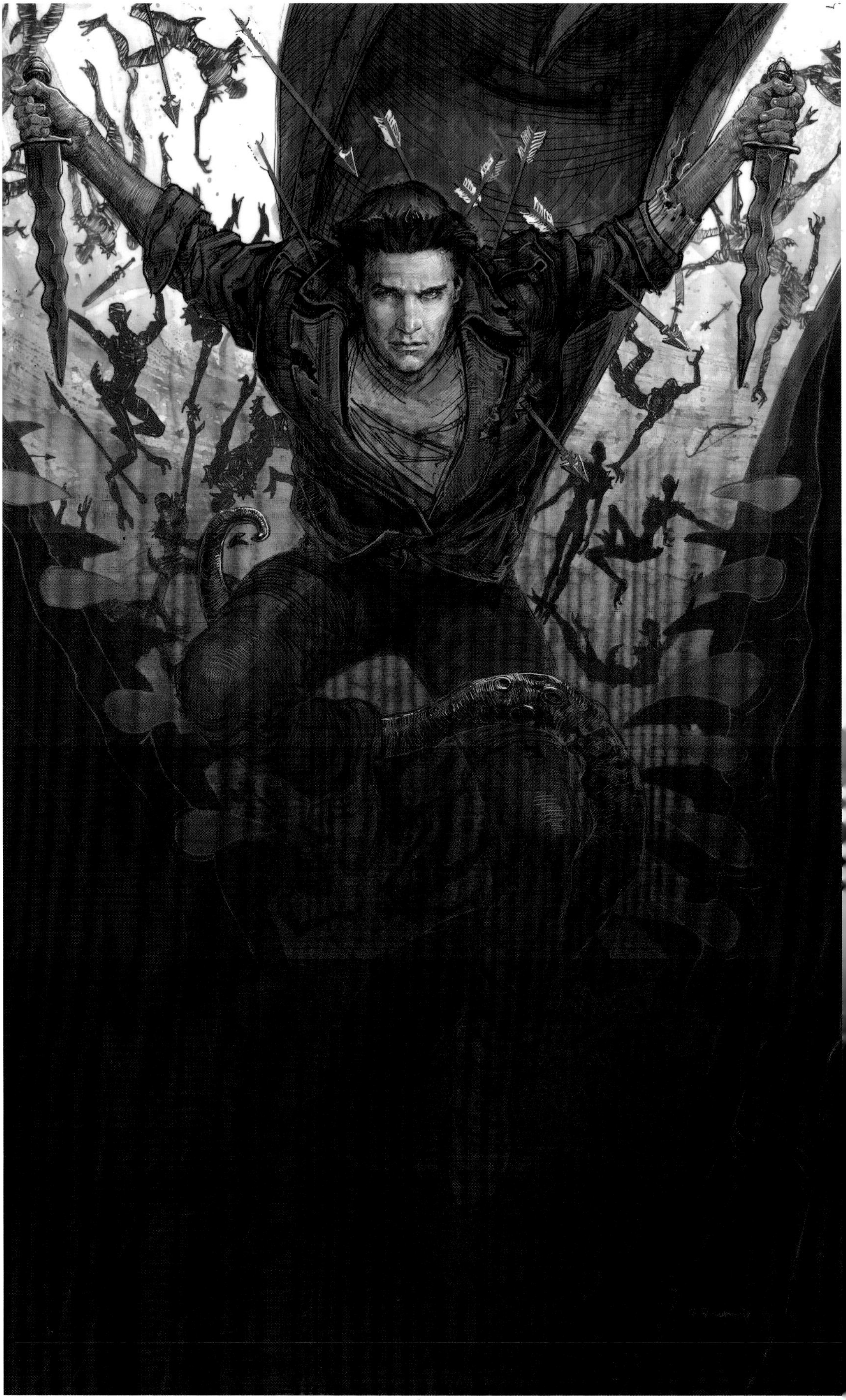

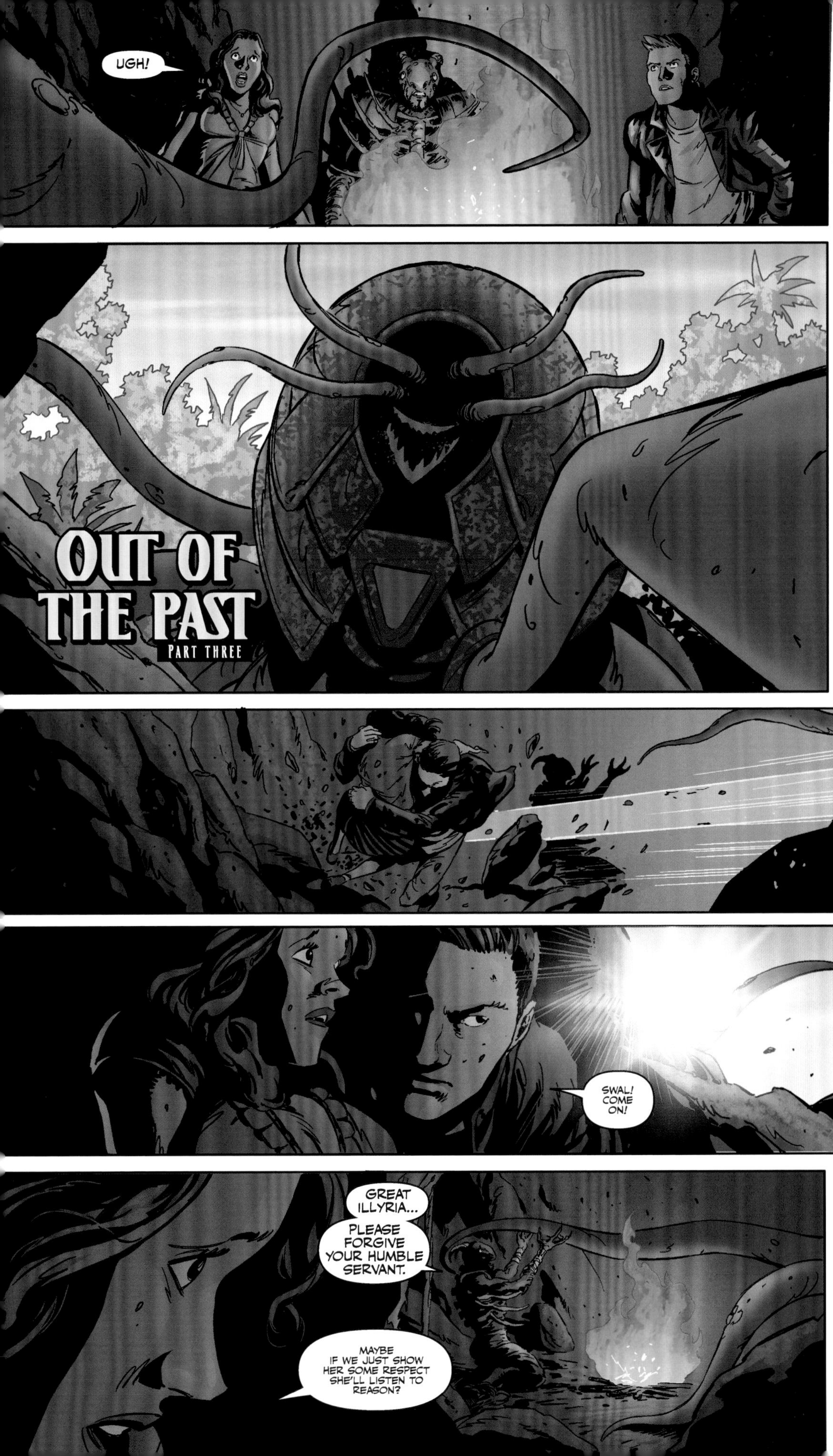
UGH!
OUT OF THE PAST
PART THREE
SWAL! COME ON!
GREAT ILLYRIA...
PLEASE FORGIVE YOUR HUMBLE SERVANT.
MAYBE IF WE JUST SHOW HER SOME RESPECT SHE'LL LISTEN TO REASON?

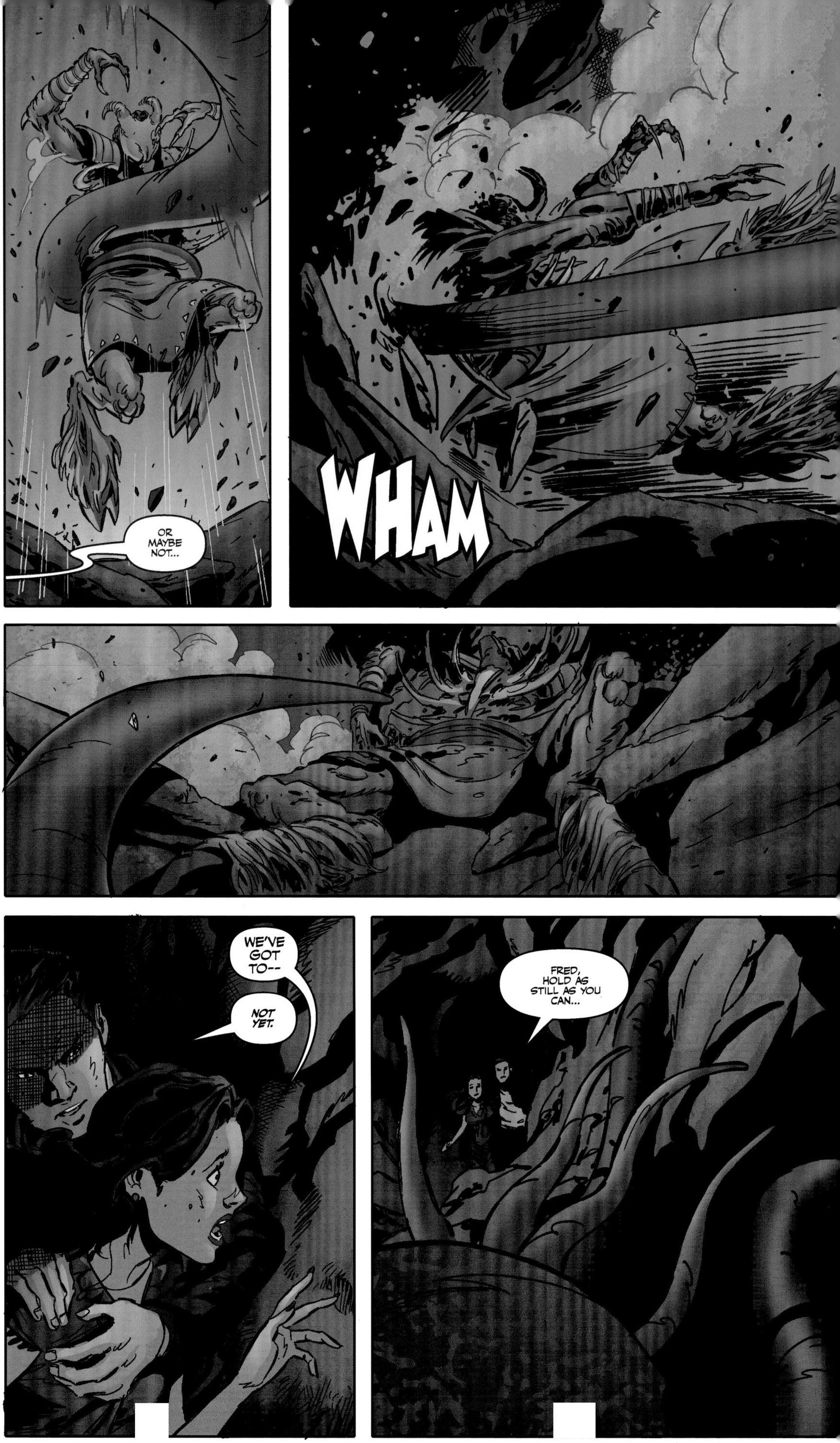
OR MAYBE NOT...
WHAM
WE'VE GOT TO--
NOT YET.
FRED, HOLD AS STILL AS YOU CAN...

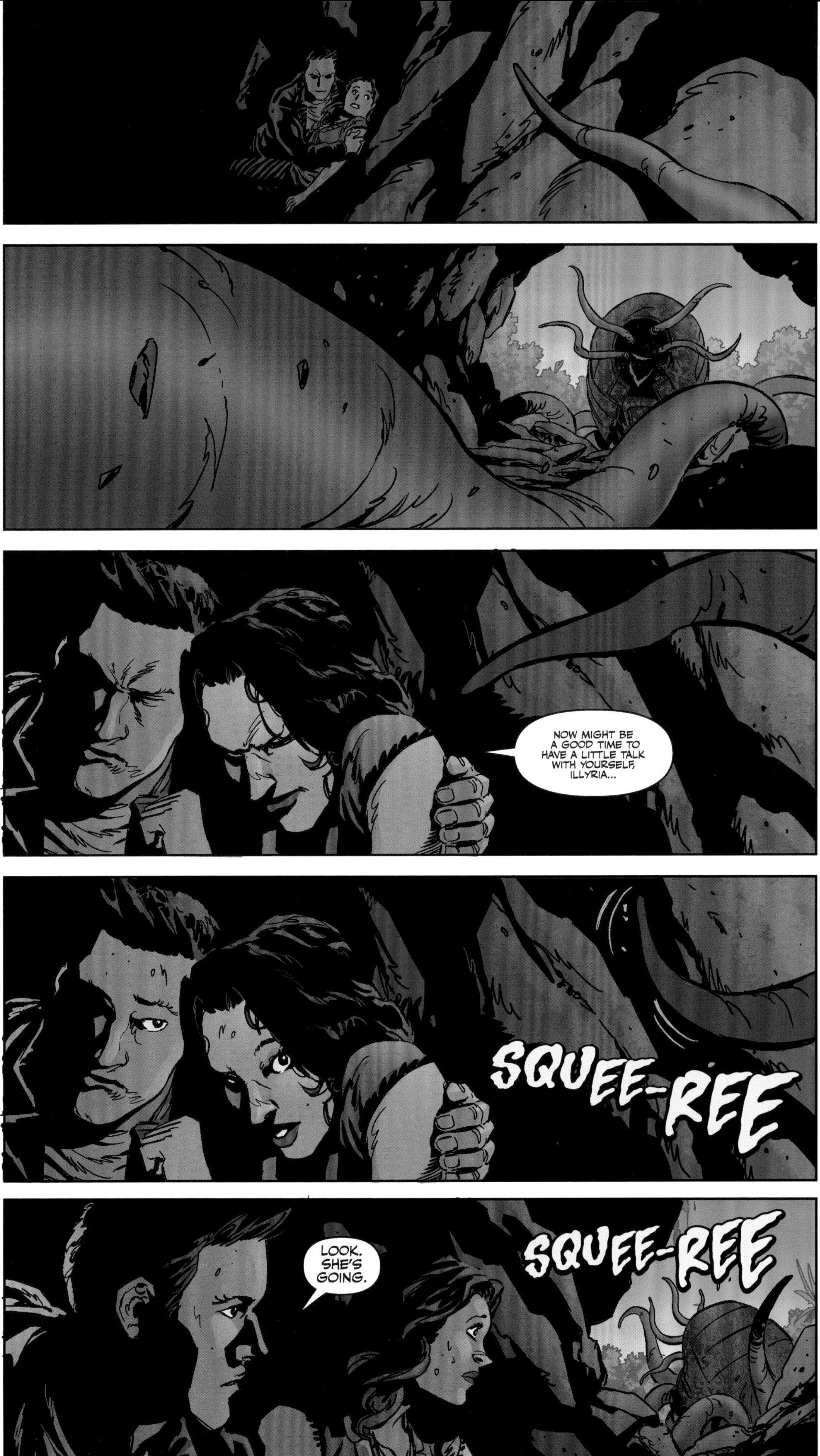
NOW MIGHT BE A GOOD TIME TO HAVE A LITTLE TALK WITH YOURSELF, ILLYRIA...
SQUEE-REE
SQUEE-REE
LOOK. SHE'S GOING.

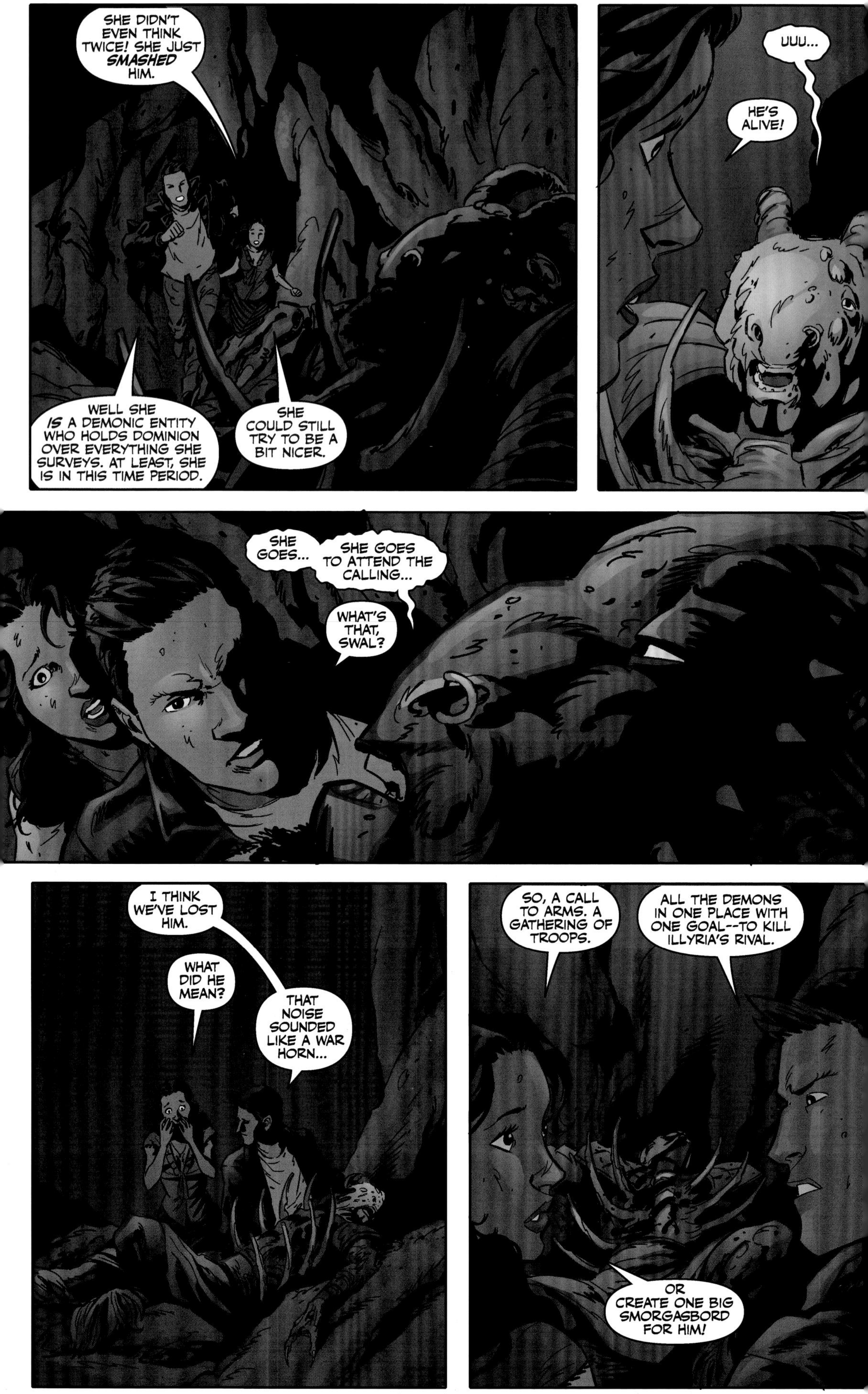

SHE DIDN'T EVEN THINK TWICE! SHE JUST SMASHED HIM.
WELL SHE IS A DEMONIC ENTITY WHO HOLDS DOMINION OVER EVERYTHING SHE SURVEYS. AT LEAST, SHE IS IN THIS TIME PERIOD.
SHE COULD STILL TRY TO BE A BIT NICER.
UUU...
HE'S ALIVE!
SHE GOES...
SHE GOES TO ATTEND THE CALLING...
WHAT'S THAT, SWAL?
I THINK WE'VE LOST HIM.
WHAT DID HE MEAN?
THAT NOISE SOUNDED LIKE A WAR HORN...
SO, A CALL TO ARMS. A GATHERING OF TROOPS.
ALL THE DEMONS IN ONE PLACE WITH ONE GOAL--TO KILL ILLYRIA'S RIVAL.
OR CREATE ONE BIG SMORGASBORD FOR HIM!

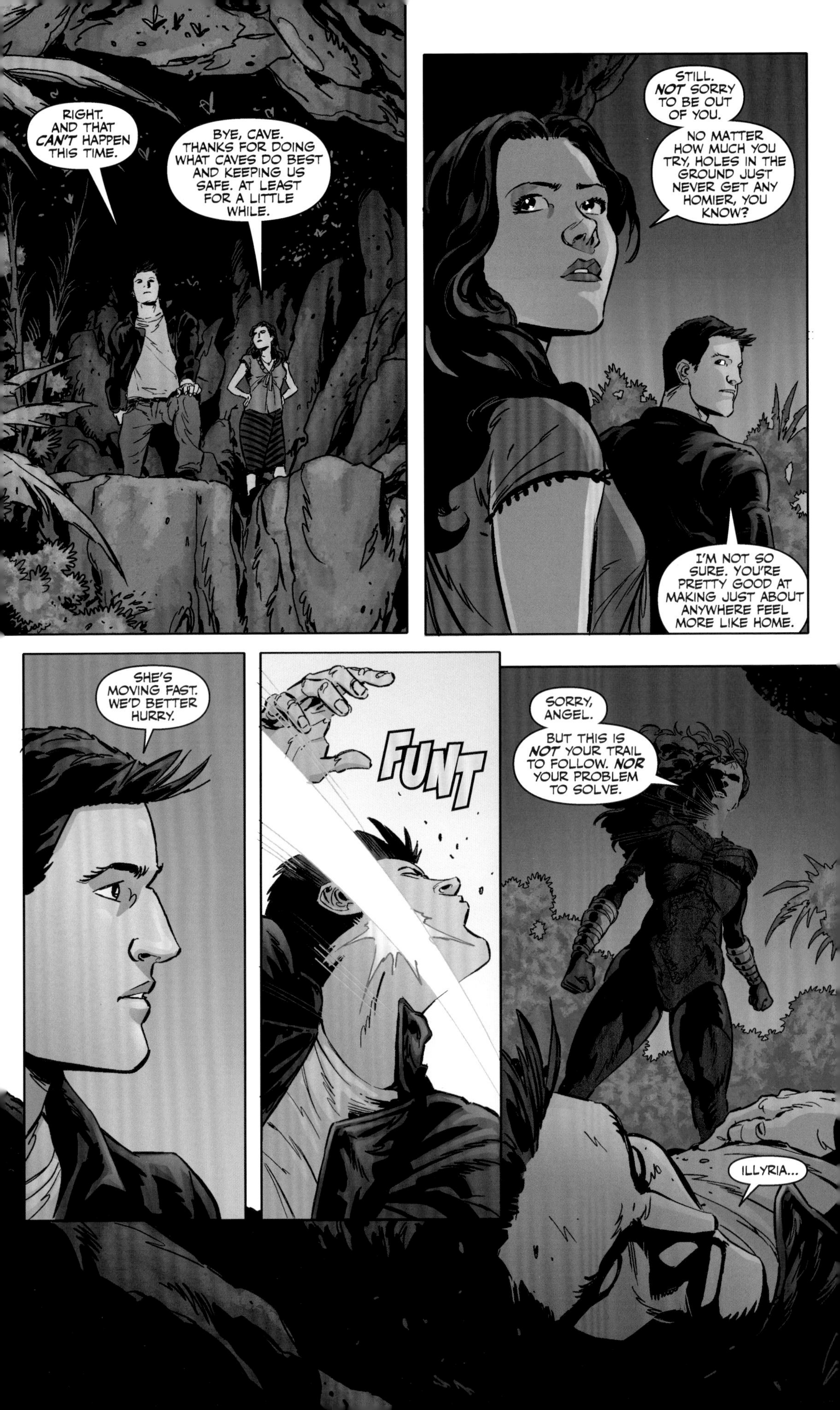
RIGHT. AND THAT CAN'T HAPPEN THIS TIME.
BYE, CAVE. THANKS FOR DOING WHAT CAVES DO BEST AND KEEPING US SAFE. AT LEAST FOR A LITTLE WHILE.
STILL. NOT SORRY TO BE OUT OF YOU.
NO MATTER HOW MUCH YOU TRY, HOLES IN THE GROUND JUST NEVER GET ANY HOMIER, YOU KNOW?
I'M NOT SO SURE. YOU'RE PRETTY GOOD AT MAKING JUST ABOUT ANYWHERE FEEL MORE LIKE HOME.
SHE'S MOVING FAST. WE'D BETTER HURRY.
FUNT
SORRY, ANGEL.
BUT THIS IS NOT YOUR TRAIL TO FOLLOW. NOR YOUR PROBLEM TO SOLVE.
ILLYRIA...

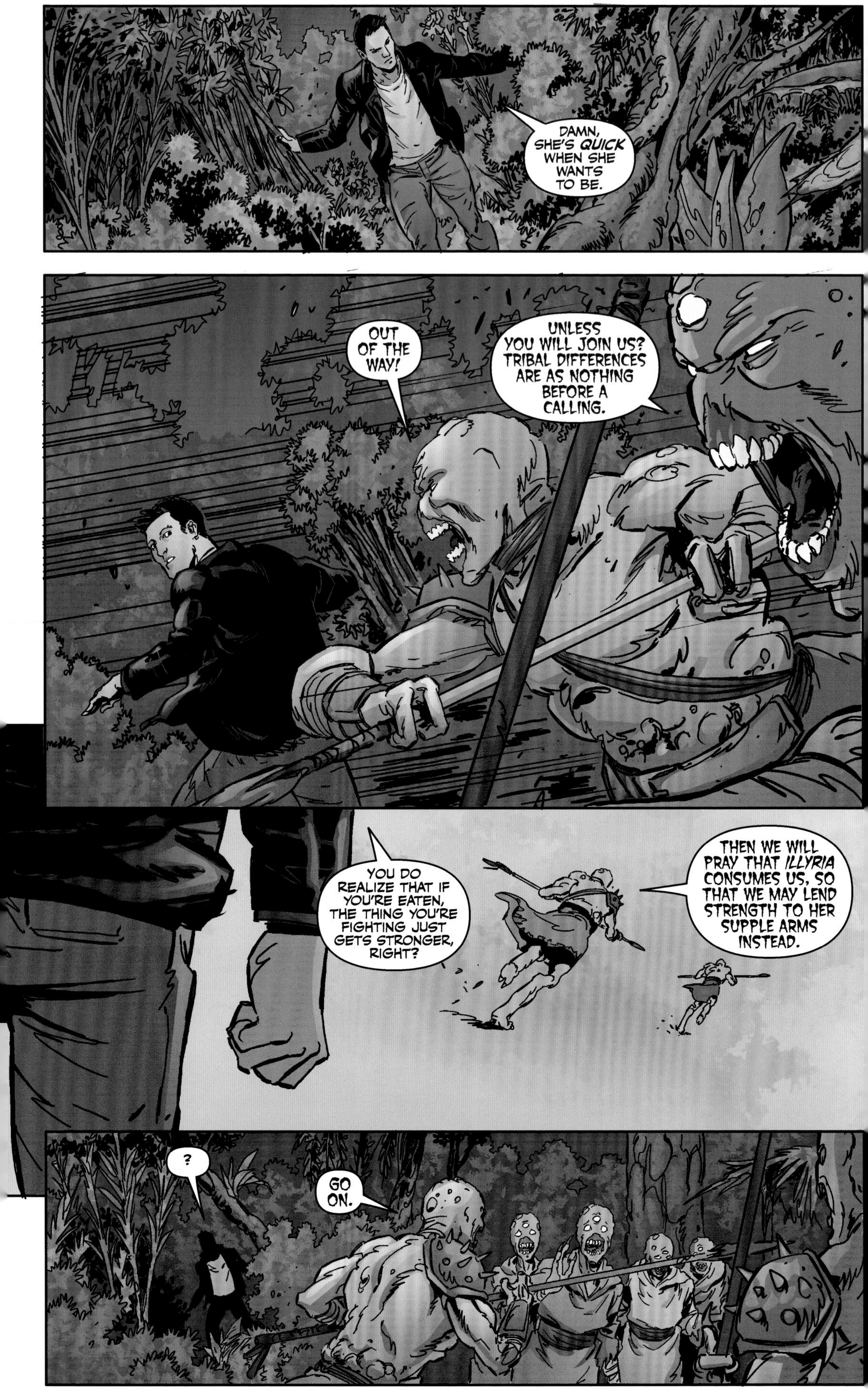
DAMN, SHE'S *QUICK* WHEN SHE WANTS TO BE.
OUT OF THE WAY!
UNLESS YOU WILL JOIN US? TRIBAL DIFFERENCES ARE AS NOTHING BEFORE A CALLING.
YOU DO REALIZE THAT IF YOU'RE EATEN, THE THING YOU'RE FIGHTING JUST GETS STRONGER, RIGHT?
THEN WE WILL PRAY THAT *ILLYRIA* CONSUMES US, SO THAT WE MAY LEND STRENGTH TO HER SUPPLE ARMS INSTEAD.
?
GO ON.

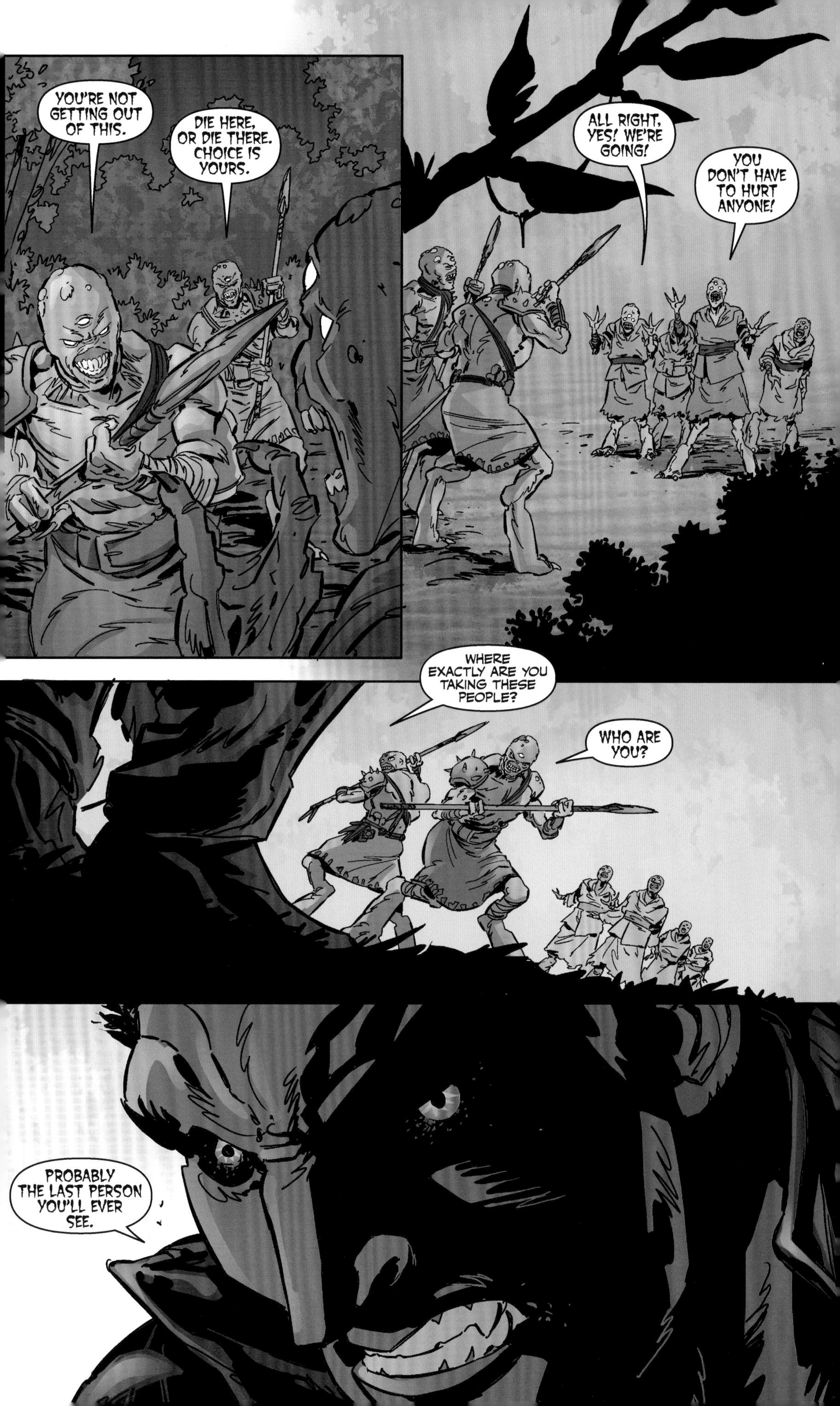
YOU'RE NOT GETTING OUT OF THIS.
DIE HERE, OR DIE THERE. CHOICE IS YOURS.
ALL RIGHT, YES! WE'RE GOING!
YOU DON'T HAVE TO HURT ANYONE!
WHERE EXACTLY ARE YOU TAKING THESE PEOPLE?
WHO ARE YOU?
PROBABLY THE LAST PERSON YOU'LL EVER SEE.

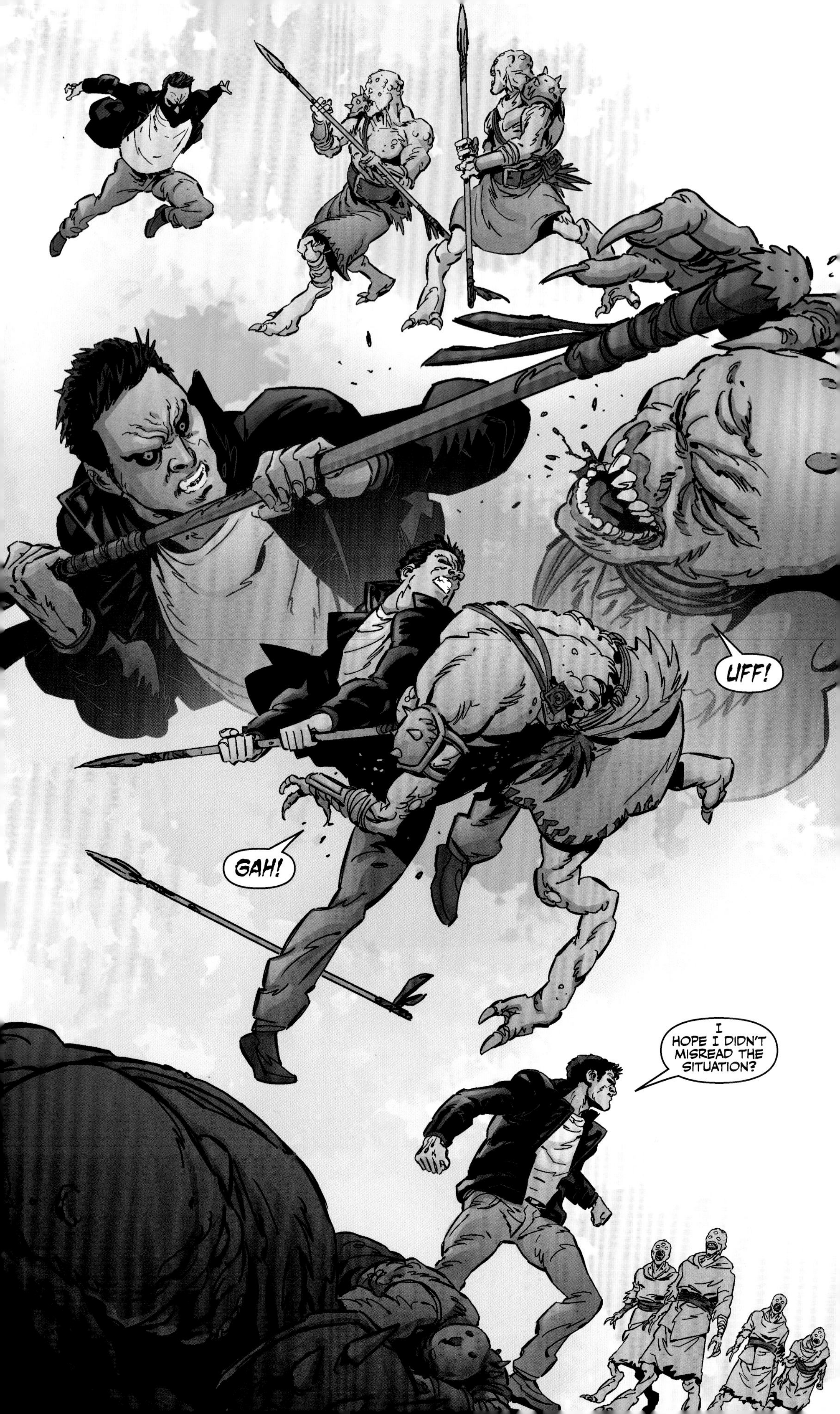
UFF!
GAH!
I HOPE I DIDN'T MISREAD THE SITUATION?

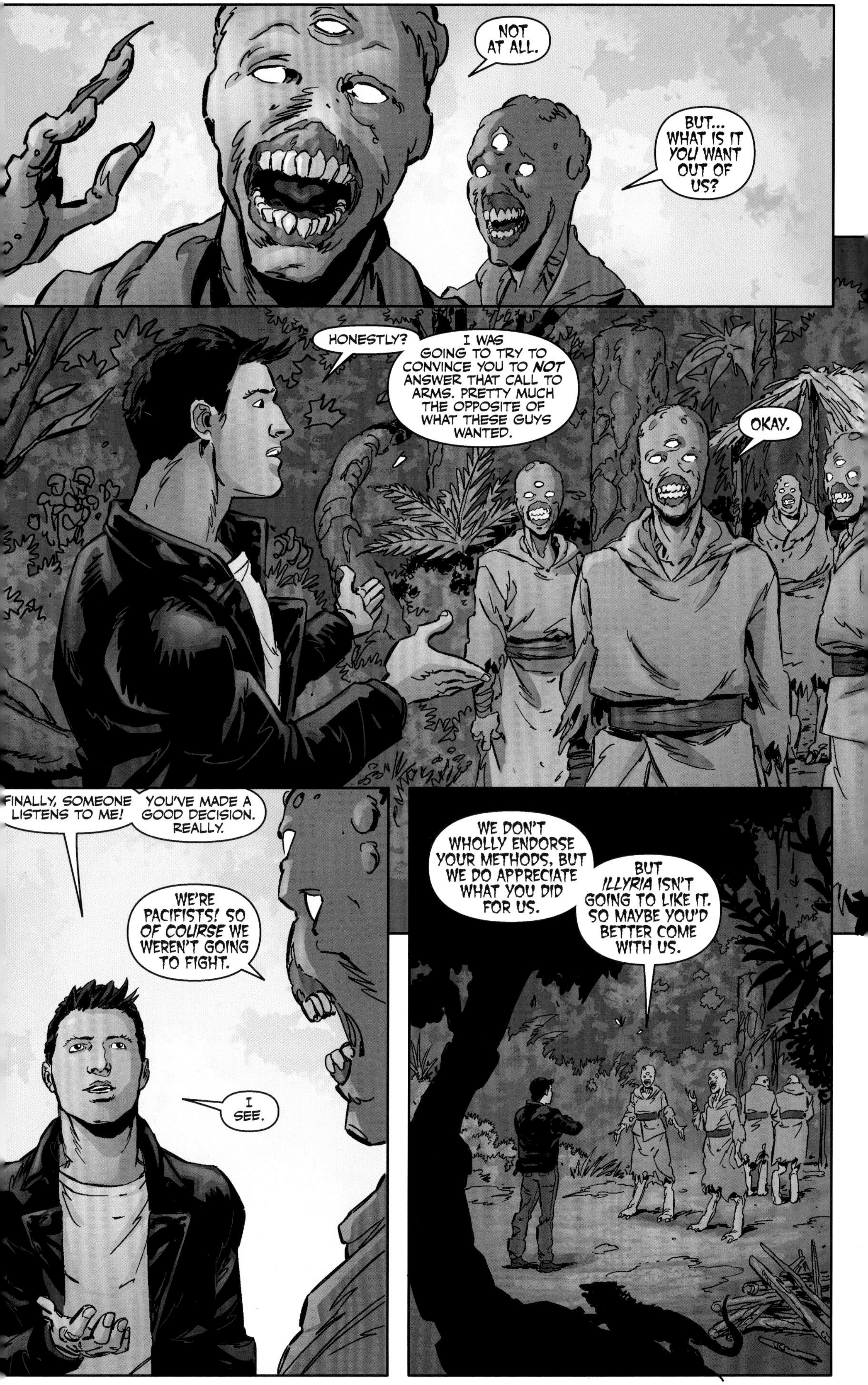

NOT AT ALL.
BUT... WHAT IS IT YOU WANT OUT OF US?
HONESTLY?
I WAS GOING TO TRY TO CONVINCE YOU TO NOT ANSWER THAT CALL TO ARMS. PRETTY MUCH THE OPPOSITE OF WHAT THESE GUYS WANTED.
OKAY.
FINALLY, SOMEONE LISTENS TO ME!
YOU'VE MADE A GOOD DECISION. REALLY.
WE'RE PACIFISTS! SO OF COURSE WE WEREN'T GOING TO FIGHT.
I SEE.
WE DON'T WHOLLY ENDORSE YOUR METHODS, BUT WE DO APPRECIATE WHAT YOU DID FOR US.
BUT ILLYRIA ISN'T GOING TO LIKE IT. SO MAYBE YOU'D BETTER COME WITH US.

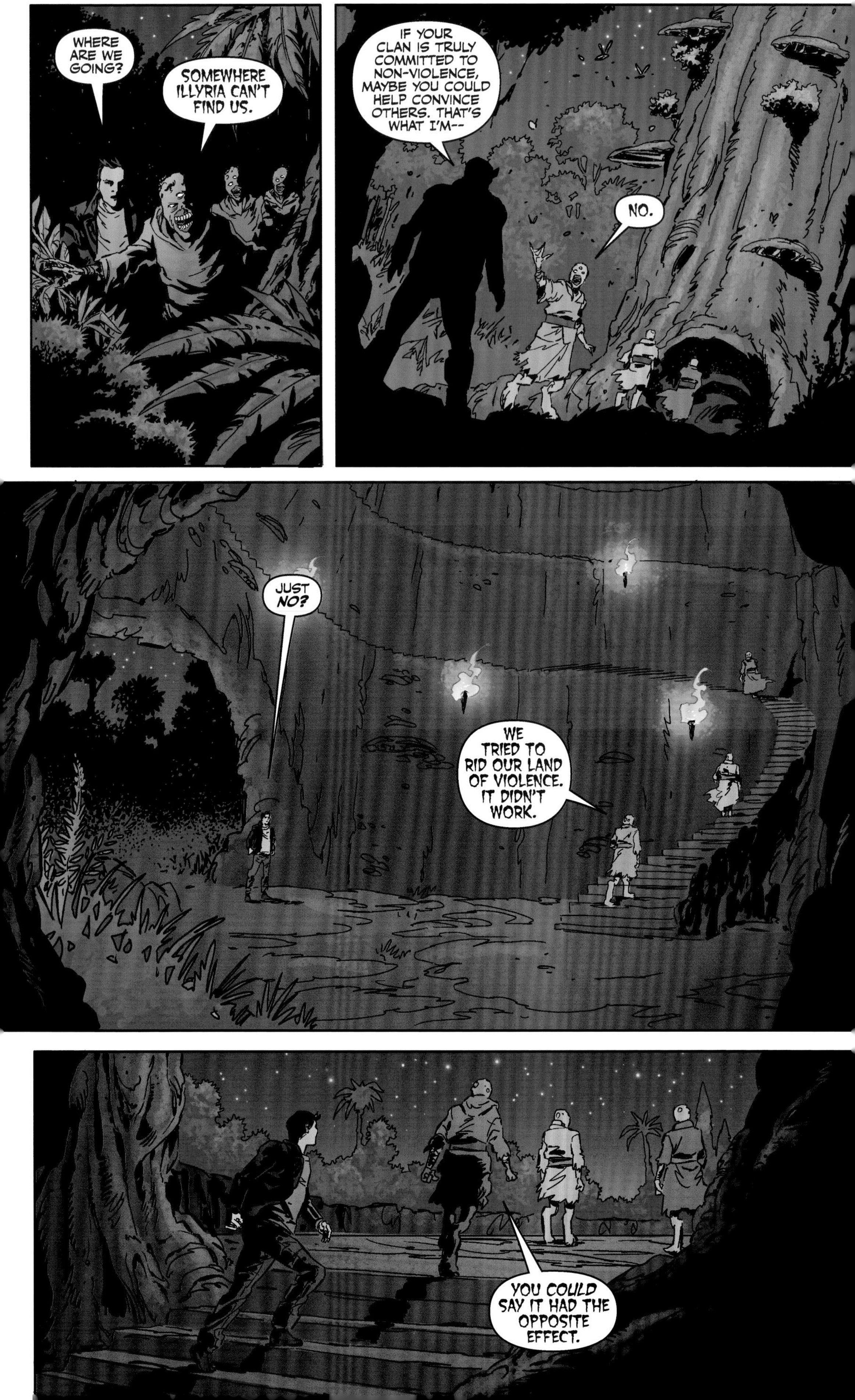
WHERE ARE WE GOING?
SOMEWHERE ILLYRIA CAN'T FIND US.
IF YOUR CLAN IS TRULY COMMITTED TO NON-VIOLENCE, MAYBE YOU COULD HELP CONVINCE OTHERS. THAT'S WHAT I'M--
NO.
JUST *NO?*
WE TRIED TO RID OUR LAND OF VIOLENCE. IT DIDN'T WORK.
YOU COULD SAY IT HAD THE OPPOSITE EFFECT.

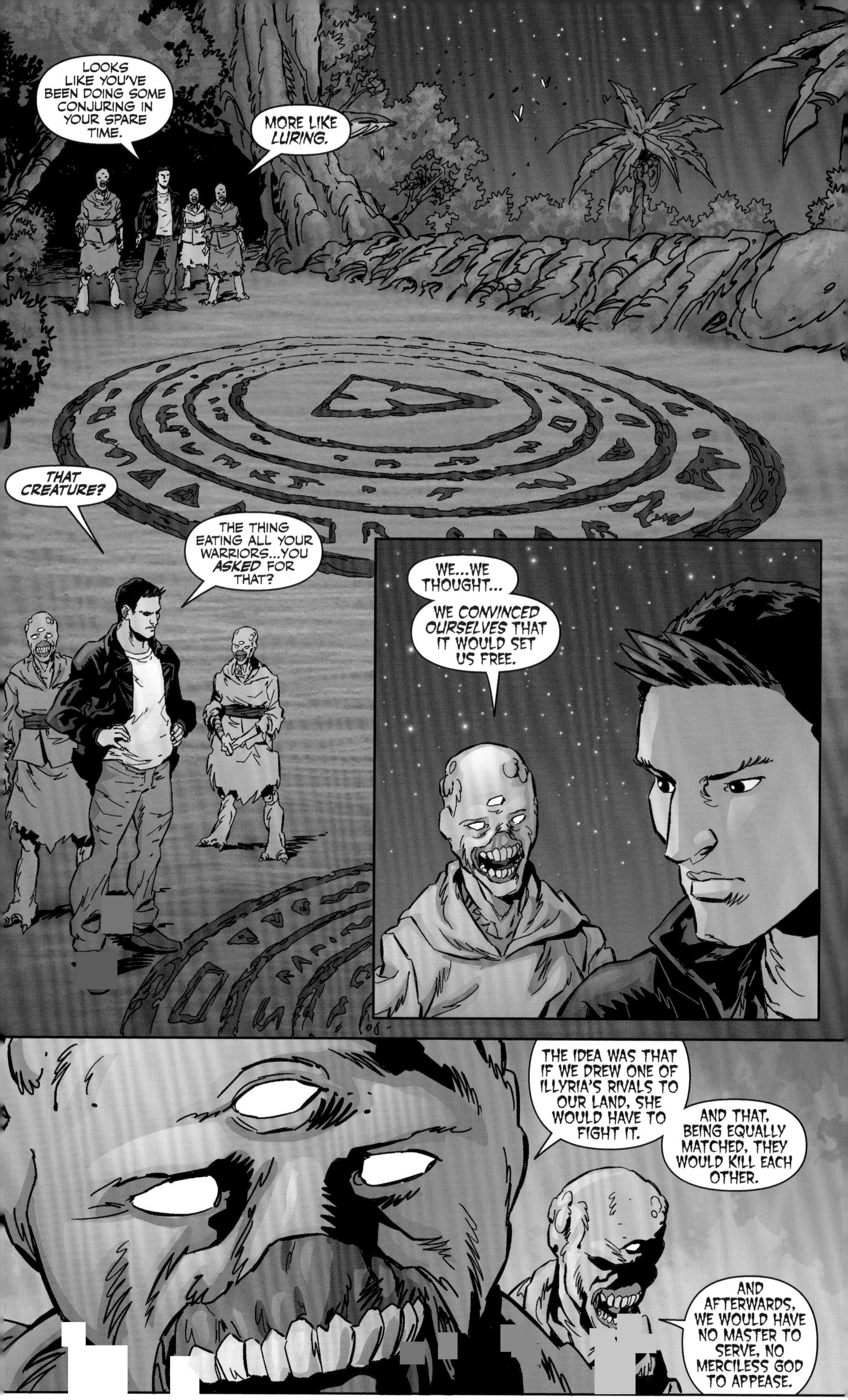
LOOKS LIKE YOU'VE BEEN DOING SOME CONJURING IN YOUR SPARE TIME.
MORE LIKE *LURING.*
THAT CREATURE?
THE THING EATING ALL YOUR WARRIORS...YOU *ASKED* FOR THAT?
WE...WE THOUGHT...
WE *CONVINCED OURSELVES* THAT IT WOULD SET US FREE.
THE IDEA WAS THAT IF WE DREW ONE OF ILLYRIA'S RIVALS TO OUR LAND, SHE WOULD HAVE TO FIGHT IT.
AND THAT, BEING EQUALLY MATCHED, THEY WOULD KILL EACH OTHER.
AND AFTERWARDS, WE WOULD HAVE NO MASTER TO SERVE, NO MERCILESS GOD TO APPEASE.

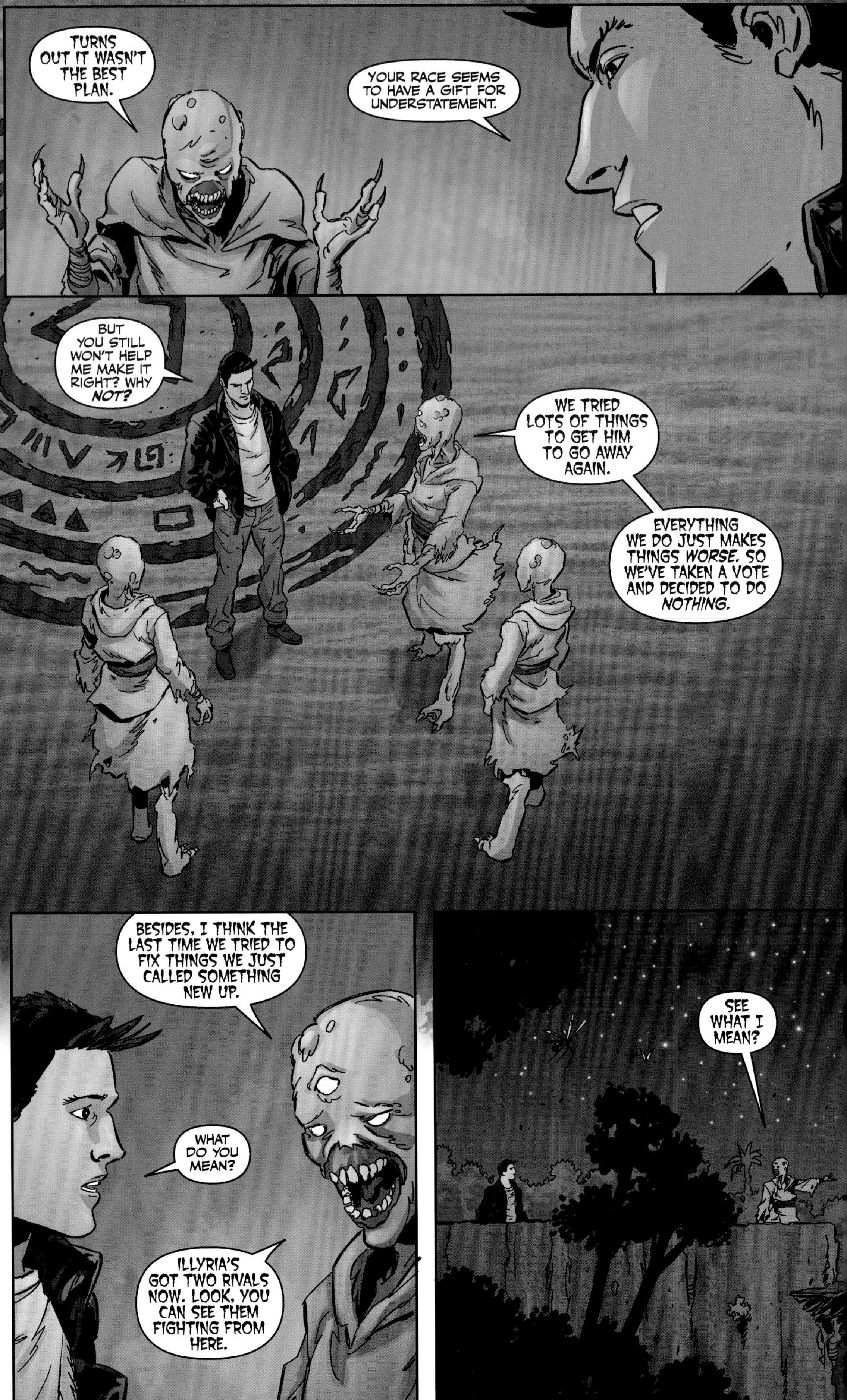
TURNS OUT IT WASN'T THE BEST PLAN.
YOUR RACE SEEMS TO HAVE A GIFT FOR UNDERSTATEMENT.
BUT YOU STILL WON'T HELP ME MAKE IT RIGHT? WHY *NOT?*
WE TRIED LOTS OF THINGS TO GET HIM TO GO AWAY AGAIN.
EVERYTHING WE DO JUST MAKES THINGS *WORSE.* SO WE'VE TAKEN A VOTE AND DECIDED TO DO *NOTHING.*
BESIDES, I THINK THE LAST TIME WE TRIED TO FIX THINGS WE JUST CALLED SOMETHING NEW UP.
WHAT DO YOU MEAN?
ILLYRIA'S GOT TWO RIVALS NOW. LOOK, YOU CAN SEE THEM FIGHTING FROM HERE.
SEE WHAT I MEAN?

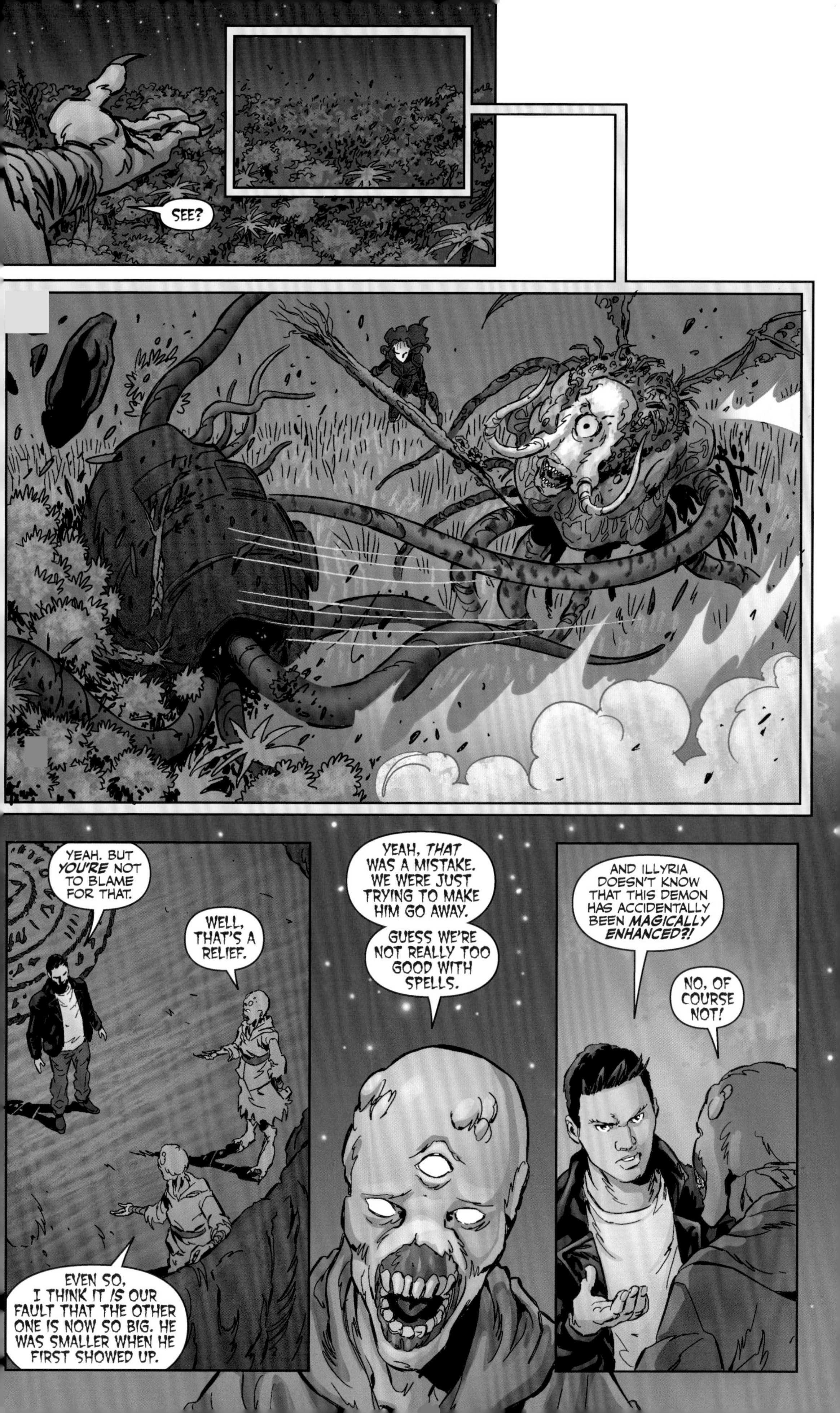
SEE?
YEAH. BUT YOU'RE NOT TO BLAME FOR THAT.
WELL, THAT'S A RELIEF.
EVEN SO, I THINK IT IS OUR FAULT THAT THE OTHER ONE IS NOW SO BIG. HE WAS SMALLER WHEN HE FIRST SHOWED UP.
YEAH, THAT WAS A MISTAKE. WE WERE JUST TRYING TO MAKE HIM GO AWAY.
GUESS WE'RE NOT REALLY TOO GOOD WITH SPELLS.
AND ILLYRIA DOESN'T KNOW THAT THIS DEMON HAS ACCIDENTALLY BEEN MAGICALLY ENHANCED?!
NO, OF COURSE NOT!

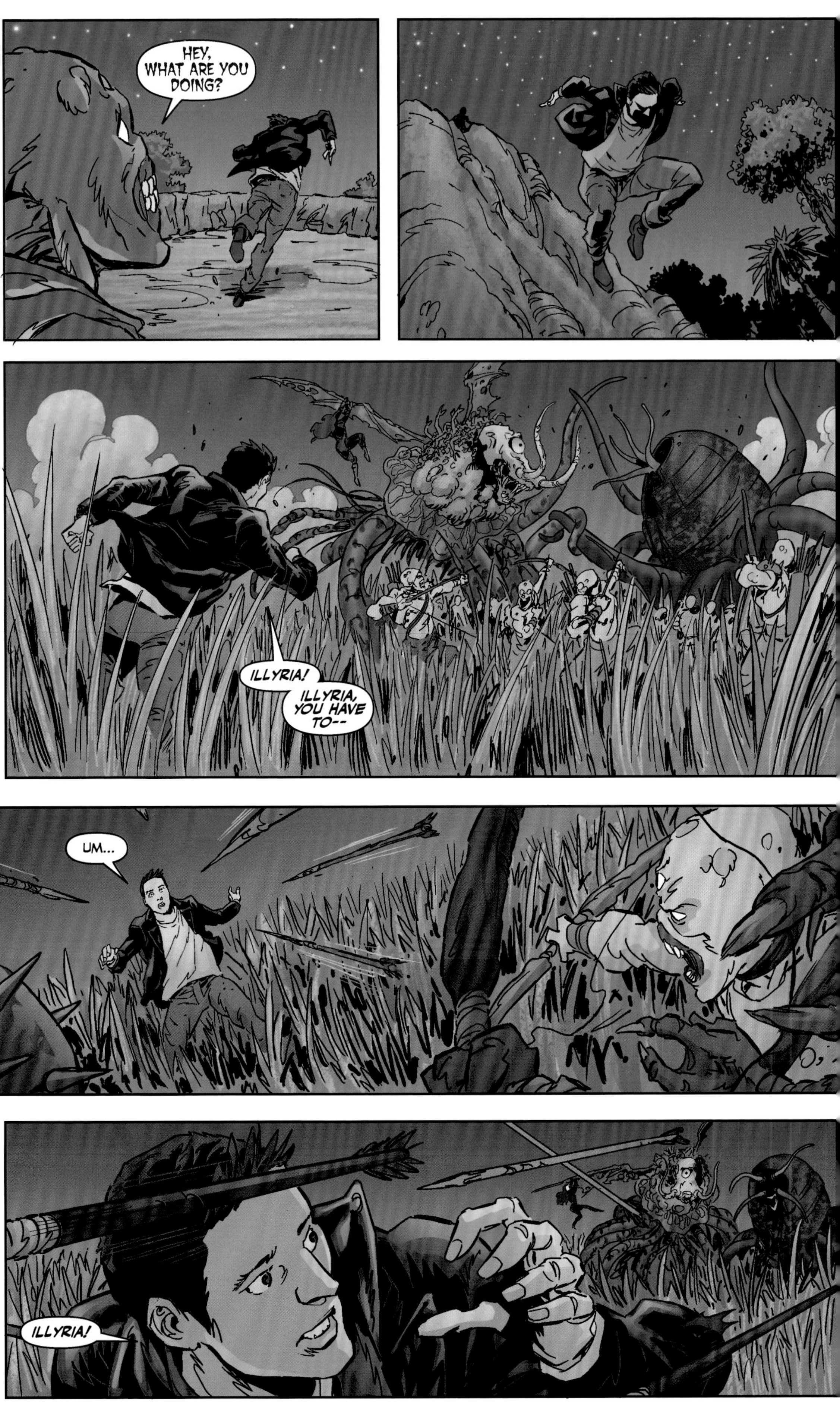
HEY, WHAT ARE YOU DOING?
ILLYRIA!
ILLYRIA, YOU HAVE TO--
UM...
ILLYRIA!

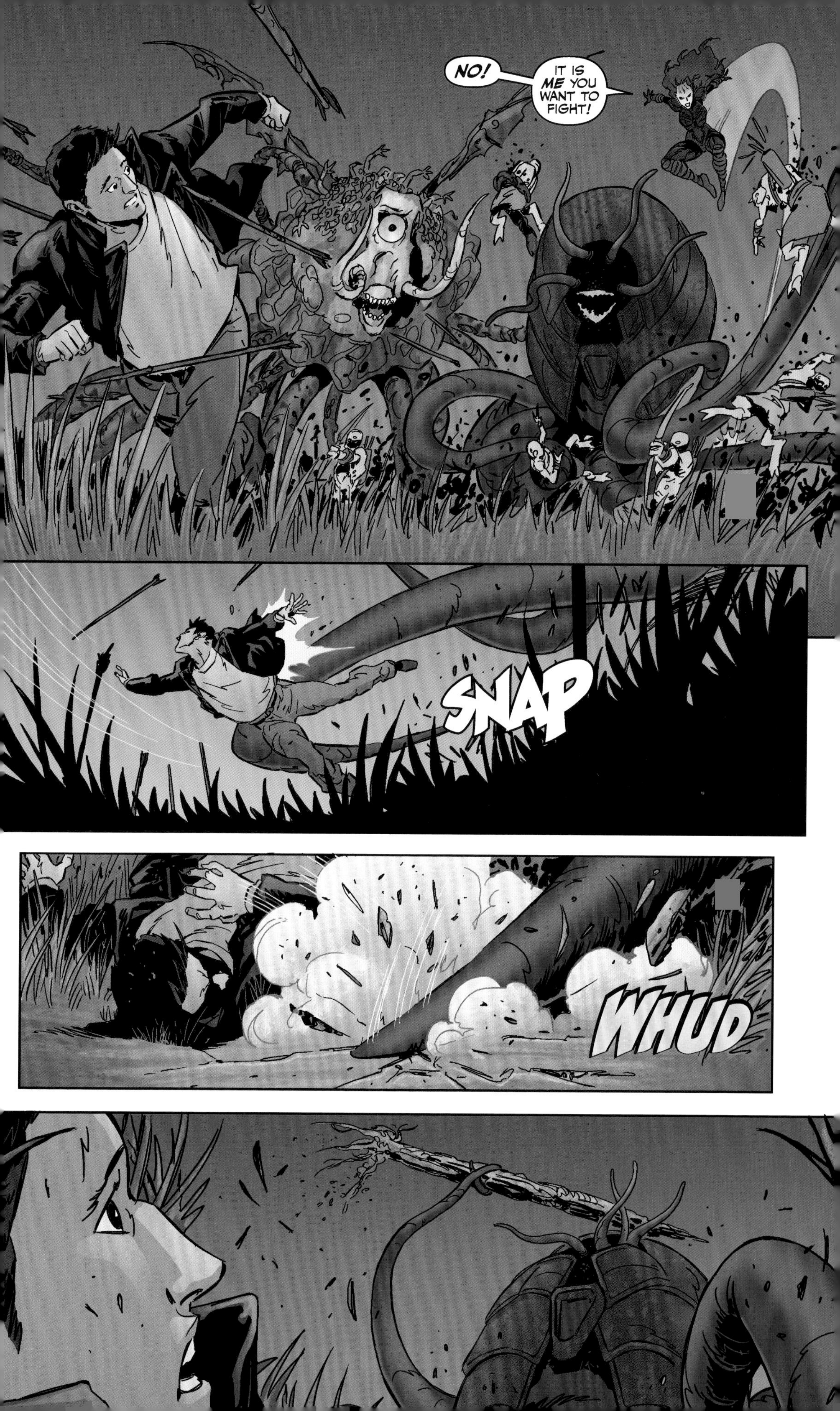
NO!
IT IS ME YOU WANT TO FIGHT!
SNAP
WHUD

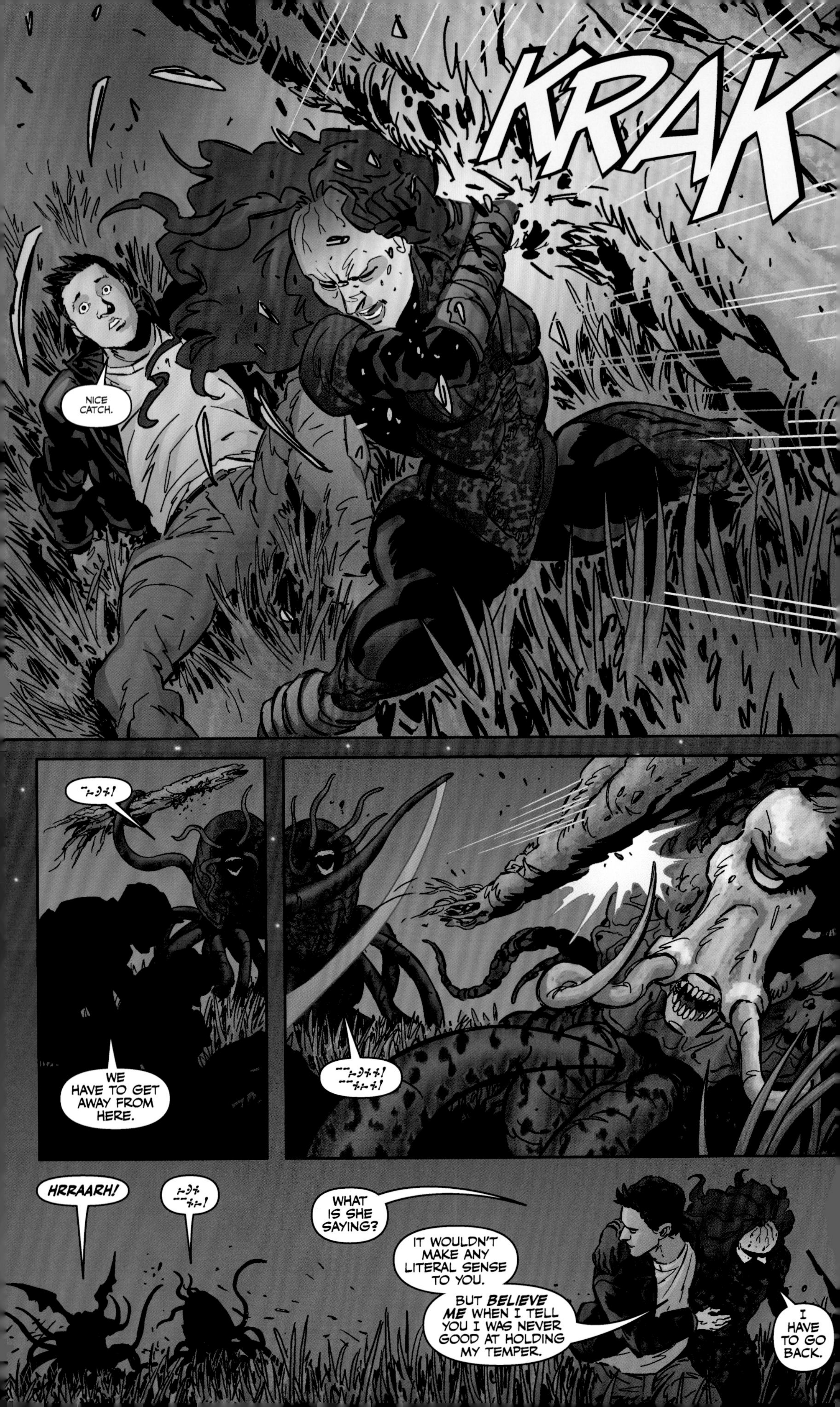
KRAK
NICE CATCH.
WE HAVE TO GET AWAY FROM HERE.
HRRAARH!
WHAT IS SHE SAYING?
IT WOULDN'T MAKE ANY LITERAL SENSE TO YOU.
BUT BELIEVE ME WHEN I TELL YOU I WAS NEVER GOOD AT HOLDING MY TEMPER.
I HAVE TO GO BACK.

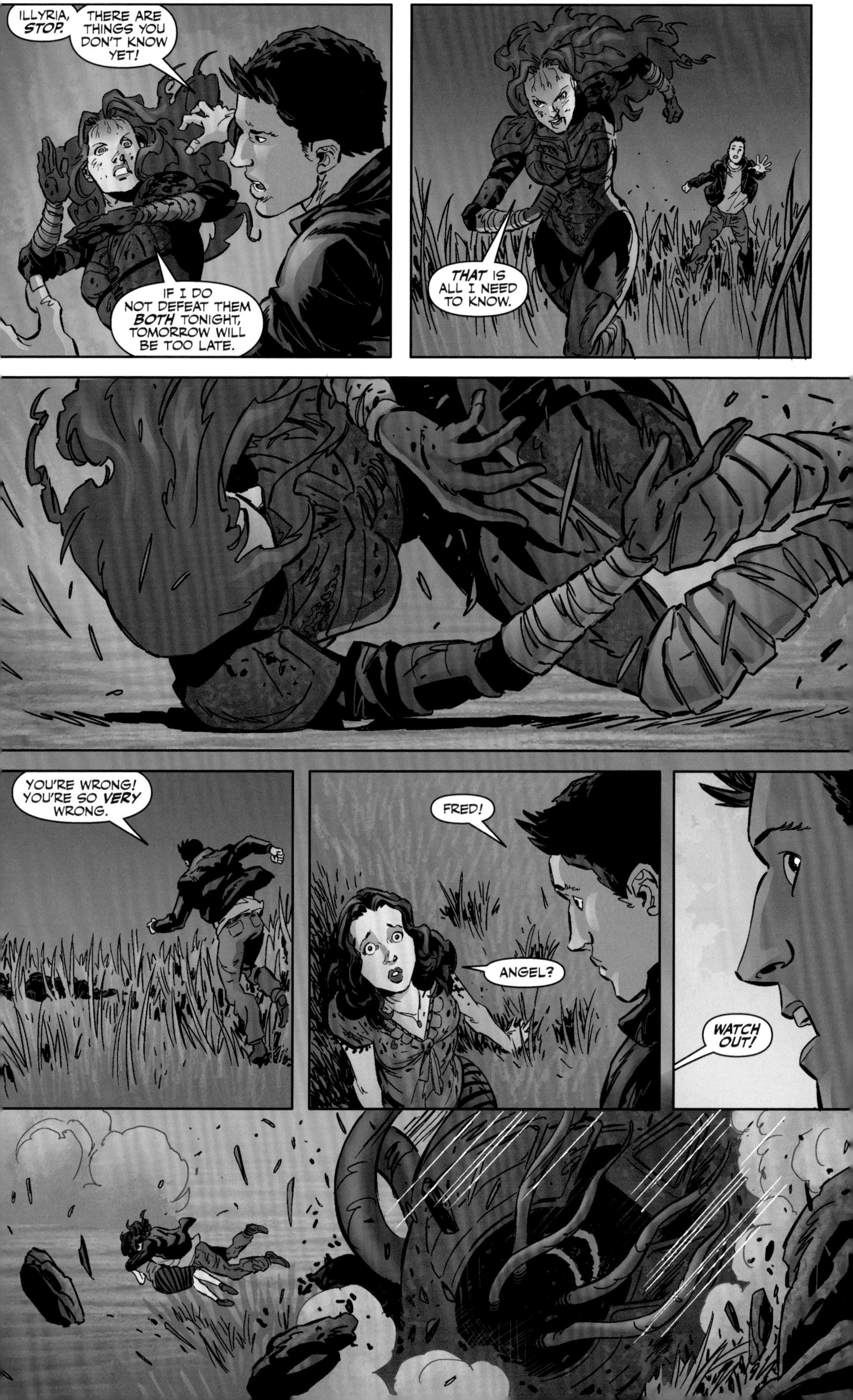
ILLYRIA, STOP.
THERE ARE THINGS YOU DON'T KNOW YET!
IF I DO NOT DEFEAT THEM BOTH TONIGHT, TOMORROW WILL BE TOO LATE.
THAT IS ALL I NEED TO KNOW.
YOU'RE WRONG! YOU'RE SO VERY WRONG.
FRED!
ANGEL?
WATCH OUT!

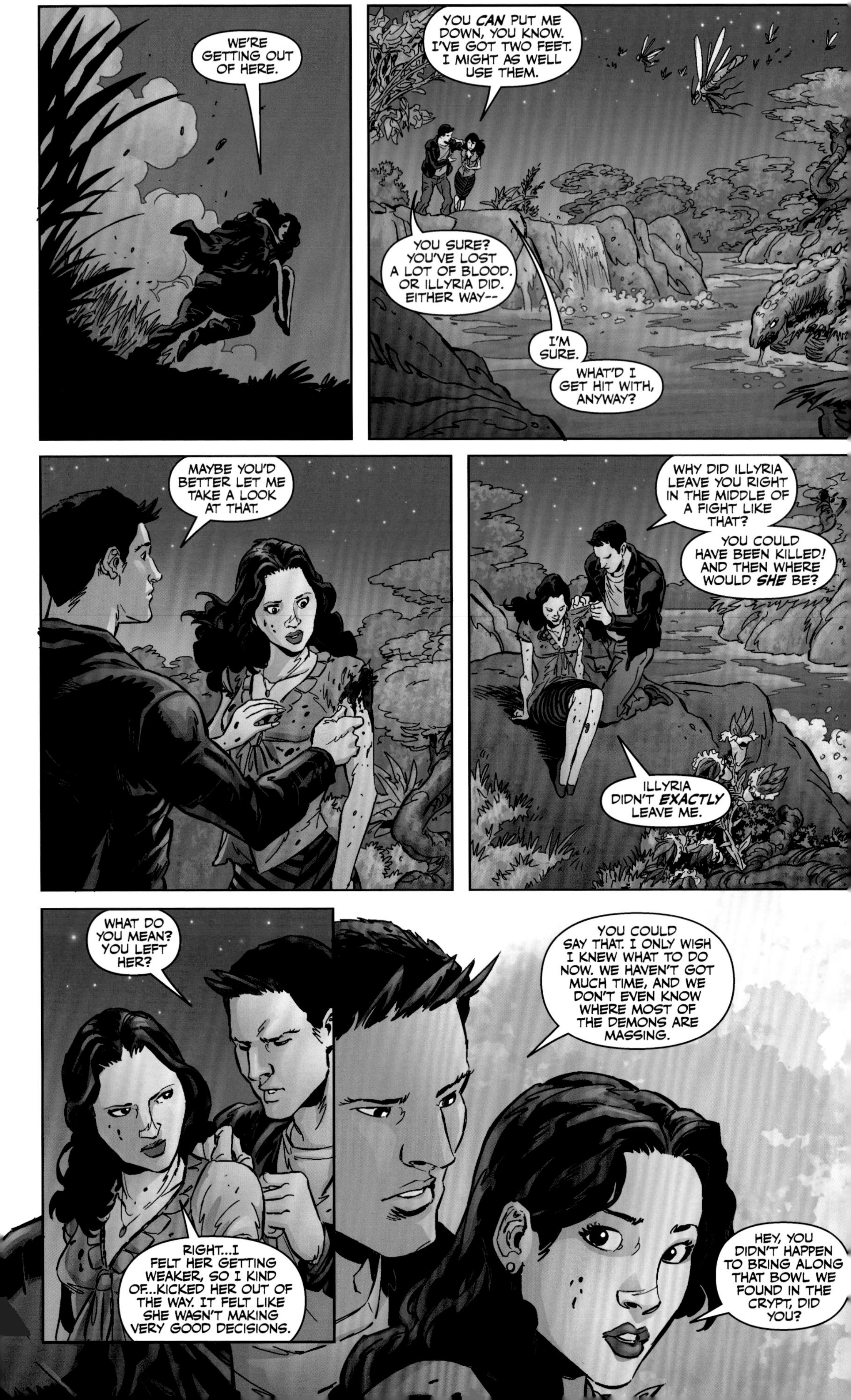
WE'RE GETTING OUT OF HERE.
YOU *CAN* PUT ME DOWN, YOU KNOW. I'VE GOT TWO FEET. I MIGHT AS WELL USE THEM.
YOU SURE? YOU'VE LOST A LOT OF BLOOD. OR ILLYRIA DID. EITHER WAY--
I'M SURE.
WHAT'D I GET HIT WITH, ANYWAY?
MAYBE YOU'D BETTER LET ME TAKE A LOOK AT THAT.
WHY DID ILLYRIA LEAVE YOU RIGHT IN THE MIDDLE OF A FIGHT LIKE THAT?
YOU COULD HAVE BEEN KILLED! AND THEN WHERE WOULD *SHE* BE?
ILLYRIA DIDN'T *EXACTLY* LEAVE ME.
WHAT DO YOU MEAN? YOU LEFT HER?
RIGHT...I FELT HER GETTING WEAKER, SO I KIND OF...KICKED HER OUT OF THE WAY. IT FELT LIKE SHE WASN'T MAKING VERY GOOD DECISIONS.
YOU COULD SAY THAT. I ONLY WISH I KNEW WHAT TO DO NOW. WE HAVEN'T GOT MUCH TIME, AND WE DON'T EVEN KNOW WHERE MOST OF THE DEMONS ARE MASSING.
HEY, YOU DIDN'T HAPPEN TO BRING ALONG THAT BOWL WE FOUND IN THE CRYPT, DID YOU?

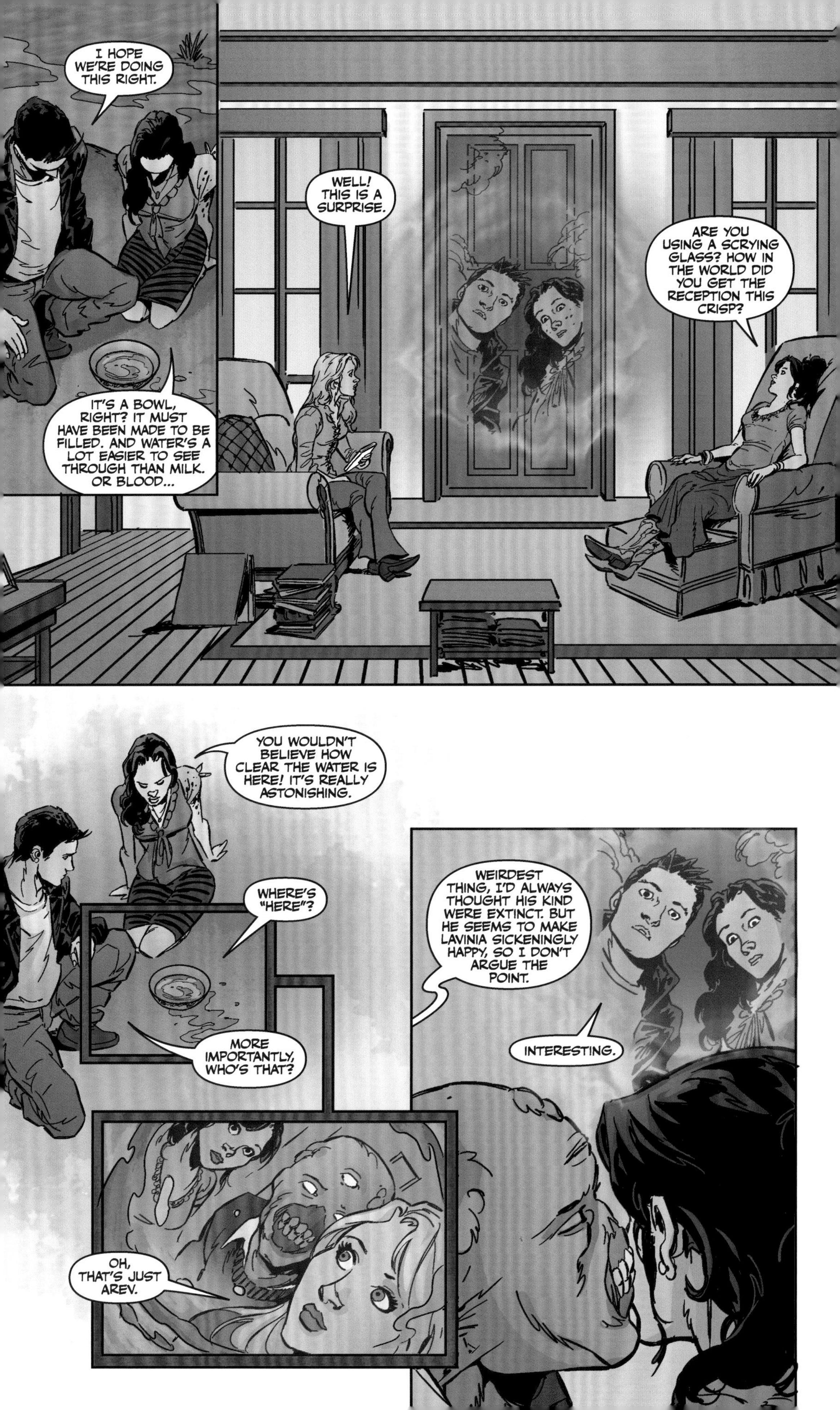
I HOPE WE'RE DOING THIS RIGHT.
IT'S A BOWL, RIGHT? IT MUST HAVE BEEN MADE TO BE FILLED. AND WATER'S A LOT EASIER TO SEE THROUGH THAN MILK. OR BLOOD...
WELL! THIS IS A SURPRISE.
ARE YOU USING A SCRYING GLASS? HOW IN THE WORLD DID YOU GET THE RECEPTION THIS CRISP?
YOU WOULDN'T BELIEVE HOW CLEAR THE WATER IS HERE! IT'S REALLY ASTONISHING.
WHERE'S "HERE"?
MORE IMPORTANTLY, WHO'S THAT?
OH, THAT'S JUST AREV.
WEIRDEST THING, I'D ALWAYS THOUGHT HIS KIND WERE EXTINCT. BUT HE SEEMS TO MAKE LAVINIA SICKENINGLY HAPPY, SO I DON'T ARGUE THE POINT.
INTERESTING.

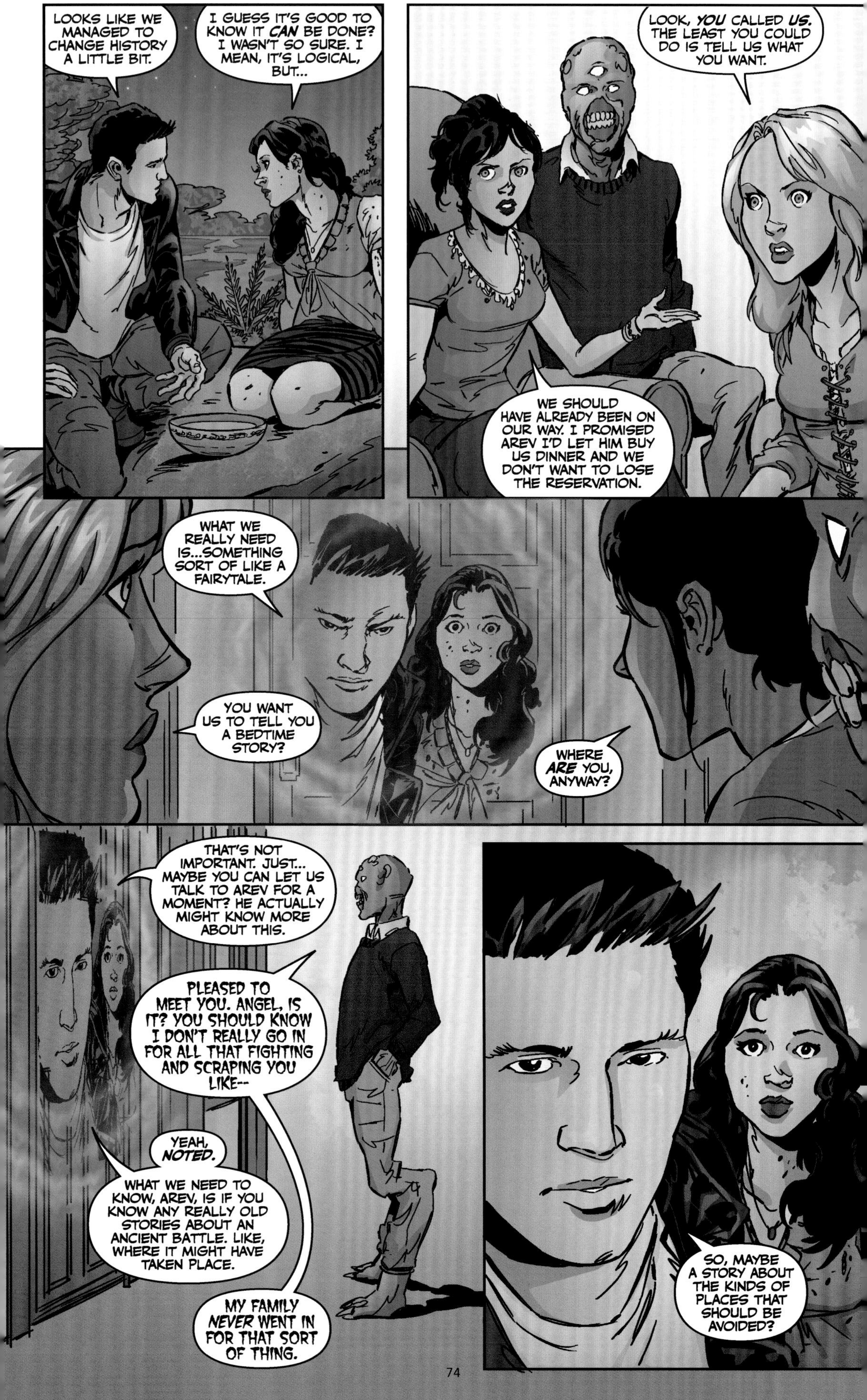

LOOKS LIKE WE MANAGED TO CHANGE HISTORY A LITTLE BIT.
I GUESS IT'S GOOD TO KNOW IT *CAN* BE DONE? I WASN'T SO SURE. I MEAN, IT'S LOGICAL, BUT...
LOOK, *YOU* CALLED *US.* THE LEAST YOU COULD DO IS TELL US WHAT YOU WANT.
WE SHOULD HAVE ALREADY BEEN ON OUR WAY. I PROMISED AREV I'D LET HIM BUY US DINNER AND WE DON'T WANT TO LOSE THE RESERVATION.
WHAT WE REALLY NEED IS...SOMETHING SORT OF LIKE A FAIRYTALE.
YOU WANT US TO TELL YOU A BEDTIME STORY?
WHERE *ARE* YOU, ANYWAY?
THAT'S NOT IMPORTANT. JUST... MAYBE YOU CAN LET US TALK TO AREV FOR A MOMENT? HE ACTUALLY MIGHT KNOW MORE ABOUT THIS.
PLEASED TO MEET YOU. ANGEL, IS IT? YOU SHOULD KNOW I DON'T REALLY GO IN FOR ALL THAT FIGHTING AND SCRAPING YOU LIKE--
YEAH, *NOTED.*
WHAT WE NEED TO KNOW, AREV, IS IF YOU KNOW ANY REALLY OLD STORIES ABOUT AN ANCIENT BATTLE. LIKE, WHERE IT MIGHT HAVE TAKEN PLACE.
MY FAMILY *NEVER* WENT IN FOR THAT SORT OF THING.
SO, MAYBE A STORY ABOUT THE KINDS OF PLACES THAT SHOULD BE AVOIDED?

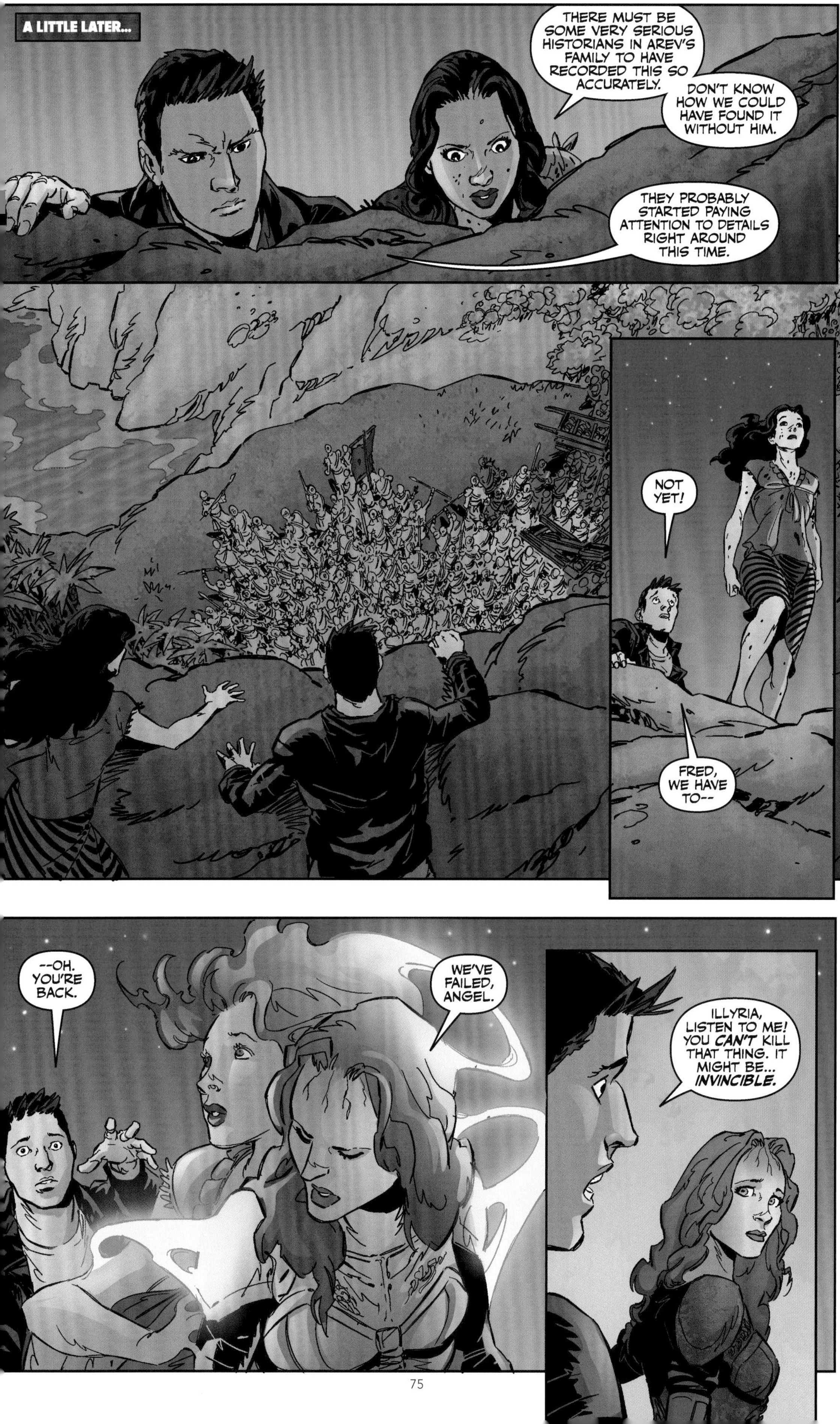

A LITTLE LATER...
THERE MUST BE SOME VERY SERIOUS HISTORIANS IN AREV'S FAMILY TO HAVE RECORDED THIS SO ACCURATELY.
DON'T KNOW HOW WE COULD HAVE FOUND IT WITHOUT HIM.
THEY PROBABLY STARTED PAYING ATTENTION TO DETAILS RIGHT AROUND THIS TIME.
NOT YET!
FRED, WE HAVE TO--
--OH. YOU'RE BACK.
WE'VE FAILED, ANGEL.
ILLYRIA, LISTEN TO ME! YOU *CAN'T* KILL THAT THING. IT MIGHT BE... ***INVINCIBLE.***

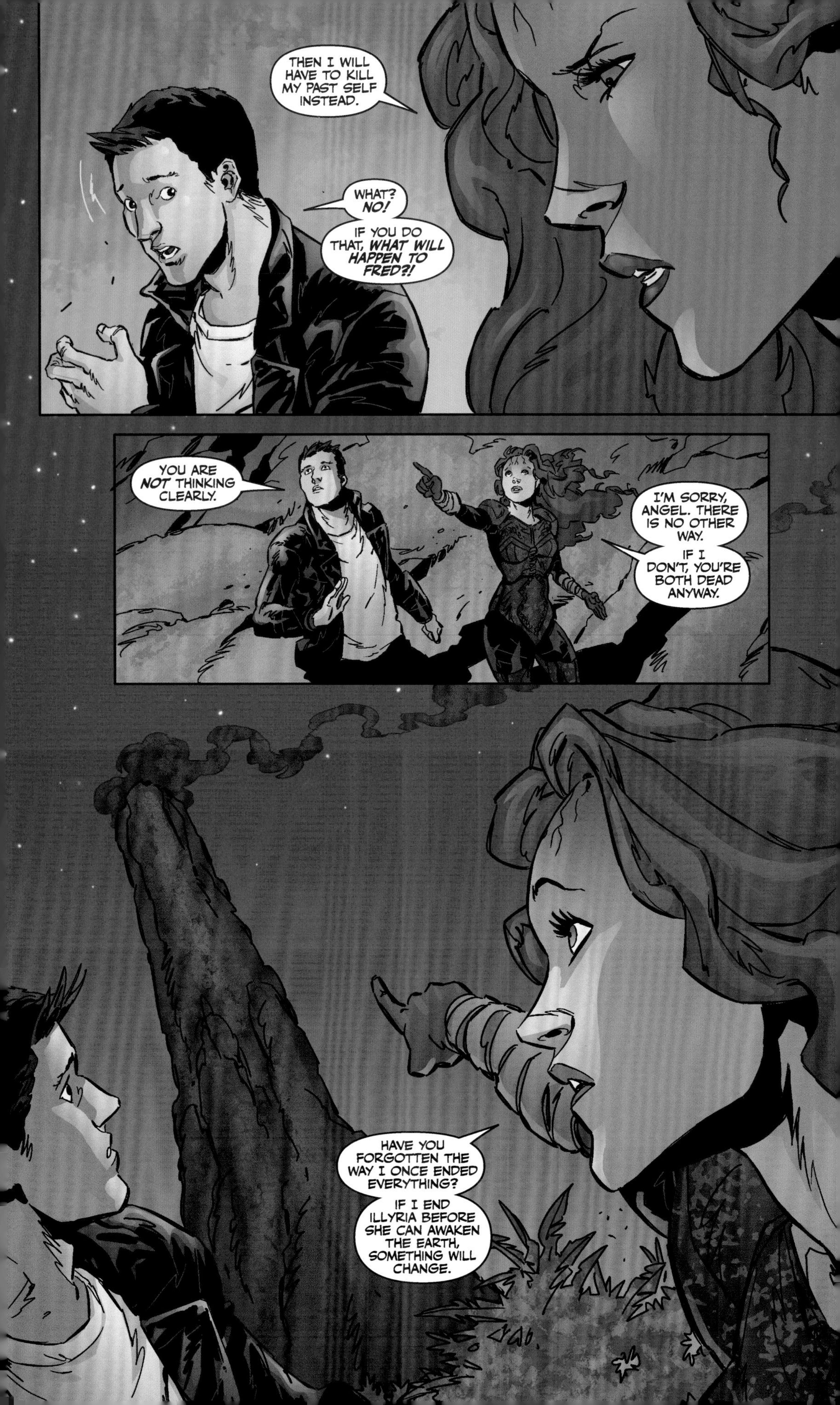

THEN I WILL HAVE TO KILL MY PAST SELF INSTEAD.
WHAT? *NO!*
IF YOU DO THAT, *WHAT WILL HAPPEN TO FRED?!*
YOU ARE *NOT* THINKING CLEARLY.
I'M SORRY, ANGEL. THERE IS NO OTHER WAY.
IF I DON'T, YOU'RE BOTH DEAD ANYWAY.
HAVE YOU FORGOTTEN THE WAY I ONCE ENDED EVERYTHING?
IF I END ILLYRIA BEFORE SHE CAN AWAKEN THE EARTH, SOMETHING WILL CHANGE.

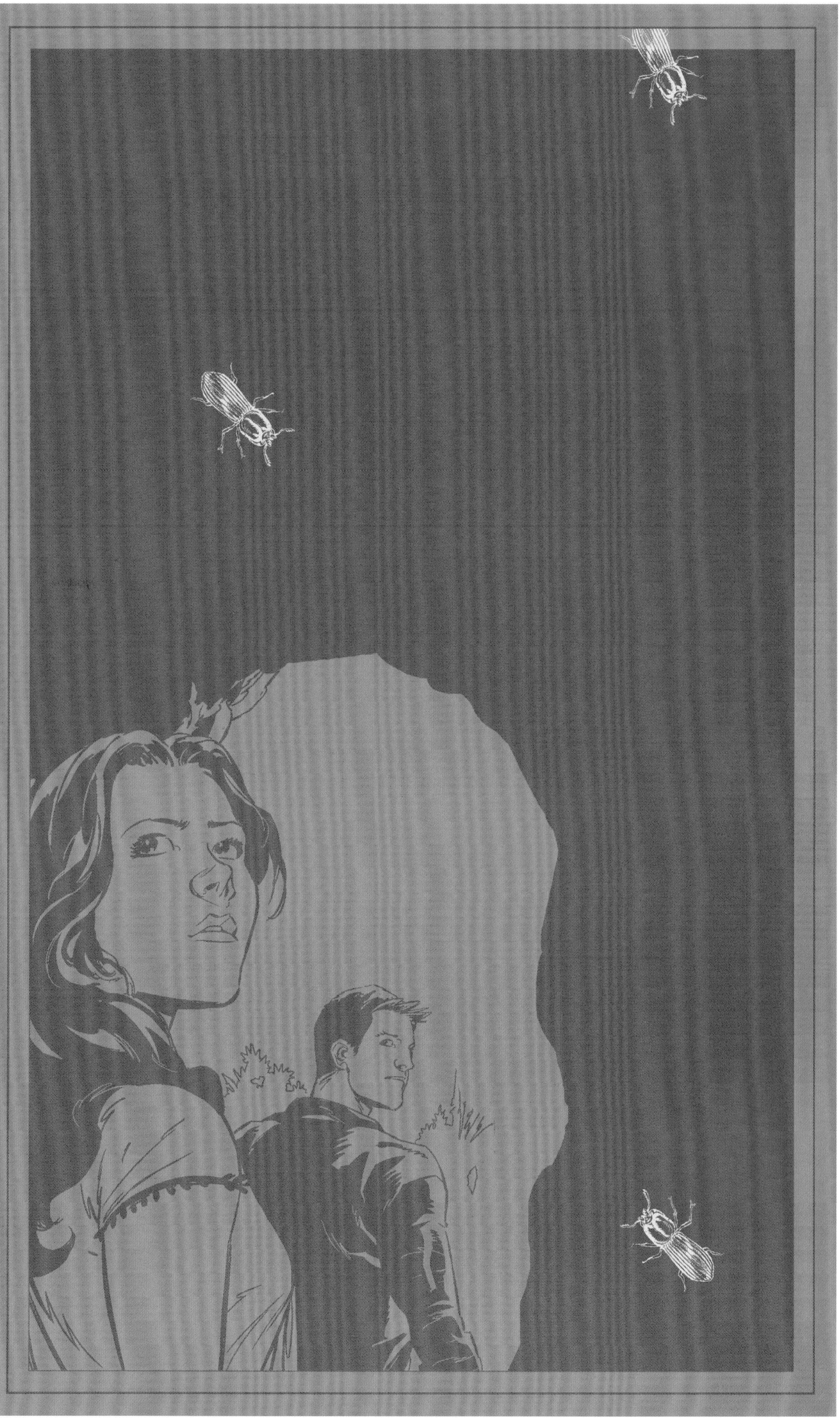

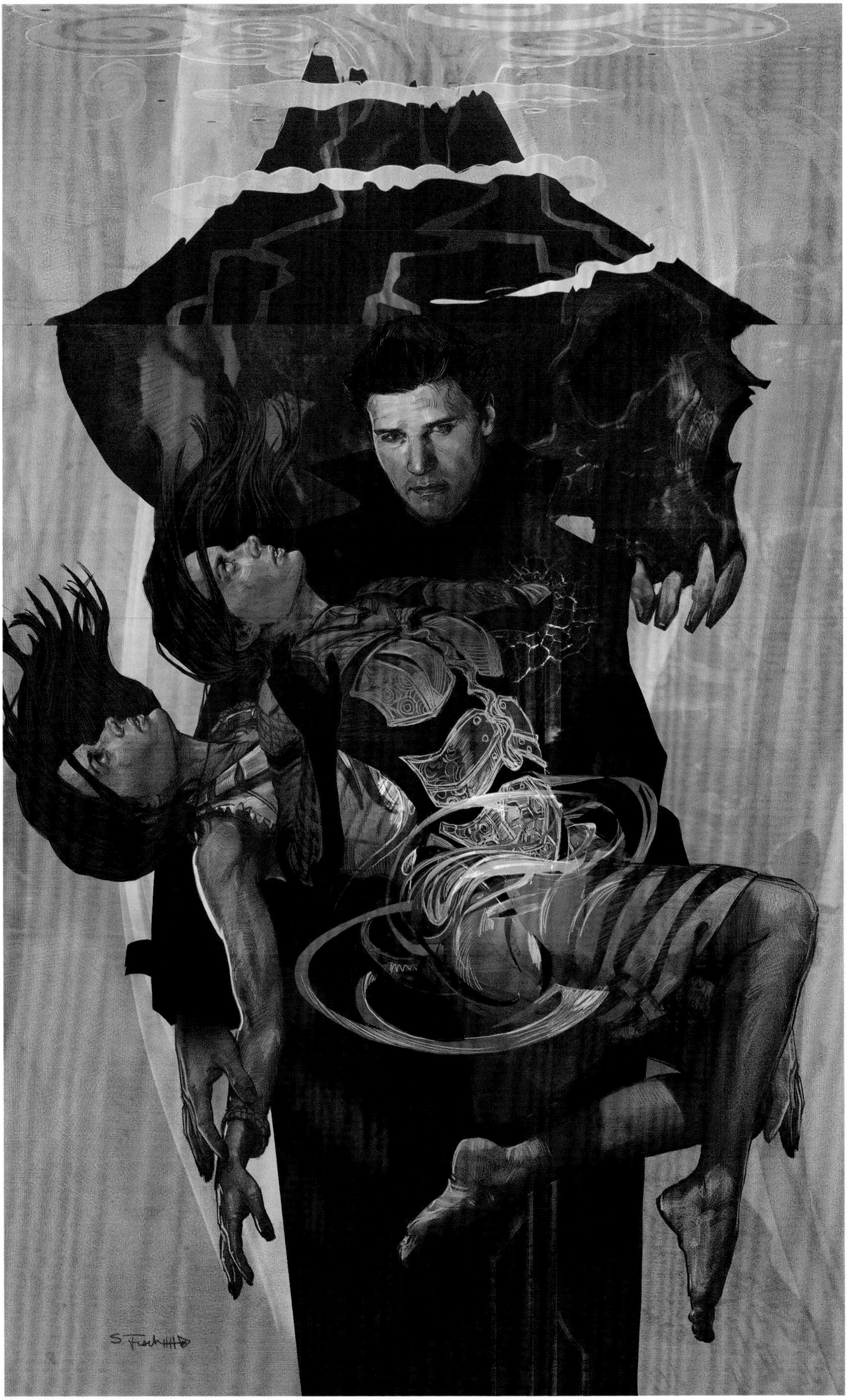

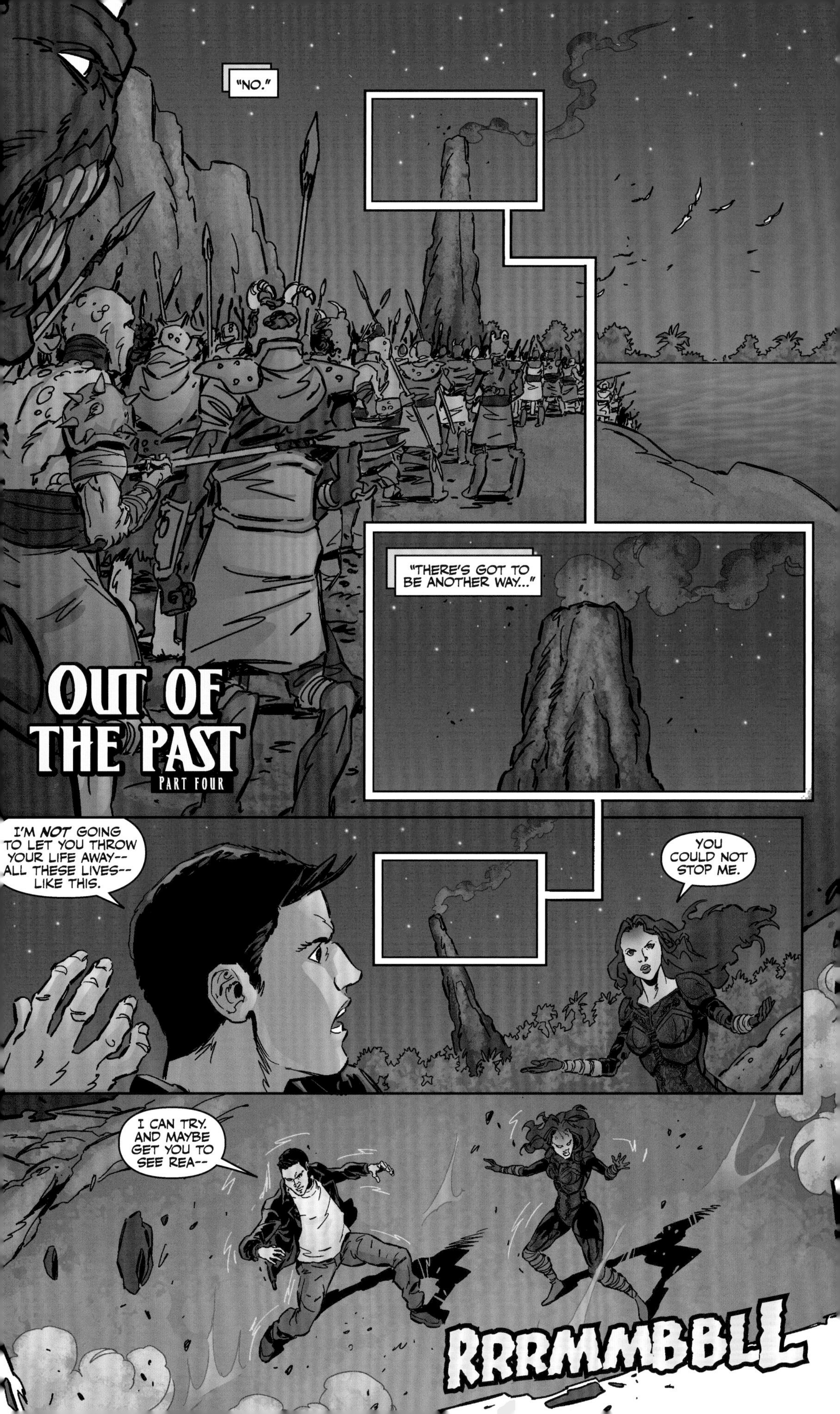
"NO."
"THERE'S GOT TO BE ANOTHER WAY..."
OUT OF THE PAST
PART FOUR
I'M NOT GOING TO LET YOU THROW YOUR LIFE AWAY-- ALL THESE LIVES-- LIKE THIS.
YOU COULD NOT STOP ME.
I CAN TRY. AND MAYBE GET YOU TO SEE REA--
RRRMMBBLL

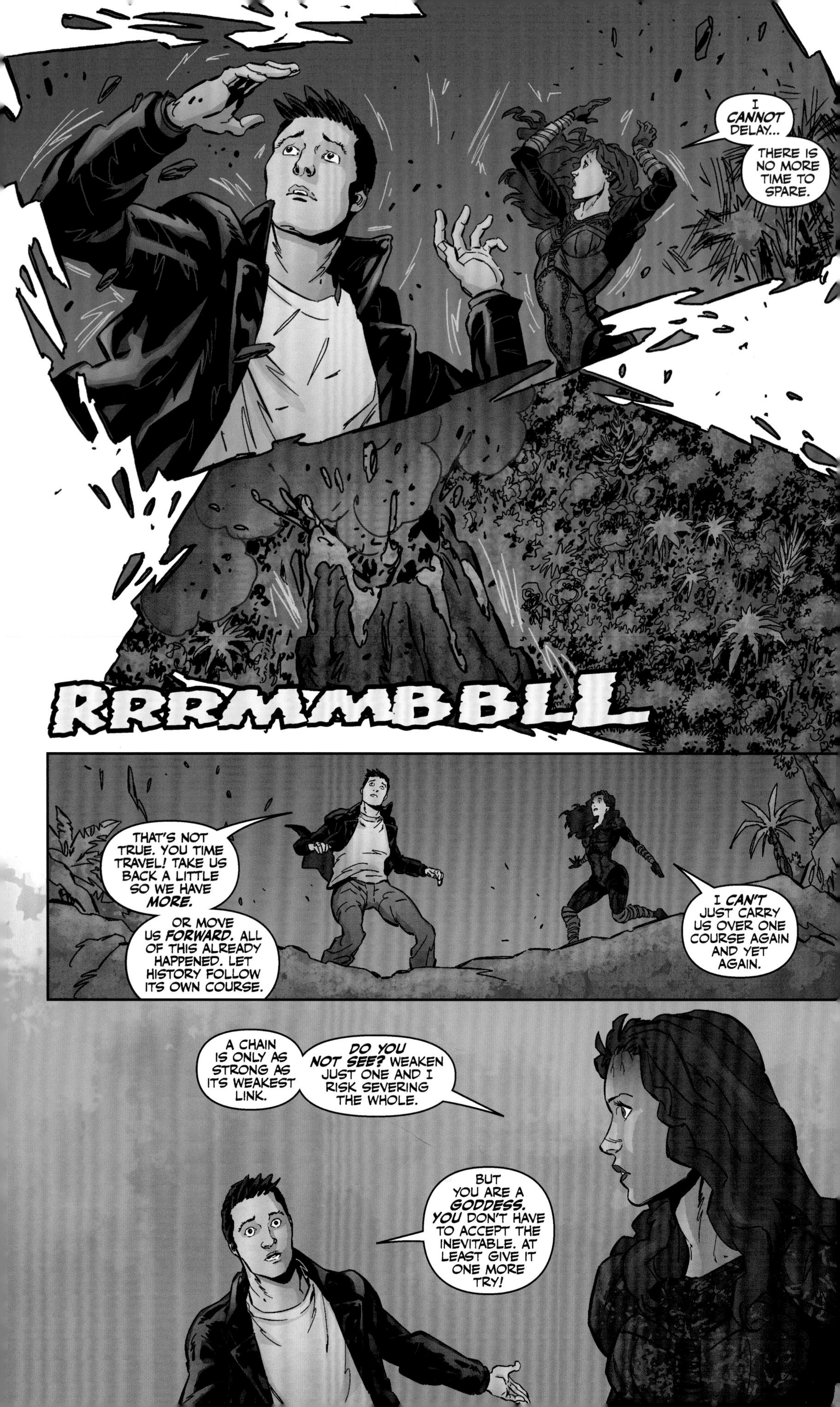

I CANNOT DELAY...
THERE IS NO MORE TIME TO SPARE.
RRRMMBBLL
THAT'S NOT TRUE. YOU TIME TRAVEL! TAKE US BACK A LITTLE SO WE HAVE MORE.
OR MOVE US FORWARD. ALL OF THIS ALREADY HAPPENED. LET HISTORY FOLLOW ITS OWN COURSE.
I CAN'T JUST CARRY US OVER ONE COURSE AGAIN AND YET AGAIN.
A CHAIN IS ONLY AS STRONG AS ITS WEAKEST LINK.
DO YOU NOT SEE? WEAKEN JUST ONE AND I RISK SEVERING THE WHOLE.
BUT YOU ARE A GODDESS. YOU DON'T HAVE TO ACCEPT THE INEVITABLE. AT LEAST GIVE IT ONE MORE TRY!

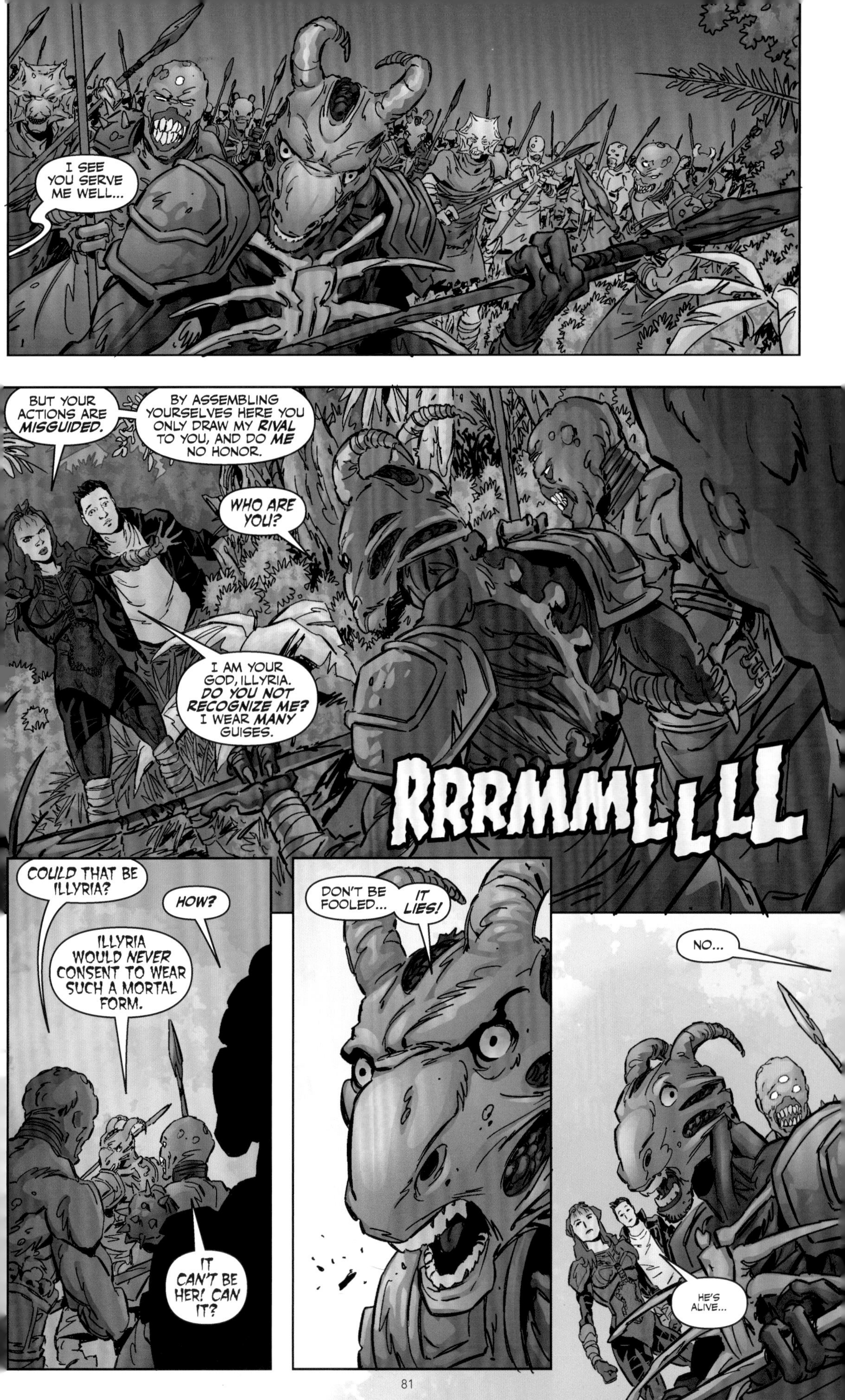

I SEE YOU SERVE ME WELL...
BUT YOUR ACTIONS ARE *MISGUIDED.*
BY ASSEMBLING YOURSELVES HERE YOU ONLY DRAW MY *RIVAL* TO YOU, AND DO *ME* NO HONOR.
WHO ARE YOU?
I AM YOUR GOD, ILLYRIA. *DO YOU NOT RECOGNIZE ME?* I WEAR *MANY* GUISES.
RRRMMLLLL
COULD THAT BE ILLYRIA?
HOW?
ILLYRIA WOULD *NEVER* CONSENT TO WEAR SUCH A MORTAL FORM.
IT *CAN'T* BE HER! CAN IT?
DON'T BE FOOLED...
IT LIES!
NO...
HE'S ALIVE...

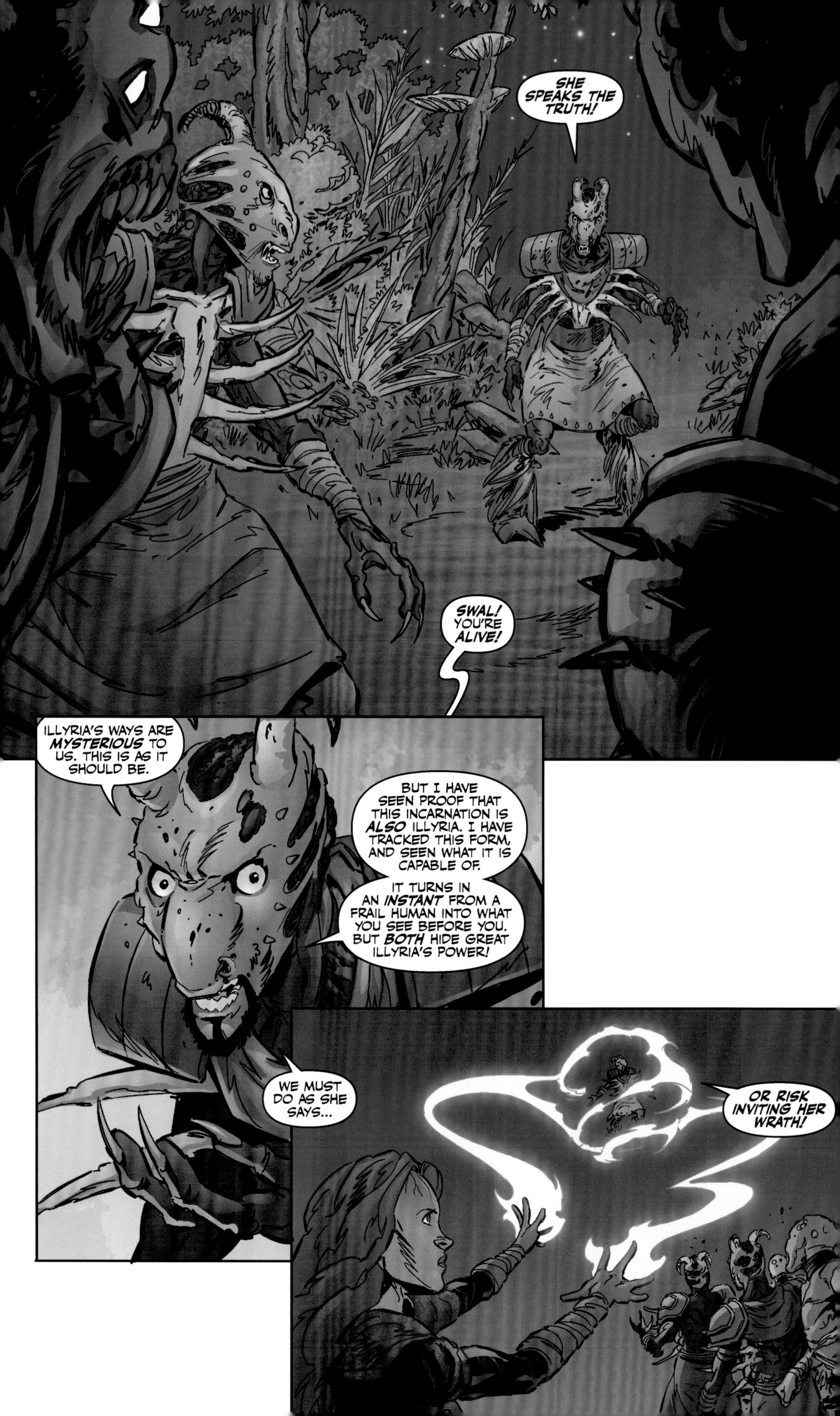
SHE SPEAKS THE TRUTH!
SWAL! YOU'RE ALIVE!
ILLYRIA'S WAYS ARE MYSTERIOUS TO US. THIS IS AS IT SHOULD BE.
BUT I HAVE SEEN PROOF THAT THIS INCARNATION IS ALSO ILLYRIA. I HAVE TRACKED THIS FORM, AND SEEN WHAT IT IS CAPABLE OF.
IT TURNS IN AN INSTANT FROM A FRAIL HUMAN INTO WHAT YOU SEE BEFORE YOU. BUT BOTH HIDE GREAT ILLYRIA'S POWER!
WE MUST DO AS SHE SAYS...
OR RISK INVITING HER WRATH!

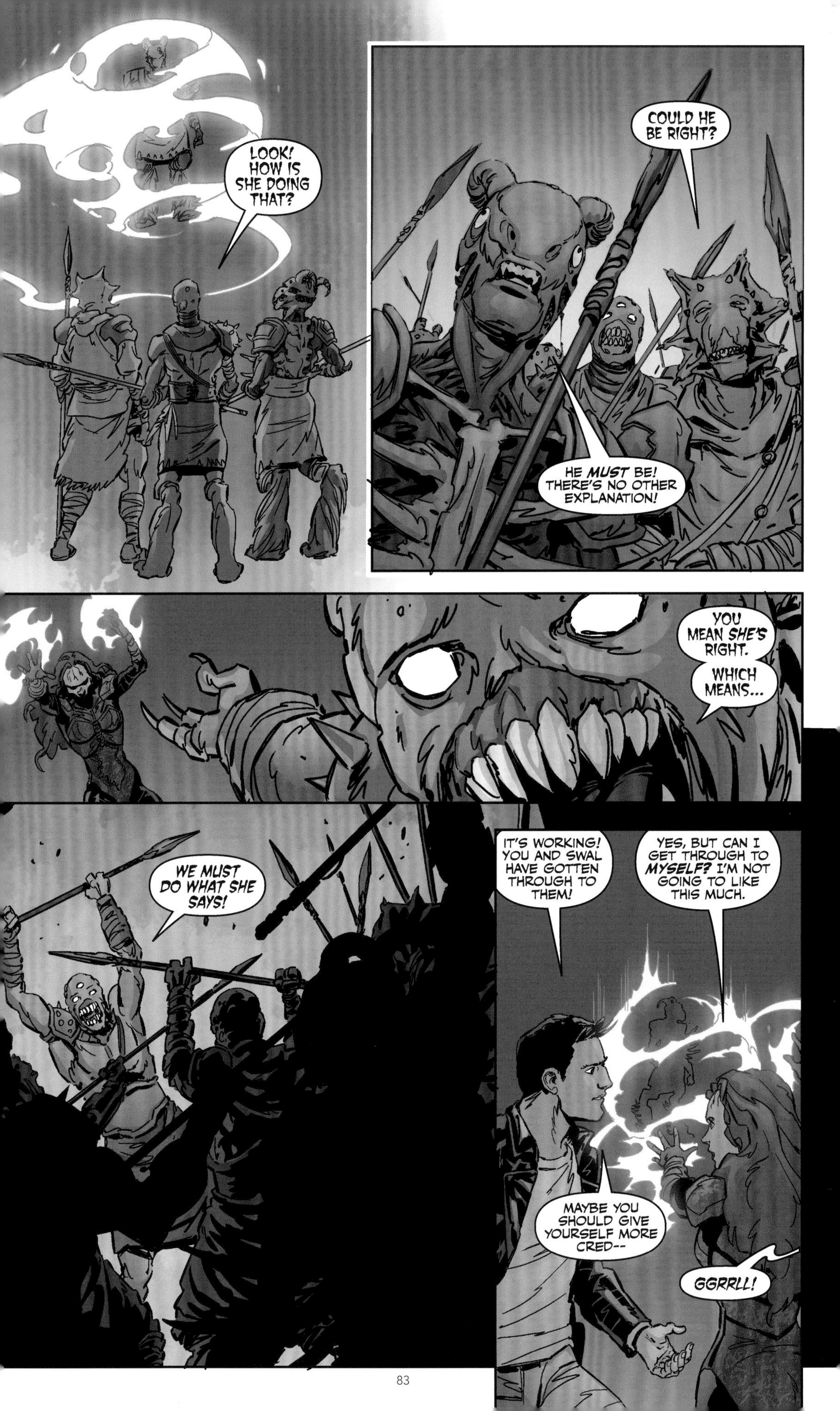
LOOK! HOW IS SHE DOING THAT?
COULD HE BE RIGHT?
HE *MUST* BE! THERE'S NO OTHER EXPLANATION!
YOU MEAN *SHE'S* RIGHT.
WHICH MEANS...
WE MUST DO WHAT SHE SAYS!
IT'S WORKING! YOU AND SWAL HAVE GOTTEN THROUGH TO THEM!
YES, BUT CAN I GET THROUGH TO *MYSELF?* I'M NOT GOING TO LIKE THIS MUCH.
MAYBE YOU SHOULD GIVE YOURSELF MORE CRED--
GGRRLL!

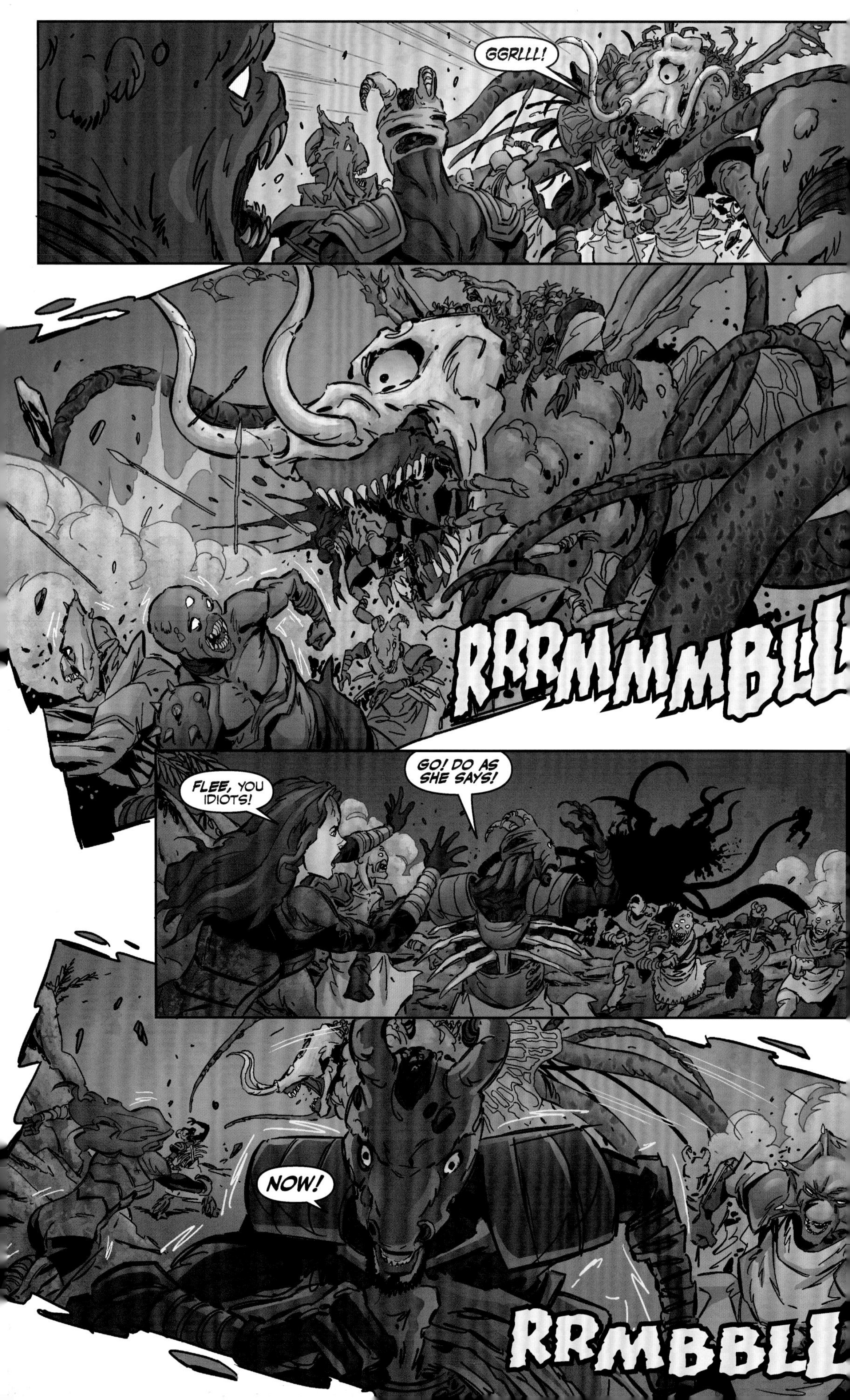
GGRLLL!
RRRMMMBLL
FLEE, YOU IDIOTS!
GO! DO AS SHE SAYS!
NOW!
RRMBBLL

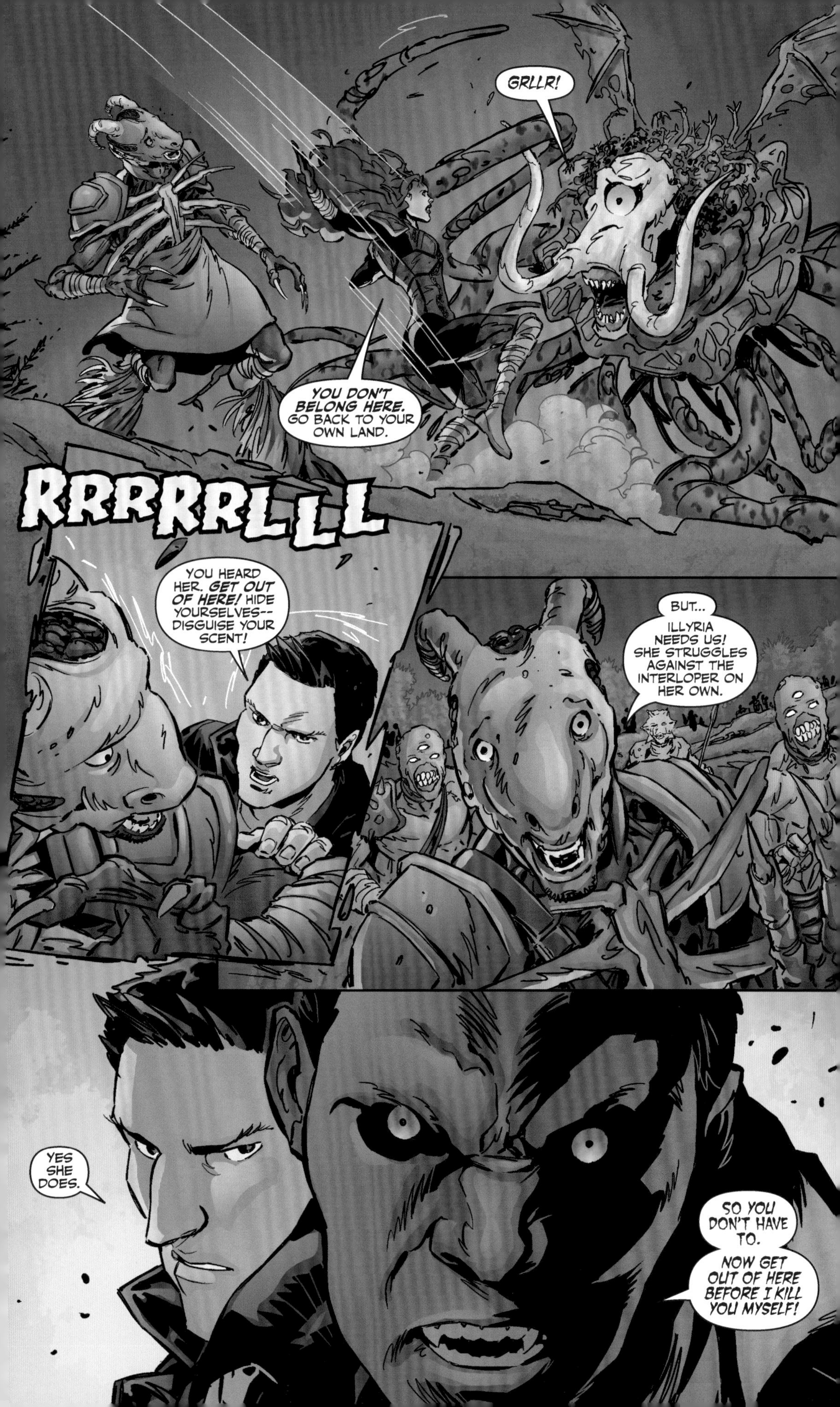
GRLLR!
YOU DON'T BELONG HERE. GO BACK TO YOUR OWN LAND.
RRRRRLLL
YOU HEARD HER. GET OUT OF HERE! HIDE YOURSELVES-- DISGUISE YOUR SCENT!
BUT... ILLYRIA NEEDS US! SHE STRUGGLES AGAINST THE INTERLOPER ON HER OWN.
YES SHE DOES.
SO YOU DON'T HAVE TO.
NOW GET OUT OF HERE BEFORE I KILL YOU MYSELF!

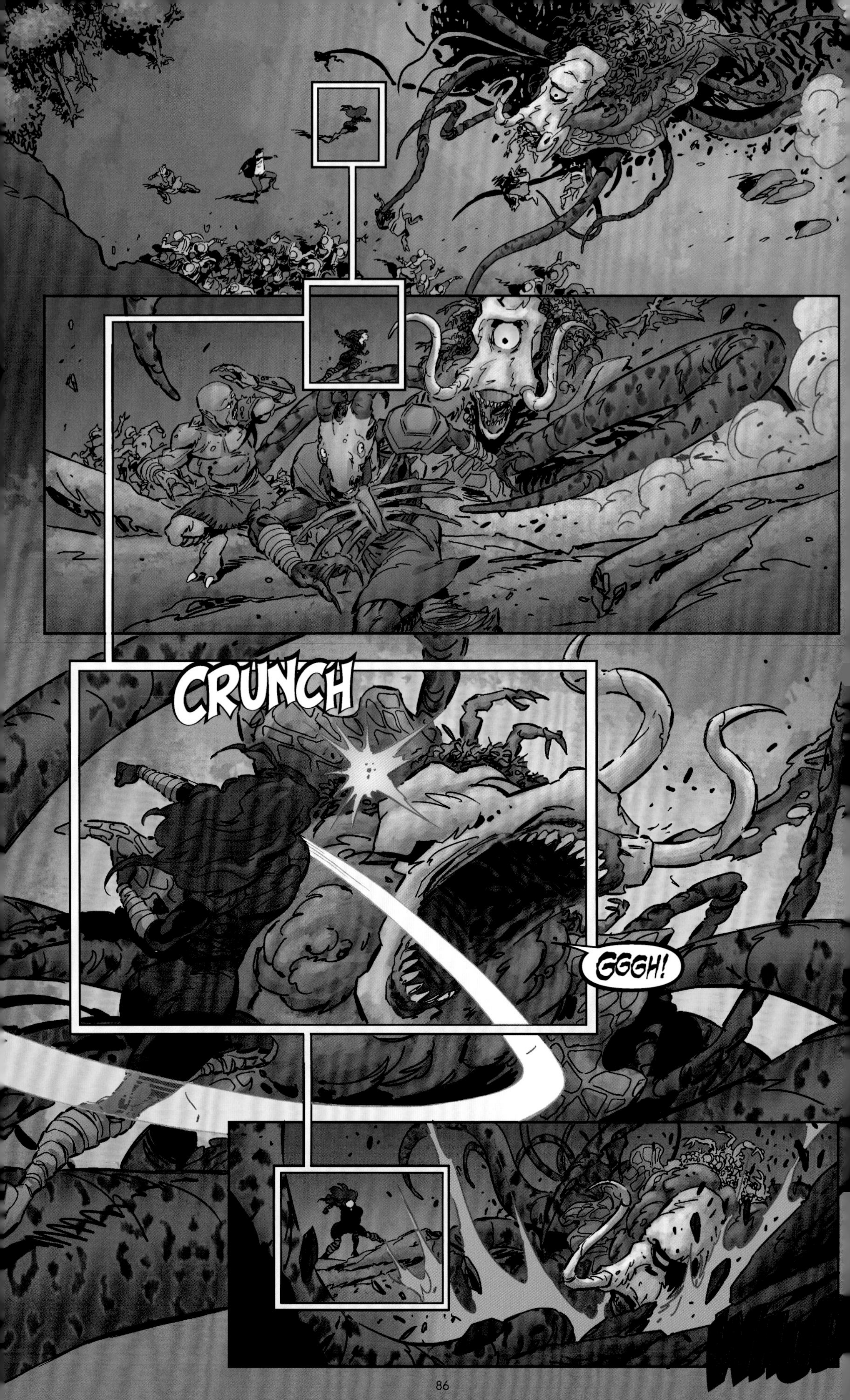
CRUNCH
GGGH!

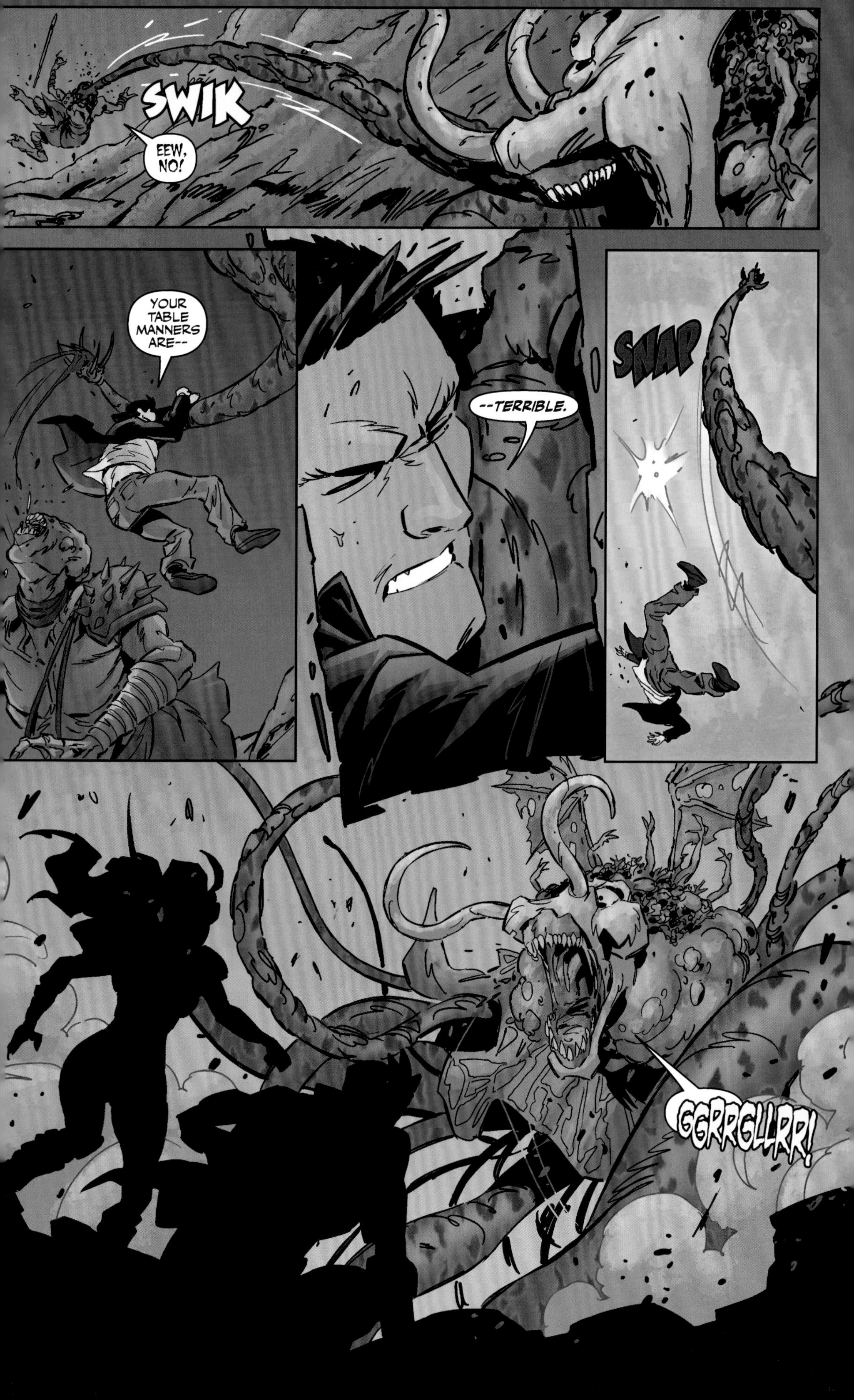
SWIK
EEW, NO!
YOUR TABLE MANNERS ARE--
--TERRIBLE.
SNAP
GGRRGLLRR!

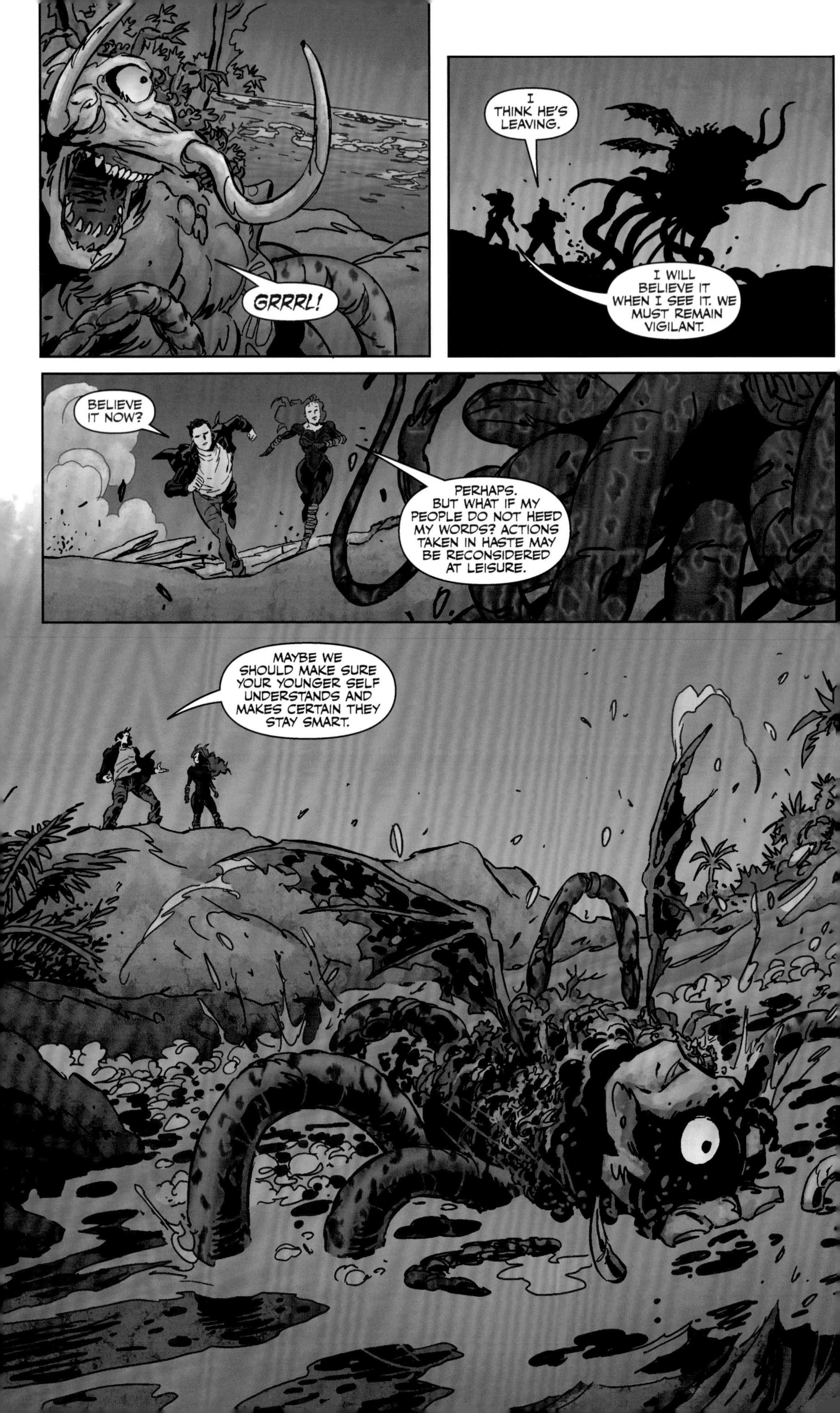
GRRRL!
I THINK HE'S LEAVING.
I WILL BELIEVE IT WHEN I SEE IT. WE MUST REMAIN VIGILANT.
BELIEVE IT NOW?
PERHAPS. BUT WHAT IF MY PEOPLE DO NOT HEED MY WORDS? ACTIONS TAKEN IN HASTE MAY BE RECONSIDERED AT LEISURE.
MAYBE WE SHOULD MAKE SURE YOUR YOUNGER SELF UNDERSTANDS AND MAKES CERTAIN THEY STAY SMART.

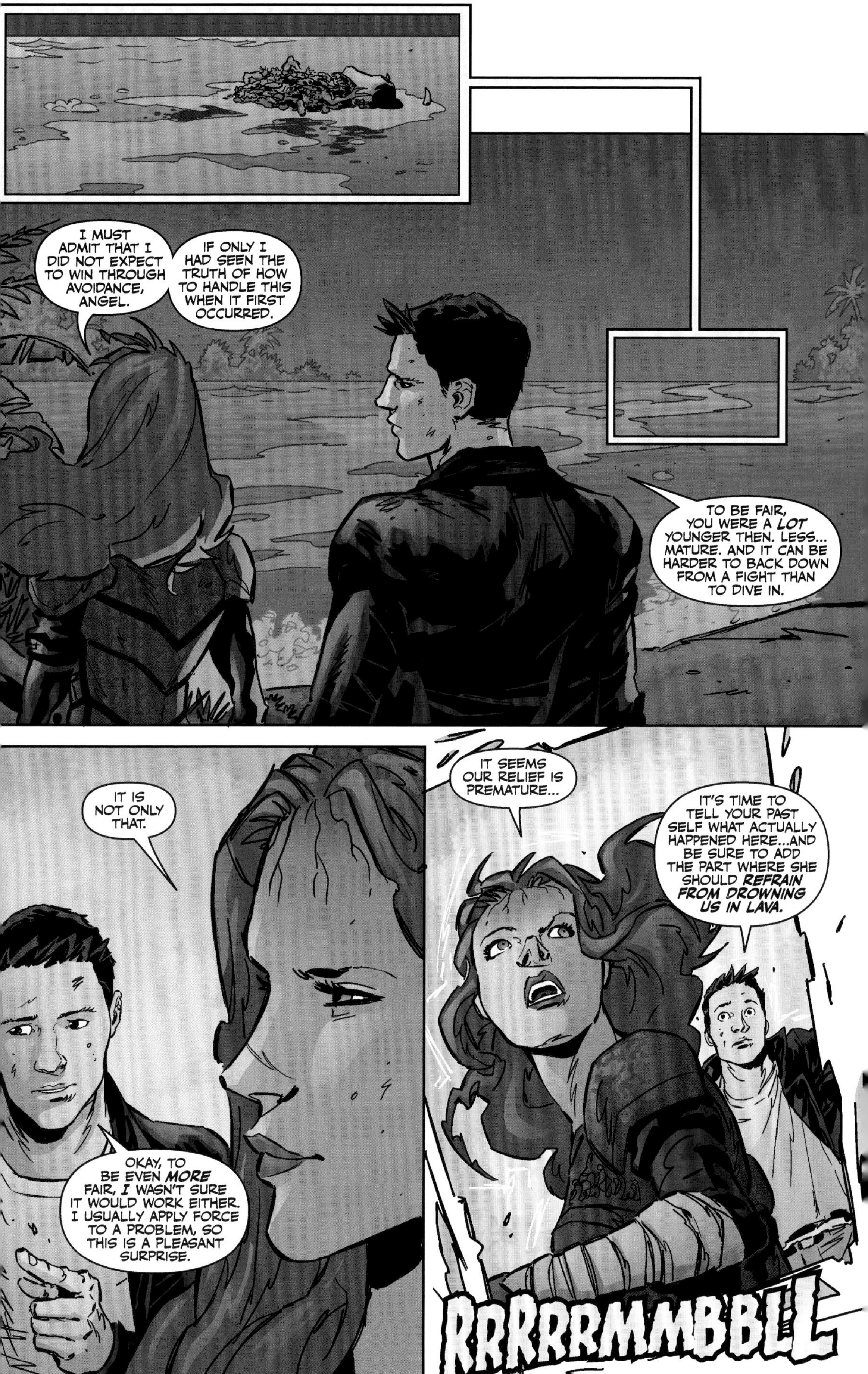
I MUST ADMIT THAT I DID NOT EXPECT TO WIN THROUGH AVOIDANCE, ANGEL.
IF ONLY I HAD SEEN THE TRUTH OF HOW TO HANDLE THIS WHEN IT FIRST OCCURRED.
TO BE FAIR, YOU WERE A *LOT* YOUNGER THEN. LESS... MATURE. AND IT CAN BE HARDER TO BACK DOWN FROM A FIGHT THAN TO DIVE IN.
IT IS NOT ONLY THAT.
OKAY, TO BE EVEN *MORE* FAIR, *I* WASN'T SURE IT WOULD WORK EITHER. I USUALLY APPLY FORCE TO A PROBLEM, SO THIS IS A PLEASANT SURPRISE.
IT SEEMS OUR RELIEF IS PREMATURE...
IT'S TIME TO TELL YOUR PAST SELF WHAT ACTUALLY HAPPENED HERE...AND BE SURE TO ADD THE PART WHERE SHE SHOULD *REFRAIN FROM DROWNING US IN LAVA.*
RRRRRMMMBBLL

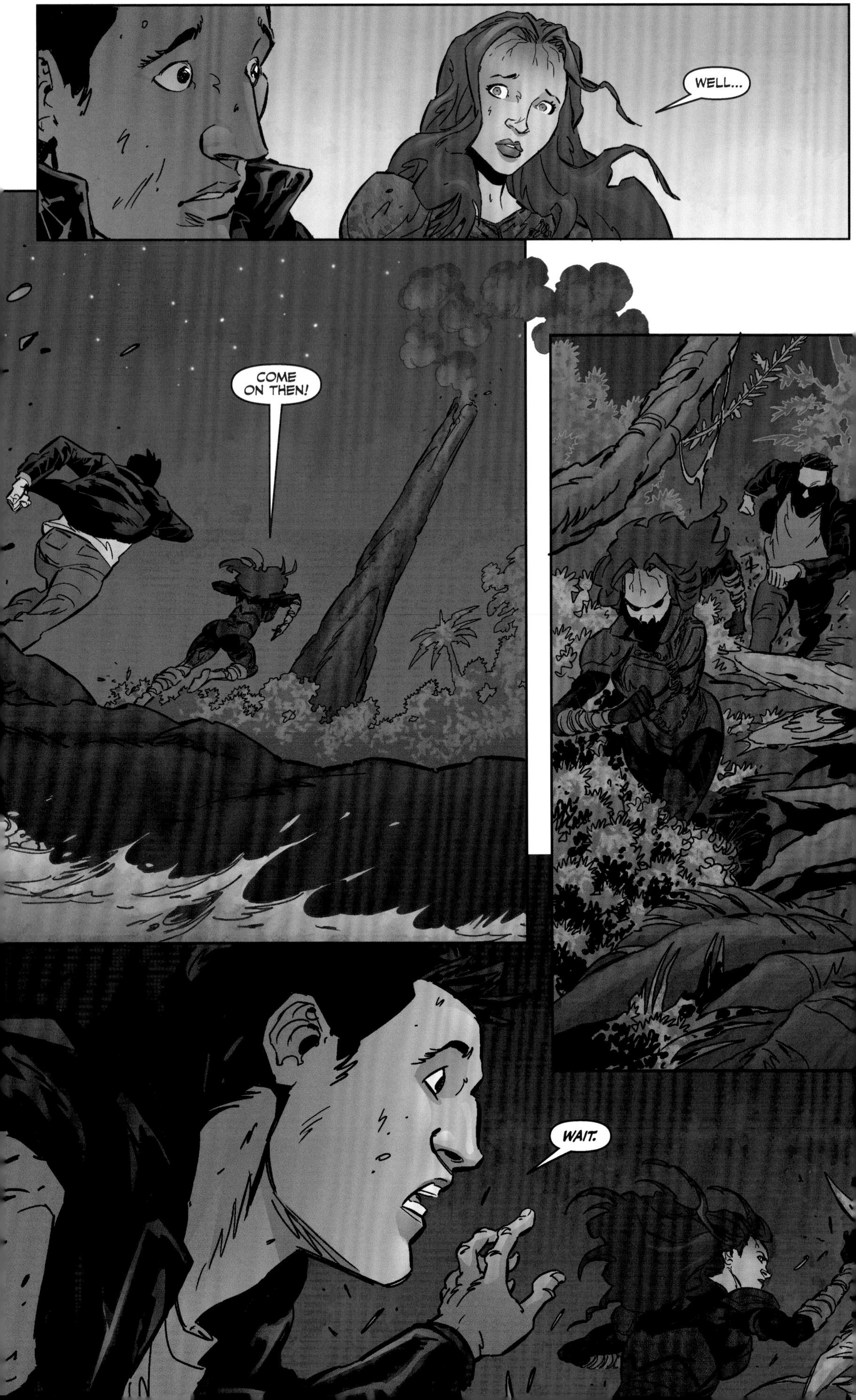
WELL...
COME ON THEN!
WAIT.

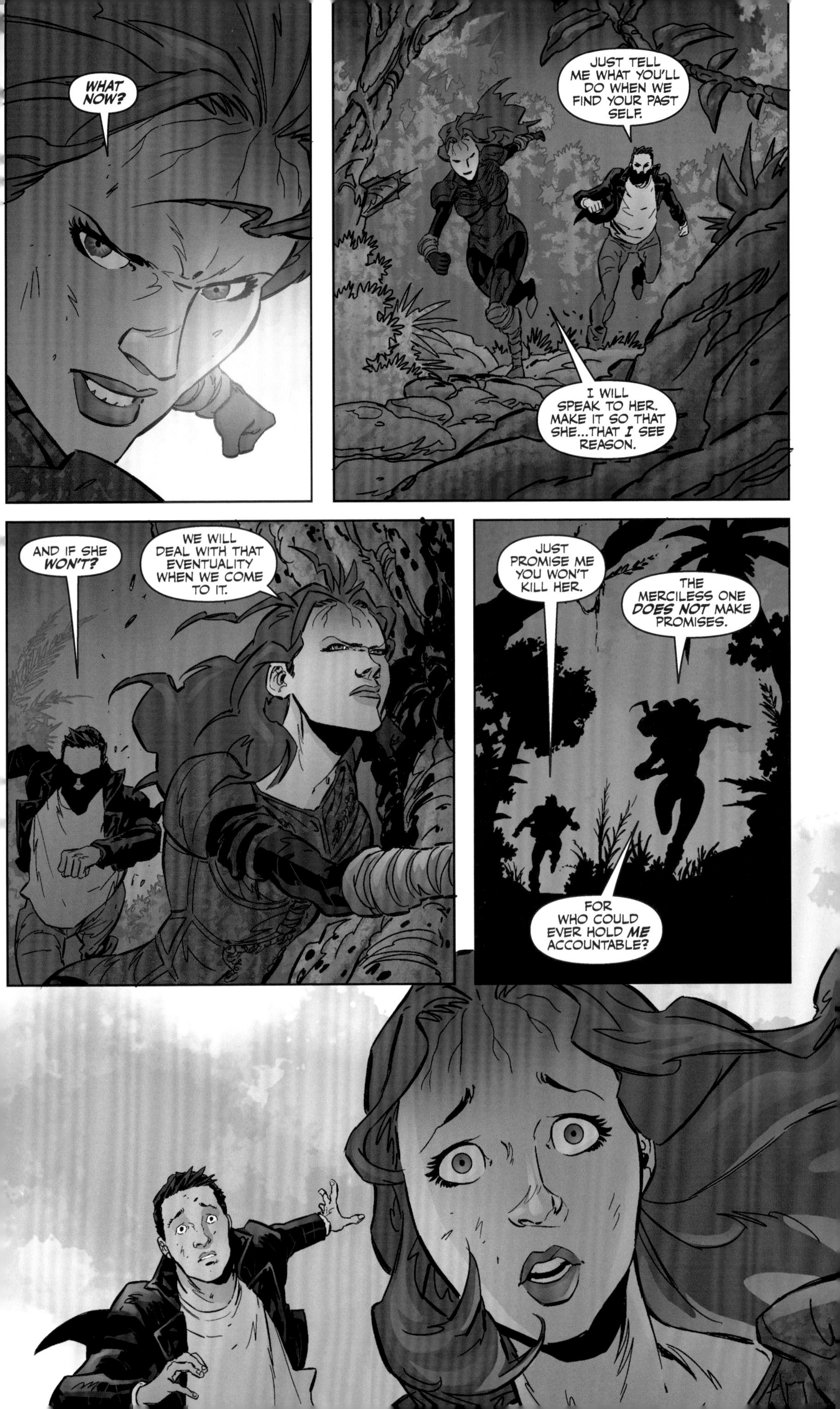
WHAT NOW?
JUST TELL ME WHAT YOU'LL DO WHEN WE FIND YOUR PAST SELF.
I WILL SPEAK TO HER. MAKE IT SO THAT SHE...THAT I SEE REASON.
AND IF SHE WON'T?
WE WILL DEAL WITH THAT EVENTUALITY WHEN WE COME TO IT.
JUST PROMISE ME YOU WON'T KILL HER.
THE MERCILESS ONE DOES NOT MAKE PROMISES.
FOR WHO COULD EVER HOLD ME ACCOUNTABLE?

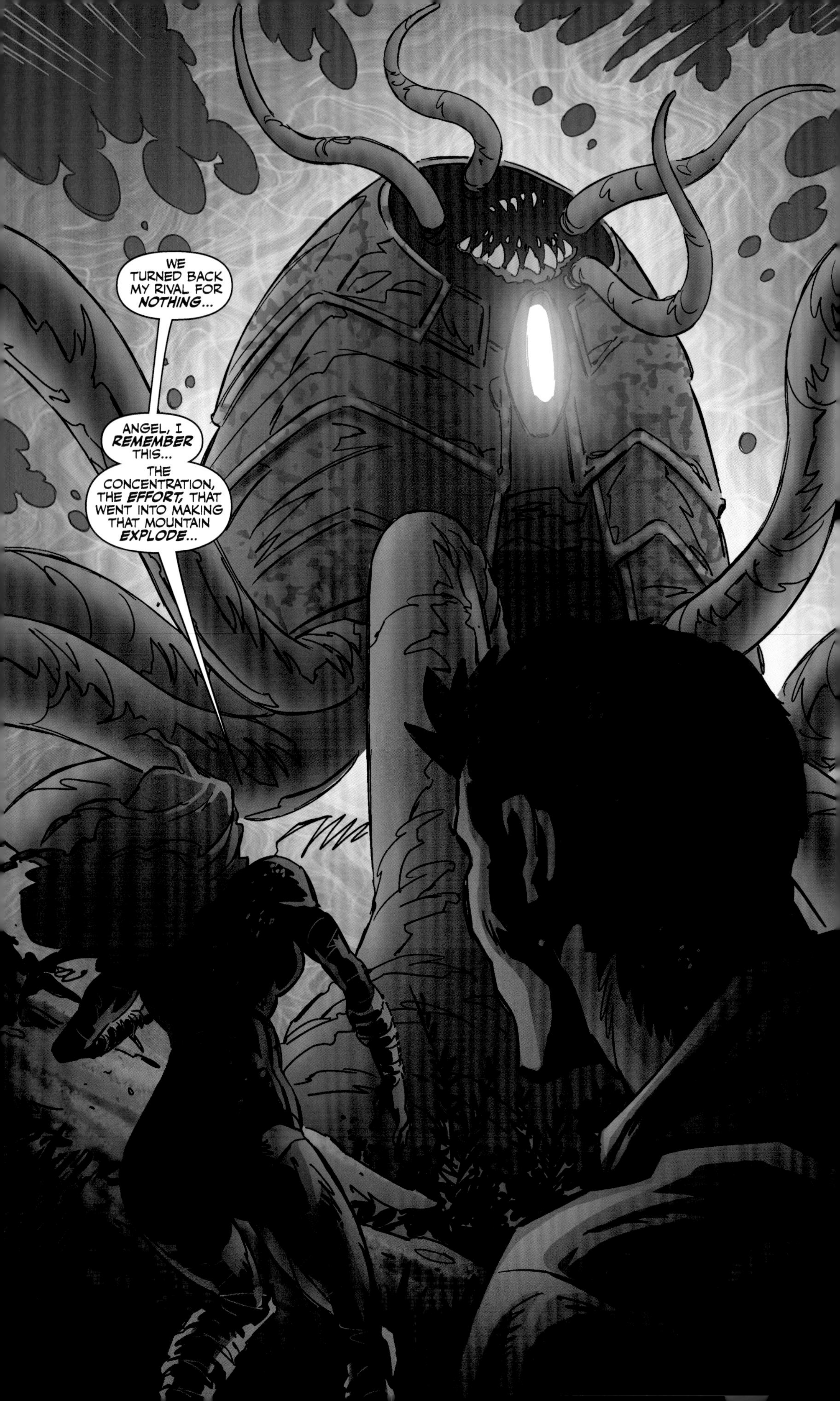
WE TURNED BACK MY RIVAL FOR NOTHING...
ANGEL, I REMEMBER THIS...
THE CONCENTRATION, THE EFFORT, THAT WENT INTO MAKING THAT MOUNTAIN EXPLODE...

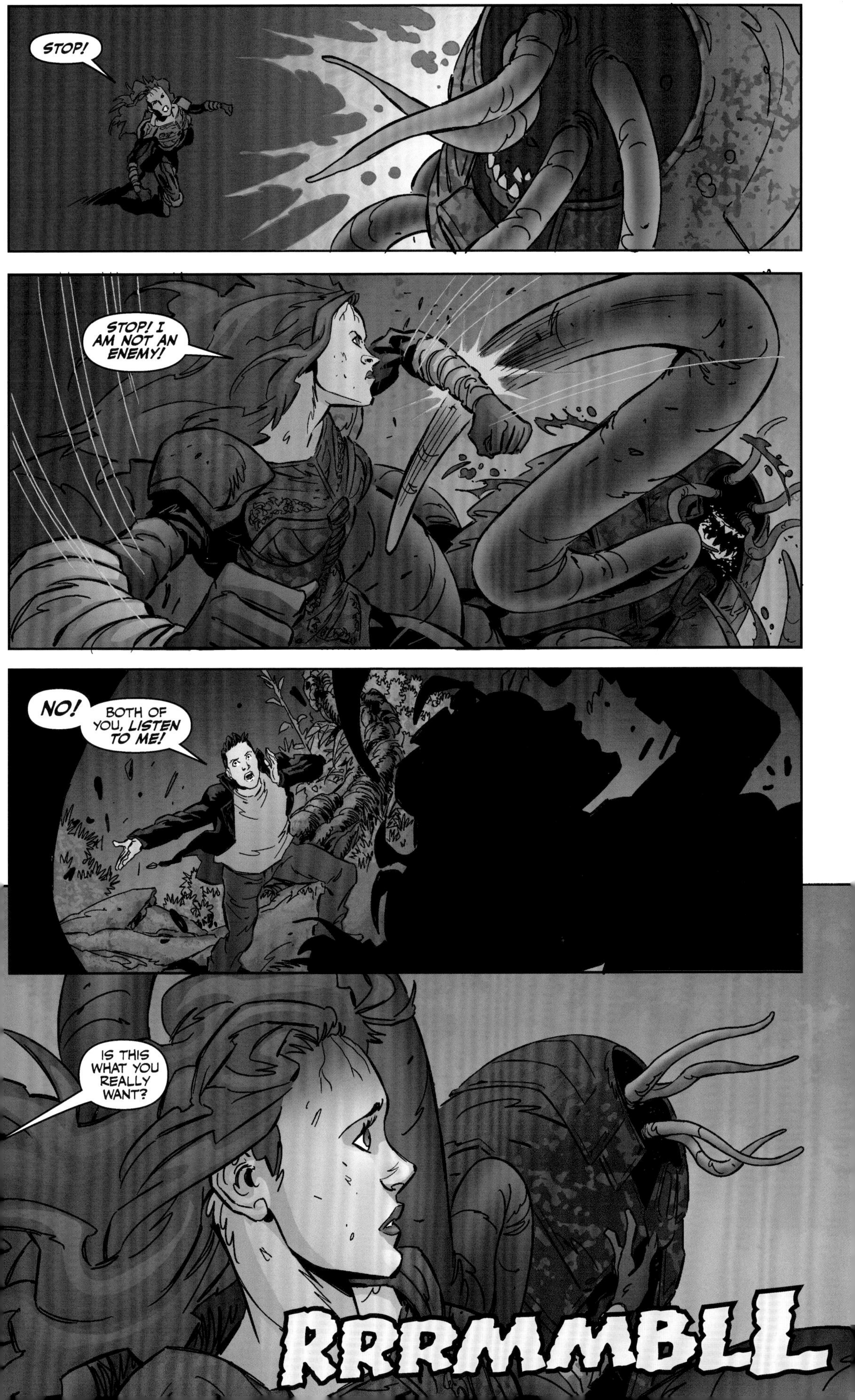
STOP!
STOP! I AM NOT AN ENEMY!
NO!
BOTH OF YOU, LISTEN TO ME!
IS THIS WHAT YOU REALLY WANT?
RRRMMBLL

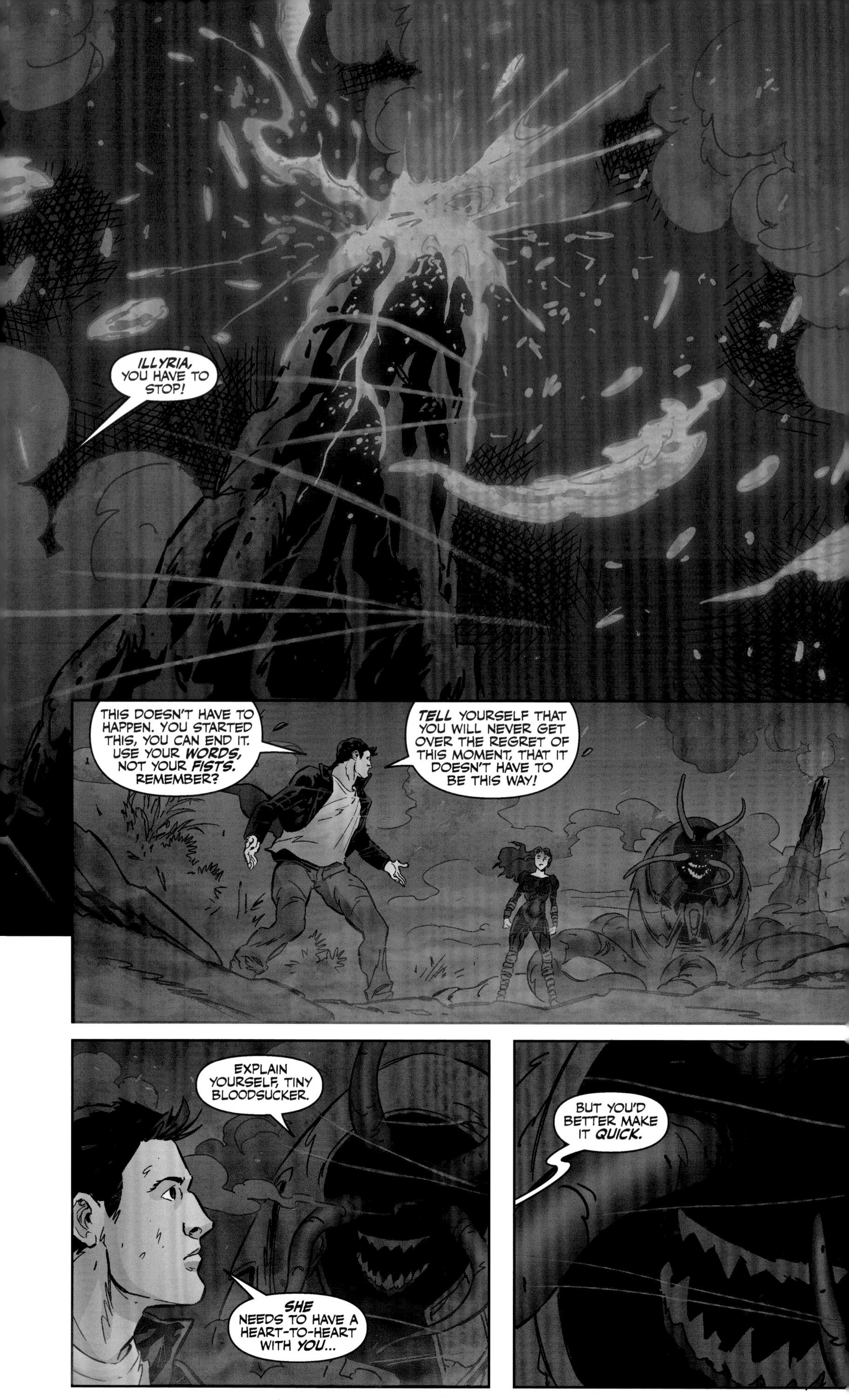
ILLYRIA, YOU HAVE TO STOP!
THIS DOESN'T HAVE TO HAPPEN. YOU STARTED THIS, YOU CAN END IT. USE YOUR WORDS, NOT YOUR FISTS. REMEMBER?
TELL YOURSELF THAT YOU WILL NEVER GET OVER THE REGRET OF THIS MOMENT, THAT IT DOESN'T HAVE TO BE THIS WAY!
EXPLAIN YOURSELF, TINY BLOODSUCKER.
SHE NEEDS TO HAVE A HEART-TO-HEART WITH YOU...
BUT YOU'D BETTER MAKE IT QUICK.

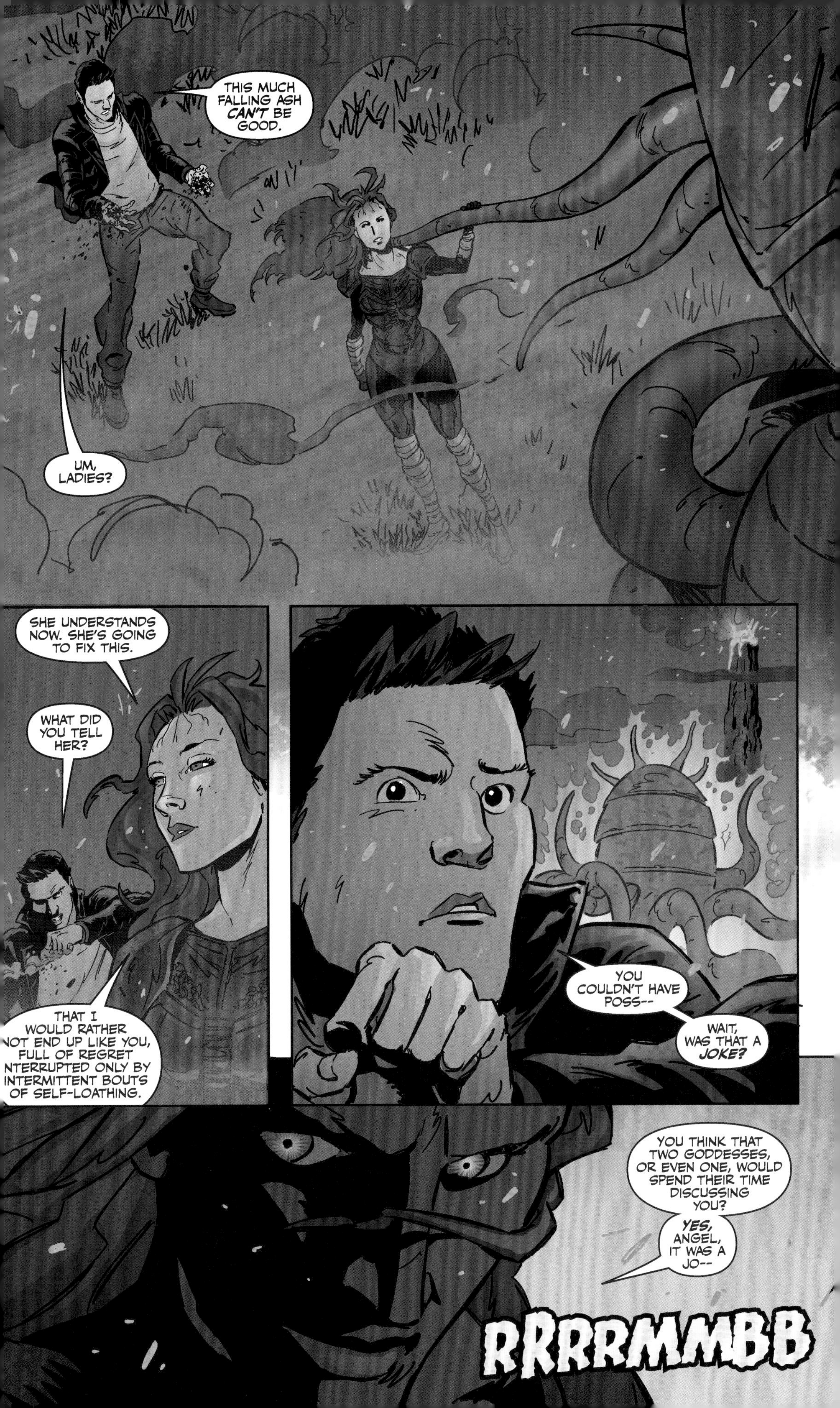

THIS MUCH FALLING ASH *CAN'T* BE GOOD.
UM, LADIES?
SHE UNDERSTANDS NOW. SHE'S GOING TO FIX THIS.
WHAT DID YOU TELL HER?
THAT I WOULD RATHER NOT END UP LIKE YOU, FULL OF REGRET INTERRUPTED ONLY BY INTERMITTENT BOUTS OF SELF-LOATHING.
YOU COULDN'T HAVE POSS--
WAIT, WAS THAT A *JOKE?*
YOU THINK THAT TWO GODDESSES, OR EVEN ONE, WOULD SPEND THEIR TIME DISCUSSING YOU?
YES, ANGEL, IT WAS A JO--
RRRRRMMBB

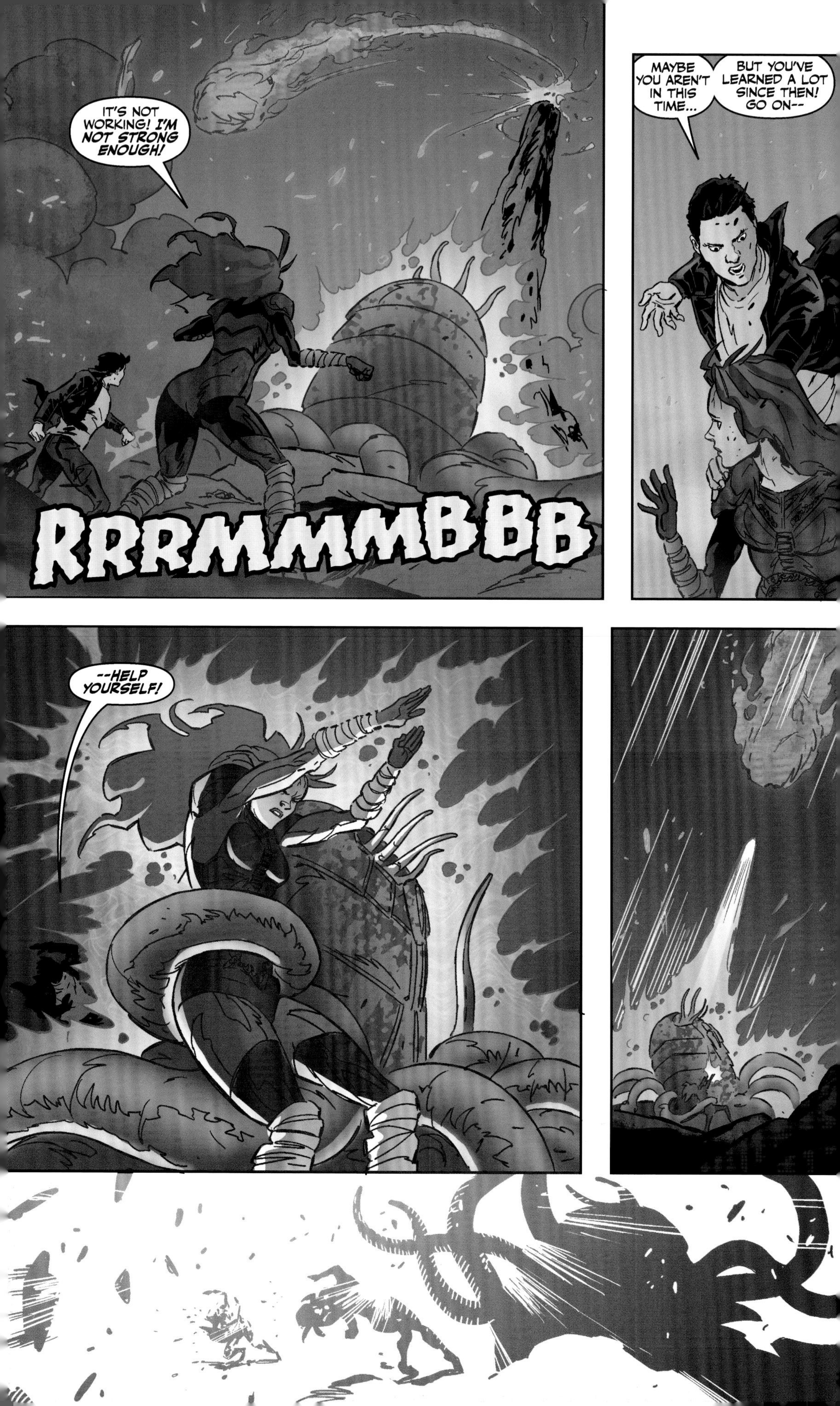
IT'S NOT WORKING! I'M NOT STRONG ENOUGH!
RRRMMMBBB
MAYBE YOU AREN'T IN THIS TIME...
BUT YOU'VE LEARNED A LOT SINCE THEN! GO ON--
--HELP YOURSELF!

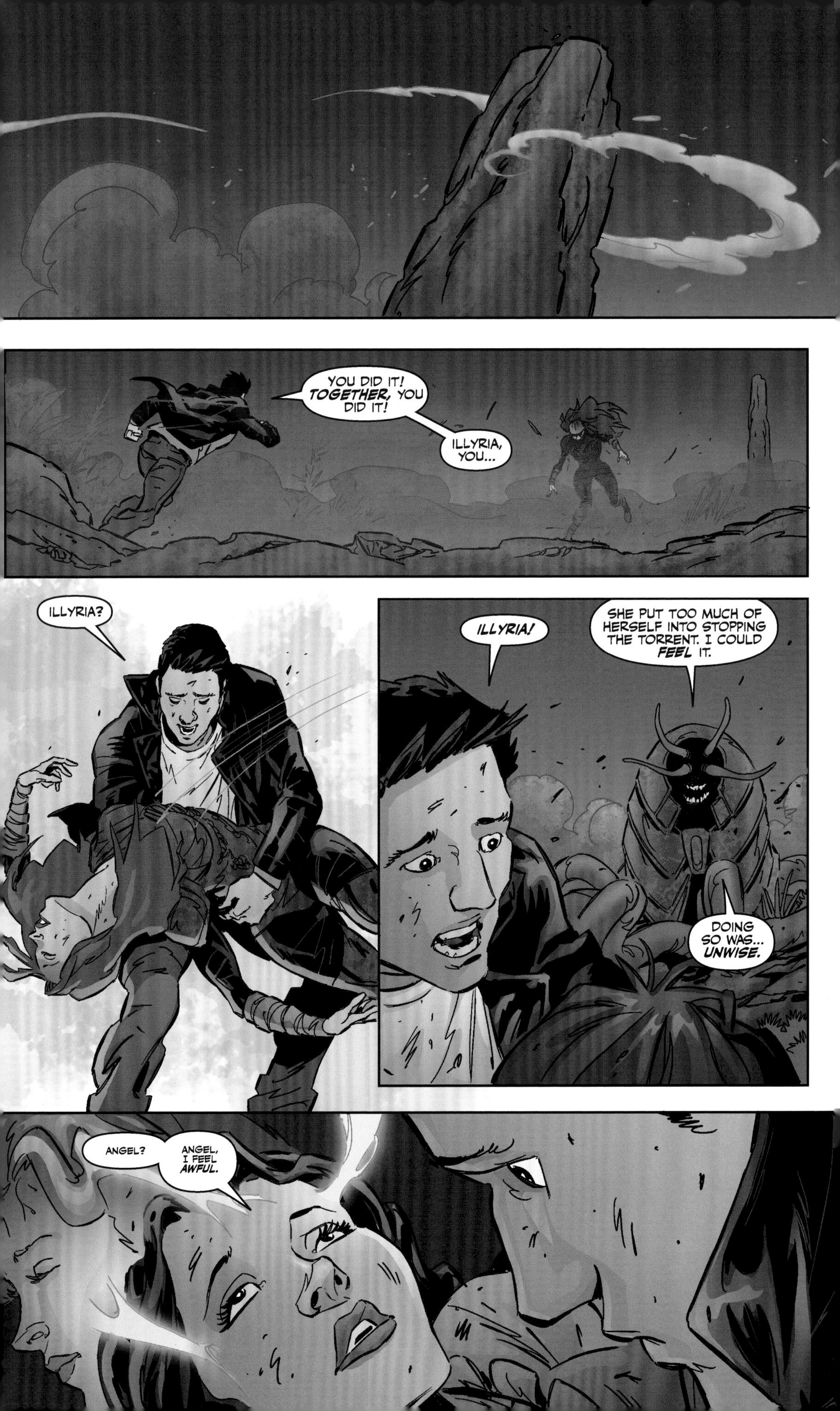
YOU DID IT! TOGETHER, YOU DID IT!
ILLYRIA, YOU...
ILLYRIA?
ILLYRIA!
SHE PUT TOO MUCH OF HERSELF INTO STOPPING THE TORRENT. I COULD FEEL IT.
DOING SO WAS... UNWISE.
ANGEL?
ANGEL, I FEEL AWFUL.

WHAT *HAPPENED?*

I FEEL LIKE I WAS IN A FIGHT-- WAS I IN A FIGHT? DID WE--

OH!

UM... WE COOL HERE?

I MEAN, I'M A LITTLE HAZY, AND THE LAST THING I REMEMBER WE WEREN'T ALL EXACTLY *FRIENDS...*

SO *THIS* IS THE SHAPE OF MY FUTURE CAGE.

SUCH A *TINY* THING, BUT OBVIOUSLY POSSESSING SOME HIDDEN MERIT...

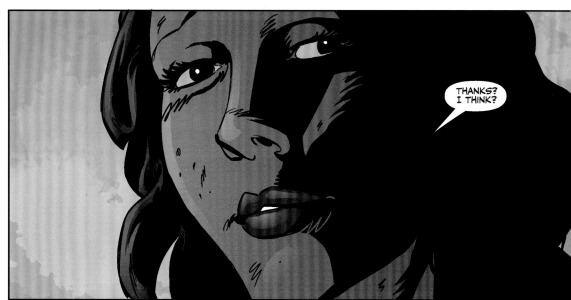

THANKS? I THINK?

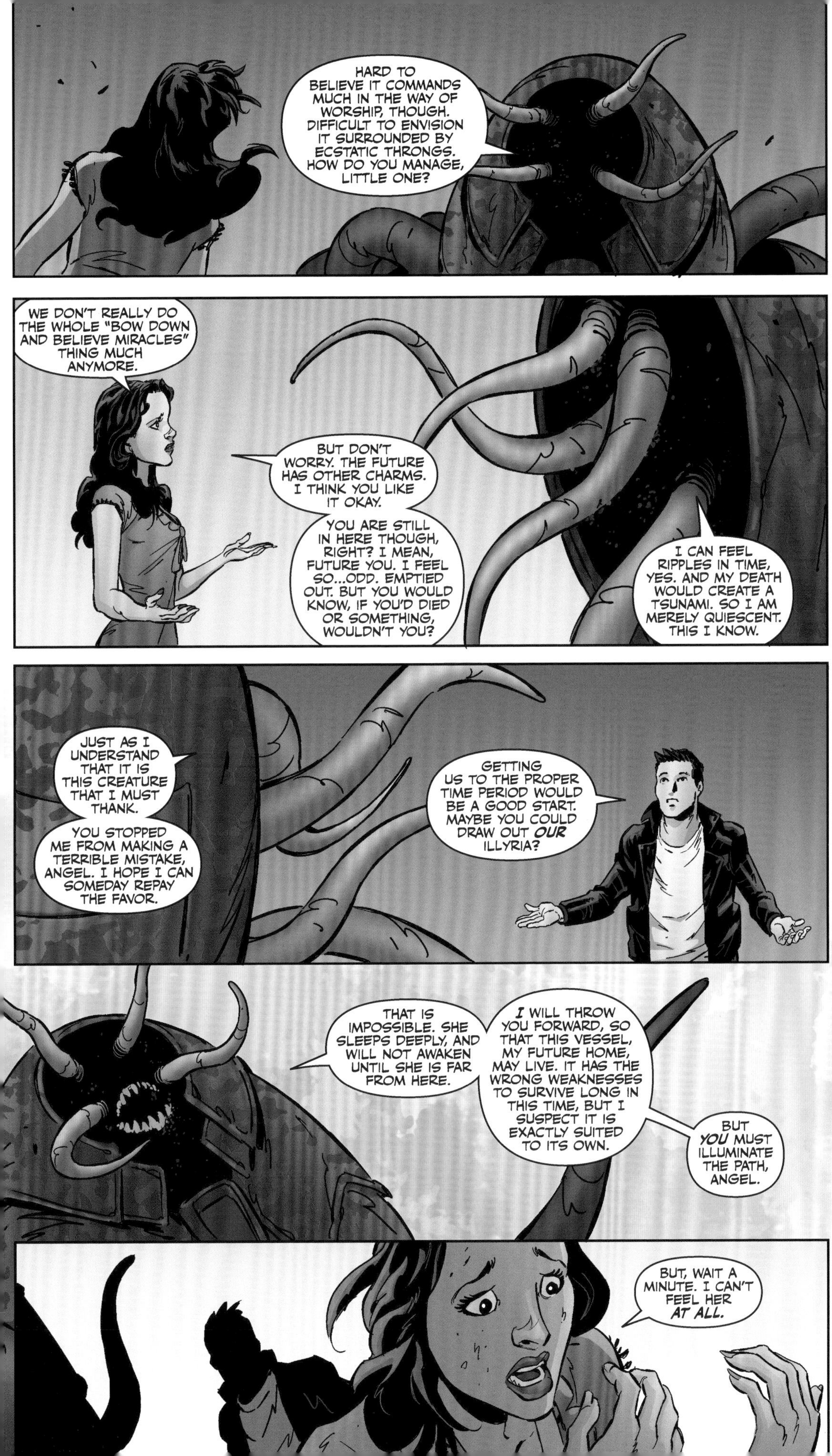
HARD TO BELIEVE IT COMMANDS MUCH IN THE WAY OF WORSHIP, THOUGH. DIFFICULT TO ENVISION IT SURROUNDED BY ECSTATIC THRONGS. HOW DO YOU MANAGE, LITTLE ONE?
WE DON'T REALLY DO THE WHOLE "BOW DOWN AND BELIEVE MIRACLES" THING MUCH ANYMORE.
BUT DON'T WORRY. THE FUTURE HAS OTHER CHARMS. I THINK YOU LIKE IT OKAY.
YOU ARE STILL IN HERE THOUGH, RIGHT? I MEAN, FUTURE YOU. I FEEL SO...ODD. EMPTIED OUT. BUT YOU WOULD KNOW, IF YOU'D DIED OR SOMETHING, WOULDN'T YOU?
I CAN FEEL RIPPLES IN TIME, YES. AND MY DEATH WOULD CREATE A TSUNAMI. SO I AM MERELY QUIESCENT. THIS I KNOW.
JUST AS I UNDERSTAND THAT IT IS THIS CREATURE THAT I MUST THANK.
YOU STOPPED ME FROM MAKING A TERRIBLE MISTAKE, ANGEL. I HOPE I CAN SOMEDAY REPAY THE FAVOR.
GETTING US TO THE PROPER TIME PERIOD WOULD BE A GOOD START. MAYBE YOU COULD DRAW OUT *OUR* ILLYRIA?
THAT IS IMPOSSIBLE. SHE SLEEPS DEEPLY, AND WILL NOT AWAKEN UNTIL SHE IS FAR FROM HERE.
I WILL THROW YOU FORWARD, SO THAT THIS VESSEL, MY FUTURE HOME, MAY LIVE. IT HAS THE WRONG WEAKNESSES TO SURVIVE LONG IN THIS TIME, BUT I SUSPECT IT IS EXACTLY SUITED TO ITS OWN.
BUT *YOU* MUST ILLUMINATE THE PATH, ANGEL.
BUT, WAIT A MINUTE. I CAN'T FEEL HER *AT ALL.*

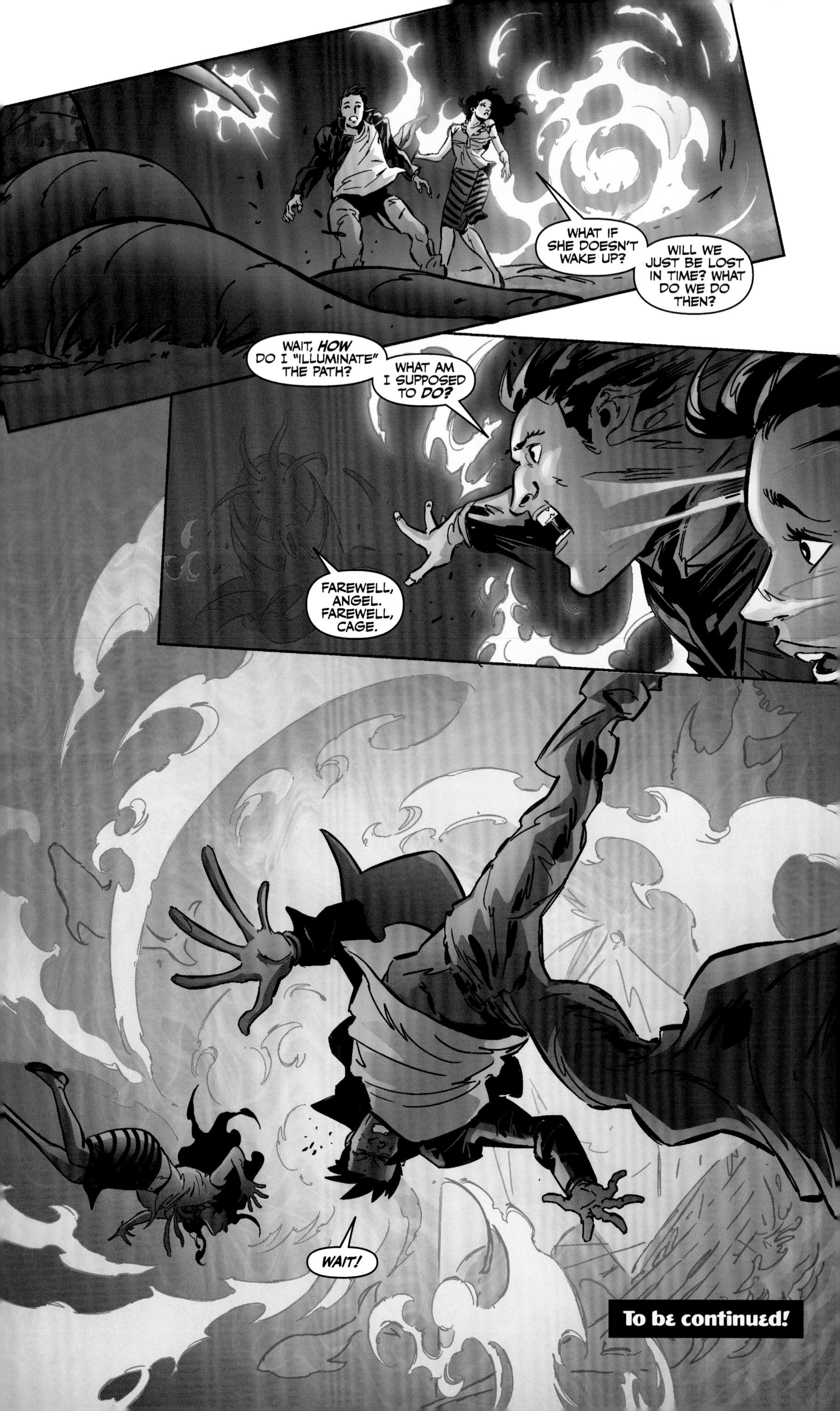
WHAT IF SHE DOESN'T WAKE UP?
WILL WE JUST BE LOST IN TIME? WHAT DO WE DO THEN?
WAIT, HOW DO I "ILLUMINATE" THE PATH?
WHAT AM I SUPPOSED TO DO?
FAREWELL, ANGEL. FAREWELL, CAGE.
WAIT!
To be continued!

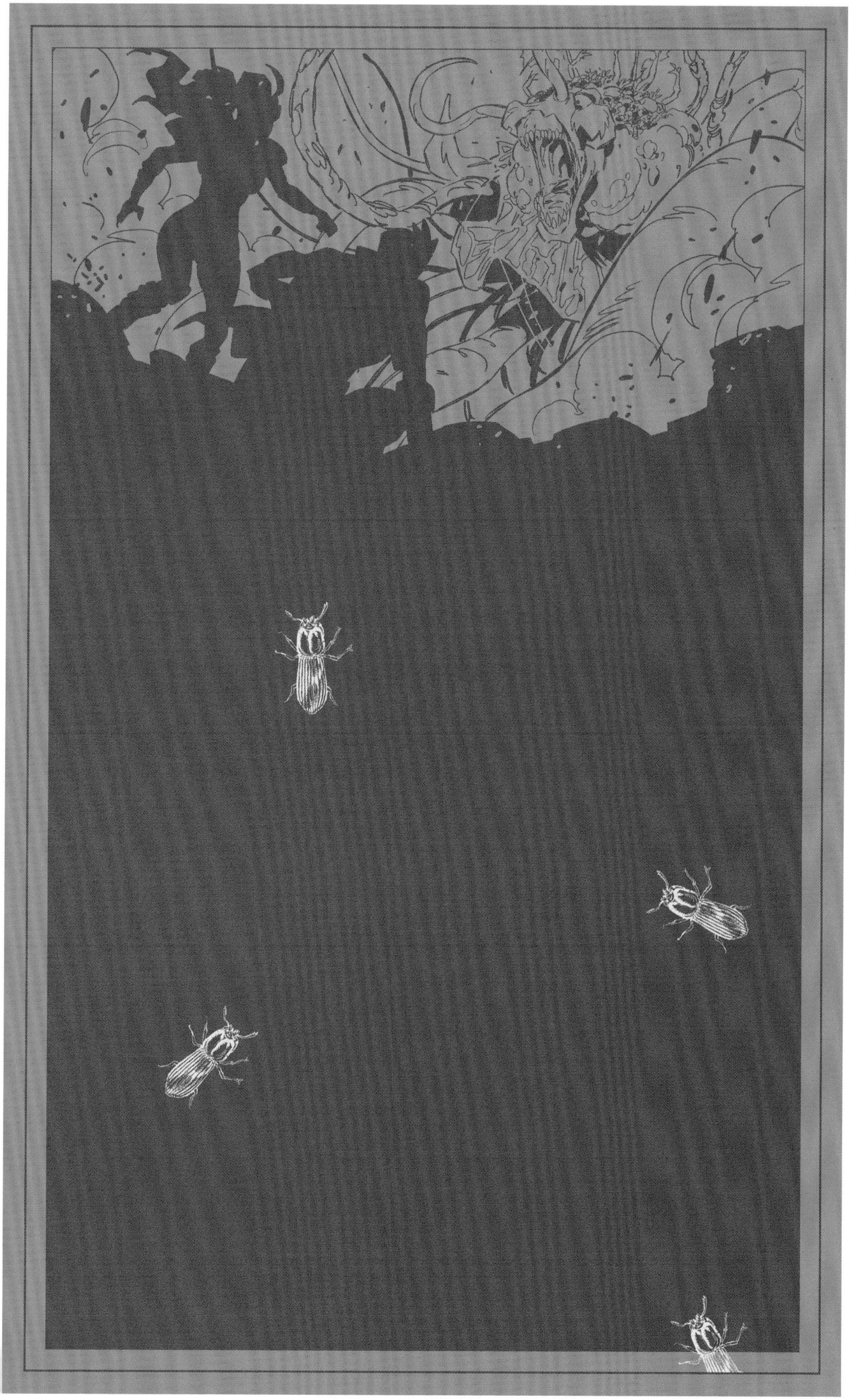

ANGEL™

COVER GALLERY AND SKETCHBOOK

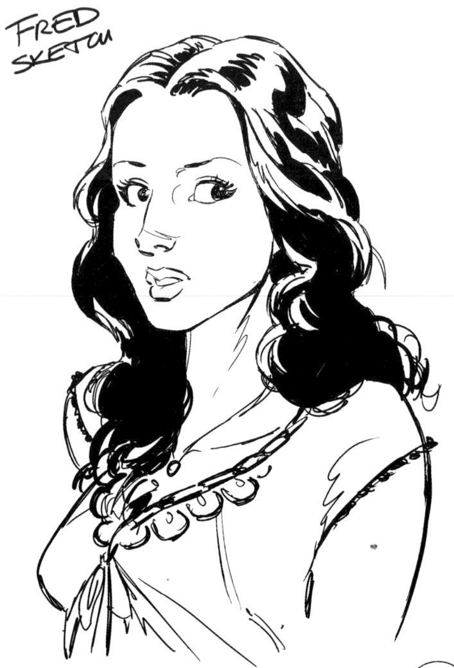
FRED
SKETCH

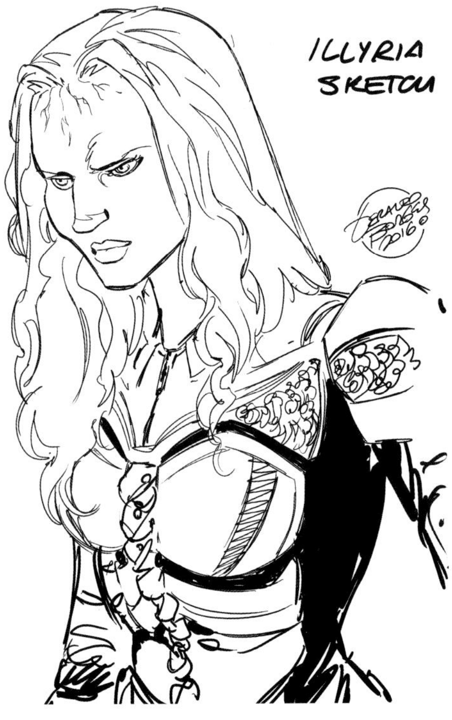
ILLYRIA
SKETCH

Before beginning interiors for the first issue of *Angel*, artist Geraldo Borges prepared sketches of our main cast, including these two of Fred and Illyria.

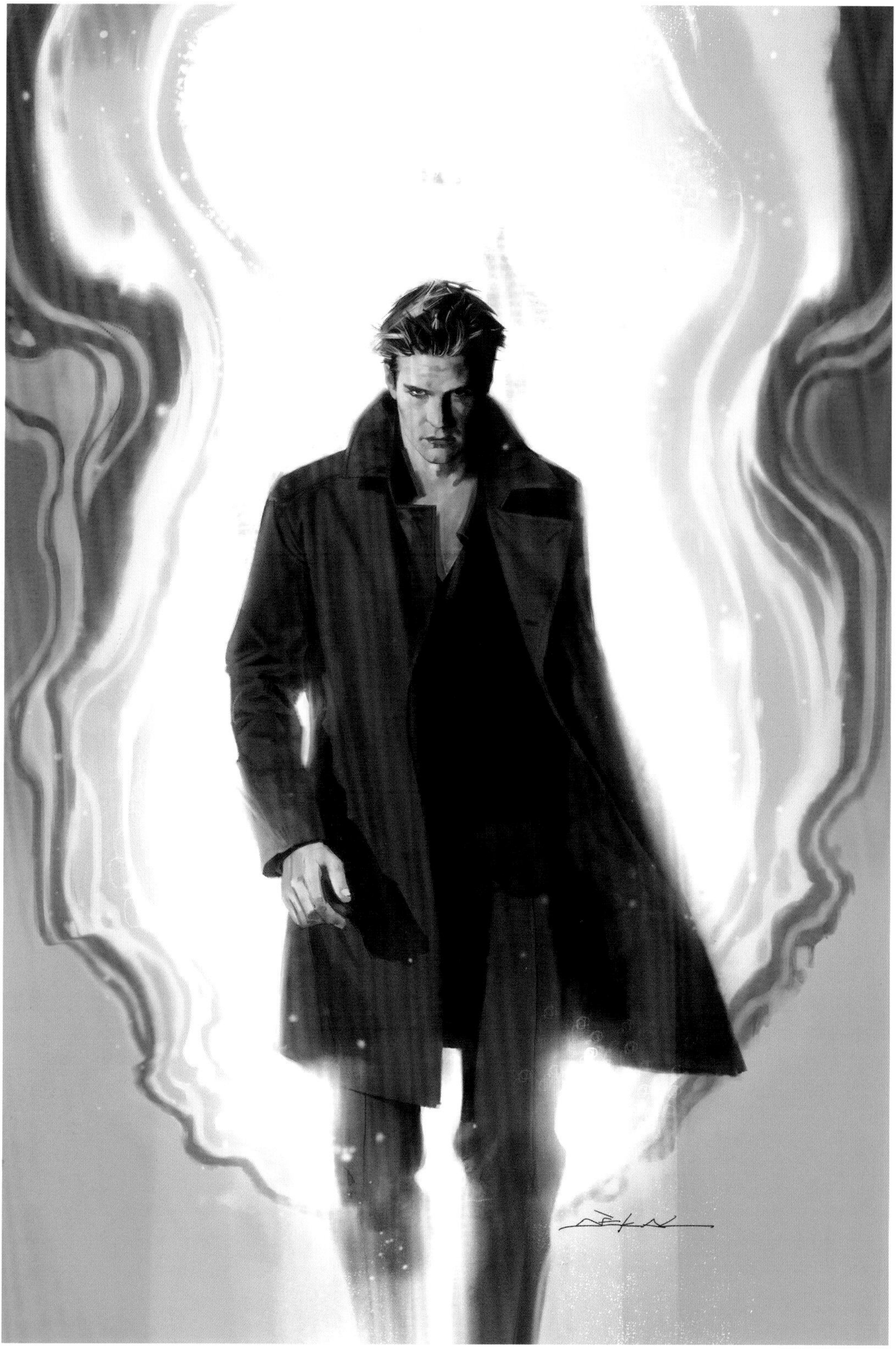

Angel Season 11 #1 variant unused cover art by Jeff Dekal. This blue version of the issue #1 variant cover was the color palette that Jeff initially planned for the final piece. He sent in final versions of the art with this color option as well as the green and mauve option which Jeff preferred and that we ultimately used for the final printing (shown on page 2). It was an incredibly tough choice!

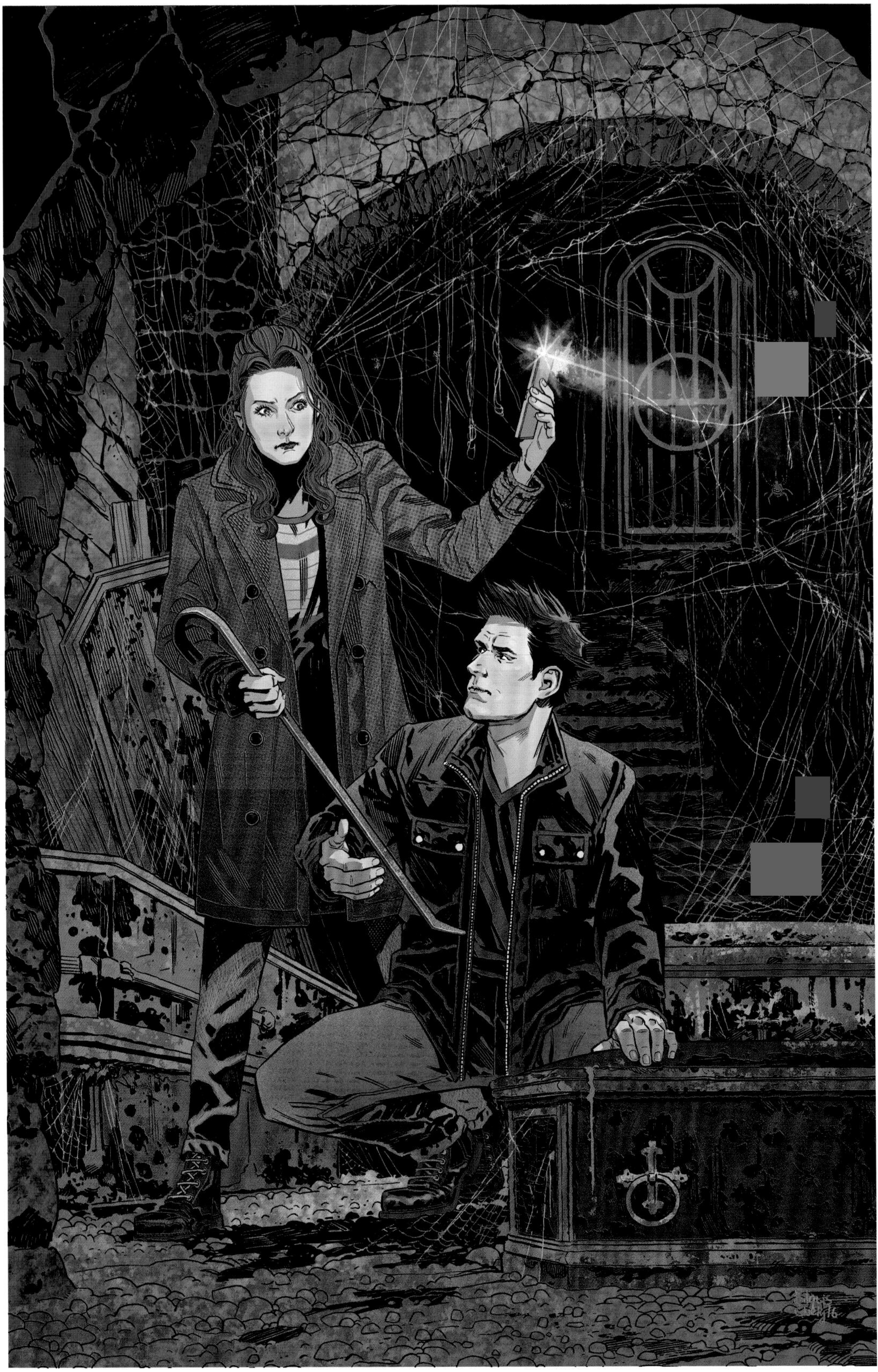

Angel Season 11 #1 ultravariant cover art by Bilquis Evely.

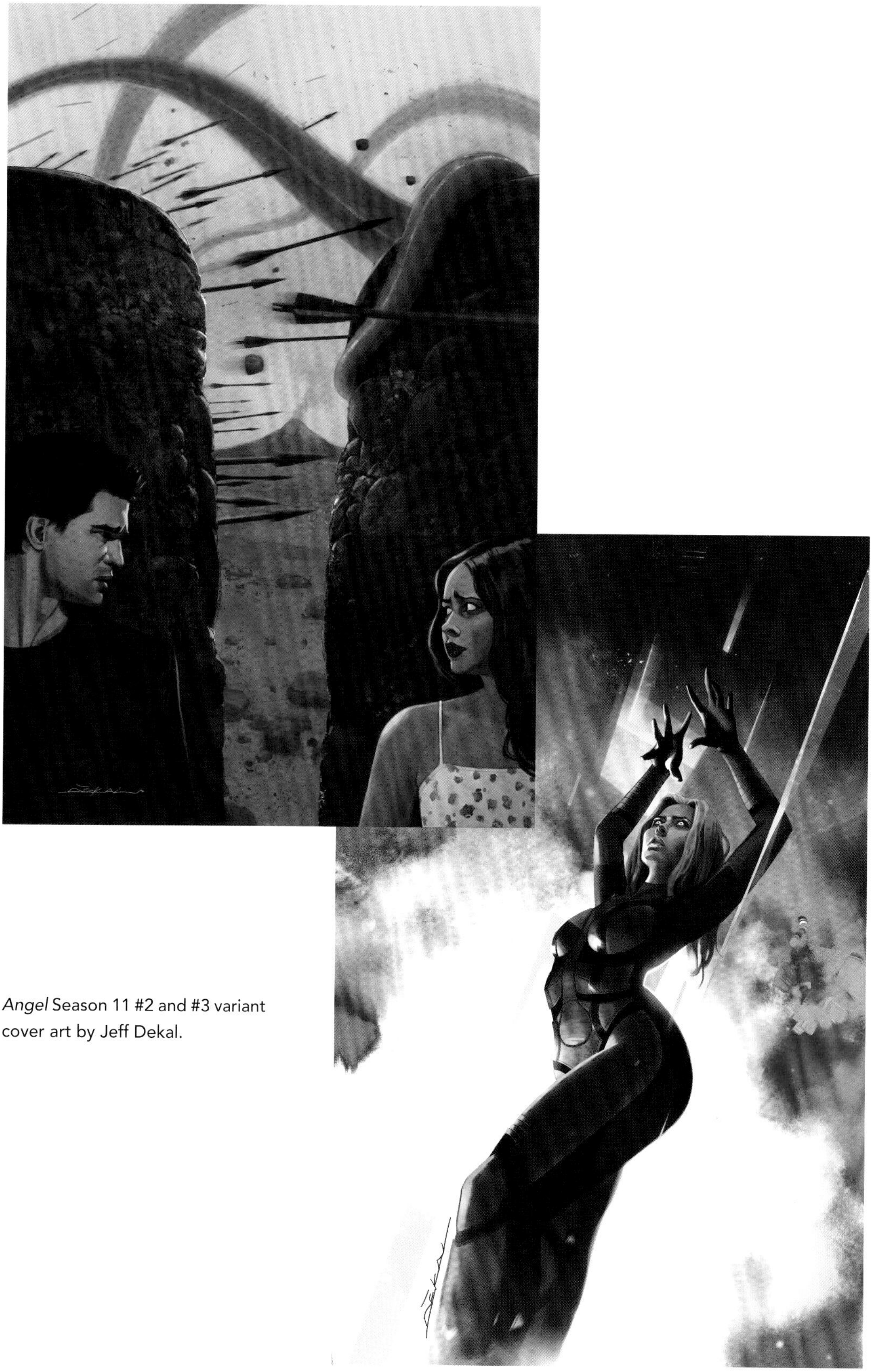

Angel Season 11 #2 and #3 variant cover art by Jeff Dekal.

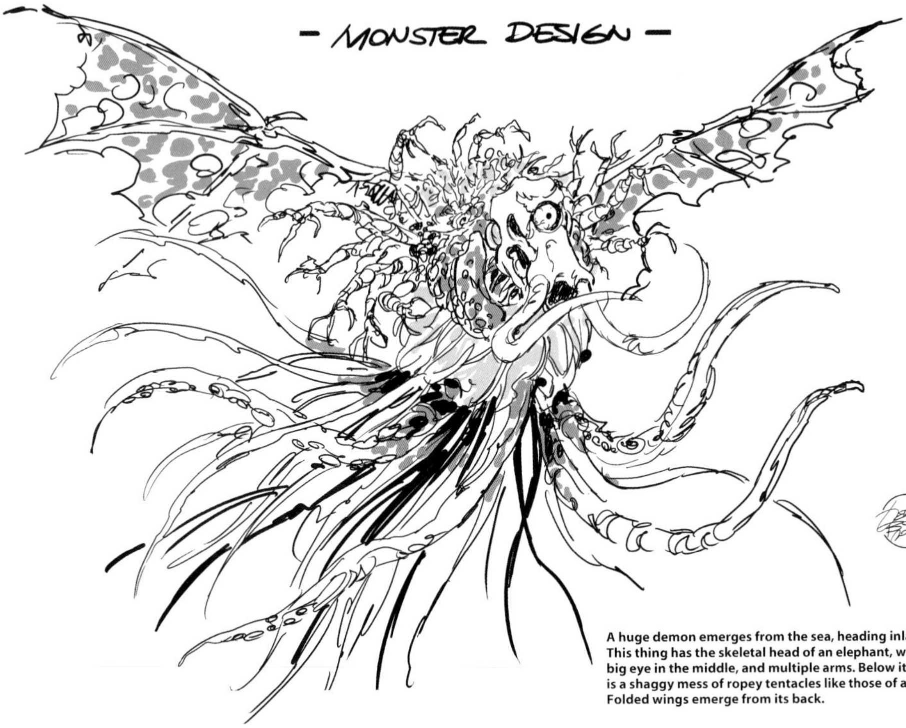
- MONSTER DESIGN -

A huge demon emerges from the sea, heading inland. This thing has the skeletal head of an elephant, with one big eye in the middle, and multiple arms. Below its waist it is a shaggy mess of ropey tentacles like those of a jellyfish. Folded wings emerge from its back.

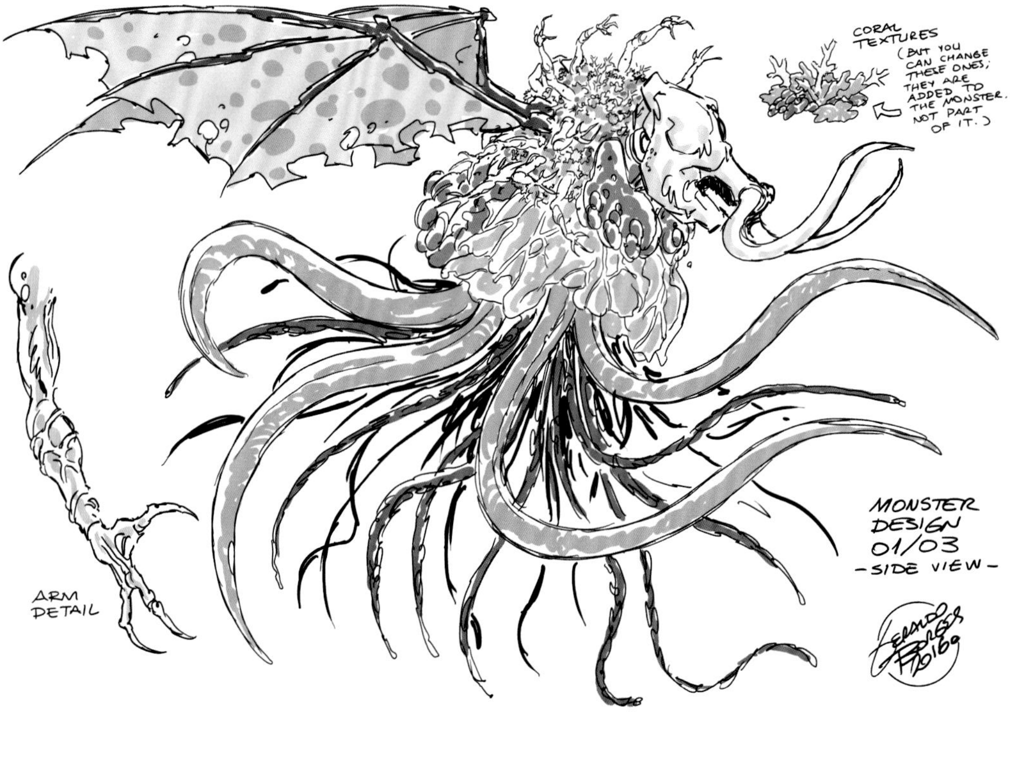
CORAL TEXTURES
(BUT YOU CAN CHANGE THESE ONES; THEY ARE ADDED TO THE MONSTER. NOT PART OF IT.)
MONSTER DESIGN 01/03
-SIDE VIEW-
ARM DETAIL

Based on Corinna's description in the script, Geraldo created this design and turnarounds for Illyria's demon rival.

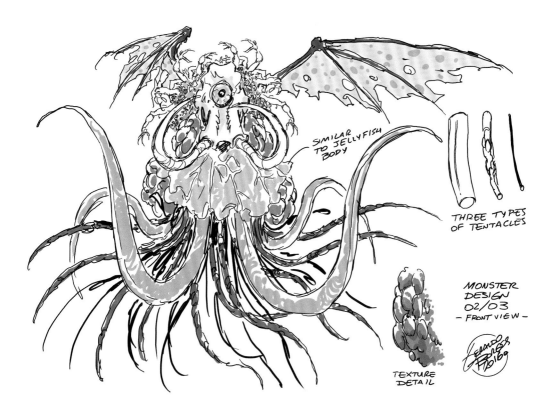

SIMILAR TO JELLYFISH BODY

THREE TYPES OF TENTACLES

MONSTER DESIGN 02/03 — FRONT VIEW —

TEXTURE DETAIL

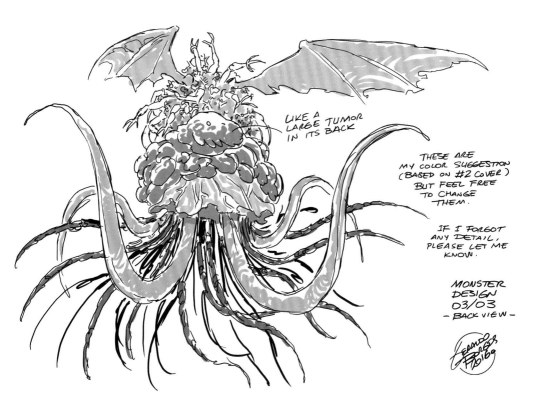

LIKE A LARGE TUMOR IN ITS BACK

THESE ARE MY COLOR SUGGESTION (BASED ON #2 COVER) BUT FEEL FREE TO CHANGE THEM.

IF I FORGOT ANY DETAIL, PLEASE LET ME KNOW.

MONSTER DESIGN 03/03 — BACK VIEW —

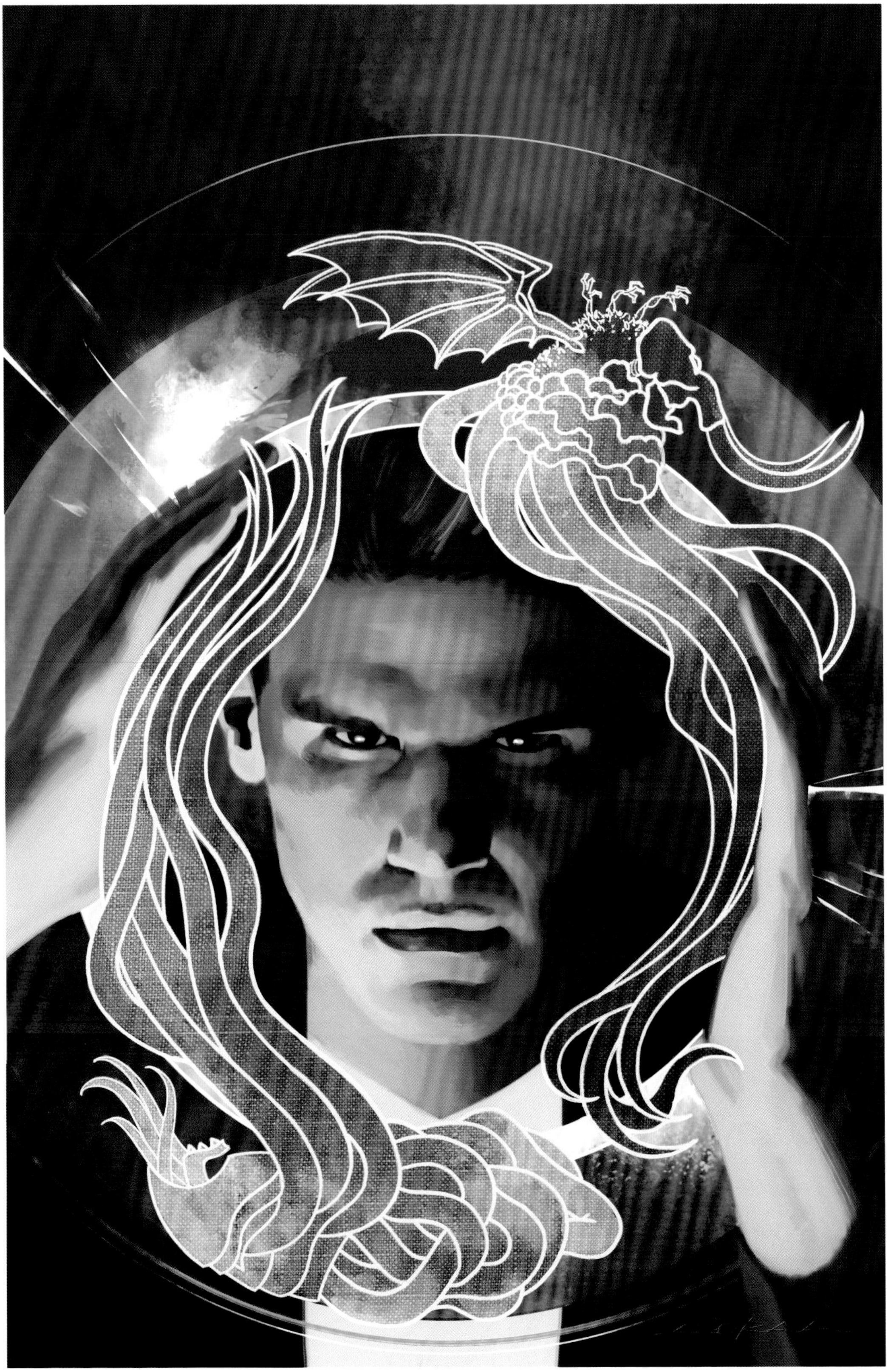

Angel Season 11 #4 variant cover art by Jeff Dekal.

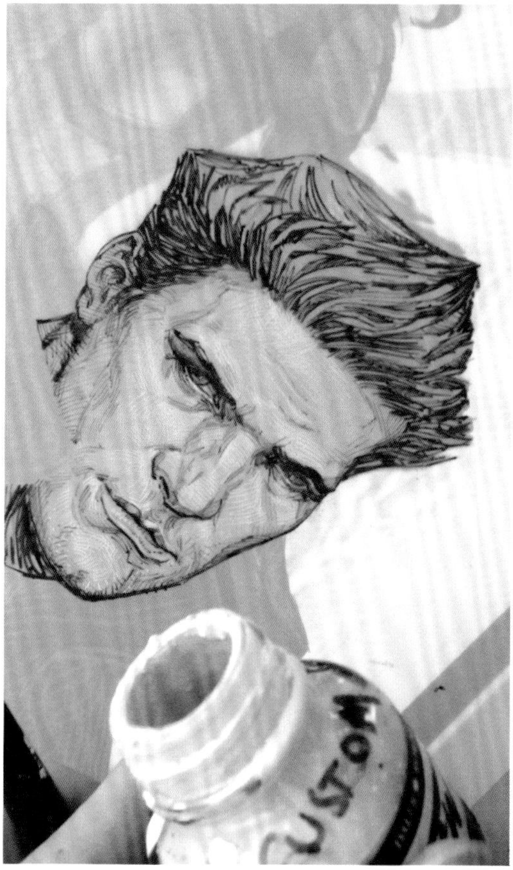
CUSTOM
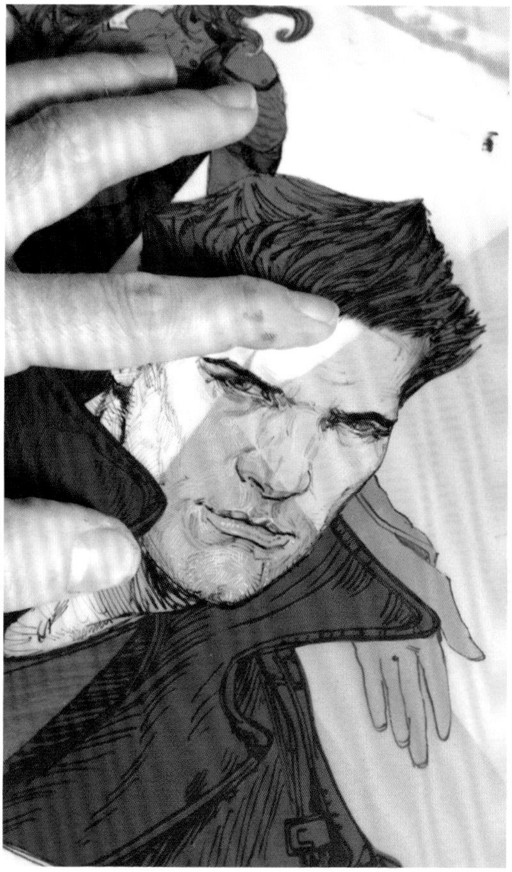
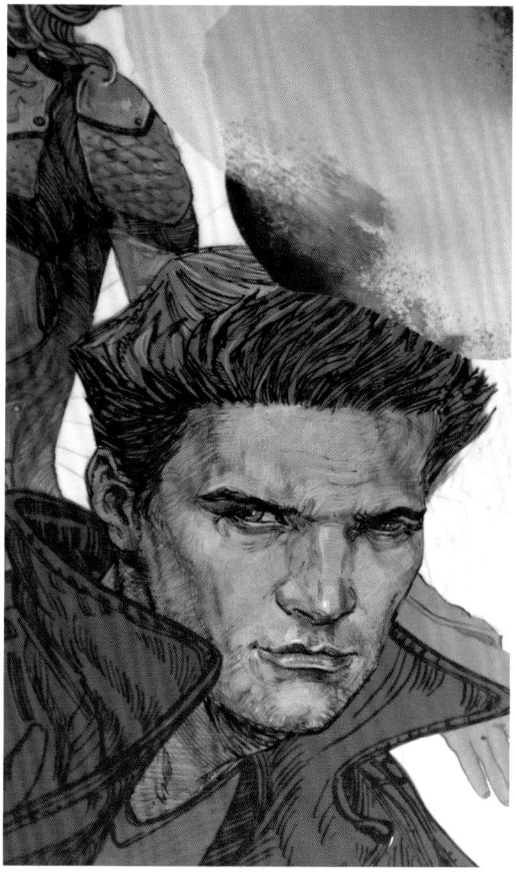
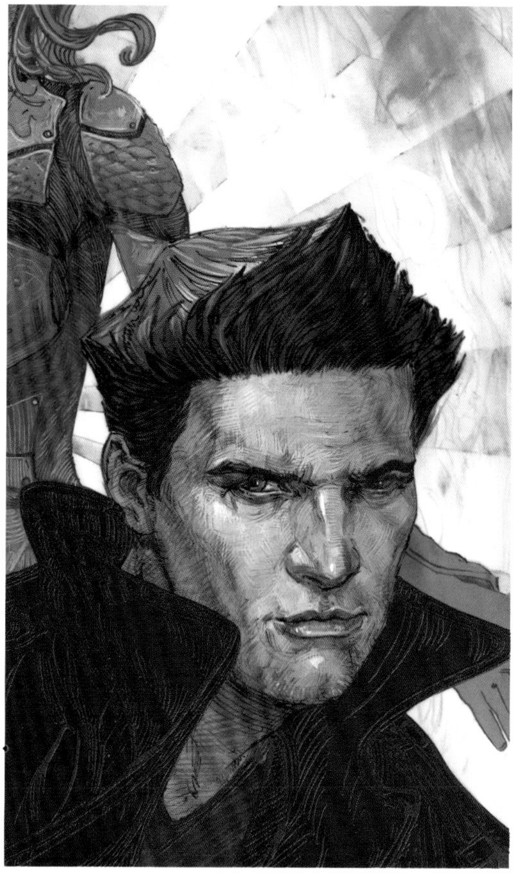

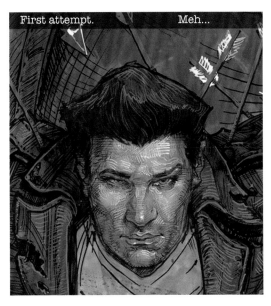

First attempt.　　　　Meh...

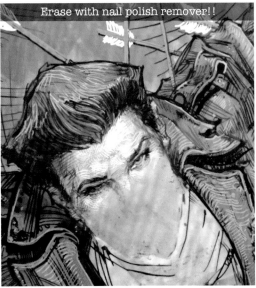

Erase with nail polish remover!!

Redraw!

Artist Scott Fischer is always working to capture Angel's likeness for his cover pieces—different angles, different expressions. Shown on this page and the previous is some process work for the issue #2 cover, focusing on Angel's face, and some process (reprocess . . .) work on Angel's face for the issue #3 cover—with a bit of commentary from Scott.

Buffy the Vampire Slayer™

BUFFY THE VAMPIRE SLAYER SEASON 8

VOLUME 1: THE LONG WAY HOME
Joss Whedon and Georges Jeanty
ISBN 978-1-59307-822-5 | $15.99

VOLUME 2: NO FUTURE FOR YOU
Brian K. Vaughan, Georges Jeanty, and Joss Whedon
ISBN 978-1-59307-963-5 | $15.99

VOLUME 3: WOLVES AT THE GATE
Drew Goddard, Georges Jeanty, and Joss Whedon
ISBN 978-1-59582-165-2 | $15.99

VOLUME 4: TIME OF YOUR LIFE
Joss Whedon, Jeph Loeb, Georges Jeanty, and others
ISBN 978-1-59582-310-6 | $15.99

VOLUME 5: PREDATORS AND PREY
Joss Whedon, Jane Espenson, Georges Jeanty, Cliff Richards, and others
ISBN 978-1-59582-342-7 | $15.99

VOLUME 6: RETREAT
Joss Whedon, Jane Espenson, Georges Jeanty, Karl Moline, and others
ISBN 978-1-59582-415-8 | $15.99

VOLUME 7: TWILIGHT
Joss Whedon, Brad Meltzer, and Georges Jeanty
ISBN 978-1-59582-558-2 | $16.99

VOLUME 8: LAST GLEAMING
Joss Whedon, Scott Allie, and Georges Jeanty
ISBN 978-1-59582-610-7 | $16.99

BUFFY THE VAMPIRE SLAYER SEASON 8 LIBRARY EDITION

VOLUME 1
ISBN 978-1-59582-888-0 | $29.99

VOLUME 2
ISBN 978-1-59582-935-1 | $29.99

VOLUME 3
ISBN 978-1-59582-978-8 | $29.99

VOLUME 4
ISBN 978-1-61655-127-8 | $29.99

BUFFY THE VAMPIRE SLAYER OMNIBUS: SEASON 8

VOLUME 1
ISBN 978-1-63008-941-2 | $24.99

BUFFY THE VAMPIRE SLAYER SEASON 9

VOLUME 1: FREEFALL
Joss Whedon, Andrew Chambliss, Georges Jeanty, and others
ISBN 978-1-59582-922-1 | $17.99

VOLUME 2: ON YOUR OWN
Andrew Chambliss, Scott Allie, Georges Jeanty, and others
ISBN 978-1-59582-990-0 | $17.99

VOLUME 3: GUARDED
Joss Whedon, Jane Espenson, Drew Z. Greenberg, Georges Jeanty, and others
ISBN 978-1-61655-099-8 | $17.99

VOLUME 4: WELCOME TO THE TEAM
Andrew Chambliss, Georges Jeanty, Karl Moline, and others
ISBN 978-1-61655-166-7 | $17.99

VOLUME 5: THE CORE
Andrew Chambliss, Georges Jeanty, and others
ISBN 978-1-61655-254-1 | $17.99

BUFFY THE VAMPIRE SLAYER SEASON 9 LIBRARY EDITION

VOLUME 1
ISBN 978-1-61655-715-7 | $29.99

VOLUME 2
ISBN 978-1-61655-716-4 | $29.99

VOLUME 3
ISBN 978-1-61655-717-1 | $29.99

BUFFY THE VAMPIRE SLAYER SEASON 10

VOLUME 1: NEW RULES
Christos Gage, Rebekah Isaacs, Nicholas Brendon, and others
ISBN 978-1-61655-490-3 | $18.99

VOLUME 2: I WISH
Christos Gage, Rebekah Isaacs, Nicholas Brendon, and others
ISBN 978-1-61655-600-6 | $18.99

VOLUME 3: LOVE DARES YOU
Christos Gage, Rebekah Isaacs, Nicholas Brendon, and Megan Levens
ISBN 978-1-61655-758-4 | $18.99

VOLUME 4: OLD DEMONS
Christos Gage and Rebekah Isaacs
ISBN 978-1-61655-802-4 | $18.99

VOLUME 5: IN PIECES ON THE GROUND
Christos Gage, Megan Levens, and Rebekah Isaacs
ISBN 978-1-61655-944-1 | $18.99

VOLUME 6: OWN IT
Christos Gage and Rebekah Isaacs
ISBN 978-1-50670-034-2 | $18.99

BUFFY THE VAMPIRE SLAYER SEASON 11

VOLUME 1: THE SPREAD OF THEIR EVIL
Christos Gage and Rebekah Isaacs
ISBN 978-1-50670-274-2 | $19.99

ANGEL & FAITH SEASON 9

VOLUME 1: LIVE THROUGH THIS
Christos Gage, Rebekah Isaacs, and Phil Noto
ISBN 978-1-59582-887-3 | $17.99

VOLUME 2: DADDY ISSUES
Christos Gage, Rebekah Isaacs, and Chris Samnee
ISBN 978-1-59582-960-3 | $17.99

VOLUME 3: FAMILY REUNION
Christos Gage, Rebekah Isaacs, Lee Garbett, and David Lapham
ISBN 978-1-61655-079-0 | $17.99

VOLUME 4: DEATH AND CONSEQUENCES
Christos Gage and Rebekah Isaacs
ISBN 978-1-61655-165-0 | $17.99

VOLUME 5: WHAT YOU WANT, NOT WHAT YOU NEED
Christos Gage and Rebekah Isaacs
ISBN 978-1-61655-253-4 | $17.99

ANGEL & FAITH SEASON 9 LIBRARY EDITION

VOLUME 1
ISBN 978-1-61655-712-6 | $29.99

VOLUME 2
ISBN 978-1-61655-713-3 | $29.99

VOLUME 3
ISBN 978-1-61655-714-0 | $29.99

ANGEL & FAITH SEASON 10

VOLUME 1: WHERE THE RIVER MEETS THE SEA
Victor Gischler, Will Conrad, Derlis Santacruz, and others
ISBN 978-1-61655-503-0 | $18.99

VOLUME 2: LOST AND FOUND
Victor Gischler and Will Conrad
ISBN 978-1-61655-601-3 | $18.99

VOLUME 3: UNITED
Victor Gischler and Will Conrad
ISBN 978-1-61655-766-9 | $18.99

VOLUME 4: A LITTLE MORE THAN KIN
Victor Gischler, Cliff Richards, and Will Conrad
ISBN 978-1-61655-890-1 | $18.99

ANGEL SEASON 11

VOLUME 1: OUT OF THE PAST
Corinna Bechko and Geraldo Borges
ISBN 978-1-50670-346-6 | $17.99

SPIKE

A DARK PLACE
Victor Gischler and Paul Lee
ISBN 978-1-61655-109-4 | $17.99

INTO THE LIGHT
James Marsters and Derlis Santacruz
ISBN 978-1-61655-421-7 | $14.99

WILLOW

WONDERLAND
Jeff Parker, Christos Gage, and Brian Ching
ISBN 978-1-61655-145-2 | $17.99

BUFFY: THE HIGH SCHOOL YEARS

FREAKS AND GEEKS
Faith Erin Hicks and Yishan Li
ISBN 978-1-61655-667-9 | $10.99

GLUTTON FOR PUNISHMENT
Kel McDonald and Yishan Li
ISBN 978-1-50670-115-8 | $10.99

PARENTAL PARASITE
Kel McDonald and Yishan Li
ISBN 978-1-50670-304-6 | $10.99

AVAILABLE AT YOUR LOCAL COMICS SHOP OR BOOKSTORE!
To find a comics shop in your area, call 1-888-266-4226. For more information or to order direct:
On the web: DarkHorse.com • Email: mailorder@darkhorse.com • Phone: 1-800-862-0052 Mon.–Fri. 9 AM to 5 PM Pacific Time

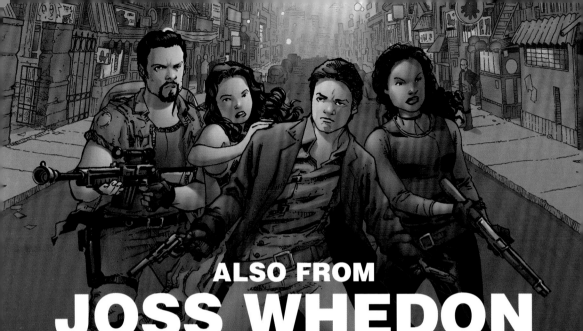

ALSO FROM
JOSS WHEDON
AVAILABLE AT YOUR LOCAL COMICS SHOP OR BOOKSTORE!